AFTER THE DAY'S WORK

THE NEW ENGLAND
YANKEE COOK BOOK

THE NEW ENGLAND YANKEE COOK BOOK

An Anthology of INCOMPARABLE RECIPES
FROM THE SIX NEW ENGLAND STATES
and a Little Something about the People whose Tradition for Good Eating is herein permanently recorded

BY IMOGENE WOLCOTT

from the Files of YANKEE *magazine and from Timeworn Recipe Books and many Gracious Contributors*

Decorations by Edwin Earle and Alanson B. Hewes

Published by COWARD-McCANN, INC., *New York*

REPRINTED BY COOKBOOK COLLECTORS LIBRARY
FAVORITE RECIPES PRESS, INC.
P. O. BOX 18324
LOUISVILLE, KENTUCKY 40218

TO MY MOTHER

CONTENTS

SPECIAL ARTICLES

ILLUSTRATIONS

ACKNOWLEDGMENTS

THE EDITOR is deeply indebted to *Yankee* magazine for permission to reprint "The Farm Kitchen," by Margaret Carmichael; "Rhode Island Clambakes," by Horace G. Belcher; "Stories of Old New England Dishes," by Ella Shannon Bowles; "RUA Yankee Cook?" "Have You A Yankee Cellar?" "Transplanting," by Harriet Donlevy; as well as many of the recipes and anecdotes. Also for the help and encouragement so generously given by the editor of *Yankee* magazine, Mr. Robb Sagendorph.

The editor is likewise sincerely appreciative of the permission given by First National Stores Inc. to reprint recipes submitted both to the printed and to the radio edition of the *First National News*. The staff of the New England Council also deserves especial thanks for its valuable suggestions and encouragement.

Unless otherwise credited, recipes for all alcoholic beverages have been contributed by Russell S. Codman, Jr., consultant for the S. S. Pierce Co., Boston. The late Louise Crathern Russell, whose collection of Yankee recipes is considered one of the most comprehensive in New England, contributed and tested many recipes and offered innumerable helpful suggestions.

Credit is also due Mrs. Norma Roberts whose knowledge of old-time New England cookery has been invaluable; Mrs. Caroline Webber Bixby, Miss Almeda King and Mrs. Eunice Sawyer for their help in assembling, checking and verifying recipes.

FORETASTE

Wilbur L. Cross

Whence cometh the strength, physical and intellectual, of New Englanders? It has come, along with their famous conscience, from the natural and sane diet which, except for the first hard years at Plymouth, has contained all the vitamins essential to sound bodies and sound minds three centuries before vitamins had been discovered. They found their main sustenance in what their Lord God of Heaven would let grow on the land and in the waters of this paradise of the New World.

Joel Barlow, in his burlesque poem called "The Hasty-Pudding," remarked that all his "bones were made of Indian corn." At first the settlers depended most on Indian corn to keep them alive. From them has come the delicious johnnycake made of yellow or white cornmeal, which is still consumed all over New England, with Rhode Island at the head. Many other uses of Indian corn have been contrived such as hasty pudding, fried mush, hominy, and hulled corn, of which johnnycake and corn bread yet maintain their original prestige. The pleasant taste of many of these cornmeal dishes has been enhanced by a liberal flow of New England maple syrup, noted for its fine flavor.

The Indians planted beans in the same hill with corn, so that the vines of one might run up the stalks of the other; and after the harvest they boiled the two together so as to blend the juices and called the dish succotash, which has held its own down to the present day. Not long after this our forefathers learned to bake their beans with pork and with molasses as soon as they began trading with the West Indies. To the Massachusetts Bay Colony must probably be given the credit of first serving with baked beans a brown bread made of corn and rye meal, sweetened with molasses. Boston Baked Beans and Brown Bread, with some minor changes in the formula, remains a favorite dish of New Englanders.

Just as cornmeal contributed to the building up of strong bodies, baked beans made their contribution to the New England conscience. The Puritan Sabbath, you know, began at sundown on Saturday and ended at sundown on Sunday. During this period no one was supposed to do any work except chores about the house and the barn. All cooking must be reduced to the minimum. But even Puritans had to have something to eat on their Sabbath. Baked beans came to their rescue. So, as late as my childhood, it was a custom among very religious families in Connecticut to cook their beans on Saturday morning and to warm them up for supper Saturday night or for Sunday noon dinner, or for both meals. In this way a little fire was made to do the work for pious housewives.

Fish abounded in sea and rivers. There were cod and trout and salmon and shad among the many varieties available. Dried and salted codfish has long remained a staple New England dish, not only in remote districts, but in cities as well. Chowder made of small fish is usual in towns by the sea.

The Pilgrims at Plymouth might not have survived the first winter but for mussels along the shore. Clams and oysters were also soon discovered. The oyster stew has since become a New England dish; and the clambake is a New England institution for political and fraternal celebrations. Most famous of all is clam chowder, without which no Friday dinner can be complete.

The Puritans were shown by the Indians how to smoke venison

for its preservation and later they adopted the practice of smoking beef and pork. Another method of preservation was to salt beef and pork and mackerel also in a brine. Thus salt pork was always at hand for cooking with peas and beans and other vegetables, and corned beef was equally at hand for corned beef hash for the New England boiled dinner. Hardly can a Yankee go through a week without corned beef hash and the New England boiled dinner. And the typical Thanksgiving dinner, which originated in New England, must still have its turkey, with pumpkin pie as a dessert.

These substantial dishes have been supplemented through New England history by wild fruits, now improved immensely by cultivation. The apple has gone into applesauce, apple dumplings, and the apple pie, which, with the doughnut having a hole in it, still survives in some places as an excellent breakfast food. In the dearth of spices, recourse was had to several aromatic roots which were grated and spread over cooked fruits as in apple pies to whet the appetite. Sassafras was a common substitute in country districts as late as the nineteenth century for nutmegs, which were slow in coming from the Molucca Islands. Hence the tradition, true or false, that Connecticut Yankees turned out wooden nutmegs and sold them to the Dutch of New Amsterdam for the genuine article.

There have always been the native beach plums for jelly, and huckleberries and blueberries for pies, muffins, puddings, and bread-and-milk. For various other dishes there have been wild blackberries, raspberries, gooseberries, and currants. Nor should be forgotten stewed cranberries necessary for the Thanksgiving dinner; nor the strawberry, loved best by New Englanders in shortcakes.

In the pages that follow may be found recipes that cover the whole range of New England cooking, from a dozen recipes for making the much disputed clam chowder down to such dishes as Squirrel Pie and Red Flannel Hash.

The way to the finest plain cooking in the world lies all before you in this book so that you may learn what to eat so as to live long lives in the joy of perfect health.

RHODE ISLAND CLAMBAKE

Christopher La Farge

Devote your search for these alone:
The sand that's salted by the sea,
The driftwood fire, the rounded stone,
Shelter of a wild-cherry tree,
But bellow like a wounded moose
If any says: Tomato-juice.

Heat up the stones till fiery red
For bottom to your sandy well,
With rockweed lay a steaming bed:
The clams' and lobsters' final hell—
But may their devil shake you loose
If you put in tomato-juice.

And when the rockweed starts to pop,
And when the whole begins to mutter,
Put on more stones and weed, and hop
To melt the freshest golden butter,
But though you're subject to abuse,
For God's sake, no tomato-juice!

O clams that are still fresh from mud!
O lobsters turning slowly red!
O delicate young Irish spud!
O corn whose husk has not been shed!
How well you fit each other's use
(Unmingled with tomato-juice)!

A blue-fish, dripping salt from it,
And planked against the flames to brown,
Marries with lobsters from the pit,
And clams provide, to wash it down,
A Narragansett nectar-sluice—
Unpoisoned with tomato-juice.

From such a feast, all duly grown
In good Rhode Island's sea and field,
Seasoned with bay-leaf on hot stone
To make the weeds their essence yield,
You shall be fed as heaven has use—
Unless you add tomato-juice.

THE NEW ENGLAND
YANKEE COOK BOOK

I. SOUPS, CHOWDERS, AND STEWS

CLAM CHOWDER, NEW ENGLAND STYLE

[Old Bay State recipe]

1 quart shucked clams	½ teaspoon salt
¼ pound salt pork, diced	⅛ teaspoon pepper
1 large onion, finely sliced	4 cups milk
3 medium-sized potatoes, sliced thin	6 split common crackers
	2 tablespoons butter

Split the head of each clam so that it is open flat and rinse in clam liquor to remove grit; remove the black cap. Separate the belly or soft part from the firm part, reserving about a cupful of the plumpest clams. With thumb and forefinger squeeze out the dark part of the bellies. Chop or grind the firm body parts coarsely. Strain ½ cup liquor. Try out salt pork, remove when crisp, sauté onion slices; add potatoes, salt and pepper and sauté slowly, stirring often, for 10 minutes. Add the chopped clams and liquor. Cover with water and cook 20 minutes. Add the cleaned bellies and cook a few minutes longer. If scum forms, skim it off at once. When clams are tender, add milk in which crackers have been soaking. Add butter, place kettle at back of stove, to allow chowder to flavor and "ripen" for about an hour. Serves 6.

3

CLAM CHOWDER, COPLEY-PLAZA

[Copley-Plaza, Boston, Mass.]

3 quarts Duxbury clams (in shell)
1 stalk celery
2 medium sized onions

¼ pound salt pork, chopped
2 medium sized potatoes
1 cup heavy cream
salt and pepper

Steam the clams with stalk of celery in a little water to prevent burning, until a quart of clam broth is obtained. Slice the potatoes; chop the onions fine and sauté in salt pork fat, taking care they do not become brown. Mix in the potatoes, then add the clam broth. Simmer about 30 minutes; remove from the fire, add cream slowly, stirring well. Add a few of the clams (well cleaned) as a garniture. Season and serve with crackers. Serves 4.

CLAM BROTH

[Recipe from Duxbury, Mass.]

1 quart clams   1½ cups cold water

Scrub clams and wash in several waters until free from sand. Place in large kettle, add water, cover tightly and cook over low heat about 20 minutes or until shells open. Remove clams from broth. When liquor has settled strain carefully. Boiling water or hot milk may be added to make one quart of broth, if desired. Serve hot or cold, with or without whipped cream and dash of paprika. (Old recipes do not call for additional water or milk or for topping of whipped cream.) Serves 4 to 6.

RHODE ISLAND CLAM CHOWDER

3-inch cube fat salt pork, diced
3 onions, sliced
4 cups potatoes, cut in small cubes
1 quart shucked clams (quahogs)
2 cups boiling water
1 cup stewed, strained tomatoes

¼ teaspoon soda
1 cup milk, scalded
1 cup thin cream
2 tablespoons butter
salt and pepper
8 common crackers, split

Try out pork until crisp; remove scraps. Cook onion in fat until lightly browned, remove, add potatoes to fat and stir and cook over low flame 10 minutes. Chop hard part of clams fine and add with onion to potatoes. Cover with boiling water and simmer until potatoes are nearly done. Stir soda into tomatoes and add with soft part of clam. Simmer gently on back of stove at least 30 minutes. When ready to serve add scalded milk, cream, butter and seasonings. Serve over crackers which have been moistened in cold milk or with crackers served dry. Serves 8.

The raging clam chowder controversy which has continued almost uninterruptedly in New England for generations centers on the use of tomatoes as an ingredient in its preparation. Rhode Island and Connecticut housewives uphold the tomato. The rest of New England scorn it. A Maine politician claims the addition of tomato to clam chowder "is the work of reds" who seek to undermine "our most hallowed tradition," and suggests that all housewives and chefs adding tomato be forced "to dig a barrel of clams at high tide" as a penalty.

Even Maine lobsters are said to object to the adding of this red coloring matter, claiming that it poaches on their preserves, and that it may mislead those who have enjoyed a real lobster stew. They claim they have a priority on said color and that the claws of every Maine lobster are raised in protest.

RHODE ISLAND QUAHOG CHOWDER

⅛ pound salt pork, diced
2 onions, sliced
5 potatoes, diced
1 quart boiling water

½ pint quahogs, drained and
    cut small
liquor from quahogs
salt and pepper

Try out salt pork until browned. Add onions and fry until soft and yellow. Add potatoes and fry a little, but not to brown. Add pork, onions and potatoes to boiling water. Cook until potatoes are done; then add quahogs. Add liquor from quahogs cautiously, to taste. (Take care!) Season and simmer a few minutes or until quahogs are cooked through. Serves 6.

Mildred C. Williams, Ocean Street, Providence, R. I., adds a cup of water to this chowder for each new guest she sees arriving. "You'll be surprised how much this chowder may be diluted and still taste very good. Quahog Chowder is even better the second day," she maintains.

MARTHA'S VINEYARD QUAHOG STEW

[*Mrs. Clarence Voges, Hillside Road, Medford Hillside, Mass.*]

½ cup butter
2 tablespoons flour
4 cups milk, heated

salt, pepper and dash of mace
1 quart shucked quahogs with
    liquor

2 eggs, well beaten

Cream flour and butter and stir into milk; add seasonings. Heat quahog liquor, skimming off froth. Chop quahogs fine and simmer in heated juice 3 minutes, stir into heated milk. Put eggs into soup tureen, pour in quahog mixture, stir well and serve. Clams may be substituted for quahogs. Serves 8.

CREAM OF QUAHOG SOUP

[A Cape Cod recipe]

24 quahogs	1 teaspoon sugar
½ cup liquor from quahogs, strained	2 tablespoons butter
	2 tablespoons flour
2 sliced onions	1 cup heavy cream
3 cups milk	salt and pepper
minced parsley	

Chop the quahogs fine; place in top of double boiler with onion and liquor. Cook over direct heat for 5 minutes. Add milk and sugar and place over boiling water and let stand but do not cook. Blend butter and flour and stir in. Cook 3 minutes; strain and add cream. Serve in bouillon cups with a small round of toast covered with minced parsley on top. Serves 6 to 8.

This is a specialty of a Cape Cod tea room.

SMOKY CHOWDER

½ pound fat salt pork, diced	1 bay leaf
1 large onion, sliced	4 cups milk
4 medium potatoes, sliced	1½ pounds smoked fillet of haddock, cubed
water	
salt and pepper	

Brown pork in skillet; add onion and sauté until onion is transparent. Add potatoes and water to cover, salt and pepper to taste and bay leaf. When potatoes are almost done add milk and fish and simmer 10 minutes. Serves 6.

GLOUCESTER FISH CHOWDER

3½ to 4-pound haddock or cod	4 cups potatoes, sliced
2 inch cube fat salt pork	4 cups hot milk
1 medium onion, sliced	1 tablespoon salt
⅛ teaspoon pepper	

Put cut-up fish in 2 cups cold water; cook until done. Cut pork into tiny dice and fry to a light brown. Remove pork scraps. Add onion to fat and cook slowly about 5 minutes. Pick fish from skin and bones. Add fish liquor and potatoes to fat and onions and enough water to cover potatoes. Boil until potatoes are nearly done; add fish, hot milk, seasonings, and pork scraps, if desired. Simmer 10 minutes. Serve with sour pickles and common crackers or pilot crackers. Serves 8.

> *Mrs. A. Stacey Barnes, Boardman Avenue, Melrose Highlands, Mass., says this recipe comes from her grandmother, a "grand cook who came from a family of Gloucester folk, famous for tasty New England fish dishes."*

DANIEL WEBSTER'S FISH CHOWDER

"Take a cod of ten pounds, well cleaned, leaving on the skin. Cut into pieces one and a half pounds thick, preserving the head whole. Take one and a half pounds of clear, fat salt pork, cut in thin slices. Do the same with twelve potatoes. Take the largest pot you have. Try out the pork first, then take out the pieces of pork, leaving in the drippings. Add to that three parts of water, a layer of fish, so as to cover the bottom of the pot; next a layer of potatoes, then two tablespoons of salt, 1 teaspoon of pepper, then the pork, another layer of fish, and the remainder of the potatoes.

"Fill the pot with water to cover the ingredients. Put over a good fire. Let the chowder boil twenty-five minutes. When this is done have a quart of boiling milk ready, and ten hard crackers split and dipped in cold water. Add milk and crackers. Let the whole boil five minutes. The chowder is then ready to be first-rate if you have followed the directions. An onion may be added if you like the flavor."

"This chowder," he adds, "is suitable for a large fishing party."

BOSTON STYLE FISH CHOWDER

[Parker House, Boston, Mass.]

A 4-pound haddock	½ pound ground fat salt pork
8 cups cold water	2 onions, chopped fine
1 bay leaf	4 tablespoons flour
1 spray thyme	3 medium potatoes, diced
1 stalk celery	2 cups milk

salt and pepper

Cut fish in 1-inch squares, place head and fish bones in a deep kettle. Add cold water, bay leaf, thyme, and celery. Simmer 15 minutes and strain. Try out salt pork in a heavy skillet; remove cracklings and add onion. Cook until onion is transparent, then add flour. Blend thoroughly. Add potatoes and fish bouillon. Simmer for 15 minutes, then add fish cut in cubes. Simmer until fish is done, about 10 minutes; add milk and bring to a boil. Season. Serves 8.

OYSTER STEW

[Union Oyster House, Boston, Mass., Established 1826]

1 pint oysters (with liquor)	3 cups milk, scalded
¼ cup butter	pepper
1 cup light cream, scalded	½ teaspoon salt
½ teaspoon paprika	

Pick over oysters; then cook in butter and oyster liquor until edges curl. Add cream and milk. Heat to boiling and season. Serve at once with crackers. Serves 4.

> *A century ago in old New England a bowl of piping hot oyster stew formed the traditional Christmas Eve supper. Coming from the Merrie England of their ancestors, the custom of serving oysters on Christmas was quite natural in a country which had an abundance of fat, delicately flavored oysters. In small communities it is still customary to hold Watch Night (New Year's Eve) services at which oyster stew is served during the evening. True New England oyster stew is never thickened.*

FALMOUTH CLAM AND MUSHROOM BISQUE

½ pound fresh mushrooms	3 cups clam broth, strained
3 tablespoons butter	1 cup cream
3 tablespoons flour	salt and pepper

Clean and chop mushrooms. Sauté in butter, blend in flour, add the clam broth and simmer slowly for 10 minutes. Add the cream, season and serve. Serves 4.

CREAM OF OYSTER SOUP

[A Rhode Island recipe]

1 pint oysters, with liquor	bit of bay leaf
4 cups milk	4 tablespoons butter
1 slice onion	4 tablespoons flour
2 stalks celery	salt, pepper
sprig of parsley	croutons, or toast sticks

Chop oysters; add liquor. Heat slowly to the boiling point and press through a coarse sieve. Scald milk with onion, celery, parsley and bay leaf. Melt butter, blend in flour, add milk. Stir over a low fire or over hot water until mixture thickens. Add the oysters and season to taste. Serve at once with fried croutons or toast sticks. Serves 4.

GREENFIELD CORN AND OYSTER STEW

1 pint oysters	2 teaspoons salt
½ cup water	2 cups celery, cut and boiled
2 tablespoons flour	tender
2 tablespoons butter	⅛ teaspoon pepper
3 cups milk	1¾ cups whole kernel corn
1 cup cream	

Cook oysters in water until edges curl. Remove from heat and strain broth. Blend butter and flour, add broth gradually; add milk, simmer 5 minutes, stirring constantly. Add cooked celery, corn and cream and simmer 5 minutes longer. Add oysters last. Season. Serves 6.

NANTUCKET SCALLOP CHOWDER

4 tablespoons butter
2 small onions, sliced
1 pint scallops, cut in pieces
2 cups boiling water

1 cup diced potatoes
4 cups milk, scalded
salt and pepper
common crackers, split and toasted

Melt butter, lightly brown onions in butter. Remove onions. Cook scallops in butter 5 minutes. Add boiling water, onion and potato and simmer 30 minutes. Add scalded milk and simmer 15 minutes more. Season to taste; serve hot with crackers. Serves 5.

LOBSTER STEW, CASCO BAY

[Copley-Plaza, Boston, Mass.]

5 pounds lobsters, boiled
5 tablespoons butter
5 cups top milk (half milk and half cream)
2 cups Duxbury clam broth
salt, paprika, cayenne

Remove meat from shell and cut in dice about ½ inch square. Sauté in butter 3 or 4 minutes. Stir in top milk and clam broth. Simmer about 6 minutes. Season with salt, paprika and a sprinkling of cayenne. Serves 6.

OLD-FASHIONED SPLIT PEA SOUP

2 cups dried split yellow peas
12 cups cold water

1 onion, sliced
1 ham bone

salt and pepper

Pick over peas and soak overnight. Drain, add cold water, ham bone and onion. Simmer 3 or 4 hours, or until peas are soft. Rub through a sieve and season. If soup is too thick add boiling water. Serves 8.

Mrs. Leonard S. Cress, Lexington, Mass., author of this recipe, writes that her ancestors the Pikes, Dows and Adams of Massachusetts, Vermont and New Hampshire were good old-fashioned New England cooks. This pea soup was always served with johnnycake and combines a New England quality of pioneer honesty with solid comfort. Some old-time recipes call for the addition of 1 potato, sliced, or 1 stalk of celery, diced.

PURÉE OF SPLIT PEA SOUP

[*Congress Square Hotel, Portland, Me.*]

1 cup yellow split peas	1 onion, sliced
1½ cups green split peas	¼ teaspoon pepper
16 cups cold water	1 teaspoon Worcestershire
¼ pound salt pork, cut in	sauce
pieces	1 clove garlic (optional)
1 small piece of left-over ham	3 tablespoons flour
2 stalks celery, diced	3 medium sized potatoes,
1 carrot, scraped and sliced	peeled and sliced

1½ cups light cream, scalded

Soak peas in water overnight; drain, add cold water, bring to a boil and simmer 30 minutes. Sauté salt pork, add ham, cut in pieces, celery, onion, carrot; add pepper, Worcestershire sauce and garlic. Shake in flour and continue to sauté for 15 minutes, stirring constantly. Combine with peas; add potatoes, simmer 2 hours longer, then strain through purée strainer. (If soup is too thick, add boiling water.) Before serving add cream, heat to boiling, season and serve with johnnycake. Serves 10 to 12.

BOSTON BLACK BEAN SOUP

2 cups dried black beans
1 tablespoon salt
2 quarts water
1 tablespoon butter
2 tablespoons flour
½ tablespoon minced onion

⅛ teaspoon black pepper
⅛ teaspoon dry mustard
1 cup heavy cream
6 thin slices of lemon
6 cloves
1 hard-cooked egg, sliced

Soak beans overnight in water to cover. Drain. Add salt and water and cook 2 hours or until beans are very soft. Force mixture through sieve. Place purée back on stove and simmer 15 minutes. Melt butter, blend in flour. Add onion, pepper and mustard. Add cream slowly, stirring constantly until slightly thickened. Add to bean purée, blending well. Heat just to boiling point. Serve in shallow bowls. Place a slice of lemon with a clove and a slice of hard-cooked egg in each bowl. Serve with croutons. Serves 6.

BAKED KIDNEY BEAN SOUP

[Edith Taylor, Indian Head Street, South Hanson, Mass.]

2 tablespoons onion, chopped
1 tablespoon celery, chopped
2 tablespoons butter
2 tablespoons flour

1 teaspoon salt
¼ teaspoon pepper
3 cups baked kidney beans
4 cups water

Place onion, celery and butter in skillet, cover and simmer slowly until tender. Blend with flour, salt and pepper. Simmer beans for 15 minutes in water. (Canned kidney beans or pea beans or yellow eye beans may be used in which case use 1 tall 28-ounce tin of beans and 1½ tins water.) Combine all ingredients and press through sieve. Reheat and serve with croutons. Serves 5.

AROOSTOOK POTATO AND GREEN PEA SOUP

2 medium sized potatoes, diced   2 tablespoons butter
1 onion, sliced   2 tablespoons flour
2 cups boiling water   4 cups milk
1 cup canned or fresh cooked peas   salt and pepper
      minced parsley or chives (if desired)

Boil potatoes and onion in water until both are tender. Add peas and rub through a sieve with the water in which potatoes and onion were cooked. Blend butter with flour and add hot milk. Cook until thickened, stirring constantly. Add purée and season. Minced parsley or chives may be served on top. Serves 5.

AROOSTOOK POTATO SOUP

4 cups potatoes, diced   4 cups milk
2 medium onions, finely sliced   1 teaspoon salt
3 cups boiling water   ⅛ teaspoon pepper
1 tablespoon flour   sprinkling nutmeg
2 tablespoons butter   chopped parsley or chives

Cook potatoes and onions in water until tender; drain, force through ricer or sieve with the water in which they were cooked. Blend flour and butter, add purée and milk, slowly stirring well; season and garnish with chopped parsley or chives. Serves 6.

MASHED POTATO SOUP

Left-over mashed potatoes make excellent potato soup. Sauté finely chopped onion in butter, blend with mashed potatoes, add thin cream sauce or rich milk and seasonings. Heat to boil, stirring constantly.

DEERFOOT CHOWDER

½ cup salt pork, cut in fine
    shreds
1 medium sized onion
1 medium sized potato
2 cups boiling water
2 cups canned corn

2 cups milk
2 tablespoons flour
2 teaspoons cold water
1½ cups canned tomatoes
1 teaspoon sugar
⅛ teaspoon soda

salt and pepper

Try out the salt pork and sauté the sliced onion in the fat. Add the potato and boiling water and cook until tender. Add corn and milk, thicken with flour blended with cold water and add the tomato heated with the sugar, soda and seasonings last. Serves 6.

MAINE CORN CHOWDER

3 tablespoons fat salt pork,
    diced
1 onion, sliced
2 cups potatoes, diced
1½ cups boiling water

1 cup canned corn
1 cup milk
1 cup cream
salt and pepper
4 common crackers, split

Try out salt pork, add onion and cook until a golden brown. Add potatoes, water, corn and cook until potatoes are tender. Add milk and cream and reheat. Season. Place a cracker in each dish and pour chowder over crackers. Serves 4.

VERMONT CABBAGE SOUP

[*Charles F. Adams, 101 Milk St., Boston, Mass.*]

Chop fine 1 small head of cabbage. (There should be about 3 cups when it is chopped.) Add water to cover and cook until tender. Drain off all but 1 cup of the water. Add 3 cups milk and 1 cup cream. Season to taste with salt and pepper. Serve hot. Serves 6.

COVENTRY BAKED SOUP

[*Mrs. George B. Taylor, South Coventry, Conn.*]

1 cup dried split peas	1 tablespoon rice
8 cups cold water	1 carrot, diced
1 pound stewing beef or lamb,	1 onion, diced
cut in cubes	1 teaspoon salt

Pick over peas and soak overnight. Drain, add remaining ingredients. Place in large beanpot, cover, and bake 3 to 4 hours in slow oven (300° F.). Add boiling water if soup is too thick. Serves 6.

YANKEE SUCCOTASH CHOWDER

¼ pound salt pork	1 quart rich milk
1 dozen ears sweet corn	¼ pound butter
1 quart cranberry beans, shelled	2 tablespoons flour
water	4 tablespoons cold water
salt and pepper	

Cut pork into small cubes. Cut uncooked corn from cob. Place beans, pork and corn cobs into a large kettle and cover with water. Cook until beans are soft and pork tender. Remove cobs, scrape, add scrapings to kettle. Add milk, butter, salt and pepper. Add cut corn and simmer 20 minutes. Thicken with the flour which has been mixed with the cold water. Allow the chowder to stand one day. Reheat and serve. Serves 8.

Mrs. James H. Prince, Auburn, Me., can trace this recipe back 200 years in her husband's family. She still uses it today. Boiling the cobs gives an interesting and unusual taste to the dish. The Indians boiled corn cobs with the succotash which they prepared.

PARSNIP CHOWDER

⅛ pound salt pork
1 small onion, sliced
3 cups parsnips, cut in cubes
1 cup potatoes, cut in cubes
2 cups boiling water

1 quart rich milk
4 tablespoons butter
½ cup rolled cracker crumbs
   (optional)
salt and pepper

minced parsley (optional)

Try out salt pork; remove cracklings. Add onion and sauté gently; add parsnips and potatoes; add water and cook about 30 minutes or until parsnips and potatoes are done. Add milk and butter. Season to taste. Some recipes call for the addition of ½ cup rolled cracker crumbs; others thicken chowder slightly with 2 tablespoons flour mixed with 2 tablespoons cold water and top with minced parsley. Serves 8.

CREAM OF PARSNIP SOUP

½ onion, minced
½ cup water
4 cups milk
1 cup cooked parsnips, rubbed
   through a sieve

3 tablespoons butter
3 tablespoons flour
1 teaspoon salt
⅛ teaspoon pepper
¼ teaspoon paprika

Boil minced onion until tender in water. Scald milk and add onion and parsnip purée. Blend butter and flour and add to hot mixture, stirring for 5 minutes or until smooth. Season. Serves 5.

Towards the end of February the frost begins to leave the ground in New England. Then it's time to dig the first "mess" of parsnips from the kitchen garden where they have ripened and sweetened all winter. Parsnips were once considered poisonous until after they had been frozen. The fact is, they were not a "keeping" vegetable and hence were better in the ground than pulled.

PARSONAGE OYSTER PLANT SOUP

1 bunch oyster plant (also called   2 cups rich milk, scalded
    salsify)   2 tablespoons butter
1 onion, sliced   salt and pepper

Wash, scrape and cut the oyster plant in thin slices. Add onion and enough water to keep from burning. Cook until vegetables are tender and water almost boiled away. Put onion and half the oyster plant through food press or sieve; add milk, butter and seasonings to taste. Add the remainder of the oyster plant and heat. Serves 3.

CONNECTICUT CREAM OF ONION SOUP

3 cups sliced onions   3 tablespoons flour
7 tablespoons butter or chicken fat   3 cups rich milk, scalded
3 cups boiling water   salt and pepper

Sauté onion slowly in 4 tablespoons butter or chicken fat until lightly browned. Add boiling water and simmer 15 minutes or until tender. Rub through a coarse sieve and reheat. Blend remaining 3 tablespoons butter or chicken fat with flour and add hot milk. Cook until thickened, stirring constantly. Add onion purée. Season. Serves 5.

EGG CHOWDER

[Norma Roberts, Bristol, N. H.]

½ cup fat salt pork, diced   5 hard boiled eggs, sliced
5 large potatoes, sliced   2 tablespoons butter
2 cups milk, scalded   salt and pepper

Dice salt pork and fry up brown; add potatoes and hot water to cover. Cook until potatoes are done. Add milk, eggs, butter and seasonings. Serves 6.

VEGETABLE BEEF SOUP

[Maybelle Burroughs, Wakefield, N. H.]

4 pounds shin of beef	¼ cup diced celery
10 cups water	¼ cup diced turnip (optional)
½ cup diced onions	2 whole cloves
¼ cup diced carrots	1 bay leaf

2 teaspoons salt

Put soup bone on to cook in cold water and cook until meat falls from bone. Set away to cool. Remove the fat and bones; cut the meat in small cubes and add the vegetables and seasonings. Makes about 2½ quarts.

In making soup use whatever vegetables your family likes, whatever is in season and plenty of imagination. Here is a partial list of vegetables and herbs that may be used to vary the flavor of this soup: ¼ cup diced green pepper, a nip of ground pepper; 1 cup lima beans, ¼ cup shell beans, ¼ cup green peas, dried tops of fresh celery, 2 tomatoes, 2 sprigs parsley, ¼ cup mushrooms, 1 tablespoon catsup, 1 tablespoon of sugar, a dash of nutmeg, 1 tablespoon of vinegar, 3 sprigs thyme, 1 sprig marjoram, 1 peppercorn.

MUTTON BROTH

Substitute 2 pounds breast of mutton for shin of beef in recipe above. Add 2 tablespoons pearl barley, soaked overnight in cold water. Omit turnip and cloves. Strain. Make 2 quarts.

MARTHA'S VINEYARD CHICKEN CHOWDER

[*Mrs. Orlin F. Davis, Vineyard Haven, Mass.*]

1 6-pound fowl	4 cups hot water
2 quarts cold water	8 cups diced potatoes
¼ pound salt pork, cubed	1 tablespoon salt
2 medium-sized onions,	4 cups milk, scalded
sliced	2 tablespoons butter

The day before this chowder is to be served, clean fowl and cut in pieces, cover with cold water, heat slowly to the boiling point, simmer, covered, 3 hours, or until tender. When done, remove chicken, cut meat in dice. Allow liquor to become cold, remove fat, then return chicken meat to the liquor.

The following day try out salt pork, remove cracklings, add onions and cook very slowly until onions are light brown. Place onions and pork fat in a large kettle, add hot water, potatoes, and salt. Simmer until potatoes are tender. Bring chicken liquor and meat to a boil and boil (not simmer) for 10 minutes. Add milk and butter. Combine the two mixtures. Some Islanders thicken the chowder slightly. Others do not. Serves 12.

During the summer months the Farmers' Co-operative Market opens twice a week in the Agricultural Hall in West Tisbury, Martha's Vineyard. The farmers supply Islanders and summer guests with fresh fruits and vegetables. Their wives offer for sale cooked foods which are distinctive of the Island, such as beach plum preserves, pastries, cakes, cookies, hot breads, and chicken chowder, one of the most famous of all Island dishes.

CREAM OF TURKEY OR CHICKEN SOUP

[A Vermont recipe]

½ cup finely chopped celery   2 tablespoons flour
3 cups turkey or chicken stock   2 tablespoons butter
½ cup cream

Simmer the celery in the turkey or chicken stock until celery is tender. Thicken soup by blending butter and flour and adding soup gradually. Simmer 10 minutes. Add cream, heat and serve. Serves 4.

R U A YANKEE COOK?

Answers on page 366

1. How do you pronounce "maple syrup?" "sumach"? "raspberry"? "saleratus"?
2. What famous New England dish rhymes with "Norwich"? How do you pronounce it?
3. What is "switchel"? "Johnnycakes"? What are "oil nuts"?
4. In place of what fruit may sumach berries be used?
5. What is a local substitute for baking-powder?
6. What is "fish hash"?
7. What is meant by "crackling"?
8. How is "souse" prepared?
9. What are "huff juffs"?
10. How do you make "milk emptyin's"?
11. What is "cider applesauce"?
12. What is "sap coffee"?
13. How is "spruce beer" prepared?
14. What is hulled corn?
15. What is brown bread brewis?

RHODE ISLAND CLAMBAKES

Horace G. Belcher

It has been said that the chief contribution of the Indians to the New England pioneers was the clambake.

All along the shore line from Maine to Connecticut are found heaps of buried shells of the soft shell clam-heaps marking the old gathering places where the tribes assembled for their feasts of shellfish. For the Indians of all the New England tribes went down to the shore in summer for clambakes, just as the New England farmers did later. And the Indians enjoyed their bakes just as much.

While the white man has elaborated the bake, its essentials and the method of making it remain unchanged from those which the Red Man enjoyed. In the Indian clambake the clams, fish and corn, were all cooked in the steam from the clams and from rock-weed spread on hot stones; this was covered over to confine the steam. In the centuries since the first white man tasted the delectable results of this rude open-air cooking he has not improved on it.

The Indian and then the farmer went to the shore, dug his clams in flats exposed at low tide, found stones in the fields and with them made his bake. Later, some of the country churches began making an annual bake as a summer outing and several of these bakes are continued to this day. The annual bake of the Hornbine church of Rehoboth, just over the Massachusetts line from Rhode Island, and of the Liberty church in famous old "South County" in Rhode Island, served in groves adjacent to the church, still draw crowds of city folk every year. The Antiquarian Society bake, another Rehoboth fixture, used to draw 1500 or more, served in relays in a great tent; it is now reduced to about one third of that number. The Frenchtown bake, another annual Rhode Island feature in what is popularly known as South County although its official name is Washington County (formerly King's), is a popular one. And there are others. Many a political career has been boosted by speeches at some of these bakes.

23

Each bake has its own bakemaster who serves year after year, sometimes for half a lifetime. He supervises its preparation from the building of the fire to the placing of the clams and the rest of the bake. His judgment fixes the time for the opening bake and to him goes credit for its success. Bakemaking is an art not given to everyone and a good bakemaster is much sought after and proud of his skill.

But these country bakes came only once a year and Rhode Islanders and their visitors pined for an opportunity to enjoy this feast whenever they felt like it. The fame of the Rhode Island bake spread and with it a demand. And so in the latter part of the last century and in the earlier years of the present, the shores of upper Narragansett Bay were dotted with clambake resorts where bakes were served daily. These resorts were reached by big fleets of Bay steamboats running out of Providence and in their heydey many excursions were run to them from neighboring states.

The automobile has driven the sidewheel passenger steamboat of a more leisurely period from Narrangansett's waters. Where once stood Field's Point, whose chowder was famous, is now a Providence municipal dock. But two of these old clambake resorts— Rocky Point and Crescent Park, both near Providence—still serve bakes daily in the summer and the secret of the Field's Point chowder has not been lost.

The Clambake Club at Newport is an adjunct to Bailey's Beach where Society bathes; and the Squantum Association and the Pomham Club, both just outside Providence, serve weekly bakes to their members. Squantum, where Presidents and titled guests have dined, has another famous clam chowder, still made as it was when this exclusive organization was founded during the time that Grant ran for re-election. Guest registers of Squantum and Pomham contain the names of many of the nation's most distinguished men. But their bakes differ only in detail and in their elaboration from the public bakes; and wherever you may get your bake you will find it made in the same way.

Opinions may differ as to whether a clam chowder should be

THE WINNER! MAINE CHAMPION CLAM DIGGER

made with milk or should include tomatoes; two propositions good for an argument wherever chowder and bakes are known, but no one ever disputes the old Indian method of making a bake.

The Rhode Island bake is made with soft-shell clams preferably about two inches long. On a layer of stones, each about the size of a man's head, is built a fire of cordwood which is allowed to burn until the stones are heated white hot. Then the embers are removed with six-tined potato diggers and pitchforks, the stones are swept clean of ashes and a thick layer of rockweed, a marine growth found along the shores of Rhode Island, is thrown on the hot stones. A good fire will have the stones white hot and ready in about an hour. At clambake resorts the stones are heated on a cement platform.

In rapid succession the ingredients of the bake are placed on the steaming rockwood whose salty moisture cooks them and whose flavor permeates them. First the clams, then another layer of rockweed, then white and sweet potatoes still in their skins, sweet corn covered with a thin layer of husks, fish in cloth or paper bags (bluefish by preference although mackerel will do), small sausages or buckworsts similarly wrapped, lobsters or chickens or both, although strictly speaking the chicken does not belong in a Rhode Island bake.

Then the whole is covered with a thick wet canvas which is kept wet during the baking. The steam from the moisture of the clams and the rockweed permeates, "tenderizes" and flavors everything. This steam is carefully confined, for the edges of the canvas are kept covered with rockweed and held down with stones. Even then, the mouth-watering odor of the bake escapes during the forty-five minutes or more it takes to cook the bake.

On the tables you will find sliced cucumbers, sliced tomatoes, sliced raw onions, brown bread, white bread, butter, pepper, salt, vinegar, pepper-sauce, small pitchers of melted butter. The first course is clam chowder, which may be made of soft-shell clams alone, or of the hard-shell clam, which here is known by its Indian name of quahog, or of both. In most cases your clam-chowder is made from quahogs, but the best chowder is from equal portions of both soft- and hard-shell clams, flavored with the quahog liquor and with the results of trying out minced salt pork.

With the chowder are served hot clam-cakes or clam fritters, delectable concoctions of dough containing chopped quahogs which gives them an incomparable flavor. Dropped from a spoon, the cakes, which take odd, irregular shapes, are fried in deep fat to a golden brown. Properly made they are light, and eaten hot they fairly melt in your mouth. A clam-cake in the left hand and a spoonful of chowder thickened with pilot bread (a flaky hard cracker of nutty flavor) in the right is the proper procedure, repeated to taste; and there is something wrong with your appetite if you do not have a second helping of chowder from the big tureen set on the table. At private bakes chowder, clam-cakes and littlenecks (young quahogs about the size of a half-dollar) are served for luncheon, the bake being opened in the late afternoon, five or six o'clock.

When the bake is opened, tin dishes holding two quarts of clams are served to each guest. You spread the clam shells apart with your fingers, remove the covering of the clam snout, take the clam by the snout and dip it in a small dish in which you have placed a quantity of hot melted butter with a little vinegar or perhaps a dash of peppersauce. Then you eat the clams with the exception of the snout, which is tough. The taste is something to remember.

Between times you may drink a cup or so of the clam broth, which you will find fit for the gods and a stomach-settler. After the hot clams come more hot clams—and all the other good things that were in the bake. If the bake is properly made, you will find you can eat clams until the cows come home. When you feel you cannot eat another mouthful, watermelon or, if you are especially fortunate, baked Indian pudding made of Indian meal, molasses and milk and baked long in a slow oven, is brought on. And at the clambake clubs the bake ends with clear coffee. It is a meal you will never forget—and if you do your duty by the bake you will not need another meal that day.

A family bake or one for a small group may easily be made in a barrel. The best barrel bake I know of is that of Captain Herbert M. Knowles, long superintendent of the Third Life Saving District before the U. S. Life Saving Service was incorporated in the Coast Guard. Here is Captain Knowles' bake:

"Make cheesecloth bags for clams, sweet and Irish potatoes, corn and everything except lobsters, chicken and fish provided you include these. The bag for clams should be broad enough to allow the clams to spread out over the barrel. The fish should be split in half and placed on shingles wrapped in cheesecloth, so each piece may be handled by unwrapping the cloth and sliding onto a platter. Lobsters may be thrown in the bake in any way.

"Stones about the size of two bowls put together are about the right size. Wood should be packed up crossways, with shavings, etc. underneath, and the stones packed in with the wood up toward the top of the barrel before lighting. Then add wood until the stones get hot. They turn white when of the proper heat. Set the barrel as deeply into sand as you wish. You cannot get it too deep. Put about three inches of sand or gravel in the bottom of the barrel and place pieces of scrap sheet iron around the sides of the barrel. These scraps can be had at any tin shop without cost. The sand and scrap iron prevent the stones from burning the bottom and sides of the barrel. The stones are picked up with a six-tine fork when hot and packed around well. If hot enough they will break and stow well.

"Be sure to have everything for the bake ready to go in the barrel as soon as the stones are put in. The green corn husks should be soaked in salt water and added with the first layer of rockweed over the stones. Then lay in the clam bag, spreading it out as much as possible. Pack your lobsters around this; then lay in the potatoes, fish, chicken and such other things as you may add.

"Spread a wet or moist bag over the bake and fill the barrel up tightly with wet sea weed. If you have a washtub handy turn it over the top of the barrel and apply wet seaweed around it to hold in the steam.

"Hold your ear to the side of the barrel when you hear the ingredients of the bake growling, which should be within a few minutes after steam starts making; you will know that all is well. The bake should be ready to open in about forty-five minutes to an hour from that time. I never saw one cooked too long and I once had one in about three hours. To my surprise, it turned out to be one of the best bakes I ever had.

"Saving the corn husks and soaking them to lay over the stones with the seaweed, gives the bake a sweetness which cannot be obtained in any other way."

Albert A. Slocum, who served bakes daily at his place on Pawtuxet Cove, Rhode Island, gave these suggestions for a barrel bake:

"In building the fire, put a flat stone under the lower ends of the wood for a draft, first placing the wood in the form of a square, and then crossing the other sticks east and west. Pile stones on the wood. Avoid granite stones which crumble in heat. Have the stones white hot.

"Put a foot or so of rockweed over the stones in the barrel, first cutting a hole four inches long in the bottom of the barrel for drainage. The hole must be near the point where the head joins the staves, and the barrel must be tipped to aid flow of drainage. Put six inches of rockweed in bottom of barrel, then stones, then a big handful of rockweed over the hot stones. Turn in the clams, a bushel being necessary to furnish sufficient steam for cooking all the features of a bake. Then add sausage, corn and the rest and cover all with a piece of clean canvas, binding down the edges to keep steam in. A dozen stones of fair size will cook anything. Cook a half hour or more.

"Be sure to permit free egress of water from the bake, through the hole made in the bottom of the barrel for that purpose. This water will rush out in a stream, the presence of which is a sure sign of success for the bake."

Try it yourself sometime—if you can get the necessary fixings. If not, come to Rhode Island, where we know how to make clambakes.

II. FISH: SHELL, SALT AND FRESH

CODFISH BALLS

1½ cups salt cod   1½ tablespoons butter
3 cups potatoes, diced   pepper
            1 egg

Soak codfish in cold water ½ hour; drain and "pick up" (flake); boil fish and potatoes together until potatoes are tender; drain and shake over fire to dry. Mash, being sure there are no lumps; add butter and pepper and beat until mixture is fluffy. Add egg and continue beating. Shape in a tablespoon and drop by spoonfuls in hot deep fat (370° F.) and fry not more than 4 or 5 at a time until a golden brown. Drain. Serves 6. Serve with gherkins or sliced green tomato pickles.

This recipe was used by the great-grandmother of Mrs. P. A. Rich of Framingham Center, Mass. She lived in Salem and served codfish cakes every Tuesday and Friday at noon.

Codfish is one of the oldest of American foods. The Pilgrim fathers subsisted largely on it. Each year, as cold weather approached, they put away stores of meaty cod, carefully preserved with salt.

29

FLUFFY FISH CAKES

[Made with shredded codfish]

1 cup shredded codfish	1 egg
2 cups hot, mashed potato	¼ teaspoon pepper

Freshen the codfish in cold water and wring dry in a cloth or drain in fine sieve. Add the codfish to the potato, then the egg and pepper. Beat until fluffy and creamy; form into small balls or cakes and cook in hot deep fat (370° F.) or pan-fry until a golden brown. Drain and garnish with parsley. Makes 16 balls.

Eating fish balls for Sunday morning breakfast is part of Boston's tradition, like reading the Transcript or taking visitors to see the glass flowers.

SCALLOPED CODFISH

1 pound salt codfish	1 tablespoon chopped parsley
2 cups thin cream sauce	1 teaspoon lemon juice
dash of pepper	¼ cup buttered crumbs

Freshen codfish (see New England Salt Fish Dinner, page 32). Simmer below boiling point for about 5 minutes or until fish is tender. Drain. Add white sauce and seasoning to taste. Pour into greased baking dish, sprinkle with buttered crumbs and bake in hot oven (400° F.) until crumbs are brown, about 20 minutes. Serves 4.

The first scalloped foods were prepared and served in large scallop shells—hence the name.

CREAMED CODFISH

    1 cup salt codfish
    1 cup thin white sauce (with salt omitted)
    dash of pepper

Freshen the fish (see New England Salt Fish Dinner, page 32).
Simmer below boiling point for about 5 minutes, or until fish is
tender. Drain, reheat fish in the white sauce, seasoned. Serve with
baked or boiled potatoes. Hard-boiled eggs may be sliced over the
fish. Serves 3.

SCALLOPED COD CHEEKS AND TONGUES

[Mrs. R. H. Sawyer, Littleton, Mass.]

2 pounds cod cheeks and tongues	2 cups white thin sauce
	1 tablespoon lemon juice
2 tablespoons butter	salt and pepper
1 cup bread crumbs	

If cheeks and tongues have been salted, they must be soaked
overnight. Drain. Simmer 5 minutes in fresh water. Drain. Sauté
in butter. Make white sauce, add lemon juice, season to taste.
Place fish in a baking dish. Pour on white sauce, sprinkle bread
crumbs over top, dot with butter and bake in a hot oven (400° F.)
until crumbs are brown. Serves 8.

*Fried codfish tongues are a specialty of the Parker House,
Boston. They are seasoned, dipped in milk, rolled in flour,
fried in butter to a golden brown. Over them is poured
freshly browned butter flavored with lemon juice and a
sprinkling of freshly chopped parsley.*

NEW ENGLAND SALT FISH DINNER

["Picked Fish"—it's sometimes called]

2 pounds salt cod	½ pound fat salt pork
8 medium sized potatoes	4 tablespoons flour
6 medium sized beets	2 cups milk

There are two ways to freshen salt cod:

I

Place fish on wooden strips (clothes pins will do) or silverware in a large kettle of water. The flesh side should be down so that salt, when extracted, can sink to the bottom of the kettle. Do not allow water to become more than warm. Soak overnight or until sufficiently fresh.

The other way:

II

Place fish in a kettle of cold water, heat water to a point just below boiling; pour off water and start all over again. Three changes of water is usually enough. Tasting is the only sure way to tell exactly how many changes of water are required. After fish has been freshened, simmer until tender in water just below the boiling point. This takes only a very few minutes. Do not at any time boil fish, as boiling makes it tough. Fish is done when it will flake if broken.

Boil the potatoes. Boil and dice the beets. Slice the salt pork into thin strips and cut in fine pieces. Try out slowly, drain and return 4 tablespoons of the fat to the frying pan. Blend the flour with the hot fat, add the milk slowly, stirring so that gravy will be smooth. Season to taste with salt and pepper. Keep hot.

Place freshened fish on a hot platter with a generous sprinkling of bits of crisp, fried salt pork on top. Surround the fish with a red border of diced buttered beets. Serve potatoes and gravy separately. Complete the meal with squares of golden corn bread flanked by cottage cheese and boiled apple cider sauce. Boiled onions and boiled carrots are sometimes served with this dinner. Serves 6 to 8.

Codfish used to come in huge, whole fish which were hung in the cellarway or nailed to the barndoor of New England farm homes. Pieces were freshened, and made into salt fish dinner, fried with salt pork scraps, served with egg sauce or made into fish cakes or chowders. Pieces were also broiled over the coals, then boiling water was poured on them, to soften, and they were sent to the table dripping with butter.

Never cut salt fish; tear it apart.

RED FISH HASH

1 cup cold boiled or baked potatoes
1 cup boiled beets

1 cup left-over cooked salt cod
¼ cup milk
pepper

Chop potatoes, beets and codfish to a fine hash; moisten with milk; season. Brown in a skillet well greased with butter. Serves 4.

A recipe prized by the great-great-grandmother of Mabelle A. Burt, Lenox Avenue, Providence, R. I.

Fish Hash, another famous Yankee dish, is made according to this same recipe, omitting the beets.

BROILED MACKEREL

Split fish and spread, skin side down, on greased broiler or rack. Season with salt, pepper and lemon juice. Broil in a pre-heated oven (450° F.), 10 minutes, or until fish is nicely browned. Turn and broil on skin side enough to crisp skin. Serve on hot platter with lemon slices. Allow ½ pound of fish per person.

BAKED SALT MACKEREL

[Mrs. Ella Wood Habern, 20 Albion St., Hyde Park, Mass.]

Fresh mackerel, following directions given in New England Salt Fish Dinner recipe, page 32. Drain. Place in a pan skin side up and bake in a moderate oven (350° F.) about 15 minutes or until light brown. Pour off any liquid there may be in the pan; add 2 cups thin cream and bake about 15 minutes longer, or until light brown again and tender. Allow ½ pound mackerel per person.

BAKED MACKEREL

Clean and split large mackerel. Rub with salt and pepper. Place skin side down in greased baking pan. Pour over fish 1 cup seasoned milk. Bake uncovered 20 to 25 minutes in moderately hot oven (375° F.). Remove carefully to hot platter. Allow ½ pound of fish per person.

Boston mackerel is a fat fish and should not be fried, nor should fat be added in the cooking process. It should be boiled, broiled or baked.

Eight or nine years ago mackerel almost entirely disappeared. There was a prediction that this branch of the industry had passed out. However, within the past four or five years larger schools of fish have made their appearance than at any time during the past twenty years. It is nothing unusual for fishermen to report acres and acres of swimming, feeding mackerel through which their boats plow their way, literally pushing the fish aside as they go. A net almost a mile long and one hundred and twenty-five feet deep is run around the "school"—the ends brought together and a rope in the bottom pulled—causing the net to take the shape of a saucepan and entrap the whole "school." Quite often mackerel fishermen will leave Boston Fish Pier one day and return the next with a large trip of fish that have scarcely stopped wiggling.

BAKED FINNAN HADDIE

Order a split smoked haddock (not individual fillets) cut in individual servings. Place skin side down in shallow baking dish and add enough rich milk to partially cover fish. Dot with butter. Sprinkle with pepper. Place shallow pan under flame of pre-heated broiler and broil until fish is tender, about 20 minutes. Baste with hot milk before serving. Allow ½ pound of fish per person. Milk remaining in the pan makes a delicious bouillon.

This recipe comes from the Liberty Café, Fish Pier, Boston. Although this restaurant is run by "Jimmie, the Greek," epicures agree that some of the best sea food in Boston is served here. Jimmie is particularly famous for his finnan haddie.

Finnan haddie is, strictly speaking, a Scotch and not a Yankee dish. It gets its title from the reputation of the haddock cured around Findon, a fishing village near Aberdeen, Scotland. Once our American supply was almost entirely imported, but now the great bulk of it, and some of the very finest, comes from New England.

FINNAN HADDIE PIE

Cover 1 pound finnan haddie with milk and soak 1 hour. Bring slowly almost to the boiling point, cool, drain and flake. Add to 2 cups medium white sauce, made without salt. Pour into a buttered baking dish. Cover with individual baking-powder biscuits rolled ½ inch thick. Bake in hot oven (400° F.) 15 to 20 minutes or until biscuits are brown. Serves 4.

2 chopped hard boiled eggs may be added to cream sauce.

BOILED COD

Wrap a fresh cod in a piece of cheesecloth. Place in a kettle of gently boiling water. For each quart of water add ½ teaspoon salt and 2 teaspoons vinegar. Simmer 8 minutes per pound. Allow ½ pound fish for each person to be served.

It is said that fishermen originally believed the cod became "the sacred cod" because it was the fish that Christ used when He multiplied the fish and fed the multitude, and even today the marks of His thumbs and forefingers are plainly visible on the codfish. His Satanic majesty stood by and said he, too, could multiply fish and feed multitudes. Reaching for one of the fish it wriggled and slid through his red-hot fingers, burning two black stripes down its side and thus clearly differentiating the haddock from the sacred cod. These markings, in actual practice, do distinguish one variety from the other. These two fish contribute to the greater portion of the New England catch and are similar in taste and texture. For many years, haddock was not considered a suitable fish for marketing and very little of it was caught, but recently the popularity has increased, until today in New England, there is approximately three times as much haddock marketed as cod.

FISH CUSTARD

1½ pounds haddock or cod	2 eggs, well beaten
1½ teaspoons cornstarch	salt and pepper
1½ cups milk	2 tablespoons melted butter

Boil and flake fish. Dissolve cornstarch in milk. Add eggs, salt, pepper and melted butter and pour over fish. Turn into buttered casserole. Bake in slow oven (350° F.) 45 minutes or until pudding is set. Serves 5. Serve with johnnycake and mustard pickles.

BAKED STUFFED HADDOCK OR COD

Select a 2- or 3-pound fish. Remove head, tail and fins. Sprinkle inside and outside with salt. Lay fish in a greased pan and fill until it bulges with oyster stuffing. Sew edges together with coarse thread. Gash the fish on top in four places and insert strips of fat salt pork. Bake in a hot oven (400° F.) for 30 to 40 minutes. Serve with parsley butter sauce. Serves 6.

OYSTER STUFFING

2 cups bread crumbs	½ pint oysters cut in small pieces
¼ cup melted butter	⅛ teaspoon pepper
1 small onion, minced	½ teaspoon salt
½ cup finely cut celery	2 tablespoons heated oyster liquor

Mix ingredients lightly with a fork.

FISH LOAF

[From the New England Kitchen of Louise Crathern Russell]

2 eggs, separated	1 cup fine breadcrumbs
½ green pepper, minced	2 teaspoons lemon juice
1 tablespoon onion, minced	½ cup milk
½ cup walnuts, chopped	⅛ teaspoon salt
2 cups cooked flaked fish	

Beat yolks; combine all ingredients, folding in beaten egg whites last. Bake in a pan (set in hot water) in a moderately hot (375° F.) oven 45 minutes. Turn loaf onto a hot platter. Arrange around it cooked flowerets of cauliflower, the tips of which have been dipped in melted butter. Serves 4.

BAKED FILLET OF SOLE

½ teaspoon salt   1 pound flounder fillets
1 cup milk   sifted bread crumbs
                3 tablespoons melted butter

Add salt to milk. Dip fillets in milk, then in bread crumbs. Place in buttered baking dish and sprinkle with melted butter. Bake in hot oven (450° F.) about 8 minutes, or until browned. Serve with tartar sauce. (See page 59.) Serves 4.

CONNECTICUT KEDGEREE

2 cups cooked rice   2 tablespoons minced parsley
2 cups cooked flaked fish   ½ cup top milk
4 hard-cooked eggs, chopped   salt and pepper

To hot rice add remaining ingredients and reheat in double boiler. Serve immediately. Serves 5.

Many dishes identified with New England had their origin in foreign lands and were brought to this country by our sea-faring forebears. This particular dish may be traced back to the Armenian dish, Kidgeri. Yankee housewives, unacquainted with egg-plant, in long-ago days, evidently thought eggs would do just as well. Then someone tried fish instead of lamb. By such steps this recipe evolved, and in its present form was handed down in the family of Mrs. Evan J. David, Westport, Conn., since the days of Clipper ships. The original recipe calls for summer savory and thyme, and was served on rusks.

WARWICK MOLDED SALMON

1½ tablespoons butter   1 cup milk
1½ tablespoons flour   1 cup salmon, finely minced
½ teaspoon salt   1 tablespoon lemon juice
⅛ teaspoon paprika   dash of nutmeg

3 eggs, separated

Melt butter, blend in flour, add salt, paprika and stir in milk slowly. Cook until smooth. Add salmon, lemon juice and nutmeg. Remove from fire and stir in egg yolks, well beaten. Beat egg whites until stiff and fold in. Butter individual molds or baking dish; fill with the fish mixture, set molds in hot water and bake in a moderate oven (350° F.) 35 to 50 minutes. Serves 4. Serve with new peas or wilted lettuce.

Everyone knows the Yankee is ingenious. A Yankee left his native soil, traveled out to the West Coast, and went to look at the big salmon-canning factories. Smart westerners saw a chance to unload a "dead horse" on the newcomer. They were running a cannery which unfortunately was not making money—most of the salmon readily available to it was of the pink variety, rather than the red that John Q. Public, for no good reason, has come to think of as being the only first-class kind. Well, the westerners sold their factory to the Yank and went off chuckling. But not for long. Reports began to get around that he was making money hand over fist. How come? Quite simple, really. He had pink salmon to sell and being a Yank, he found out how to sell it. Every can bore the label—"Finest Pink Salmon—guaranteed not to turn red in the can."

BOILED SALMON

Wrap a fresh salmon steak in cheesecloth. Simmer gently in 1 quart of boiling water to which has been added ½ teaspoon salt and 2 teaspoons vinegar. Simmer 6 to 8 minutes per pound of fish. Serve plain or with egg sauce. For each person to be served, allow ½ pound of steak.

EGG SAUCE

Add 2 cubed hard-cooked eggs to 1 cup of medium white sauce.

The correct menu for the Fourth of July in some parts of New England, particularly around Boston, is fresh salmon, new peas and boiled potatoes. Strawberry shortcake is served for dessert.

"CAPE COD TURKEY" WITH EGG SAUCE

[Mrs. Mae Bangs Twite, Pasque Ave., Oak Bluffs, Mass.]

Remove head and tail from a 4-pound haddock or codfish; split and wipe with wet cloth. Sprinkle inside with a cup of salt. Let stand overnight. In the morning remove salt, rinse thoroughly, tie in cheesecloth and simmer gently about 30 minutes, or until fish is done. Place fish on a platter, surround with boiled potatoes of uniform size and small boiled buttered beets; also with fried salt pork scraps. Serve with egg sauce made by adding hard-cooked eggs to drawn butter. Serves 6.

Dishes of mashed summer or winter squash, boiled onions and hot cornbread were often served with this dinner. Left over fish was made into a dish called "Picked Fish." Bits of the fish were flaked and heated in cream sauce and sprinkled with parsley and served over mashed

*potato or buttered toast. Salt Fish Dinner (see page 32) was
also referred to as "Picked Fish."*

*The origin of the name "Cape Cod turkey" is obscure.
It has come to mean cooked fish; what kind doesn't matter
unless you are literal. If you are, it means baked stuffed
codfish well-larded with salt pork.*

*One explanation of the term centers about Thanksgiving.
The traditional food for that day was, and still is, turkey.
Turkey meant thankfulness to God for his bounty. However, without the fishing industry the colonists would have
had very little to be thankful for. No doubt the term "Cape
Cod turkey" was started by some wit, which shows that
even in early times life was not all drab.*

*Both the Pilgrims, who settled at Plymouth and the
Puritans, who settled in Boston turned to fishing as a means
of livelihood and codfish was the most profitable product
of the deep.*

*When some of the Plymouth group made money enough
to settle in Boston with established businesses, they were
referred to as "codfish aristocracy." Although the codfish
were a great source of trade, references were derogatory.*

*Then, too, the Irish in and around Boston used the term
"Cape Cod turkey" to refer to their Friday meal of fish.
Fish, and particularly salt fish, seemed to taste better if it
bore the more aristocratic name "Cape Cod turkey."*

FILLET OF HALIBUT—POINT SHIRLEY STYLE

[*Parker House, Boston, Mass.*]

Fillet the halibut, removing skin and all bones. Season with salt
and pepper. Dip in melted butter and sprinkle with bread crumbs.
Lay in richly buttered pan. Baste each fillet with butter and bake
in moderately hot oven (375° F.,), until tender, about 20 minutes.
Serve with own juice and a freshly boiled potato.

BROILED SCROD

[The Copley-Plaza, Boston, is famous for this dish]

Select a young, fresh codfish and scrape to remove the scales, being careful not to break the skin. Cut into fillets without removing the skin. Season lightly to taste with salt and pepper, and then sprinkle with melted butter. Dip in fresh bread crumbs; sprinkle again with a little more melted butter. Start the broiling with the flesh side down, and when broiling with the skin side down, use care not to allow the skin to break. Serve very hot with a bowl of melted butter with a little lemon juice stirred in. Allow ½ to ¾ pound of fish for each person to be served.

The sacred cod, six-foot emblem of the Commonwealth of Massachusetts, hangs in the Spectators' Lobby of the State House, in Boston, where it is viewed each year by thousands of sightseers. Only once in over 240 years has this august plaque been absent from its accustomed place. In April, 1933, a group of Harvard students carried it off, as a prank. When it was reported lost, hell broke loose in Boston. Twenty-four hectic hours passed and the police had no clue. Then came a tip that the fish was in a crate in an M. I. T. building. Investigation did, indeed, disclose a huge crate, but upon being opened the crate contained not the six-foot cod, but a sardine! Several days passed. The sacred cod was front-page news in the Boston newspapers; the Harvard "Lampoon" offered a reward. At last it was found. It was thrown from a speeding car into the arms of an astonished policeman. Whether the "Lampoon" was responsible for its disappearance, or the little green men who live at the bottom of the Charles River, no one dares to state positively.

BROILED SCROD

[Parker House, Boston, Mass.]

Split a young codfish and remove all bones. Sprinkle with salt and pepper and dip in olive oil. Again sprinkle with salt and pepper and dip in bread crumbs and broil on a medium fire (charcoal is best) about 20 minutes, or until tender. Put on hot platter and cover lightly with butter to which chopped parsley and a little lemon juice have been added. ½ to ¾ pound scrod serves 1 person.

In the fish industry, scrod has come to mean haddock under 2½ pounds. The correct definition of scrod is a small fish prepared for planking.

POTTED FISH

[Norma Roberts, Bristol, N. H.]

Clean enough suckers, removing heads, tails and fins to fill a gallon jar. Sprinkle jar lightly with salt, add a layer of fish, sprinkle lightly with salt and a few mixed pickling spices. Repeat until the jar is nearly full. Cover with vinegar that has been diluted to taste with water. Bake for 8 hours in a slow oven. The bones will become soft. This is delicious served cold for supper. The above recipe may easily be halved or made in smaller quantities using a heavy earthen dish or bean pot for cooking. Other white-fleshed fish may be substituted, but suckers are best.

MARTHA'S VINEYARD EEL STIFLE

[Mrs. Mae Bangs Twite, Oak Bluffs, Martha's Vineyard, Mass.]

1 quart potatoes	flour
4 onions	¼ pound salt pork, diced
2 pounds eels	and fried
salt and pepper	water

Slice potatoes and onions, cut eels in small pieces and line a kettle with layers of potatoes and onions, then layers of eels. Season with salt and pepper, sprinkle a little flour between each layer; top with salt pork scraps and add pork fat. Add water almost to cover. Cook until tender. Serves 6 to 8.

All good Island cooks know what Eel Stifle is, and very few visitors ever leave the Island without having a taste of this popular Vineyard dish.

FRIED EELS

[*"My grandmother's rule"—Norma Roberts, Bristol, N. H.*]

Skin and soak eels in salted water for several hours. Wash and cut in slices. Parboil in skim milk for 5 minutes. Remove, roll in corn meal and pan-fry in salt pork drippings until crisp and brown.

Eels are occasionally found in New England waters today but like salmon, shad and alewives were barred from many rivers years ago by impassable dams. In the early fall eels used to migrate up the rivers and were taken by means of sluiceways that ran into an "eel pot." Hauls of a hundred or more at night were not uncommon at the time of the year when they returned. At Amoskeag they were taken in such numbers that they became known as "Derryfield Beef" after the old name for Manchester, N. H. A New Hampshire poet, writing of the early settlers, speaks of the prevalence of eels:

> *"From the eels they formed their food in chief,*
> *And eels were called the Derryfield beef;*
> *It was often said that their only care,*
> *And their only wish, and their only prayer,*
> *For the present world and the world to come,*
> *Was a string of eels and a jug of rum."*

FRIED SMELTS

Clean, wash and dry smelts. Roll in seasoned flour. Beat 1 egg slightly, add 2 tablespoons water. Dip floured fish in egg, then roll in fine bread crumbs or cornmeal. Fry in hot deep fat (370° F.) until smelts are a golden brown, about 4 minutes. Or pan-fry, turning so that smelts will brown evenly. Drain and serve with tartar sauce. 12 smelts serves 3.

BAKED STUFFED SMELTS

Sprinkle 12 clean, dry smelts with salt and pepper. Stuff, brush over with lemon juice, place in a buttered shallow pan and bake 5 minutes in a hot oven (425° F.) with a cover over the pan. Uncover, sprinkle with buttered crumbs and bake until crumbs are brown. Serve with lemon butter sauce. (Page 48.) Serves 3.

STUFFING

2 tablespoons finely chopped mushrooms, stems or caps	¼ cup buttered crumbs
	1 teaspoon hot oyster liquor
¼ cup oysters, parboiled, drained and chopped	2 teaspoons chopped parsley

Mix ingredients lightly with a fork.

TROUT OVER A CAMPFIRE

Sharpen a hardwood stick and push it down the backbone to the tiny fatty fin near the tail. Push the other end of the stick into the earth close to the embers. Cook until done.

BAKED LAKE TROUT

Remove skin; also fat along backbone. Split, clean and stuff. Lay in pan with a little milk. Lay strips of fat pork across and bake about 1 hour in a moderate oven (375° F.). Before removing from oven, add 1½ cups cream. Heat and serve.

STUFFING

2 cups fine bread crumbs	1 small onion, finely cut
4 tablespoons butter	1 teaspoon salt
1 teaspoon sage	pepper

Mix all together.

PAN-FRIED BROOK TROUT

Remove eyes and scales; make an incision down the underneath side and clean carefully. Wash fish and roll in equal parts of yellow cornmeal and flour sifted together. Preheat salt pork fat or bacon fat in a skillet. Add the fish and cook 4 minutes. Cover and cook about 2 minutes longer. Remove cover, brown on both sides. Remove to hot platter, garnish with lemon, cress or parsley and serve hot.

No fish, probably, is more fitted to grace a silver platter, garnished with yellow half moons of lemon and crisp cress than eastern brook trout, which is equally at home pan-fried or broiled over the embers of a fisherman's camp-fire where its tantalizing odor drifts away to blend with the spice of balsam thickets.

PLANKED TROUT

Put plank in cool oven and heat to 500° F. Remove head of trout, split, clean and soak for 5 minutes in 2 cups water and 5 tablespoons salt. Drain, dry and brush with cooking oil. Oil hot plank, place fish on it, skin side down. Return plank to oven. Baste fish with melted butter. Season. Broil about 20 minutes. When nearly done surround with mounds of mashed potatoes. Serve with green peas in lettuce cups.

COLD BUTTER DRESSING FOR FRIED FISH

[Norma Roberts, Bristol, N. H.]

Cream ½ cup butter; gradually work in ¼ teaspoon salt, sprinkling of pepper and 2 teaspoons lemon juice. When well blended, work in 1 teaspoon minced parsley or cress. Form into balls and place in refrigerator to harden. Serve one with each portion of fish.

LEMON BUTTER

[To serve with planked, baked or broiled fish]

6 tablespoons melted butter   ⅛ teaspoon pepper
½ teaspoon salt   2 teaspoons lemon juice

Blend and serve hot.

CONNECTICUT STUFFED BAKED SHAD

[From the New England Kitchen of Louise Crathern Russell]

1 large shad, about 5 pounds   ¼ teaspoon pepper
1 cup cracker crumbs   1 small onion, minced
¼ cup melted butter   1 teaspoon sage
¼ teaspoon salt   1 cup hot water
                ¼ pound bacon strips

Leave head and tail on fish; clean and dry. Make a dressing of the cracker crumbs, melted butter, salt, pepper, onion and sage. Stuff shad and sew the edges together. Place on a strip of clean cloth or rack in baking pan. Add water. Fasten strips of bacon (or salt pork) on the fish with toothpicks. Bake in a hot oven (400° F.) for 10 minutes. Then reduce heat to moderately slow (325° F.) and bake for about 35 minutes, basting frequently to keep fish tender and well browned. Serve on hot platter. Serves 6.

BROILED SHAD ROE

Dip shad roe in melted butter and lay on a greased broiler rack.
Broil under moderately high flame 8 to 10 minutes, turning once
and brushing frequently with melted butter. Season with salt and
pepper. (Worcestershire is optional.) Garnish with crisp bacon
and serve with maître d'hôtel butter. 3 shad roe will serve 6.

*Shad is one of the fish that run up the New England
rivers in spring. The blooming of the shad bushes, all snowy
white, is supposed to herald their coming in northern New
England. In southern New England they come in March.
Like salmon, shad look for fresh water to spawn. Shad
average about 1½ feet long and weigh about 4 pounds.
The flesh is dark pink in color and has a distinctive flavor.
The roe is exceedingly choice.*

FILENE'S SEA FOOD NEWBURG

[Restaurant operated by Wm. Filene's Sons, Boston, Mass.]

2 littleneck clams	4 tablespoons butter
¼ cup lobster meat	1 tablespoon sherry wine
¼ cup crab flakes	1 cup cream
¼ cup shrimp	3 yolks of eggs, slightly beaten
paprika	1 tablespoon lemon juice

salt and pepper

Sauté clams, lobster, crab flakes, shrimp and paprika in 2 tablespoons butter for a few minutes. Add sherry wine; toss over fire
few minutes more, then add ¾ cup cream, let come to a boil. Add
the balance of cream in which the yolks of eggs have been slightly
beaten. Keep stirring all the time until thick, remove from fire.
Put in lemon juice, salt, pepper and 2 tablespoons butter. Serve hot
on toast or in chafing dish. Do not allow to boil after adding yolks.
Serves 2.

FRIED SCALLOPS

[Union Oyster House, Boston, Mass.]

Roll a handful of sea or Cape scallops in flour, then dip them in egg wash (1 egg and 1 pint milk beaten together). Take the scallops from the egg wash and roll in equal parts of crumbs and flour mixed together. Fry in hot deep fat (375° F.) for 5 minutes, or until brown. Drain. 1 pint scallops serves 4.

The scallop is one of the sweetest shellfish found anywhere.

BOILED LIVE LOBSTER

Plunge lobster in a large kettle of rapidly boiling water; adding 1 tablespoon salt for each quart water. When water has returned to a full boil cover kettle and allow 20 minutes to complete the boiling. Remove from water and place on back to drain. Serve hot or cold. Take out intestinal vein and stomach, crack the claws and serve with hot melted butter or mayonnaise. Allow 1 small lobster per person. Corn pudding (page 104) is a delicious accompaniment to hot boiled or broiled lobster.

LOBSTER A LA NEWBURG

[Union Oyster House, Boston, Mass.]

Melt 1 tablespoon of butter in a pan, then add ¼ pound lobster meat. Stir until the meat is braised, about 5 minutes. Add 2 tablespoons sherry.

In another bowl, mix the yolk of an egg and 2 tablespoons of cornstarch. Dissolve this mixture in a pint of milk and then add it to the braised lobster meat. Put on a slow fire and let it simmer slowly, stirring constantly. Season to taste. Serve on hot toast. Serves 1 or 2.

BROILED LIVE LOBSTER

[Toll House, Whitman, Mass.]

If possible have lobsters split at the market. Otherwise hold large claws firmly. With a sharp pointed knife begin at mouth and make incision, then split the shell the entire length of the body and tail. Remove the stomach and intestinal canal and a small sac just back of the head. Crack the large claws and lay the lobster as flat as possible. Brush the meat with melted butter. Season with salt and pepper. Place in a broiler, shell side down. Broil slowly until a delicate brown, about 20 minutes. Serve hot with melted butter. Allow ½ large or 1 small lobster per person.

PANNED OYSTERS

[A Rhode Island recipe]

1 pint oysters   pepper
4 tablespoons butter   salt
2 tablespoons lemon juice   lemon slices
          Worcestershire sauce (if desired)

Drain oysters, place in a heavy frying pan with butter and cook over a low fire until the edges curl. Add lemon juice, pepper and salt to taste. A dash of Worcestershire sauce may be added, if desired. Serve on hot toast and garnish with lemon. Serves 4.

Lemon juice may be omitted and a wine glass of sherry added before serving.

DEEP DISH OYSTER PIE

[A Famous Rhode Island recipe]

¼ pound of butter   1 pint of oysters
½ cup flour   salt and pepper
 1 pint whole milk   biscuit dough

Melt the butter, add the flour and blend. Add milk and heat in a double boiler until the cream sauce thickens. Add the oysters and continue to heat in the double boiler, stirring gently until the oysters and cream sauce are near the boiling point. Add salt and pepper to taste.

Pour into a baking dish that is deep enough so that the contents will not fill it more than ⅔ full. Roll out baking-powder biscuit dough, cut biscuits ½ inch thick and place on top of creamed oysters. Bake in a hot oven (450° F.) until the biscuits are done. It is important to have the creamed oysters hot when the biscuits are put on top and there should be no delay in placing dish in the oven. Serves 4.

SCALLOPED OYSTERS

½ cup bread crumbs   1 pint oysters, drained
1 cup cracker crumbs   salt and pepper
¼ cup melted butter   4 tablespoons oyster liquor
2 cups rich milk or cream

Mix bread and cracker crumbs and stir in melted butter. Put a thin layer of crumbs in bottom of a buttered, shallow baking dish; cover with oysters and sprinkle with salt and pepper. Add half of the oyster liquor and milk or cream; repeat, cover top with remaining crumbs. Bake 20 minutes in a hot oven (400° F.). Serves 4.

This is a recipe handed down from the grandmother of Mrs. C. A. Patterson, Bucksport, Me. It has been tested many times. Good cooks never use more than 2 layers of oysters in making this dish.

Whether or not sherry should be added to scalloped oysters is a moot question in Concord, Mass. The town is about equally divided into camps of pro-sherry and anti-sherry advocates. The subject is frequently discussed at meetings of the Old Social Circle.

OYSTERS OR SCALLOPS ON SKEWERS

Alternate large oysters and small squares of bacon on skewers. If scallops are used, wash, drain and dip in seasoned crumbs, eggs and again in crumbs. Pour melted butter over them or alternate with bacon squares. Place skewers under a broiler 5 or 10 minutes, or until bacon is crisp. Turn to brown evenly. Serve with tartar sauce. (Page 59.) Sweetbreads, oysters (or scallops), bacon and mushrooms may be alternated.

OYSTER AND MUSHROOM MOUSSE

12 large oysters	1 teaspoon salt
1 pound mushrooms	dash of pepper
2 tablespoons butter	1 cup heavy cream, whipped
3 tablespoons flour	stiff
4 egg yolks, beaten	2 egg whites, whipped stiff

Put oysters and mushrooms through food chopper. Melt butter, stir in flour. Sauté the mushrooms and oysters in this mixture lightly. Remove from fire, add egg yolks, salt, pepper. Fold in cream and egg whites. Butter a 9-inch ring mold. Fill it ⅔ full with the mousse. Cover with buttered paper. Place in a pan of hot water. Bake in a slow oven (325° F.) for 1 hour. Invert the mousse onto a platter. Fill the center with buttered peas. Serves 6.

OYSTERS BAKED IN GREEN PEPPERS

6 small green peppers	½ cup oyster liquor (about)
7 common crackers, rolled fine	⅓ cup butter, melted
1 tablespoon butter	salt and pepper
24 large or 48 small oysters	1 tablespoon minced parsley

Cut thin slice from stem end of peppers. Remove seeds and inner membrane. Parboil 10 minutes in salted water. Drain and place upright in a buttered baking dish.

Mix crackers with melted butter. Sprinkle inside of peppers with salt, put a thick layer of crumbs in each pepper. Add 2 large or 4 small oysters. Season with pepper and salt and a sprinkling of parsley; moisten with a little of the oyster liquor. Add another layer of crumbs, then 2 or 4 more oysters. Season and top with crumbs. Moisten with a little more of the oyster liquor and dot with bits of butter. Bake in a hot oven (400° F.) about 20 minutes or until crumbs are browned. Serves 4 to 6.

OYSTERS WITH TRIPE

1 pound honeycomb tripe	1 cup milk
1 tablespoon butter	25 large oysters
1 small onion, chopped	½ teaspoon salt
1 tablespoon flour	¼ teaspoon pepper

Boil tripe until tender. Cut into dice. Melt butter in saucepan. Add the chopped onion. Cover saucepan and cook until onion is soft but not brown. Sprinkle in the flour and mix. Add the milk, stir until boiling; then add tripe and oysters. When oysters are cooked sufficiently to curl the gills, add salt and pepper; serve at once. Serves 6.

OYSTER FRITTERS

1½ cups oysters	2 cups flour, sifted
2 eggs, slightly beaten	2 teaspoons baking powder
1 cup milk	½ teaspoon salt

Chop the oysters. Make a batter of the eggs, milk, flour, baking powder and salt. Stir the oysters into the batter and drop by spoonfuls into deep hot fat (375° F.). Turn the fritters over to brown evenly on both sides. Drain. Serves 4.

PIGS IN BLANKETS

12 large oysters	bacon
salt and pepper	toast

Sprinkle oysters with salt and pepper. Encircle each oyster in a strip of bacon. Secure bacon firmly with a toothpick. Broil 8 minutes or until bacon is crisp. Serve on rounds of well-buttered toast.

CREAMED OYSTERS

[A Rhode Island recipe]

4· tablespoons butter	2 cups milk
4 tablespoons flour	1 pint oysters with liquor
½ teaspoon salt	1 cup diced celery, cooked
pepper	1 slice pimiento

Melt butter, stir in flour, salt and pepper; when well blended add milk. Stir over a low fire until smooth and thick. Add oysters, celery and minced pimiento. Cook gently about 3 minutes or until the edges of the oysters curl. Serve at once on hot toast or in toasted bread cases, or patty shells. Serves 4.

OYSTERS AND MACARONI

4 ounces elbow macaroni	1 cup soft bread crumbs
25 large oysters	1 tablespoon butter
1 teaspoon salt	½ cup grated cheese
¼ teaspoon black pepper	1 cup milk

Place the macaroni in a kettle of boiling salted water. Cook until tender. Pick over the oysters. Drain. Grease a baking dish. Cover the bottom with the boiled macaroni; then a layer of oysters; season with salt and pepper. Continue until the dish is full, having the top layer macaroni. Sprinkle the cheese over the top; then the bread crumbs. Dot the top with pieces of butter. Pour on the milk. Bake 20 minutes in a hot oven (425° F.) and serve at once. Serves 4.

CHATHAM OYSTER SHORTCAKE

[Household Department, Boston Sunday "Post"]

Bake a shortcake dough (omitting sugar) in two layers, one on top of the other. Split and spread with butter.

FILLING

Scald 1 quart oysters in their liquor. Remove oysters and keep hot. Strain 1 cup of the liquor into saucepan. Mix 2 tablespoons flour with 3 tablespoons cold water. Stir into oyster liquor and season to taste with salt, pepper and celery salt. Cook slowly for 5 minutes, stirring constantly. Add 3 tablespoons heavy cream and the oysters. Stir until well heated, then place between and on top of the shortcake and serve. Serves 6.

STEAMED CLAMS

See Clam Broth, Page 4. Steamed clams are served in soup plates accompanied by cups of clam broth and individual dishes of melted butter. "To eat steamed clams: first take a lesson from a native of New England," advises Miss Ula M. Dow, eminent Boston authority on cooking.

Succulent steamed clams, dripping butter all the way from plate to lips, are amongst earth's choicest contributions to man's gastronomic pleasure.

The lowly clam is one of New England's great recreational assets. Thousands of visitors from inland points come each summer to enjoy clambakes, steamed clams, fried clams and clam chowders. The fame of the New England clambake has spread far. The number of inland dwellers who come to New England each summer with the idea that it is something to be dished up in a café or hotel like a boiled dinner is surprisingly large.

A middle-aged, well-dressed man was recently given a seat in the main dining-room of a well-known Boston hotel. Pushing away the menu, he looked up expectantly.

"Please bring me a clambake," he said.

"Clambake, sir?" repeated the astonished waiter.

"Certainly. That's what I'm ordering. One of your famous New England clambakes I have read so much about!"

NEW HAMPSHIRE SHORE DINNER

Clam or Fish Chowder
Crackers—Celery—Sour Pickles

Steamed Hampton River Clams
with
Clam Bouillon and Drawn Butter
Broiled Rock Cod—Fried Clams
Broiled Lobster—Potato Chips
Corn on the Cob—Tomato and Cucumber Salad
Rolls

Apple Pie—Cheese—or Ice Cream
Coffee

"FANNIE DADDIES"

[The Cape Cod name for Fried Clams]

3 dozen clams, removed from shells
1 cup fine bread crumbs, cracker crumbs or corn meal
½ teaspoon salt
pepper
2 eggs
1 tablespoon water

Drain clams and dry between towels. Dip in seasoned crumbs, eggs diluted with water and then in crumbs again. Fry in deep fat (385° F.) until golden brown. Drain on soft paper and serve with tartar sauce. Serves 4.

Fried oysters are prepared in the same way.

TARTAR SAUCE

½ cup mayonnaise
1 tablespoon minced pickles
1 tablespoon minced olives
1 tablespoon minced parsley
1 teaspoon minced onion

Combine and serve on lettuce leaf.

CLAM OMELET

6 eggs
½ teaspoon salt
pepper
1 cup hot, chopped seasoned clams

Beat the eggs, season, turn into a well buttered hot frying pan and place over moderate heat. As omelet cooks, lift edges towards center and tip pan so the uncooked mixture flows under the cooked portion. Cook slowly until eggs have thickened and bottom is lightly browned. Spread clams over omelet. Fold. Slip onto hot platter; serve immediately. Serves 4.

SCALLOPED CLAMS

[Mrs. Harriet Mohler, Swan's Island, Me.]

4 tablespoons butter	pepper
3 tablespoons flour	1 cup milk
1 tablespoon chopped parsley	2 cups clams, removed from
1 teaspoon scraped onion	shell
½ teaspoon dry mustard	2 hard-cooked eggs, minced
½ teaspoon salt	½ cup buttered bread crumbs

Melt butter, add flour and stir until blended; add seasonings and milk, stirring until smooth. Add clams and eggs. Pour into buttered scallop shells or a shallow baking dish. Cover with buttered crumbs. Bake in a moderately hot oven (375° F.) 20 minutes or until crumbs are brown. Serves 4 to 6.

CLAM CAKES

[In Maine and on Cape Cod they make them this way]

1 quart clams, shucked	½ cup clam liquor
1 cup fine cracker crumbs (about)	2 eggs, well beaten

Drain clams and save ½ cup liquor. Remove the black from soft part. Put the necks through a food chopper. Put clams in a dish, add clam liquor and enough cracker crumbs to absorb all the moisture. Let stand 10 minutes. Add eggs. Shape into flat cakes. Drop into hot deep fat (375° F.) and cook until a golden brown. Drain. Serves 4.

This recipe was given to the mother-in-law of Mrs. Charles W. Spinny, Grant St., Portland, Maine, by an old fisherman who was born and lived in Harpswell, Me.

DEEP SEA CLAM PIE (CAPE COD STYLE)

[Mrs. Emma Cross, Onset, Mass.]

¼ pound salt pork, cut in slices
1 tablespoon butter
2 tablespoons flour
1 cup clam broth

½ cup water
4 large sea clams
pepper
pastry crust

Try out the salt pork, add butter; blend in flour, add the clam broth and water and cook until broth is thickened. Grind the meaty portion of the clams (discarding the tough portions) and add the broth. Season with pepper—no salt is required. Line a deep dish with a rich pastry crust. Pour in clam mixture and cover with top crust. Cut a hole in the center and surround hole with a twist of crust. Bake in a hot oven (450° F.) for 15 minutes; then reduce heat to moderate and bake 20 minutes longer. Serves 4.

MARTHA'S VINEYARD QUAHOG FRITTERS

1 pint shucked quahogs
2 cups flour, sifted
3 teaspoons baking powder
½ cup quahog liquor

⅓ cup milk
2 eggs, separated
⅛ teaspoon salt
⅛ teaspoon pepper

Chop quahogs; mix and sift dry ingredients; add quahog liquor, milk, egg yolks and clam mixture, stirring until smooth. Fold in egg whites, beaten until stiff. Drop by spoonfuls into hot deep fat (375° F.) and cook 3 minutes, or until brown. Drain. Serves 8.

This recipe comes from West Tisbury, Martha's Vineyard. Clams or oysters may be substituted for quahogs. Scallops, cut in quarters, and parboiled may also be used, substituting milk for the quahog liquor.

"BOAT STEERERS"

[*Clam Fritters is another name*]

1 quart shucked clams	½ cup milk
1 egg, slightly beaten	1 cup flour, sifted
2 tablespoons olive oil	4 teaspoons baking powder
(or melted butter)	¼ teaspoon salt

⅛ teaspoon pepper

Put shoulder and rim of clams through food chopper, leave soft parts whole. Add egg, olive oil and milk. Mix and sift dry ingredients and add to clam mixture, stirring until smooth. Drop by spoonfuls in deep hot fat (375° F.) and cook until golden brown. Drain. Serves 8.

MARTHA'S VINEYARD CLAM BOIL

[*Mrs. Mae Bangs Twite, Oak Bluffs, Martha's Vineyard, Mass.*]

1 quart medium sized potatoes	1 pound frankfurters
1 large bunch carrots	1 pound link sausages
6 small onions	6 ears corn
½ peck small clams	1 quart water

Place potatoes in their jackets in the bottom of a large kettle or boiler, add carrots cut in halves, onions, clams in the shell which have been thoroughly washed. On top place the frankfurters, sausages and the ears of corn. Pour on water. Tightly cover the kettle or boiler and steam-cook until tender, about 45 minutes. Serves 6.

A clam boil may be prepared at home on the kitchen stove, but it tastes better on a moonlight night on the beach.

CLAM PIE

2 dozen clams	2 tablespoons flour
3 medium onions, sliced	2 cups rich milk or thin cream
2 medium potatoes, cut ¼ inch slices	salt and pepper
	1 tablespoon minced parsley
3 tablespoons butter	3 common crackers

Scrub clams thoroughly. Place in saucepan, adding 1 cup hot water. Simmer until shells open slightly. Remove clams from shells, reserving water in which clams were steamed. Chop clams fine. Strain liquor and cook sliced onion and potatoes in this broth until tender, but not broken. Melt 2 tablespoons butter, stir in flour. Add milk gradually stirring until thickened. Add clams, potatoes, onions and liquid in which they were cooked. Season, simmer 2 minutes, pour into well-buttered glass baking dish and sprinkle with parsley. Split crackers and soak in cold milk until softened. Arrange over clam mixture. Dot with remaining tablespoon butter, sprinkle with paprika and bake in a moderately hot oven (425° F.) until crackers are lightly browned. Serves 6.

CAPE COD CLAM PIE

[Household Department, Boston Sunday "Post"]

2 quarts soft-shelled clams	2 tablespoons cornstarch
3 tablespoons butter	3 tablespoons cold water
2 cups hot water	pastry
salt and pepper	

Steam the clams, remove from shells, clean, cut off black end of neck with scissors and discard. Cut the remainder coarsely, removing the black from the stomach. Sauté the clams in butter, add 2 cups hot water and season to taste. When the mixture begins to boil, thicken with cornstarch dissolved in cold water until mixture is the consistency of thick heavy cream. Line a deep pie plate with pastry, fill with the mixture. Put on top crust, slash top to permit escape of steam. Bake in a hot oven (450° F.) for 15 minutes; then reduce heat to moderate (350° F.) and bake 25 minutes longer. When done set away for several hours or a day, then reheat. Serve with pickled beets and brown bread. Serves 4 to 6.

This recipe may be varied by using milk or part milk and water. Do not use the clam liquor, as that makes it bitter. Some Cape Cod recipes call for the addition of diced potatoes.

R U A YANKEE COOK?

Answers on page 367

16. The housewife is "sugarin' off" in the kitchen. What does she mean by "lifting"? "airing"? "graining"? "stirring-off"? "granulating"?
17. What is a sausage-gun?

THE PERFECT CHURCH SUPPER

C. M. Webster

Father was a tolerant man who excused dull sermons and for-gave bad amateur plays—the ministers and actors had done their best, he said—but he asked for perfection in a church or Grange supper. Since preaching and acting were pleasures that he could not enjoy in his own home, he was willing to be lenient in judging them, but when a man forsook his own wife's excellent cooking, changed his clothes, hitched up and drove two miles, and then paid twenty-five cents for a meal, he had a right to expect a lot. Father was almost always disappointed in the suppers he went to; something he wanted was not there, or the food he got was not seasoned right; but on one historic occasion he was completely satisfied.

I was home from college for Easter vacation, so I know all about that perfect supper. It was held in April on a Friday night. By the time Spring came, Father was a trifle bored by home cook-ing, no matter how good it was; and Friday was better than Satur-day as a night for suppers, for he liked to have plenty of time to take a bath and then study his Sunday School lesson for the next day. That Friday evening was just right for the season of the year and held no menace of too warm or too cold weather to come; the going was good, and our Morgan gelding passed Seth Osgood's rig on the way to the village. Little things like those helped put Father in a pleasant mood.

After he had bought our tickets from the minister's wife, Father spent a profitable five minutes selling Jerome Ennis a load of hay at the top market price; then he looked around for a seat. At least two suppers had been partially ruined by poor neighbors, but tonight he found a place next to Oscar Tillinghast, a man who did not talk too much and passed things promptly. After a few polite remarks about health and the weather, Father's face became sober as he wondered what there was to eat and who was waiting on this table.

The jolly and buxom Mrs. William Moseley brought a big dish of baked beans. Father took an experimental helping and tasted critically. Yes, they were yellow-eyes and baked to the right consistency with New Orleans molasses and none of that heretical brown sugar. He took a real helping and looked to see what went with the beans. There was a dish of pork—slices of melting softness with a crisp edge. Father ate three and then discovered the brown bread. That was as it should be; a church supper was no place for fragile rolls or biscuits or uninteresting white bread. There was a quarter of a pound of Mrs. Elijah Holcomb's butter to go with the brown bread. Father ate a slice and finished half of his beans before he reached for the rest of the supper.

So far everything had been perfect, but he was fussy about salads. This one suited him; the potatoes were tender and yet escaped being an indefinite mush; not too many onions spoiled the taste of the slices of hard-boiled eggs that matched the potatoes in a ratio of one to three, and the mayonnaise was good. Father ate a big spoonful and continued his search, for a good supper meant more than beans, bread, and salad.

Young Mrs. Moseley's bare round arm put a steaming cup of coffee beside his plate, and after the thick cream and sugar and the first swallow, Father remarked: "Some women I could mention didn't have a hand in making that coffee; it's too good."

Then he asked for the cole slaw. A minor crisis was at hand. Had mayonnaise been used? No, only vinegar, cream (not milk), and sugar, and not too much vinegar. The critic ate a little of it; took another helping of yellow-eyes, and began to relax. Now was the time for the extra dishes that turned an adequate supper into a real good one. Father sampled and liked the sweet pickles and the watermelon rind in its thick juice spotted with cloves, but he approved most of the green tomato relish.

"Must be yours, Mrs. Tillinghast," he said. "Nobody else gets quite this flavor."

"I'm glad you like it. But you just try these pickled beets I brought and see what you think of them."

Father accepted a very small beet and ate it cautiously. "Umm. Pretty fair." A second ... "Good!" and he took two larger ones for leisurely consumption.

"They seem to have a new flavor that I can't remember ever happenin' on before," he remarked.

"That's because I use a few bay leaves the way my grandmother did," explained Mrs. Tillinghast.

Father often jeered at the way some women spoiled a good dish by sticking in some funny thing, but this time he welcomed the exotic.

"I don't generally take to new dishes, but those pickled beets go good with baked beans," he said.

Father took a bite more of beans, a dab of cole slaw, a slice or two of green tomatoes, a touch of salad, and another beet before he looked expectantly at the pretty Mrs. Moseley.

"We've got punkin, mince, 'n' apple pie," she announced.

"Do you know whose apple pies they are?" asked Father.

"Mrs. Dwight Porter brought two."

"She uses cinnamon," said Father dourly.

"And I guess one of Mrs. Lincoln's is left.'

"Good!" said Father. "You might bring me a piece. She puts a dash of nutmeg in her pies."

Father scarcely looked at his pie when Mrs. Moseley brought it; he was interested in the last vital question—would there be cheese, and if so, what kind? Of course he knew what he wanted, but no supper he had ever gone to had as yet given it to him. But this one was different, for there beside the pie was a large rectangle of sage cheese tastefully marbled with delicate streaks of green. When he had very slowly eaten the pie and cheese, Father allowed himself to be argued into having a second cup of coffee and a small piece of mince pie.

"Wouldn't you like a bite more of that sage cheese?" asked Mrs. Moseley.

"It is about the best I've tasted in a long time," admitted Father.

Five minutes later he sighed and remarked to Oscar Tillinghast, "That's what I call an A-One supper."

"It might've been a whole lot worse," agreed Oscar.

For the next quarter of an hour, Father and Oscar and Seth Osgood and Jerome Ennis discussed farming, the weather, Jerome's new Ayrshire bull, and, in lowered voices, the tendency of the minister to shout and wave his arms in the pulpit. Then Father remarked that tomorrow was a day of work and he'd better be getting along home.

While we drove through the April evening, Father forgot the caution of Puritanism and its fear of open praise and talked lovingly about each dish in that perfect supper.

"Yes, sir," he said at last. "Everything was there that should be, and it was all good. Got real satisfactory service, too, and could look twice at the woman who was giving it. And it seemed kind of good to talk things over for a minute with some men. In a way you might say that everything sort of fitted together into as good a supper as a man has any right to expect."

LAWYERS AND BUTCHERS

In Eastport, Maine, a few years ago, a lawyer's dog took a side of beef from a butcher's cart.

The butcher went to the lawyer and said, "IF a dog should steal a piece of meat from my cart, could I collect from the owner of the dog?"

"Why, yes," said the lawyer, "if you should go to the owner and tell him, I think he would be glad to pay you for the loss of the meat."

"All right," said the butcher, "you owe me seven dollars. It was your dog."

"Well," said the lawyer, "my legal advice to you is worth ten dollars, so you owe me three."

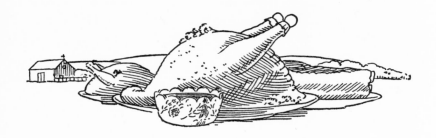

III. MEAT, POULTRY AND GAME

MRS. VALLÉE'S SPICED BEEF

[*Kay Vallée Lenneville, Westport, Me.*]

4 or 5 pounds chuck roast	1 teaspoon cloves
cider vinegar to cover meat	1 teaspoon salt
2 onions, ground	1 teaspoon pepper
1 teaspoon cinnamon	2 onions, sliced
1 teaspoon allspice	4 carrots

1 medium-sized yellow turnip

Cover the meat with the vinegar, ground onions and spices and let stand overnight. Remove meat from liquid; place in a covered roaster, add ½ cup of the vinegar liquid and 2 cups water. Place sliced onions over meat. Roast in slow oven (275° F.), about 3 hours. When meat is nearly done, before the last half hour, put carrots and turnip through food chopper and fry in equal parts of vegetable shortening and butter until golden brown. Cover top of meat with these vegetables and cook until done. Serves 8. Serve with mashed or baked potatoes.

This recipe comes from Rudy Vallée's paternal grand-mother, a Vermonter, who gave it to Rudy's mother.

YANKEE POT ROAST

4 pounds beef—round, chuck	sprig parsley
or rump	5 or 6 raisins
salt, pepper, flour	6 carrots
⅛ pound salt pork	6 onions
1 bay leaf	6 potatoes
1 small turnip, sliced (optional)	

Wipe meat with a clean damp cloth. Sprinkle with salt, pepper and flour. Try out a small piece of salt pork in an iron pot. Put in meat and brown on all sides. (Roll it over, so as to keep juices in. Do not insert fork.) When brown, add enough boiling water to cover the bottom of the pot. Add bay leaf, parsley and raisins. Cover and simmer slowly for 3 hours, keeping about 1 cup water under the meat. The last hour of cooking add carrots, onions, turnip (if desired); add the potatoes the last half hour. Serve on a platter with the vegetables arranged around the meat. Mix about 2 tablespoons flour in ¼ cup cold water to a smooth paste to thicken gravy. Season a little more if necessary. Serves 8.

Ethel R. DeTeso, Richardson St., Woburn, Mass., contributed this recipe which came originally from her great-grandmother who lived on a farm in New Hampshire.

Generations of Yankee cooks have been taught that sometime during the cooking, a pot roast should "catch on" (stick to the pot just enough to brown) thereby giving the gravy richness and savor.

OLD NEW ENGLAND MOTTO:—

"WASTE NOT—WANT NOT"

VERMONT CORNED BEEF

[Mrs. Henry Doucette, 348 Main St., Lewiston, Me.]

4 or 5 pounds corned beef   whole cloves
½ cup maple syrup

Cover corned beef with water and bring to boiling point. Drain, cover with hot water and let simmer until done, allowing about 40 minutes per pound. When done place on a rack in an open roasting pan. Stick with whole cloves in diagonal design. Pour maple syrup over meat and put in moderate oven (350° F.) to brown and glaze. Baste occasionally with maple syrup. Serves 8.

MAINE CORNED BEEF HASH

[Kenneth Roberts, Kennebunkport, Me.]

3 cups boiled potatoes   ¼ cup butter
4 cups corned beef   ¾ cup boiling water
                    pepper

Place cold potatoes and cold corned beef (free from gristle and fat) in chopping bowl. Chop until both meat and potatoes are in very small pieces. Melt butter in heavy skillet. Add boiling water. Add chopped meat and potatoes seasoned with pepper. Fry over very low heat for about 15 minutes or until brown crust has formed on lower side of hash; then fold over as omelet is folded. Serves 4 to 6.

When you speak of the market
That's known as Faneuil,
Kindly pronounce it
To rhyme with Dan'l.
             From "An Almanac for Bostonians."

NEW ENGLAND BOILED DINNER

[Mrs. William D. Eddy, 58 Myrtle St., Pawtucket, R. I.]

Select a 4- or 5-pound piece of corned beef, preferably brisket, corned between 4 and 7 days without saltpeter. Place in a large kettle, cover with cold water and boil slowly. After cooking 2 hours add ½ pound salt pork. When beef is almost done (3 to 4 hours) add the following vegetables: onions, cabbage, quartered and cored, medium sized white turnip pared and quartered, and last carrots and potatoes. When potatoes are done, place meat in center of a large platter and arrange vegetables around meat. Beets are served with a boiled dinner but should be cooked separately. A 4-pound piece of corned beef serves 8.

Nelson Eddy, radio and movie star, enjoys this boiled dinner at the home of his mother in Pawtucket when he is visiting New England. Mrs. Eddy serves Indian Pudding with whipped cream for dessert. Her recipe varies from the Durgin-Park recipe in that she uses a variety of Rhode Island corn meal that is made from a strain of the original Indian maize that has been grown continuously on the Carr Homestead, Quononoquott Farm, Jamestown, Rhode Island, since Governor Carr's time. It is slowly ground between fine grained stones of Rhode Island granite.

"Boil dinners" were always served once a week from early fall until late spring. Monday and Wednesday were favored days. Cabbage often went into a netted cotton bag and used to come from the kettle with the quarters whole. A boiled dinner is a very old version of a perfect one-plate meal.

For Corned Beef and Cabbage omit all vegetables except cabbage.

AUNT DILLY'S SAVORY MEAT

[Mrs. Volney E. H. Cone, 28 Providence St., Springfield, Mass.]

3 pounds corned beef, chopped
fine
8 crackers, rolled
2 eggs, beaten

½ cup warm water
pepper
½ teaspoon sage or parsley

Mix ingredients well and pack into 2 greased loaf tins, 5 x 4 x 3 inches. Bake in a moderately hot oven (375° F.). When cold, slice and serve with mustard pickles. Serves 8. 1 medium-sized onion, minced, may be added if desired.

RED FLANNEL HASH

1 tablespoon butter
1 cup chopped cooked corned
beef

3 cups chopped boiled potatoes
1 cup chopped cooked beets
½ chopped onion

Heat butter in frying pan. Spread mixture smoothly over the bottom of the pan. Brown slowly. When crust forms, turn as an omelet. Serves 4.

The best Yankee cooks state positively that the meat and potatoes used to make hash should always be chopped separately in a wooden chopping bowl, by hand, never put through the food grinder. A little cream may be added to moisten.

A sauce made by blending 2 tablespoons freshly grated horseradish with ½ cup whipped cream is excellent with hash. Sliced green tomato pickles are a perennial favorite.

ORIGINAL PLYMOUTH SUCCOTASH

[Mrs. F. A. Hagen, Atlantic Street, Plymouth, Mass., and Mrs. Richard Sinnott, Ocean Street, Marshfield, Mass., both vouch for this recipe]

4 pounds corned beef	1 turnip, sliced
4 or 5 pound fowl	6 potatoes, sliced
1 quart pea beans	salt
2 quarts hulled corn, cooked	

Boil the meat and fowl together the day before the dish is to be served. Soak the beans overnight, then cook until soft enough to mash. Reheat the meat and fowl, then remove both and skim the fat from the broth. Add to the broth slices of turnip and potato, cook slowly and when nearly done add the mashed bean pulp and the hulled corn. Stir often so that vegetables will not burn on the kettle. Unless the broth is very salty it will be necessary to add salt to season properly. Serve the meat and fowl on a large platter and the vegetables in a large tureen. Serves 12.

This dish was made by the Pilgrims and handed down through succeeding generations. It is served by every true Plymouth family on Forefathers' Day—December 21st. This dish keeps well and is improved with each warming over.

From a Rotary Club luncheon comes the story of a conversation between a Westerner and a New Englander. In the course of their talk, the Yankee had occasion to use the expression "New England conscience" several times and finally the Westerner, somewhat puzzled, asked him to define it. "Well," said the Yankee, "the way I see it, a New England conscience doesn't prevent your doing anything, but it does prevent your enjoying it."

"JOE BOOKER"

[A stew famous in the vicinity of Booth Bay Harbor, Maine.]

½ pound salt pork, diced   1 cup onions, sliced
2 cups lean veal or beef, diced   2 cups carrots, diced
2 cups turnip, diced   8 cups water
2 cups potatoes, diced   salt and pepper

Try out salt pork; remove the cracklings. Add to the fat the meat, vegetables, and water. Simmer 2 hours, or until meat is tender. Season to taste. This hearty stew may be served with dumplings or not, as desired. Serves 8.

When the men came in from cutting ice or chopping trees, "Joe Booker" was their favorite dish. Elderly residents of Booth Bay Harbor cannot recall for whom or by whom the dish was named, but the stew is still popular in Maine.

BAKED SALT PORK

[Mrs. John Haynes, 105 Charlotte St., Hartford, Conn.]

Wash a piece of salt pork of proper size for the family to be fed; then soak overnight in sweet milk. Score the rind an inch deep in half-inch cuts and fill the incisions with a highly seasoned bread dressing. Dust with pepper, and lay in a baking pan with a cup of milk. Bake in a moderate oven (350° F.) about 30 minutes to the pound. About an hour before dinner pour out most of the gravy, and surround the pork with sweet and Irish potatoes; bake and brown them. Skim the fat from the gravy, thicken and season, and serve the pork in thin slices.

SALT PORK WITH MILK GRAVY

[Mrs. J. A. Regan, 21 Columbus Circle, Newport, N. H.]

Cube and fry until crisp, ¾ pound lean salt pork. Remove from fat. Drain off excess fat, leaving 2 tablespoons in pan. Add 2 tablespoons flour and blend until smooth. Add 1 cup cold milk. Heat, add pork cubes and serve over hot baked or mashed potatoes. Serves 2 or 3.

HOMEMADE BEEF-AND-PORK SAUSAGE

[A New Hampshire recipe]

10 pounds pork (the cheeks, small chin segments, mixed fat and lean scraps)	1 ounce sage
	¼ ounce summer savory
5 pounds lean beef strips	¼ ounce sweet marjoram
3 ounces salt	
1½ ounces black pepper	¼ ounce thyme

Grind meat, then add seasonings; mix with a wooden paddle. Press mixture down in the pan. Stand in a cold place. Use only top quality meat. Dry the herbs in the oven and "fine up" before using.

Every member of the family takes part in sausage making. Mother scalds the iron sausage-grinder. Sister and brother proceed to take turns alternately in feeding the machine or in turning the crank and then watching the red and white parti-colored stream of meat pour forth into the bushel-sized cheese basket which is always used for a container. Following the grinding process the folks pour the meat into ordinary tin milk pans in order to season the

*sausage more carefully. Each member of the family pro-
ceeds to fry a small part of the mixture to test its flavor.*

*A three-fold disposition of the sausage follows: for the
family, father and mother fill the milk pans with the meat,
press down firmly and let it freeze until desired for cooking. For the neighborhood market they fill cloth bags about
3 inches in diameter. These slice across easily. For the fancy
market the sausage is forced into skins by means of a tin
sausage gun.*

*Anyway, sausage is sausage, whether contained in milk
pans, cloth bags, or skins. Nothing tastes finer on a zero
morning than sausage and fried apples, sausage and scram-
bled eggs, sausage and griddle cakes, or even honest-to-
goodness fried sausages with golden gravy and baked
potatoes.*

SAUSAGE AND HOMINY

[*Mrs. Marie Howe, 227 Danforth St., Portland, Me.*]

1 pound little link sausages	¼ cup melted butter
water	1 tablespoon sugar
2 cups cooked hominy	parsley garnish

Place sausages in frying pan and cover with cold water. Let come
to a boil. Pour off water and let cook until brown. Place in the
center of platter a mound of hominy which has been cooked in
boiling salted water and seasoned with melted butter and sugar.
Arrange the sausages around the hominy and garnish with parsley.
Serves 3 or 4.

FRIED SAUSAGE

With wet hand shape sausage meat into flat cakes; pan-broil in hot frying pan about 15 minutes, pouring off fat as sausage fries. Drain on absorbent paper; 1 pound sausage meat makes 8 small cakes. Serve with Apple Rings.

APPLE RINGS

[Mrs. Minnie Pires, Bedford St., New Bedford, Mass.]

Core and pare cooking apples. Slice into rings about ½ inch thick. Dip rings into milk and roll in flour. Fry in sausage fat. When lightly brown, remove and sprinkle with confectioners' sugar.

APPLES STUFFED WITH SAUSAGE

Mash 1 pound of lightly seasoned sausage meat in a skillet. When it has browned, add enough fresh bread crumbs to absorb the fat. Core, but do not peel 6 or 8 Greenings. Fill centers with sausage meat and bread crumbs. Bake in a moderately hot oven (375° F.) about 40 minutes, or until apples are tender. Serve with cornbread and custard pie for lunch. Serves 3.

HOG'S HEAD CHEESE

[Also Called Souse Meat]

1 pound fresh pork scraps (ears, feet, nose or pig's head)	1 teaspoon salt
1 pound neck of beef	1¼ tablespoons poultry seasoning
water	½ teaspoon pepper

Simmer pork and beef in small amount of water until meat falls from bone. Remove bones, lift meat from kettle and chop. Stir in seasonings; add broth in which meat was cooked and mix thoroughly. Heat through, pack in bread tins (or milk pans) and place overnight in a cool place. Remove fat that rises to top of loaf and slice. Serve with fried Baldwins and baked potato.

Some prefer vinegar gravy with their meat but it is generally served plain. This recipe came from an 1850 bride of a Maine pioneer and is still used in the family of Mrs. R. R. Tibbetts, Bethel, Maine. Additional broth remaining after making head cheese is sometimes thickened with corn meal and made into mush. It is sliced, browned in hot fat, and served for breakfast. Yankees call it Panhas.

STUFFED PORK CHOPS

½ cup chopped celery	1 cup cranberry sauce (canned
2 tablespoons finely chopped	or homemade)
onion	1 teaspoon salt
2 tablespoons chopped parsley	pepper
(optional)	6 pork chops, 1 inch thick
1 cup soft bread crumbs	flour
1 tablespoon melted butter	2 tablespoons fat

Combine the celery, onion, parsley, crumbs, cranberry sauce and butter. Add salt and a dash of pepper. Cut pockets in the pork chops and stuff; sprinkle with salt and pepper and dredge with flour. Brown lightly in fat, then bake uncovered in a moderate oven (350° F.) about 60 minutes or until tender. Serves 6.

NEW ENGLAND PORK CHOPS

[Mrs. W. F. Hill, Sacramento St., Cambridge, Mass.]

4 pork chops, well trimmed of
    fat
flour
4 medium sized onions, sliced

2 tablespoons butter or vege-
    table shortening
water
salt and pepper

Sift flour over pork chops, covering both sides. Fry onions in butter until light brown. Place chops in skillet with onions. Brown
quickly on both sides; season. Add water enough to cover, and
cook over low flame for 45 minutes, tightly covered. Chops will be
tender with a slightly thick brown gravy. Serves 2 to 4.

HAM BAKED IN CIDER I

[A Vermont recipe]

Center slice of smoked ham, cut
    2 inches thick
16 whole cloves

2 tablespoons dry mustard
½ cup maple syrup
½ cup cider (or apple juice)

Stick whole cloves into fat and rub mustard over ham. Lay in
casserole and pour maple syrup and cider over ham. Bake in moderate oven (350° F.) until tender, about 1½ hours. A 1½ pound
slice of ham serves 3.

HAM BAKED IN CIDER II

[A Delicious Colonial Dish]

1 smoked ham about 10 pounds

Marinate ham overnight in 1½ quarts sharp cider. Remove from
cider and place in a baking dish. Place it uncovered, in a roasting

pan in slow oven (300° F.) and roast 3 hours, basting with cider. Remove rind from ham. Cover with a mixture of equal parts of brown sugar and bread crumbs. Stick whole cloves into surface and brown in oven about 1 hour longer, or until ham is tender. Serve hot or cold with cider sauce made from juices in pan. Serves about 25.

RAISIN SAUCE FOR HAM

[From the New England Kitchen of Louise Crathern Russell]

1 cup seedless raisins	¼ cup cider vinegar
water	½ teaspoon salt
1 cup sugar	⅛ teaspoon clove
	1 glass currant or grape jelly

Soak raisins in lukewarm water until plumped. Pour off water. Add remaining ingredients. Heat before serving. Good with hot or cold ham.

HAM APPLE PIE

In a buttered baking dish place 3 alternate layers of ham sliced about ¼ inch thick and 3 Greenings, peeled, sliced and sprinkled with 1 tablespoon brown sugar. Sprinkle the juice of half a lemon over the top layer. Place in a moderately hot oven (375° F.) for 45 minutes. The dish should be covered until the last 30 minutes of cooking. The juice should cook down thick. Serves 4.

This is an entrée, not a dessert.

BERTHA'S HAM LOAF

[Mrs. Bertha Glendining, Mountain St., Sharon, Mass.]

1 pound uncooked ham (string   1 cup fine bread crumbs
   end)   1 egg
1 pound fresh pork   ¾ cup milk
1 onion, chopped fine   pepper

Grind ham and pork together twice. Blend all ingredients thoroughly and turn into an oiled bread tin. Bake 1½ hours in a moderate oven (350° F.). Unmold and serve with mustard sauce.

MUSTARD SAUCE

1 egg   1 bouillon cube
½ cup prepared mustard   ⅓ cup sugar
              ½ cup mild vinegar

Beat the egg; heat the remaining ingredients and when bouillon cube is dissolved, pour onto the egg. Serve hot without allowing sauce to boil. 2 tablespoons butter may be added just before serving.

FRIED HAM WITH APPLE RINGS

[A Connecticut recipe]

1 slice ham, 1 inch thick   ½ cup flour
4 red cooking apples   ¼ teaspoon salt
1 egg, beaten   brown sugar
¼ cup milk   cinnamon

Rub frying pan with ham fat and brown ham on both sides; cover, cook slowly 30 minutes, turning several times. Core, but do not peel apples. Cut thick rings crosswise. Combine egg, milk, flour and salt, dip apple rings in this batter and fry in ham fat, after removing slice of ham, adding more ham fat or bacon fat so that fat is about 1 inch deep in frying pan. When brown, drain and sprinkle apple rings with brown sugar and cinnamon and serve in an overlapping ring about the ham. Serves 4.

Although older recipes did not call for it, 2 teaspoons of brandy added to the batter gives a special flavor to the apples.

WINDSOR PIE

1½ cups chopped cooked ham, some fat included

3 cups drained, cooked macaroni

6 common crackers, crushed

2 tablespoons butter

3 cups milk (about)

Place the chopped meat in well-buttered baking dish. Place cooked macaroni on top of meat, then crackers. Pour milk over the crackers, slowly wetting the whole top surface. Add milk until all of mixture is covered. Dot with butter. Bake in a slow oven (300° F.) about 1 hour, or until milk is absorbed and the top nicely browned. Serves 4. Serve with coleslaw.

Corned beef or well-seasoned chopped cold meat of any kind may be used in place of ham. Minced onion and seasonings should be added to chopped beef or lamb.

The grandmother of Mrs. Doris G. Whitney, Grafton, Mass., a "down-easter," was famous for this dish.

BEAN POT STEW

[Mrs. W. E. Lane, West Falmouth, Me.]

1 pound beef (bottom of round) cut in cubes	1 cup peas, fresh or canned
1 onion	4 tablespoons rolled oats
2 tablespoons fat	1 teaspoon salt
2 small carrots, sliced	water to cover
1 small turnip, sliced	pepper
	3 potatoes, cubed

Brown meat and onion in fat; add carrots, turnips and peas. Turn into greased bean pot or casserole. Add remaining ingredients except potatoes, cover with water and bake in moderate oven (350° F.) 4 hours. Add potatoes the last hour of cooking. Serves 4.

CHURCH SUPPER MEAT LOAF

6 pounds beef, ground	4 large onions
2 pounds pork, ground	6 cups soft bread crumbs
3 teaspoons salt	2 cups water
1 teaspoon pepper	

Combine ingredients and turn into four greased loaf pans. Bake in moderately hot oven (375° F.) for 40 minutes. Serve plain or with tomato sauce. Serves 24.

NEW HAMPSHIRE CHURCH SUPPER MENU

Chicken Pie or Meat Loaf or Other Cold Meat
—Scalloped Potatoes—
Mixed Vegetable Salad—Whole Wheat and White Rolls
—Pickles—
—Washington Pie—
—Coffee—

HAMBURG LOAF

[From the New England Kitchen of Louise Crathern Russell]

1 egg, beaten
2 pounds hamburg
1½ teaspoons salt

½ teaspoon pepper
10 soda crackers, rolled
1 can mushroom soup (12 oz.)

Mix the egg into the hamburg; add seasonings and crackers. Lastly add the can of mushroom soup. Bake in a moderately hot oven (375° F.) 40 minutes. Serves 6.

BEEF STEAK AND OYSTERS

[A Rhode Island recipe]

Broil a steak until nearly tender. Cover with drained oysters, dotted with butter. Bake in a moderate oven (375° F.) until oysters are plump. Season oysters. Serve with lemon butter and chopped parsley sauce. Allow ½ pound steak per portion.

MEAT BALLS WITH CRANBERRY SAUCE

1 pound ground beef
½ cup dry bread crumbs
1 egg
2 tablespoons finely chopped
   onion
2 teaspoons salt

⅛ teaspoon pepper
1 cup strained cranberry sauce
   (canned or homemade)
1 eight-ounce can tomato
   sauce
½ cup water

Combine the beef, crumbs, egg, onion and seasonings. Form into small balls and allow to stand for a few minutes. Brown in fat. Make a sauce by mashing the cranberry sauce and mixing it with the tomato sauce and water; pour over the meat balls; cover and simmer for 1 hour. Serves 5.

VEAL POT PIE I

½ pound fat salt pork	dumpling dough
2 pounds veal from the breast	(recipe page 91)
water	½ pint cream
salt and pepper	1 tablespoon butter

Cut salt pork in ½ inch pieces. Slice into a deep kettle, cover kettle and let salt pork fry a light brown. Add veal, cut in small cubes; cook for ½ hour, turning often to brown on all sides. Add boiling water to cover the meat to the depth of 1 inch. Season. Cover kettle and simmer until meat is tender, about 45 minutes. Make dumpling dough; carefully drop in dumplings. Cover and let cook until dumplings are done. Lift dumplings from the kettle, lay around edges of a hot platter. With a skimmer lift out the veal and lay in the center of the platter. Add cream to the liquid in the kettle. Thicken gravy. Stir in 1 tablespoon butter. Pour gravy over veal on the platter and serve at once. Serves 6.

Mrs. James E. Marshall, Bell St., Chicopee, Mass., found this recipe when she was looking for famous recipes for an Old Time Fair in Norwich, Conn. This recipe is a treasured family recipe belonging to one of the oldest families in Norwich.

Veal Pot Pie recipes of olden times call for a deep baking dish lined with baked pastry crust. Rice was placed over the crust so that it would keep its shape. The veal was then added and topped with pastry or cream of tartar biscuits, soda biscuits or dumplings. The veal was browned in a variety of herbs from the kitchen garden, parsley, a little thyme, a bay leaf; also a dash of cayenne. Sometimes vegetables were omitted and diced oysters and hard-boiled egg yolks added to the veal.

VEAL POT PIE II

[*A New Hampshire recipe*]

1½ pounds veal
6 tablespoons flour
1 teaspoon salt
dash of pepper
¼ cup fat

boiling water
2 small onions, finely cut
2 carrots, diced
soda biscuits
(recipe page 164)

Cut veal in 1-inch dice. Dredge with seasoned flour and sauté in fat until well browned, turning frequently. Cover with boiling water and simmer, covered, 1½ hours or until tender, adding onions and carrots the last ½ hour of cooking. Thicken with paste of a little additional flour and water, if gravy is not thick. Place meat, gravy and vegetables in a deep baking dish. Cover with small rounds of soda biscuits rolled ½ inch thick. Bake in hot oven (450° F.) about 15 minutes. Serves 5.

LIVER LOAF

[*From the New England Kitchen of Louise Crathern Russell*]

¼ pound salt pork
1 pound liver
20 crisp soda crackers
1½ cups hot stock (or water)
2 eggs, beaten

1 tablespoon minced onion
1 teaspoon poultry seasoning
1 teaspoon salt
¼ teaspoon pepper
1 tablespoon butter

Pan-fry the salt pork. Remove from pan. Add liver to the fat. Sear on both sides. Coarsely grind the liver and pork together. Pour the hot stock over crumbed crackers. Combine meat, crackers, eggs and seasonings. Shape into a loaf and dot with butter. Bake in a hot oven (425° F.) for 25 to 30 minutes. Serves 6.

BRAISED BREAST OF LAMB WITH SPINACH STUFFING

[*Mrs. B. Stanwood, Forestville, Conn.*]

Simmer a breast of lamb in salted water to cover until tender, about 20 minutes per pound. Remove from broth, slip the bones out at once and allow the meat to cool. Spread out breast of lamb, cover with a thin layer of spinach stuffing, roll and tie at both ends with clean, white string. Place rolled meat in a baking pan, sprinkle lightly with flour and pour ¼ cup of the broth around it and brown in a hot oven (400° F.).

SPINACH STUFFING

2 cups dry bread crumbs	1 tablespoon green pepper, chopped
½ pound spinach leaves	
4 tablespoons butter	1 tablespoon onion, chopped
2 tablespoons celery, chopped	½ teaspoon salt
	¼ teaspoon pepper

Wash spinach thoroughly, cut in fine pieces and place in a saucepan with celery, green pepper, onion and 2 tablespoons butter. Cook to wilt the spinach slightly, about 2 minutes, stirring constantly. Push spinach to one side of the pan, melt remaining butter in empty part of pan and add the bread crumbs. (This is an easy way to butter the crumbs.) Mix spinach and crumbs. Season.

FRIED PICKLED TRIPE

[*Helen H. Radcliffe, The Galley, Fairhaven, Mass.*]

Parboil pickled honeycomb tripe about 3 minutes. Dry thoroughly and dip in beaten egg. Roll in flour and fry in a well greased skillet until brown on both sides.

BROILED TRIPE

[Famous recipe of the Parker House, Boston, Mass.]

Cut honeycomb tripe in pieces about 4 by 6 inches. Season with salt and pepper. Sprinkle with flour, then dip in olive oil and sprinkle generously with sifted bread crumbs. Broil slowly 2 or 3 minutes on each side or until the crumbs are brown (a charcoal fire is best). Serve with mustard sauce.

MUSTARD SAUCE

Sauté 1 tablespoon minced onion in 3 tablespoons butter. Add 2 tablespoons cider vinegar and simmer 5 minutes. Moisten 2 teaspoons dry mustard with 1 tablespoon water and blend; then add 1 cup brown gravy. Let simmer a few minutes and strain. Serve very hot. Makes 1¼ cups sauce.

Some Vermonters were debating their various personal tastes in the giblet portion of the beef critter for table consumption. Topics had ranged from tongue, through kidneys to oxtail soup. At last the inevitable ne plus ultra of cow-cuts came up for discussion. The interviewer inquired directly if his friends thought it a fit table dish. "How about tripe?" he asked.

The man considered, spat, and then replied, "Wa'al, tripe's all right, I guess. But allus seemed to me as if 'twas eatin' the critter up too clus."

NEW HAMPSHIRE "OLD HOME" CHICKEN PIE

*[Daisy Deane Williamson, State Home Demonstration Leader,
State of New Hampshire]*

1 recipe plain pastry	3 cups chicken gravy
1 fowl (about 4 pounds)	salt and pepper

Line an earthen baking dish with the pastry rolled about ¼ inch thick. Lay into this unbaked shell pieces of hot boiled chicken, seasoned to suit the taste, and pour gravy over it. Put on the top cover, rolled ⅛ inch thick, and gashed to allow the steam to escape. Bake in a hot oven (450° F.) for about 15 minutes, then reduce heat to moderate (350° F.) and continue baking about 30 minutes longer. This recipe makes 6 servings.

PLAIN PASTRY

2½ cups sifted flour	¾ cup shortening
¾ teaspoon salt	⅓ cup cold water (about)

Mix and sift flour and salt. Cut in shortening. Add water in small amounts, stirring with a fork and laying dough to one side as it is formed. Use water sparingly. Roll dough ¼ inch thick, and form bottom and top of pie as suggested above.

For variety these pies were often made with latticed top.

In the Connecticut Valley sweet chicken gravy is used on chicken pies. At church suppers you are asked whether you prefer your chicken gravy sweetened or unsweetened.

POTTED CHICKEN

[In Plymouth, Mass., they call it "tendering a fowl"]

Cut up a fowl as for fricassee. Roll each piece in seasoned flour. Pack closely in a large bean pot and cover with boiling water and bake 3½ hours. Cover after water begins to boil.

CAPE COD CHICKEN

[Mrs. George W. P. Babb, Montclair Ave., Roslindale, Mass.]

2 slices of fat salt pork   6 onions
1 fowl cut in pieces for stewing   6 potatoes
6 slices of turnip   salt and pepper
         dumplings

Try out pork in large kettle and then lay in the chicken pieces. Cover with boiling water and boil ½ hour. Then lay in the turnip slices and the onions. When nearly done add potatoes. 12 minutes before serving put in the dumplings or steam separately. Put chicken on large platter surrounded by vegetables and dumplings; make the gravy and serve in bowl. Serves 6.

DUMPLINGS

2 cups flour   3 teaspoons baking powder
¾ teaspoon salt   1 cup rich milk

Sift dry ingredients together 4 times. Add milk, stirring quickly to make a soft dough. Drop by spoonfuls on top of chicken gravy or stew, making sure the dough rests on pieces of meat or vegetables and does not settle in the liquid. Cover tightly and steam 12 minutes without removing cover. Dumplings may also be dropped on a plate and cooked in a steamer over rapidly boiling water for 20 minutes. Makes 12 dumplings. If *rich* milk is not available cut in 2 tablespoons shortening as for baking-powder biscuits.

A clever New England way of making a tough chicken tender enough to fry is to soak it overnight in buttermilk. The buttermilk also gives it a delicious flavor.

CHICKEN SMOTHERED IN OYSTERS

[Famous "company dish," 300 years old]

Clean and cut young chickens into quarters. Season. Heat butter in a skillet and sauté chicken. Place in a baking dish. Pour over ½ cup milk for each chicken. Cover dish and place in a moderately hot oven (375° F.) for 1 hour. Baste frequently. Add 1 pint small oysters and 1 cup cream for each chicken and roast 15 minutes longer. Remove chicken to hot platter. Pour oysters and cream around and serve.

CREAMED CHICKEN AND RICE

[Mrs. William H. Vanderbilt, Oakland Farms, Newport, R. I. The favorite recipe of Rhode Island's governor and his family]

Singe and wash one 5-pound chicken. Tie drumsticks and wings close to body. Place in kettle with 1 carrot, 1 cup celery, ¼ teaspoon salt, 3 quarts of water and simmer gently 1½ hours.

For the cream sauce, melt 2 tablespoons butter, blend well with 3 tablespoons flour, add 2 cups of broth from the chicken pot, stirring all the while. Add 1 cup of cream last, and season with salt and pepper, to taste. Add mushrooms to sauce if desired.

Disjoint chicken, place in sauce and keep warm till serving time. Serve with boiled rice molded in ring, piling the chicken in the center with the sauce. Serves 6.

HEN AND BEANS

[An old New Hampshire recipe]

Cut up a tough old rooster as for fricassee. Prepare Boston Baked Beans according to recipe on page 100. Smother pieces of chicken under the beans and proceed as for Boston Baked Beans.

MAINE CHICKEN STEW

2 3½-4 pound chickens	2 tablespoons butter
6 potatoes, sliced	1 cup thin cream or rich milk
3 onions, sliced	salt and pepper
cold water	minced parsley
6 to 8 common crackers	

Cut chicken for stewing. In an iron kettle place alternate layers of chicken, slices of potato and thinly sliced onion. Cover with cold water. Simmer gently until chicken is tender. Add butter in small bits and cream or milk. Season with salt and pepper and minced parsley. Split crackers, moisten in cold milk, and reheat in stew. Serves 8.

WILD DUCK, TEAL DUCK AND QUAIL

To roast wild duck, rub inside with salt and fill cavity with a small onion, an apple and celery. Season with salt and pepper. Place in a roasting pan. Truss, cover breast with thin slices salt pork. Bake, uncovered in a hot oven (450° F.) 20 to 30 minutes. Baste frequently.

Wild duck should be served rare.

Teal duck is filled with a dressing of bread crumbs and sour apples.

Roasted quail is usually served on buttered toast with rich cream gravy.

Serve birds with currant, wild plum or beach plum jelly. Wild rice or fried hominy should accompany duck.

VERMONT ROAST TURKEY

Singe, clean and rub inside with salt; stuff and truss. Rub entire turkey well with olive oil, butter, or cooking oil. Place breast side up in an ordinary dripping pan with a rack in the bottom. Do not cover. In such a roaster any steam that forms will go off into the air and not stay inside to draw juices from the turkey and make it dry.

Roast turkey at a moderately slow temperature (325° F.). Do not sear. Keeping the temperature constant throughout the cooking gives a finished bird that is cooked evenly. There will be little or no sputtering and the drippings will be just right for making a nice brown gravy. Allow 25 to 30 minutes per pound. A young turkey weighing between 10 and 14 pounds, market weight, requires 3 to 3½ hours roasting at 325° F. (Market weight means picked but not drawn and including head and feet.)

Turn a turkey cooked in an open roaster breast side down the last 30 minutes of roasting. To turn without breaking the skin, pick the turkey up by the neck and legs using several folds of soft clean cloth as a "holder."

To determine if turkey is done, run a steel skewer or cooking fork into the thickest part of the breast and also into the thigh next to the breast. If the meat is tender and the juice does not look red, the turkey is roasted enough. Basting is not necessary if the bird is fat. Otherwise baste every 30 minutes with pan drippings or water and butter.

In buying a turkey allow ¾ pound for each person to be served. That is as the bird is weighed when bought, undrawn with head and feet attached. A 15-pound turkey will make 20 generous servings.

BREAD CRUMB STUFFING

5 cups bread crumbs	1 teaspoon salt
1 onion, minced	¼ teaspoon pepper
1 cup finely chopped celery	½ teaspoon poultry seasoning or
¾ cup butter, melted	thyme, marjoram or sage

Mix bread crumbs, onion, celery, seasonings and melted butter with a fork. Makes stuffing enough for a 10-pound turkey. Halve this recipe for 5-pound chicken or fish.

½ cup fat salt pork (put through the meat grinder) was often substituted for the melted butter. Certain New England recipes call for the addition of ½ teaspoon grated nutmeg.

BUTTERNUT STUFFING

[From the New England Kitchen of Louise Crathern Russell]

1½ cups butternut meats,
  chopped
4 cups bread crumbs, sifted
1 teaspoon dried powdered
  sage
½ teaspoon summer savory

½ teaspoon thyme
1 egg, well beaten
½ cup cream
4 cups hot mashed potatoes
1 teaspoon salt
½ teaspoon pepper

Mix well nuts, bread crumbs and dried powdered herbs. Combine well-beaten egg with cream. Add this to the freshly boiled mashed hot potatoes. Add salt and pepper and beat. Put the mixtures together and stuff bird. Makes stuffing enough for a 13-pound turkey. Butternut stuffing was an old-time favorite, and too good to be forgotten.

ROAST VENISON

[A Maine recipe]

Roast venison in the same manner in which lamb is roasted, allowing 25 minutes to the pound for cooking (in an oven 350° F.) as venison is served rare. If venison is lean, place a few slices of salt pork over the roast. Serve with currant sauce and fried hominy. (See recipe page 97.)

CURRANT SAUCE

1 cup hot gravy   ¼ glass currant jelly

Combine and serve.

VENISON STEAKS AND CUTLETS

Broil or pan-fry in the same manner in which chops are broiled, first brushing with olive oil. If venison is strong, marinate with French dressing for 1 hour before broiling. Venison from a freshly killed deer should ripen for 2 weeks before being eaten.

Shoulder cuts of venison may be braised with celery, onion, carrot. Add 1 tablespoon vinegar and cook about 2½ hours. Serve with grape jelly.

VENISON SAUCE

½ tablespoon chicken fat or
   butter
1 cup barberry, wild currant or
   grape jelly

⅛ teaspoon salt
1 tablespoon cider or cider
   vinegar
½ teaspoon ground cloves

½ teaspoon cinnamon

Let butter melt (but do not let it brown) in skillet. When melted, add the jelly, salt, cider and spices. Simmer slowly until mixture thickens slightly.

This sauce may be made ahead of time. When desired for use, reheat in double boiler. The above quantity is for a 6-pound haunch of venison, a good-sized chicken, a roast partridge, pheasant, or roast of lamb. This recipe is 150 years old and comes from Kent, Connecticut.

FRIED HOMINY

[To serve with roast duck and birds and venison]

2 cups cold cooked hominy   2 egg yolks
½ teaspoon salt

Combine hominy, egg yolks and salt. Shape in croquettes and fry in hot deep fat (370° F.) for 5 minutes until delicately browned, or pan-fry. Serves 3 or 4.

SQUIRREL PIE

[Norma Roberts, Bristol, N. H.]

Dress 4 squirrels and cut into suitable pieces to serve. Soak over-night in lightly salted water. Wash well and parboil 15 minutes. Rinse well with hot water and simmer in 2 cups water until tender, about 1 hour. Remove meat to a pastry lined deep dish (which has an inverted cup in the center). Thicken and season the gravy, adding 2 tablespoons butter and pour over meat. Top with tiny baking powder biscuits or a pastry crust. Bake in a hot oven (450° F.) until crust is well browned. At least 4 squirrels are needed to fill a 2-quart pie dish. 4 squirrels serve 6. Bottom crust may be omitted.

To dress squirrels, cut off forefeet at first joint; cut skin around first joint of hind legs, loosen it and with a sharp knife slit the skin on the under side of legs at the tail. Loosen the skin and turn it back until it is removed from the hind legs. Draw the skin over the head, slipping out the forelegs when reached. Cut off the end of nose and thus re-move the entire skin. Wipe squirrel with a damp cloth, remove entrails (heart and liver are edible). An ingenious way to remove skin readily is to slip tip of bicycle pump under the skin of legs. The pressure of the air does the trick neatly.

COOT STEW

[Edward Bailey, Hanover, Mass.]

Skin 2 coots (do not pick). Wash in salt and water and let stand overnight in solution of ¼ cup salt and water to cover.

Place in stew kettle and boil for 10 minutes. Remove and pour

off water. Return to kettle. Add 1 teaspoon salt, ¼ teaspoon pepper
and fresh water to cover.

When tender enough to break at joints, remove. Add to liquor
-4 medium-sized onions chopped, 6 large potatoes, diced, 1 sweet
potato, diced, 1 cup diced turnip and cook until almost done, then
add coots, which have been cut in pieces. Thicken slightly and
serve. Serves 6.

*The expression "crazy as a coot" comes from observation
of the coot that is shot off the coast of Maine. Gunners,
in boats, wait until a flock of these birds take it into their
heads to dive under the water, all at the same time. They
row their boat over the coot, which eventually pops from
the water in horrified amazement. The famous coot stew
recipe always brings a chuckle to a State of Mainer, no matter how many times he has heard it: "Place the bird in a
kettle of water with a red building brick free of mortar and
blemishes. Parboil the coot and brick together for 3 hours.
Pour off water, fill the kettle, and again parboil for 3 hours.
Once more throw off the water, refill the kettle, and this
time let the coot and brick simmer together overnight. In
the morning throw away the coot and eat the brick." To
appreciate the joke, one must know that where a partridge
will drop from one shot, fifty goose shot will rattle off a
coot as though his feathers were made of steel. When
cooked properly, coot is as tender and savory as duck.*

IV. VEGETABLES: INDIVIDUAL
AND COLLECTIVE

BOSTON BAKED BEANS

1 quart pea beans
½ pound fat salt pork
2 teaspoons salt

1½ tablespoons brown sugar
¼ cup molasses
½ teaspoon dry mustard

boiling water

Wash and pick over beans. Soak overnight in cold water. In the morning, drain, cover with fresh water and simmer until skins break; turn into bean pot. Score pork and press into beans, leaving ¼ inch above the beans. Add salt, sugar, molasses and mustard. Add boiling water to cover. Cover and bake in slow oven (250° F.) for about 8 hours without stirring, adding water as necessary to keep beans covered. Uncover during last half hour to brown. Serves 8.

The secret of delicious baked beans is to keep them covered with water at all times except the last hour of baking. Cape Cod cooks add ½ cup cream to baked beans the last half hour of baking. A large onion nestled in the center of the bean pot is popular with Connecticut cooks. A bay leaf hidden here and there also adds flavor. In the early days,

*beans were left to bake all night in the slow steady heat
of the great brick oven.*

*The Puritan housewife baked her beans all day Saturday,
served them fresh for the Saturday night meal (the beginning of Sabbath); warmed them over for Sunday breakfast, and served them warm or cold, depending on the heat-
holding qualities of her oven, for Sunday's noonday lunch,
providing she did not consider it necessary to fast from
breakfast until sundown on Sunday.*

*Of all the Puritan influences which fastened themselves
on New England, the Saturday night baked bean supper is
one of the most lasting and widespread in its effect on other
parts of the country. Beans are still eaten every Saturday
night and Sunday morning by thousands of New Englanders. All religious significance has been lost many years
ago, but the baked bean holds popular favor in its own
right.*

BAKED BEANS WITH MAPLE SYRUP

[*A Vermont recipe*]

1 quart pea beans	½ cup maple syrup
½ pound fat salt pork	½ teaspoon dry mustard
1 onion	2 teaspoons salt
boiling water	

Soak beans overnight. In the morning put on to cook in fresh
water. Let simmer until skins burst, 1 to 1½ hours. Drain beans.
Put an onion in bottom of bean pot; add beans. Mix syrup, mustard
and salt and sprinkle over beans. Put pork down into beans so that
only the rind is above the surface. Pour on boiling water to cover.
Bake in a slow oven (250° F.) for 6 to 8 hours, adding water, a
little at a time, to keep beans covered. Serves 6.

NEW HAMPSHIRE BAKED YELLOW EYE
PORK AND BEANS

[From the New England Kitchen of Louise Crathern Russell]

1 quart dried yellow eye beans	1 teaspoon mustard
½ pound salt pork (streaked	¼ teaspoon pepper
with lean)	½ teaspoon ginger
1 tablespoon sugar	½ cup tomato catsup
¾ cup brown sugar	2 teaspoons salt

boiling water

Wash and pick over beans. Soak overnight in cold water to cover. In the morning drain; cover with fresh water and simmer for 1 to 1½ hours, or until the skins wrinkle. Turn into beanpot. Add sugar, brown sugar, mustard, pepper, ginger, catsup and salt. Score the pork and press it down into the beans. The rind should be uppermost and projecting ¼ inch above the beans. Pour on boiling water to cover. Cover and bake in a slow oven (250° F.) about 8 hours. During the baking add boiling water so that the beans are covered with water. Uncover during last half hour to brown. Serves 8.

Serve sliced green tomato pickles or sharp cucumber pickles with the beans.

BAKED BEANS, MAINE LUMBERCAMP STYLE

[From Howard Reynolds' series on camping on the Allagash printed August, 1923, in the Boston "Post"]

"First a hole is dug in the ground, fairly free of rocks, 2 feet deep by 18 inches in circumference. In the hole kindling of soft wood is first placed, and over the hole a cobhouse of split hard wood is built. When the fire is lighted in the kindling the cobhouse catches fire, and as the air circulates freely through it, the hardwood sticks, being of uniform size, all burn down together.

"In the meanwhile over the campfire a pail of beans (about 2 quarts dried beans) has been parboiling so that their skins crack when dished out in a spoon and exposed to the air. The water from these is drained off and they are poured into another pail on the bottom of which has been placed several thick slices of fat salt pork. On the top of the beans is placed a piece of pork weighing about a pound, the rind of which has been well gashed. Over all is poured a teaspoonful of salt, 3 tablespoons of molasses, 2 of sugar and a dash of mustard, dissolved in hot water. The pail is then filled with enough boiling water to cover the beans.

"Next the coals are raked out of the hole and the pail, covered tight with an empty corn-can put on top and wedged in so as to keep the pail upright, is placed in the hole. The live coals are then shoveled around it and over it, together with a few inches of earth tramped down tight and allowed to remain alone all night. In the morning dig the pail out and serve."

MORNING DIP

Goldie E. Benson, who lives in Clinton, Mass., recalls that on Saturday morning her mother used to say, "Now run down cellar and get me a piece of salt pork for the beans." Goldie would pick up the old butcher knife and proceed to the dark, damp cellar. Off would come the board which served as a cover to the firkin, then the heavy, flat stone which weighted the pork down in the brine. Next came the terrifying moment when she held her breath and plunged her bare hand and arm into the cold salt water to fish out a strip of pork; then cut off a generous piece for the four-quart bean pot. As long as she lives, Goldie Benson says, she will never forget the courage it took to make that final plunge into the brine to pull out the pork.

FROZEN BEAN PORRIDGE

[A very old recipe]

Put 3 cups of dry red kidney beans to soak overnight, parboil them in the morning until the skins crack; drain. Cook 3 pounds soup bone (beef with marrow) until the bones may be removed and the meat cut in pieces. Add enough water to the amount the meat was boiled in to make 6 quarts; add the beans, 2 tablespoons salt, ¼ teaspoon black pepper and cook until the beans are tender but not mushy. Add 1 cup yellow corn meal, wet with water, and cook 30 minutes, stirring often to avoid "catching on" (sticking and burning). Set out to freeze. Small amounts are cut from this as needed and "het" boiling hot. An iron kettle is best but any heavy kettle will do.

This porridge was made in huge iron kettles and hauled on ox sleds into the wilderness for a staple food when men and boys went to clear the land and build a cabin for their families, who would follow in the spring. Without doubt, much of New Hampshire was "settled" on frozen bean porridge.

NANTUCKET CORN PUDDING

1 egg	½ teaspoon sugar
1 cup milk	½ tablespoon melted butter
½ teaspoon salt	few grains cayenne

1 cup cooked corn scraped from the ear

Beat the egg; add the milk, seasonings, butter and corn. Turn the mixture into a buttered baking dish. Bake in a moderate oven (350° F.) until the mixture will not adhere to a knife inserted in the center (45 to 50 minutes). This dish resembles a custard but is served with the main course of the dinner. Serves 4.

OVEN ROASTED CORN

[A New Hampshire recipe]

Place ears of corn (with husks) in a moderate oven (350° F.) and bake for 30 minutes. Remove husks and silk and serve hot with butter. Oven-roasted corn has the flavor of corn served at corn roasts or clambakes.

CORN OYSTERS

[Mrs. Nellie Barrett, East Sumner, Me.]

½ cup flour, sifted	1 cup canned corn
½ teaspoon baking powder	1 egg, well beaten
½ teaspoon salt	2 tablespoons melted butter
1 tablespoon milk	

Sift dry ingredients. Combine the corn and milk and mix thoroughly. Add egg and butter and mix well. Drop from tip of spoon into hot fat in skillet. These little fritters should be the size of large oysters. Sauté until brown, turning to brown both sides. Makes 12 to 16 oysters.

If pulp from corn-on-the-cob is used, score the kernels on the cob down the middle with a sharp knife, and press out the pulp using the dull back of the knife. Make a batter of the remaining ingredients adding flour in small quantities until the consistency is that of pancake batter. If the corn is not milky, add an additional tablespoon of milk.

> *"All the fine old frugal ways*
> *Of the early Pilgrim years*
> *Have the power to wake in me*
> *A deep sober ecstasy*
> *Close akin to tears."*

HULLED CORN—OLD METHOD

Boil white wood-ashes in an iron kettle with plenty of water until the mixture is stout enough to float an egg. Drain it off from the ashes. Place the shelled corn in the liquid. Boil the corn carefully until the hulls rub off. Rinse in several waters so that no lye remains. Boil again in salted water until tender.

HULLED CORN—NEW METHOD

Pick over 1 quart dried, yellow corn. Cover with 2 quarts cold water to which has been added 2 tablespoons soda. Soak overnight. Boil in the same water, adding more as needed, until the hulls are loosened, about 3 hours. Drain, wash, rub off the hulls between hands. Boil corn again in clear water. Change the water, add a teaspoon of salt and boil gently until corn is tender, about 4 hours. Serve hot with milk or butter. 1 quart corn makes 4 quarts when cooked.

Hulled corn is a favorite old New England dish. It is made from yellow corn, whereas hominy, another venerable dish, is made from white corn. Both hulled corn and hominy (samp) may be purchased today in two forms— hulled and ready to cook (about 4 hours cooking time required) or in tins, all cooked, ready to heat and serve. Hulled corn or hominy is an excellent change from potatoes. It may be warmed up by frying in butter.

Many New Englanders recall peddlers who used to sell hulled corn and horseradish.

SUCCOTASH

2 tablespoons butter

2 cups cooked beans (lima or kidney)

2 cups corn (fresh scraped from the cob or canned)

½ cup water

1 teaspoon salt

⅛ teaspoon pepper

1 teaspoon sugar

¼ cup rich milk

Melt butter; add the beans, corn and water and the seasonings. Cook over low heat. Stir in the milk as water is absorbed. Heat thoroughly, but do not boil after milk is added. Serve very hot. Serves 6.

Succotash comes from the Indian word m'sickquatash— "maize not crushed or ground."

9 POTATO RECIPES FROM AROOSTOOK, ME.

[Pearl Ashby Tibbetts, the busy wife of a very busy country doctor in Bethel, Me., contributes all 9]

POTATOES AND PEPPERS IN CREAM

Cut 6 Maine potatoes, boiled in skins, into small cubes. Parboil 1 sweet green pepper, remove seeds and chop. Place cubes of potato and chopped pepper in top of double boiler with 1 cup top milk and cook 15 minutes. Then place in casserole with 2 tablespoons grated cheese. Cook about 20 minutes in moderate oven (350° F.). Serves 4 to 6.

POTATOES IN HALF SHELL

Bake even sized Maine potatoes. Slice lengthwise. Carefully scoop out interior of each. Mash well and add butter, salt, pepper, and hot milk or cream. Beat vigorously and when fluffy return to shells. Sprinkle with paprika and chopped parsley, brown in the oven and serve.

SMALL POTATOES

Peel and wash 8 small Maine potatoes. Boil quickly and drain. Add 3 tablespoons butter; 1 tablespoon lemon juice and 2 tablespoons minced parsley. Serve with any cooked fish. Serves 3 or 4.

PUFF BALLS

6 medium potatoes	salt and pepper
3 tablespoons butter	egg
½ cup hot milk	bread crumbs

¼ cup mild grated cheese

Pare and boil potatoes. Drain and mash very smooth and light. Add butter, hot milk, grated cheese, salt and pepper to taste, and beat until fluffy. While hot, shape into little balls, roll in egg and bread crumbs, place on a well-buttered tin and brown delicately in a hot oven (450° F.). Serve immediately. Serves 4.

PANNED POTATOES

Put 2 tablespoons butter in a baking pan; pare and slice 6 Maine potatoes as for frying, put in pan, sprinkle with salt and pepper and cover with rich milk. Cook in moderate oven (350° F.) about 40 minutes until potatoes are tender and milk absorbed. Serves 4.

SAVORY SUPPER DISH

Slice a layer of raw onion in bottom of buttered baking dish. Fill dish with thin slices of raw Maine potatoes. Add salt and pepper. Nearly cover with water, place cubes of salt pork on top and cook slowly 3 hours in an oven 250° F.

MASHED MAINERS WITH MINT

Boil and mash Maine potatoes; add salt, butter and hot milk. Beat until fluffy and add 2 tablespoons finely chopped fresh mint leaves. Excellent with roast lamb.

POTATO BROWN MOUND

Pile mashed potatoes lightly in greased baking dish. Pour over ½ cup heavy cream and sprinkle with ½ cup dry bread crumbs. Bake in hot oven (450° F.) until crumbs are brown. Serve with cold sliced meat.

MAINE SOUFFLÉ

Combine 3 cups hot boiled and mashed Maine potatoes, ¼ cup melted butter, yolks of 2 eggs, little cayenne pepper, 1 cup hot milk. Stir well and then fold in the beaten whites of the eggs. Pile in well buttered baking dish and bake 15 minutes in a moderate oven (350° F.). Serves 4.

GRANDMOTHER'S POTATOES

Pare large potatoes and cut a tunnel through the center of each one with an apple corer. Draw a small sausage through each one; place potatoes in the pan and lay a slice of salt pork or bacon on each one. Bake in a moderately hot oven (375° F.), about 50 minutes or until done, basting with hot water when necessary.

This was the old Maine recipe of Kate Douglas Wiggin's grandmother copied by Mrs. Prescott W. Hilton, Providence, R. I., from a "Book of Dorcas Dishes" edited by Kate Douglas Wiggin.

The Dorcas Society was founded by Kate Douglas Wiggin at Buxton, Maine, and the meetings were well attended. Mrs. Hilton is a Dorcas Society member.

"NECESSITY MESS," "POTATO BARGAIN," OR "TILTON'S GLORY"

[From a book of Vineyard recipes]

"To make this dish properly," according to Joseph C. Allen, Cape Higgon, Mass., "an iron pot should be used. Otherwise it must be started in a frying pan. ½ pound mixed pork, 3 onions the size of duck eggs, 1½ quarts potatoes, peeled and cut in slices ½ inch thick. Slice the pork about ¼ inch thick. Peel and slice onions very thin. Place in the pot and fry briskly until very brown. Then put in the potatoes and fill the pot with water until it is about an inch above the potatoes. Boil slowly until the potatoes are thoroughly cooked but not enough to crumble. Thicken the gravy, using about 3 tablespoons flour and serve in one dish. A small turnip, a carrot, or both, may be added, as may also dumplings. But as these are not, properly speaking, 'necessities,' I have not included them in the recipe."

SCOOTIN'-'LONG-THE-SHORE

¼ cup bacon fat   1 cup onions, sliced
                 4 cups raw potatoes, sliced

Heat bacon fat in a skillet; stir in the onions and potatoes. Cover and cook slowly, stirring occasionally until the fat is absorbed and the potatoes are tender. Uncover when brown and crusty on the bottom. Serve with fried or boiled fish. Serves 4.

Mrs. Mae Bangs Twite, Oak Bluffs, Martha's Vineyard, Mass., says this plain but appetizing combination of potatoes and onions rejoices in the name of Scootin'-'Long-the-Shore because for years upon years Cape Cod fishermen prepared this meal while at their work. Mrs. Twite has often heard her grandmother ask her "granddad" what they should have for lunch. Always his comeback was, "Well, Mother, make it Scootin'-'Long-the-Shore."

Down in Maine a similar recipe is popular. Potatoes are sliced as thin as possible, and thrown into cold water while salt pork is tried out. Pork is removed from pan and potatoes fried slowly for about 30 minutes, stirring frequently. Sometimes an onion is added. When the potatoes are done, the salt pork is placed on top. This dish is known as Very Poor Man's Dinner.

HALLELUIA

[Mrs. Ella Wood Habern, 20 Albion St., Hyde Park, Mass.]

¼ pound salt pork, sliced
2 cups hot water
4 large onions, sliced
4 potatoes, sliced
⅛ teaspoon pepper

1 tablespoon flour
¼ cup cold water
½ teaspoon salt
½ teaspoon sugar

Try out the pork; add water, onions and potatoes. Cook slowly 50 minutes, or until vegetables are soft. Before serving thicken with flour dissolved in cold water; add salt, sugar and pepper. Serves 5.

This is a popular luncheon or supper dish in certain New England communities. On Cape Cod it is called Cape Cod Stifle. It is sometimes baked in a casserole.

MAPLE CANDIED SWEET POTATOES

[A Vermont recipe]

6 medium-sized sweet potatoes
½ cup maple syrup
1 tablespoon butter
½ cup water

1 teaspoon salt
1 cup apple cider (or apple juice)

Boil potatoes in jackets until nearly done. Peel, slice and put into baking pan. Let maple syrup, butter, salt, cider and water come to a boil. Pour over potatoes and bake in slow oven (300° F.) for 1 hour or until potatoes are glazed and syrup of desired consistency. Serves 6.

FAMILY AT SUPPER

BAKED SWEET POTATO AND APPLE SLICES

[A Vermont recipe]

2 large apples	½ teaspoon salt
2 large cold cooked sweet	2 tablespoons butter
potatoes	¼ cup maple syrup

Select tart, perfect apples; core, pare and cut in crosswise slices and sauté each slice in butter until nearly soft. Brown well, but do not allow the slices to break. Cut the potatoes into rather thick crosswise slices, sprinkle with the salt and place a slice of fried apple on each slice of potato. Arrange in a shallow baking dish, slightly overlapping one another. Pour the maple syrup over all and dot with the butter. Bake in a moderately hot oven (375° F.) about ½ hour, or until the potato absorbs nearly all the syrup and the apples are quite brown. Serves 4.

JERUSALEM ARTICHOKES

Pare, boil in salted water about 30 minutes, or until tender; drain, add melted butter, minced parsley and a few drops lemon juice. Serve in place of potatoes.

This tuber was cultivated in New England by the Indians before Columbus came.

MASHED TURNIP

[A Connecticut recipe]

Wash and slice 2 medium-sized turnips. Boil in salted water until tender. Drain, mash; season with butter, salt, pepper and a little cream. Serves 8 to 10.

HASHED TURNIP

2 cups turnip
1 teaspoon salt
¼ teaspoon pepper

1 tablespoon butter or salt pork
fat or sausage fat
pepper to taste
4 tablespoons water

Wash, peel and slice turnip. Cook until done, about 30 minutes, in unsalted water. When done, chop coarsely and measure. Add other ingredients.

Cook slowly in spider or saucepan stirring constantly about 4 minutes. Serve at once. Serves 4.

BAKED TURNIP PUFF

2 cups hot mashed potato
2 cups hot mashed turnip
2 tablespoons melted butter

½ teaspoon salt
⅛ teaspoon pepper
2 tablespoons sweet cream

1 egg, well beaten

Mix potato and turnip. Add other ingredients in the order given. Turn into a well greased baking dish and bake in a hot oven (400° F.) for 20 minutes. Serve hot in same dish. Serves 6.

These recipes for Hashed Turnip and Baked Turnip Puff are copied from a very old "written-in" recipe book belonging to the Kimball family of Hampton, Conn. They were recopied for the Yankee Cook Book by Mrs. Lucy Kimball Ide, Charlton City, Mass.

PICKLED BEETS

½ cup vinegar
½ cup water
4 whole cloves
1 stick cinnamon

2 teaspoons sugar
1 teaspoon scraped onion
salt and pepper
2 cups hot cooked beets, sliced

Combine all ingredients, except beets, in a saucepan. Simmer about 8 minutes. Pour over beets, and let stand until cold.

HARVARD BEETS

¾ tablespoon cornstarch
¼ cup sugar
⅛ teaspoon salt

½ cup vinegar
¼ cup beet liquid
2 cups cooked cubed beets

2 tablespoons butter

Mix cornstarch, sugar and salt. Add vinegar and beet liquid gradually until blended. Stir and cook until thickened. Add beets and butter. Serve hot. Serves 4.

Where the name Harvard Beets originated, no one knows. New England cooks have prepared them this way for more than 100 years. Their color ("red for Harvard") is the logical explanation. Yet Yale Beets are red, too, and differ from Harvard Beets in that orange juice is substituted for vinegar.

PAN-FRIED TOMATOES

Slice green or firm ripe tomatoes in thick slices, without peeling. Sprinkle with salt and pepper. Dip each slice in flour. Pan-fry in a small amount of fat until brown on both sides. Pour off excess liquid from tomatoes while frying. Excellent served with cold meat.

SCALLOPED TOMATOES

2 cups canned tomatoes	1 teaspoon sugar
½ small onion, scraped	pepper
1 teaspoon salt	2 cups dried bread crumbs

4 tablespoons butter

Mix tomatoes and seasonings. Arrange tomatoes and crumbs in alternate layers, in buttered baking dish, having bread as top layer and dotting each layer with butter. Bake in a moderately hot oven (375° F.) about 20 minutes. Serves 5.

In a small cemetery in Newport, R. I., stands a tombstone bearing the legend: "To the first man to eat a tomato—Michele F. Corne."

Tomatoes were introduced into New England gardens about 150 years ago and were called "love apples." They were chiefly eaten sliced raw with sugar, or stewed with a little water, salt, pepper and a generous lump of butter. Sugar was sprinkled over them.

SUMMER SQUASH

[Summer or bush squashes were much used in olden times]

Summer squash may be boiled or steamed. Wash, cut off stem but do not pare. Cut in slices; place in steamer (or top of double boiler) or in rapidly boiling salted water. Cook until tender (15 to 30 minutes). If boiled, drain well, mash and drain again. Turn into a serving dish, season with melted butter, salt and pepper.

BAKED SQUASH

[*As Vermonters prepare it*]

Cut a Hubbard squash in pieces. Remove seeds and stringy parts.
Place in a covered pan. Bake 2 hours in a slow oven (300° F.).
Remove from shell, mash, season to taste with butter, salt, pepper,
and maple syrup.

PARSNIP FRITTERS

[*A Vermont recipe*]

Wash and scrape 10 medium-sized parsnips. Cook in boiling,
salted water for 45 minutes. Drain and mash; season with butter,
salt, and pepper. Shape into small, flat, round cakes. Roll in flour,
fry lightly and quickly, turning frequently. Serves 4 to 6.

PARSNIP STEW

[*Mrs. Mary Shea, Pemberton St., Worcester, Mass.*]

8 parsnips	¼ pound salt pork
6 potatoes	salt and pepper
water	

Parboil parsnips and potatoes; peel and slice in fairly thick pieces.
Place alternate rows crosswise and at an angle in a casserole with
thin slices of salt pork between. Season with salt and pepper. Fill
dish ⅔ full of water. Bake in a slow oven (300° F.) about 30
minutes, or until potatoes and parsnips are done. Serves 6.

*Parsnips were a familiar dish long ago. As early as 1600
the phrase "soft words butter no parsnips" came into
existence.*

MUSHROOM SOUFFLÉ

½ pound mushrooms	4 tablespoons flour
4 tablespoons butter	1 cup milk
½ teaspoon salt	3 egg yolks, beaten
pepper	3 egg whites, beaten stiff

Peel mushrooms; chop fine. Cook in butter until slightly brown. Add salt, pepper, flour; brown lightly. Add milk; cook until thick, stirring constantly. Cool. Add egg yolks and fold in egg whites. Pour into a greased baking dish; bake in a moderate oven (350° F.) 50 minutes. Serve immediately.

BROCCOLI

Cut off large outer leaves, peel woody outer skin of thick stems. If stems are large, split. Stand with blossoms uppermost in kettle and cook uncovered in boiling salted water 15 to 30 minutes, or until just tender. Drain, season with salt, pepper and melted butter to which an equal amount of lemon juice has been added. Allow ½ pound broccoli per person.

When Thoreau toured Cape Cod in 1849 broccoli was growing in an old oysterman's garden in Wellfleet. The oysterman had obtained his seed from the wreck of the ship "Franklin," out of London, for Boston.

VINEGARED CARROTS

[A Vermont recipe]

Wash and scrape 12 medium-sized carrots. Boil until tender. Cut lengthwise in quarters. Place in heated shallow serving dish. Season with salt, pepper, paprika and 2 tablespoons melted butter. Pour over carrots ⅓ cup hot cider vinegar. Serves 6 to 8.

STUFFED EGGPLANT

[*A Connecticut recipe*]

1 medium-sized eggplant	1 cup minced ham
1 cup uncooked mushrooms	¼ teaspoon salt
½ cup chopped onion	⅛ teaspoon pepper
4 tablespoons butter	¾ cup bread crumbs

Cut eggplant in half lengthwise. Scoop out pulp to within ½ inch of the outer skin. Peel mushrooms. Chop mushrooms and eggplant coarsely, and sauté in butter with onion for 10 minutes. Add ham and seasonings. Fill eggplant shells with the mixture and sprinkle top with buttered bread crumbs. Bake in a moderately hot oven (375° F.) until heated through and brown. Serve with thin strips of pimiento arranged crosswise on top. Serves 6.

CREAMED ASPARAGUS

Break asparagus in 1½-inch lengths, reserving tips. Place in boiling salted water. Boil until tender, about 20 minutes, adding tips the last 10 minutes of cooking. Drain, season with butter, salt and pepper and reheat with a few tablespoons of heavy cream. Many New England cooks prefer asparagus served in this way to the long, awkward stalks.

America's first asparagus was raised in West Brookfield, Mass. The man who brought it over from Holland lies buried in West Brookfield's "Indian" Cemetery. On his tombstone is this inscription: "Diederick Leertower, Esq., Late Consul of Their Mightinesses, the States-General of the United Netherlands for the states of Massachusetts and New Hampshire, Departed this life August 24, 1798, æ. 38 years."

GREAT-GREAT-GRANDMOTHER'S STRING BEANS

[*Norma Roberts, Bristol, N. H.*]

1 quart string beans	1 teaspoon sugar
cold water	1¼ teaspoons salt
1 tablespoon butter	pepper
⅛ teaspoon soda	1 cup boiling water

1 cup creamy milk

Break off both ends of beans, pull off strings, if present, and break into small pieces or cut into julienne strips. Let stand in cold water to which 1 tablespoon salt is added for 1 to 2 hours. 30 minutes before dinner, drain. Into a saucepan, put butter and heat to a froth but do not brown. Add beans, soda, sugar, salt, pepper and boiling water. Cook slowly, being careful that the beans do not burn. They will be tender in 30 minutes and most of the water will have boiled away. Add milk, let boil up once, then set where they will keep hot until served. Makes 3 cups cooked beans.

Old time cooks often added bits of salt pork to beans while cooking.

STUFFED PEPPERS

[*A New Hampshire recipe*]

6 green peppers	1 small onion, chopped
2 cups chopped cooked meat	⅛ teaspoon pepper
½ cup bread crumbs	½ teaspoon salt
½ cup stock	buttered bread crumbs

Wash peppers. Cut a piece from the stem end of each. Remove seeds. Parboil for five minutes. Stuff with a mixture of the meat, bread crumbs, stock, onion and seasonings and top with buttered bread crumbs. Pour water around the peppers to cover the bottom of the baking-pan. Bake for 45 minutes in a moderate oven (350° F.). Serve with tomato sauce. Serves 4 to 6.

BUTTERED CONNECTICUT VALLEY ONIONS

Peel onions and cook uncovered in boiling salted water about 30 minutes, or until tender. Drain, add butter and cream, salt and pepper.

EDGARTOWN STUFFED ONIONS

Remove skins from large onions and boil in salted water 10 minutes. Drain and cool. Remove center of onion without destroying shape of outer ring. Make filling by combining equal parts of cold chicken, chopped celery and finely chopped onion centers. Season with salt and pepper and moisten with cream and melted butter. Refill the cavities and cover top with buttered crumbs. Place in baking dish with a little chicken stock or water and bake in a moderate oven (350° F.) until onions are cooked, about 15 minutes.

SCALLOPED EGGS AND ONIONS

[New England Fresh Egg Institute]

12 small onions	2 cups medium white sauce
8 slices bacon, cut in pieces	6 sliced hard cooked eggs
½ cup buttered bread crumbs	

Peel and slice onions. Cook bacon until crisp and break into small pieces. Cover bottom of a well-greased casserole with white sauce; place a layer of raw onions in it. Sprinkle with half the bacon, cover with half the eggs. Repeat, making the last two layers onions and white sauce. Sprinkle with buttered crumbs. Bake in moderate oven (350° F.) for about 1¼ hours or until onions are tender. Serves 5.

ONION SOUFFLE

[*A Connecticut recipe*]

12 silver-skinned onions	¼ teaspoon salt
1½ tablespoons butter	⅛ teaspoon pepper
1½ tablespoons flour	¼ cup soft bread crumbs
1 cup rich milk	1 egg yolk

3 egg whites, stiffly beaten

Peel onions. Cook in boiling salted water until tender. Drain thoroughly, chop and drain again. Force through a sieve. There should be 1 cup thick purée. Blend butter and flour, add milk to make a cream sauce. Add crumbs, egg yolk, salt and pepper. Combine with the onion purée. Fold in egg whites. Pour into a buttered baking dish. Set dish in a pan of hot water and bake 40 minutes in a moderate oven (350° F.). Serves 6. Serve as an entrée or with the meat course. Delicious with fowl.

Sign that hangs outside the Cackle and Crow Hennery near Groton, Mass.: "All our hens lay fresh eggs."

DOCK GREENS

Dock greens are a long narrow leaf that may be found almost any place alongside of a clump of dandelions in fields or backyards. They have a taste of their own but resemble spinach slightly. Cook the same as spinach, adding a small piece of salt pork for extra flavor. Drain, serve with melted butter, salt and pepper. One reason they were much used in early days was because anyone could go out and gather them without cost. Dock greens, served with new potatoes rolled in garden parsley and melted butter, with hot cornbread and cup custards make a tempting but healthful meal.

Stewed sorrel was another old-time favorite. Wash sorrel in several waters. Cook leaves until tender in boiling, salted water. When done, season with butter, salt, pepper and sweet cream. Sorrel Pie was a popular Maine dish.

Marsh marigold or cowslip greens were still another springtime vegetable. The greens were gathered when the cowslips were in bud, the pithy stems discarded. The leaves were cooked with a piece of well-scored, salt pork until the pork was nearly done. Peeled potatoes were added. When the potatoes were done, they were removed and the greens were drained and served with butter, salt and pepper or vinegar.

FARMER'S CABBAGE

Put 1 cabbage through the meat grinder, coarsely. Place in a well-buttered baking dish. Season with salt and pepper. Add 2 cups medium white sauce. Mix well. Cover with buttered bread crumbs. Bake until brown in a moderate oven (350° F.) about 20 minutes. Serves 6.

FRIED SAUERKRAUT

½ cup sliced onions   4 tablespoons butter
1 pound sauerkraut, drained

Sauté onions in butter until delicately browned. Add sauerkraut and mix well. Cover and simmer gently for about ½ hour. Serves 5.

YANKEE SLAW DRESSING

[Mrs. Rosalie Nolin, Poplar St., New Haven, Conn.]

1 cup milk	2 tablespoons sugar
1½ tablespoons flour	¼ cup vinegar
½ teaspoon salt	1 egg
½ tablespoon mustard	1 tablespoon butter
2 quarts cabbage, shredded	

Scald three-fourths of milk. Measure and sift flour, salt and mustard and make a smooth paste with remaining cold milk. Add to hot milk and cook thoroughly. Heat vinegar and add slowly to dressing after it has thickened. Beat egg with sugar and add to dressing; stir while adding. Add butter. Pour hot dressing over cabbage. Serve slaw hot or chill and serve cold. Serves 6.

WILTED LETTUCE

3 bunches garden lettuce	¼ teaspoon salt
4 slices bacon	¼ cup vinegar
pepper	1 hard-cooked egg, sliced

Shred lettuce into salad bowl. Sauté bacon, remove from the pan and cut into small pieces. Add vinegar, salt and pepper to the bacon fat, bring to a boil and pour over lettuce. Mix and serve at once with egg slices and the bacon pieces over it as a garnish. Serves 6.

YANKEE DOODLE IN A KETTLE

Joseph C. Lincoln

The very words "New England Cooking" set an old New Englander's memory flying backward. It lingers in the old home kitchen, with its smells and its surreptitious tastes. It pauses by the cooky jar beneath the buttery—not pantry, if you please—shelf. Sugar cookies, molasses cookies, raisin cookies, ginger snaps, jumbles. It flits along to blueberry muffins, new rye muffins, blueberry pancakes, blueberry dumplings with thick yellow cream—skimmed, not separated cream. (If you were a Cape Codder that cream was skimmed with a sea clam shell, white and polished like porcelain.)

Dumplings? Oh yes, dumplings. Why, a whole chapter could be given over to dumplings. A dumpling, you understand, is not necessarily a lump of soggy dough, shaped like a glass paperweight and almost as heavy, tasteless as a rubber bath sponge. A dumpling, a genuine old-fashioned New England "riz" dumpling, is light and fluffy and flavorsome, something to eat and enjoy. A New England chicken stew with dumplings is—

Well, well! A sermon might be preached on dumplings, but "Dumpling" is not my text just now.

Nor is Pie. New England, as everyone knows, is supposed to be the Pie Belt and when a Down-Easter thinks of pie he sets the buckle forward a notch. Apple pie, mince pie, pumpkin pie—the latter not spiced and sugared to death, of course—squash, currant, cranberry—I just *mustn't* get going on cranberry pie made as it can be—Washington pie, cream pie. Then, to put the horse behind the cart, chicken pie, clam pie—

Eh? Why, yes! I know I should edge around to my real text pretty soon. It was clam pie that reminded me. In the short time allotted me, as the after-dinner speakers say, I shall confine my remarks—most of them—to the clam, the clam as expressed and glorified in a New England clam chowder.

I think it was the recollection of blissful experiences and bitter disappointments which led me to choose clam chowder as my principal topic. The bliss comes from many, many happy memories of beach and boat picnics and chowder feasts indoors and out. The bitterness from sad disillusionments when I have ordered and tasted clam chowder in roadside eating-houses, city restaurants and fashionable and high-priced hotels.

A New England clam chowder, made as it should be, is a dish to preach about, to chant praises and sing hymns and burn incense before. To fight for. The Battle of Bunker Hill was fought for— or on—clam chowder, part of it, at least; I am sure it was. It is as American as the Stars and Stripes, as patriotic as the national anthem. It is "Yankee Doodle" in a kettle.

When made as it should be. Ah! don't forget that stipulation, for when made as it *shouldn't* be it is an abomination. And, alack and alas, how often it is so made.

A genuine A No. 1 New England clam chowder is *not* a purée, thickened with flour and loaded with diced potatoes and bits of onion and chopped parsley, with, here and there, tiny fragments of clam as a feeble excuse for its name. It is *not* a thin, milk and watery broth, with bits of salt pork and onion skin on the surface and two or three tough clams, black necks still attached, lying on the bottom like drowned castaways. It is not—

You see, there are so many things it is not; and yet, over and over again, in restaurants, in roadside eating-houses, even as an item in a so-called "shore dinner," profanations like those just described are placed before the innocent customer. In metropolitan hotels the New England clam chowder is often a sad mistake. Something should be done about it, of course. "There ought to be a law."

A "Manhattan" chowder or a "Rhode Island" chowder is a different dish altogether. It is made of hard clams, "quahogs," has tomatoes in it instead of milk, and is often good, or quite as often bad, depending upon its ingredients and its cook. But I am not discussing a quahog chowder now. What I am talking about is—

Which reminds me that I have talked too much already, but I meant to add some priceless advice about selecting the clams for a *real* chowder. They should be dug the same day or, at the earliest, the previous day. They should be clean-shelled, tender, sweet and young. The potatoes should be sliced, *not* diced. There is a hint of salt pork, of course, a hint, not a hunk. The crackers should be the round "Boston" crackers—they called them "common crackers" when I was a boy. Split them, you understand, and put a few in the chowder and add a few dry halves to float on top just before serving. The hard parts of the clams should be chopped and the soft parts—

Here is where I stop. I meant to say more, but, with difficulty, I refrain. The tried and true recipes for good New England cooking you will find in the pages of this book. Follow its instructions carefully, cook, taste, eat, and be thankful.

The same applies to the other recipes. Good New England cooking *is* good cooking. It needs no French or Greek or Italian additions. My fellow Yankees know this and here is the opportunity for the rest of the world to acquire knowledge. If I were wealthy beyond the dreams of avarice or the Rajah of Whatever I should buy this book in thousand lots and leave a copy at each roadside stand advertising "New England Home Cooking."

Thus, provided the proprietors of those stands read and profited and reformed, I should pose for my statue in the Hall of Fame.

R U A YANKEE COOK?

Answers on page 367

18. How does one use the following kitchen utensils—trencher? piggin? skeel? losset? keeler? noggin?

19. What is a splinter-broom?

20. In what way does the housewife prepare the brick-oven for Saturday's baking?

21. To what three household uses does the housewife put the berries, bark, and wood of the red sumach?

22. For what ailments does one use the following dried herbs: catnip? pennyroyal? thoroughwort? yarrow? hoarhound? sweet flag-root?

23. What is a cheese-basket? Tallow-dip? Cracker-stamp? Scotch-kettle? Swizzle-stick?

24. What is the meaning of the expression "Mighty small potatoes and few in a hill!"?

25. What is meant by: "Give her honest measure, but don't kick the salt!"?

26. What food product has made Vermont famous?

27. What are baked crullers? Cherry cider? Fried pies? Sage cheese? Election cake?

28. What is a menhaden? Porgy? Squinteague? Quahog? Turbot?

29. What is bean swagger? What is "scraps"? What are bloaters?

30. What is Connecticut's most famous fish?

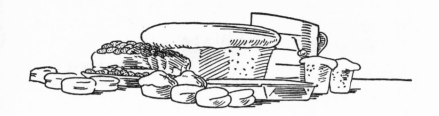

V. BREADS, BISCUITS, GEMS, SHORTCAKE AND MUSH

RANGER PANCAKES

1 teaspoon soda	½ cup cornmeal
1 cup sour milk	2 cups flour
1 egg, beaten	½ teaspoon baking powder
2 tablespoons melted shortening	½ teaspoon salt
	1 cup sweet milk

Add soda to sour milk. Add egg, shortening and cornmeal. Sift remaining dry ingredients. Add alternately with sweet milk. Use more or less flour if a thicker or thinner batter is preferred. Beat until free from lumps and bake on a hot greased griddle. Makes about 24 griddle cakes.

This recipe comes from Mrs. E. C. Ranger, North Clarendon, Vt., who in turn received it from her mother. Griddle cakes taste better to a true Vermonter if they are baked in large thin cakes, spread while hot off the griddle with butter and soft maple sugar and stacked in a pile of 6 or 8 cakes. The stack is cut in pie-shaped wedges and served at once. A topping of whipped cream is optional.

MRS. PACKARD'S PANCAKES

[Mrs. Caroline Packard, Conway, Mass., was a good cook at 90 years of age.]

2 cups flour, sifted	2 teaspoons baking powder
2 tablespoons bread crumbs or	½ teaspoon salt
shredded biscuit crumbs or	1 cup milk
yellow cornmeal	½ cup cream

Combine the ingredients and beat lightly. Do not beat out all the "nubs" of flour. Fry on a hot, greased griddle. Serve with butter or bacon fat or maple syrup. Serves 5.

These griddle cakes have been praised by the family, summer guests and college girls.

PARKER HOUSE PANCAKES

[Parker House, Boston, Mass.]

2 cups flour, sifted	1 tablespoon powdered sugar
3 teaspoons baking powder	2 eggs, well beaten
½ teaspoon salt	1¾ cups milk (about)

Mix and sift dry ingredients. Combine eggs and milk; add flour mixture and beat until smooth. Bake on a hot well-greased griddle. One tablespoon of the mixture makes one cake. This recipe makes about 24 small thin, delicate cakes.

Our great-grandmothers used hard wood ashes (in place of baking soda) to make pancakes rise. They poured boiling water over sifted ashes in a cup, let ashes settle and used the liquid as we use soda that has been dissolved.

GREEN CORN GRIDDLE CAKES

[A Martha's Vineyard recipe]

20 ears sweet corn	½ teaspoon baking powder
2 cups milk	2 teaspoons salt
1 cup flour, sifted	1 teaspoon sugar

2 eggs, beaten separately

Cut each row of corn lengthwise through each kernel. Grate with grater and scrape each ear, taking care not to scrape too close to the cob. Combine ingredients folding in stiffly beaten egg whites last. Drop by spoonfuls on a well greased hot griddle. Makes about 12 griddle cakes.

SQUASH GRIDDLE CAKES

[Mrs. William O. Abbott, Chestnut St., Wakefield, Mass.]

1 cup milk, scalded	½ teaspoon salt
1 cup sifted squash	1 egg, beaten
1 tablespoon butter	2 teaspoons baking powder
1 tablespoon sugar	1 cup flour, sifted

Pour the hot milk over the squash. Add the butter, sugar and salt. When cool add the egg, then the baking powder sifted with the flour. Bake on a hot greased griddle. Makes about 12 griddle cakes.

THRIFT

[As told by a Connecticut woman]

Eat it up,
Wear it out,
Make it do,
Or go without.

RHODE ISLAND JONNYCAKE

1 cup Rhode Island white
jonnycake cornmeal, not
bolted (waterground if you
can get it)

1 teaspoon salt
1 cup boiling water
½ cup milk (about)

Add salt to cornmeal; scald with boiling water until every grain swells; add milk very gradually until batter is a little thicker than ordinary pancake batter. Bake on slightly greased skillet, allowing more time than for frying griddle cakes. Let cakes cook thoroughly on one side before turning. Turn so that cakes are golden brown on both sides. Makes 16 small cakes.

Rhode Island jonnycakes are NOT easy to make. The trick is to get the batter thin enough so that cakes will be about ⅛ inch thick, yet not too thin, or it will be difficult to turn the cakes. The batter should just start to spread when it touches the hot skillet. It is worth experimenting, for the result is a delicate satisfying cake. Some Rhode Islanders add a teaspoon of sugar to the above recipe; some use all water and no milk; some use evaporated milk. Serve with butter only if you are a native son; otherwise serve with butter and maple syrup.

A true Rhode Islander would not dream of using an "h" in jonnycake. "Shepherd Tom" (Thomas Robinson Hazard) in his famous book, The Jonny Cake Papers *has settled this point once and for all, especially for those from South County. It is said of Rhode Island jonnycakes that they were served as a matter of course for breakfast; midday dinner was considered incomplete without them, and if a wife wished to give her husband a special treat for supper she served jonnycakes. This still holds true in some of the older Rhode Island villages today, notably Wickford.*

NEW BEDFORD JOHNNYCAKE

Follow recipe for Rhode Island Jonnycake adding 2 tablespoons flour and 1 tablespoon sugar to the cornmeal.

Johnnycakes were originally called Journey Cakes. As the Pilgrim Fathers traveled from the Plymouth Colony to their garrison post at Russell's Mills, Dartmouth, Mass., they stopped on a hill in what is now New Bedford and ate the journey cakes they had brought with them. In time the hill became known as Johnnycake Hill. Today the Bourne Whaling Museum and Seaman's Bethel, containing records and relics of New Bedford, are located on this hill, just above the Acushnet River. This historical note and the recipe for New Bedford johnnycake comes from Mrs. Herbert A. Manchester, Jenny Lind Street, New Bedford, Mass.

In Chelsea, Vermont, there was once a street called Johnnycake Lane. In the days when wheat began to take the place of cornmeal in the making of bread, many people still held to corn. A peddler came into Chelsea at the noon hour and went down a certain street. The midday meal was in progress. Later, in the tavern, the peddler remarked that every family on the street had johnnycake for dinner— "Why, it's a regular Johnnycake Lane," he said. The street remained Johnnycake Lane for a century.

SERVANT PROBLEMS—1693

On the 14th of March in 1693, Jennie Lightheifer, half-Indian maidservant, confounded all by-standers by standing on her head beside the town pump. Her mistress was summoned and Jennie led away; Jennie's explanation: "I just wanted to see how things looked." Her report, "Just like ordinary, only the other way 'round."

From "An Almanac for Bostonians."

SUET JOHNNYCAKE

[Helen H. Radcliffe, The Galley, Fairhaven, Mass.]

8 tablespoons Rhode Island white   ½ teaspoon salt
     corn meal   3 tablespoons molasses
boiling water   1 cup suet, chopped
               milk

Scald cornmeal until every grain swells. Add salt, molasses and suet. Thin batter with milk so that it will drop on griddle by spoonfuls, retaining its shape. Fry on griddle slowly until well browned on both sides. Makes 10 griddle cakes.

FRIED INDIAN CAKES

[Also called Cornmeal Slappers]

2 cups cornmeal   ½ teaspoon salt
½ teaspoon soda   2½ cups boiling water (about)

Mix cornmeal, soda and salt quickly with boiling water until just stiff enough to form into inch-thick cakes with the hands. Fry in skillet in hot fat, deep enough to cover about halfway up around cakes, turning so that both sides become golden brown. Serve hot with butter and maple syrup and bacon.

"This recipe has been in the all-Yankee family of Mrs. E. C. Alward, 450 Summer Ave., Reading, Mass., since long before she was born."

OLD-FASHIONED RAISED BUCKWHEAT CAKES

½ cake compressed yeast
1 cup milk, scalded
1 cup water
1 teaspoon salt

2 tablespoons molasses
1 cup flour
1 cup buckwheat flour
¼ teaspoon soda

¼ cup lukewarm water

Crumble yeast cake into lukewarm milk and water, add salt, molasses and flours to make a batter as thick as cream. Stir until free from lumps. Cover and let rise overnight at room temperature. In the morning, before baking, stir in soda dissolved in water. Pour into small cakes and fry on hot griddle, greased with salt pork. Serve with maple syrup. Makes 20 small cakes.

In households where cakes were served every morning a cup of batter was left to "rise" them, instead of fresh yeast.

SOUR MILK BUCKWHEAT CAKES

[To serve with pork gravy]

1 cake compressed yeast
4 cups lukewarm water
1 cup cornmeal
4 cups buckwheat flour

1 teaspoon salt
1 cup sour milk (or buttermilk)
1 teaspoon soda
¼ cup warm water

Crumble yeast into lukewarm water, add cornmeal, buckwheat flour, salt and milk; beat until a smooth batter is formed. Cover and let rise overnight at room temperature. In the morning, before baking, add soda dissolved in ¼ cup warm water. Mix well and fry on hot buttered griddle. Makes 36 small cakes.

Mrs. R. H. Ayers, Day St., Pittsfield, Mass., suggests that if a less pronounced buckwheat taste is preferred add 1 cup flour and 1 additional cup lukewarm water.

NEW HAMPSHIRE SKI SNACK

Raised Buckwheat Cakes with
New Hampshire Maple Syrup
Broiled Homemade Sausage
Coffee

WAFFLES

2 cups flour, sifted
3 teaspoons baking powder
½ teaspoon salt

3 eggs, separated
1¼ cups milk
¼ cup melted butter or butter
substitute

Mix and sift dry ingredients. Combine well beaten egg yolks and milk, and add to flour mixture. Beat until smooth, then add shortening. Fold in stiffly beaten whites and bake in a hot waffle iron. Makes 6 waffles.

So that the waffles might be baked over the fireplace coals, early waffle irons had long handles.

JOLLY BOYS

[Also called Rye Meal Drop Cakes]

1 cup sour milk
½ teaspoon soda
2½ cups rye meal (about)

1 egg, beaten
½ cup molasses

Stir soda into sour milk; combine remaining ingredients, adding rye meal until mixture is about the consistency of doughnut dough.

Drop balls from tip of mixing spoon into hot fat (365° F.). When golden brown drain and serve with maple syrup if desired. Or they may be broken in half and a piece of butter sandwiched between halves. Makes 25 small cakes.

This is a very old recipe from Mrs. Emma G. Smith, Cranston, Rhode Island. It has been handed down in her family from her great-grandmother Whipple, née Hannah Read, born in Burlington, Vermont, in 1800.

CONNECTICUT SPOON CAKES

1 teaspoon soda	1 egg, slightly beaten
2 cups sour milk	1 teaspoon salt

3 cups sifted flour (about)

Combine soda and sour milk; add egg and salt and enough flour so that batter will "drop off" teaspoon into hot fat without sticking to spoon. Fry in hot deep fat (370° F.) 3 or 4 minutes, or until golden brown. Drain and serve with molasses sauce or maple syrup.

MOLASSES SAUCE

6 tablespoons molasses   1½ teaspoons vinegar

Mix molasses and vinegar and dip each "mouthful" into the sauce.

The mother of Mrs. Albert Myers, South Windham, Connecticut, first made these spoon cakes 35 years ago. They are a kind of fritter but she always called them Spoon Cakes. The sauce may not be popular with modern cooks who may prefer maple syrup or "apple molasses" (thick boiled cider).

HOLY POKES

Form bread dough, which has risen once, into balls the size of large marbles. Let rise again until it has doubled in volume. Slip dough balls into a kettle of fat heated to 360° F. and fry until a golden brown. Drain and serve with plenty of butter. Or serve with maple syrup, as a fritter.

Holy Pokes are a Connecticut favorite. On the Maine Coast they are called Huffjuffs. Baptist Bread is another name.

BANANA FRITTERS

[A modern Yankee recipe]

melted fat or oil	¼ cup flour
4 medium ripe bananas	fritter batter

For shallow frying, have 1 inch of melted fat or oil in frying pan. For deep-fat frying, have deep kettle ½ to ⅔ full of melted fat or oil. Heat fat to 375° F. (or until a 1-inch cube of bread will brown in 40 seconds). Cut bananas crosswise into quarters, halves or 1-inch thick pieces. Roll pieces in flour, then dip into fritter batter, completely coating the banana with the batter. Shallow fry or deep-fat fry in the hot fat 4 to 6 minutes or until brown and tender. Drain on unglazed paper. Serve very hot. Serves 6 to 8.

FRITTER BATTER

1 cup flour, sifted	2 teaspoons baking powder
¼ cup sugar	1 egg, well beaten
1¼ teaspoons salt	⅓ cup milk
2 teaspoons melted fat or oil	

Sift together the flour, sugar, salt and baking powder. Combine egg and milk, and add gradually to dry ingredients, stirring until batter is smooth. Then stir in fat. This is a stiff batter.

APPLE FRITTERS

1 cup flour, sifted	1 egg, beaten
1½ teaspoons baking powder	3 large apples, peeled, cored
¼ teaspoon salt	and sliced
⅔ cup milk	2 tablespoons powdered sugar

1 tablespoon lemon juice

Make a batter by sifting together flour, baking powder and salt; add milk and egg and beat until smooth. Add sugar and lemon juice to apple slices; dip in batter and fry in hot deep fat (375° F.) until a golden brown. Drain and sprinkle with powdered sugar. Serves 6.

CAPE COD CRANBERRY DROP CAKES

2 cups cranberries	1¼ tablespoons melted butter
½ cup water	½ teaspoon salt
½ cup sugar	dash of cinnamon

1 cup cracker crumbs

Wash and pick over cranberries. Add water and cook until berries are soft. Force through sieve. Add sugar to pulp and then add butter and seasonings. Stir in cracker crumbs. Drop by spoonsful into deep hot fat (370° F.) and cook until browned. Drain and serve hot or cold. Serve with chicken or turkey in place of potatoes or in place of dumplings. Serves 6.

GOT ONE?

Way, way back, great-great-grandmothers "whisked their eggs in brown bowls with yellow stripes." Old-time recipes called for just that kind of bowl for many toothsome delicacies, including bag pudding.

MAINE MOLASSES DOUGHNUTS

2 eggs	4 cups flour (about)
1 cup sugar	¼ teaspoon cloves
½ cup molasses	¼ teaspoon ginger
1 cup sour milk	⅛ teaspoon salt
1 teaspoon soda	1 tablespoon melted lard

Beat the eggs, add the sugar and beat well, then the molasses and sour milk, to which has been added the soda, then the flour, mixed and sifted with the spices, and last the melted shortening. Handle dough as little as possible. Roll out a few at a time and fry in deep hot fat (360° F.). Turn frequently as they fry; drain. Makes 36 doughnuts.

This same recipe was used years and years ago by the grandmother of Ada M. Dyer, North Baldwin, Me.

Great-grandmother was less accurate in her measurements than present-day cooks. She did not use a spoon or cup to measure her molasses but measured it by the "plop" or "blurp" as it came from the jug. Old recipes sometimes specified how many "plops" to add.

An old Maine recipe called "Old Bachelor's Doughnuts" has the following curious wording:

"Pour hog's lard in an old-fashioned iron fry pan, heated 'til she sputters will do the trick. Then take a deep yellow dish and put in one cup of sugar, and if eggs don't cost over 2 cents each, put in one and the yolk of another, and put the white away until eggs are worth more. Then add one cup of cow's milk without anything in it except about a big spoonful of cream and a little salt and nutmeg, then add two teaspoons of tartar and one and a little over of soda in some flour. Then take a big spoon and give her hail Columbia for about 20 seconds. Next find a good clean place to roll them out. Fry one at a time, cut out with a

four-quart pail cover and cut the hole with a pint dipper with handle busted, and if you are looking for a house-keeper, take one of the doughnuts, hold it up to the window and call in the first maiden lady who comes in sight and kiss her through the hole and she is yours."

BANANA DOUGHNUTS

5 cups sifted flour	3 eggs, well beaten
4 teaspoons baking powder	1½ teaspoons vanilla extract
1 teaspoon soda	¾ cup mashed bananas
2 teaspoons salt	(about 2 bananas)
1 teaspoon nutmeg	½ cup sour milk or buttermilk
¼ cup shortening	½ cup flour for rolling
1 cup sugar	melted fat or oil

Sift together flour, baking powder, soda, salt and nutmeg. Beat shortening until creamy. Add sugar gradually and continue beating until light and fluffy. Add eggs and beat well. Add combined vanilla, bananas and sour milk to creamed mixture and blend. Add flour mixture and mix until smooth. Turn a small amount of dough onto a floured board. Knead very lightly. Roll out with a floured rolling pin to ⅜-inch thickness. Cut with floured 2½-inch doughnut cutter.

Heat fat to 375° F. or until a 1-inch cube of bread will turn golden brown in 40 seconds. Slip doughnuts into fat with spatula. Fry about 3 minutes, or until golden brown, turning frequently. Drain on absorbent paper. Sugar the doughnuts, if desired. Makes about 3½ dozen doughnuts.

Doughnuts, described in one old recipe book as "a kind of fried matter," enjoy perennial popularity.

MRS. SCULLY'S DOUGHNUTS

[*Mrs. W. H. Scully, Pico Road, Newton Highlands, Mass.*]

2 eggs
1¾ cups milk
1½ cups sugar
6 cups flour
3½ teaspoons baking powder

½ teaspoon salt
½ teaspoon lemon extract
        (optional)
¼ teaspoon grated nutmeg
few drops of vinegar

Beat the eggs until lemon colored; add the milk and sugar. Add the flour which has been sifted three times with the baking powder and salt. Beat thoroughly. Add the lemon extract, nutmeg and vinegar and beat again. Roll out ¼-inch thick on lightly floured board and cut with floured doughnut cutter. Fry in hot deep fat (360° F.) for 2 to 3 minutes, or until lightly browned, turning doughnuts when they rise to top and several times during frying. Drain. Makes 48 doughnuts.

POTATO DOUGHNUTS

2 tablespoons butter
¾ cup sugar
2 eggs, well beaten
¼ cup sour milk

1 teaspoon soda
1 cup warm riced potato
1½ teaspoons salt
¼ teaspoon nutmeg
1½ cups flour, sifted (about)

Cream butter and sugar; add eggs, sour milk, soda, potato, salt, nutmeg and enough flour to make an easily handled dough. Roll, cut into rounds with a doughnut cutter, slip into a kettle of fat heated to 360° F. Do not attempt to fry more than 4 or 5 at a time. As soon as doughnuts rise to the surface turn them. Turn frequently thereafter until they are sufficiently brown. Drain. Makes 18 doughnuts.

RAISIN DOUGHNUTS

[Norma Roberts, Bristol, N. H.]

½ cup sugar
yolks 2 eggs, well beaten
½ cup sour milk
½ teaspoon soda

2 cups flour
½ teaspoon cinnamon
¼ teaspoon salt
⅓ cup seeded or seedless raisins

Add the sugar to the beaten egg yolks; add the milk to which the soda has been added. Sift the flour, cinnamon and salt and add. Stir in raisins. Drop by teaspoons in hot deep fat (360° F.). Fry until little balls are lightly browned, turning as they rise to top and several times during frying. Drain. Makes 20 doughnut balls. Serve with sweet cider.

If a whaling man is lucky, he gets aboard a ship where the captain's wife is aboard. When the blubber is being "tried out," she often gives the crew a treat by frying a batch of doughnuts in the hot fat of the tried-out blubber.

WHITE BREAD FOR TWO

[Mrs. A. L. Ward, Clarence St., Everett, Mass.]

1 tablespoon lard	1 cup boiling water
1 tablespoon butter	1 cup milk, scalded
2½ tablespoons sugar	1 cake compressed yeast
2 teaspoons salt	¼ cup lukewarm water

6 to 8 cups bread flour, sifted

Place lard, butter, sugar and salt in a large mixing bowl and pour on the boiling water and scalded milk. When lukewarm add yeast cake crumbled in lukewarm water. Gradually add just enough flour so that dough can be handled easily. The dough should be moist and a little sticky to the fingers. Turn out on floured board and knead until smooth and elastic. Place dough in greased bowl, cover and let rise in a warm place until doubled in bulk (about 4 hours or overnight). Knead, adding more flour if necessary, shape into loaves and place in greased bread pans; cover and let rise in a warm place until doubled in bulk (about 2 hours). Bake in a moderately hot oven (375° F.) 20 minutes; reduce heat to moderate (350° F.) and bake 40 minutes longer. Remove from pans and rub with melted butter and slightly cool. While yet a trifle warm, place in bread box. The crust will be crispy but soft. This is a delicious bread. Makes 2 loaves.

ANADAMA BREAD

[Mrs. Helen Kershaw, Harrison St., Manchester, N. H.]

2 cups water	2 teaspoons salt
½ cup yellow cornmeal	2 cakes compressed yeast
2 tablespoons shortening	½ cup lukewarm water
½ cup molasses	7½ cups flour (about)

Boil the 2 cups water and add the cornmeal gradually, stirring constantly. Add the shortening, molasses and salt and let stand until lukewarm. Add crumbled yeast cakes to lukewarm water and add the cornmeal mixture. Stir in the flour to make a stiff dough. Knead well. Place in a greased bowl, cover, and let rise in a warm place until doubled in bulk. Cut through the dough several times with a knife, cover and let rise again for about 45 minutes, or until light. Toss onto a floured board and knead well. Add more flour if necessary. Make into 2 loaves and place in greased loaf tins. Cover, let rise in a warm place until doubled in bulk. Bake in a hot oven (400° F.) for 15 minutes then reduce the heat to moderate (350° F.) and bake about 45 minutes longer, or until done. Brush with melted fat and remove the bread from the pans to a cake rack. Makes 2 loaves.

Anadama bread was invented a long time ago by a fisherman who had a lazy wife and often had to do his own cooking. He experimented with this result, which he named after his wife, "Anna, damn her." Polite society modified this to Anadama Bread. This is an old Concord, Mass., recipe.

OATMEAL BREAD

[*Helen H. Radcliffe, The Galley, Fairhaven, Mass.*]

4 cups boiling water or milk	1 tablespoon salt
2 cups rolled oats	1 cake compressed yeast
2 tablespoons lard	½ cup lukewarm water
⅔ cup molasses	9 to 10 cups flour, sifted

Pour boiling water or scalded milk over rolled oats and lard, cover and let stand an hour. Add molasses, salt, and yeast cake (dissolved in lukewarm water). Add flour, gradually, beating it in with a knife. Let rise until double its bulk; cut down, shape into loaves and let rise again. Press into buttered bread tins; let rise again and bake 40 to 45 minutes in a moderate oven (350° F.). Makes 4 loaves.

OATMEAL BREAD WITH NUTS AND HONEY

Before Oatmeal Bread goes into oven spread with equal amounts of honey and finely chopped nut meats. This bread has been popular in the family of Mrs. E. W. Beach, Marvel Road, New Haven, Conn., for two generations. It will keep a long time—if you let it!

SALT-RISING BREAD

[*A. M. Hooton, Roxbury, Mass.*]

1 cup of milk, scalded	3 tablespoons melted short-
4 tablespoons cornmeal	ening
2 tablespoons sugar	1 cup lukewarm water
1½ teaspoons salt	5 cups flour (about)

Scald cornmeal, sugar and ½ teaspoon of salt with milk. Let stand in a warm place overnight or until fermented. Into this "yeast" stir shortening, remaining teaspoon of salt, lukewarm water and 2 cups of flour. Return to a warm place and let rise until sponge is very light. Gradually stir in remaining flour and shortening. Knead until smooth, shape into loaves and place in 2 greased bread pans. Cover and let rise until 2½ times its original bulk. Bake in a moderately hot oven (375° F.) for 10 minutes. Lower heat to moderate (350° F.) and bake 25 minutes longer. Salt-rising bread is not so light as yeast bread. It is moist and crumbly. The "yeast" will keep 2 or 3 weeks in cool weather and is not injured by freezing. In warm weather only ⅓ the quantity of yeast is required.

It is important that the cornmeal mixture be fermented. To hasten fermentation, mixture may be placed in a covered jar which is put in a bath of water as hot as the hand can stand. If mixture is not fermented do not use.

FEATHERBEDS

[A New Hampshire potato roll]

2 large potatoes	1½ cups potato water
1 teaspoon salt	¾ cup milk, scalded
2 tablespoons sugar	1 cake compressed yeast
3 tablespoons butter	7 cups flour, sifted

Boil potatoes until tender; drain and save water. Mash potatoes, add salt, sugar, butter and beat well. Add potato water and hot milk and cool. When lukewarm, add crumbled yeast cake and stir in 4 cups flour, beating well; then add enough remaining flour to make a dough stiff enough to knead. Knead until smooth and elastic; brush top with melted butter and place in large greased mixing bowl; cover and let rise until doubled in bulk (about 5 hours or overnight). Place on board, pat into ½-inch thick pieces (do not knead); pinch off small pieces and shape into small rolls. Place in greased pan and let rise until very light and more than doubled in bulk; bake in hot oven (400° F.) for 20 minutes or until done. Makes 48 small rolls.

In 1832, the Boston "Transcript" defined a gentleman thus: "He gets up leisurely, breakfasts comfortably, reads the paper regularly, dresses fashionably, eats a tart gravely, talks insipidly, dines considerably, drinks superfluently, kills time indifferently, sups elegantly, goes to bed stupidly and lives uselessly."

CONNECTICUT HOT CROSS BUNS

1 cup milk, scalded	¼ cup warm water
½ cup sugar	1 egg, well beaten
3 tablespoons melted butter	3 cups flour
½ teaspoon salt	½ teaspoon cinnamon
1 cake compressed yeast	½ cup currants

Combine the milk, sugar, butter and salt. When lukewarm, add the yeast cake dissolved in the lukewarm water and the egg and mix well. Sift the flour and cinnamon together and stir into yeast mixture. Then add the currants and mix thoroughly. Cover and let rise in a warm place until double in size. Shape the dough into large biscuits and place on a well-buttered baking pan. Let rise again. Beat 1 egg and use to brush the top of each biscuit. Make a cross on each biscuit with a sharp knife. Bake in a hot oven (400° F.) for 20 minutes. Remove from oven and brush over lightly with a frosting made with milk and confectioners' sugar.

Mrs. Edward G. Banning, Clearfield Road, Wethersfield, Conn., found this recipe in an old book of recipes handwritten by her grandmother and marked, "Goes good at church suppers."

CAPE PORPOISE SQUASH BISCUITS

1½ cups strained squash	1 teaspoon salt
1 cup milk, scalded	4 tablespoons butter
½ cup sugar	½ to 1 cake compressed yeast
5 cups flour, sifted (about)	

Place squash, milk, sugar, salt and shortening in a mixing bowl and cool; when lukewarm add crumbled yeast, which has been dissolved in the water, and half the flour and beat thoroughly. Gradually stir in remaining flour, adding just enough to make a dough that can be handled easily; turn out on floured board and knead until smooth and elastic, adding flour as necessary. Place dough in greased bowl and brush with melted shortening; cover and let rise in a warm place overnight or until doubled in bulk. Knead, shape into biscuits and place in a greased pan, brush with melted shortening, cover and let rise in a warm place until very light (1 to 2 hours). Bake in a hot oven (400° F.) for about 15 minutes. Makes about 3 dozen rolls.

Grace L. Rowell, 11-A Putnam St., Somerville, Mass., adds this note to her recipe: "My grandmother, Mrs. Henry Lewis Langsford, of the Langsford House, Cape Porpoise, Me., used to make delicious squash biscuits by this rule 50 or 60 years ago. She was noted for her fine cooking."

SOUR MILK RUSKS

[*Olive Winsor Frazar, Duxbury, Mass.*]

2⅛ cups flour, sifted	½ teaspoon cloves
1 teaspoon soda	1 cup sugar
½ teaspoon salt	½ cup shortening
1 teaspoon nutmeg	1 egg, beaten
1 teaspoon cinnamon	1 cup sour milk
½ cup raisins	

Mix and sift dry ingredients; cream sugar and shortening. Add egg and stir in the milk and dry ingredients alternately. Stir in raisins. Pour into a square tin and bake in a moderate oven (350° F.) 1 hour. Cut in 16 squares.

Many of the old fashioned rusks were made with yeast dough. Rusks have come to have an entirely different meaning from what they had several generations ago. Today a rusk is looked upon as a dried sweetened bread, not unlike toast.

YANKEE THRIFT

"My mother used to make her own bread," writes J. Almus Russell, Mason, N. H. "Every week she set a sponge in a large iron-ware bread pan, placed on a small table behind the kitchen stove. One Friday evening she set the sponge as usual, threw a clean remnant of freshly laundered Turkey-red tablecloth over the bread bowl, and retired for the night.

"The next morning as we entered the kitchen, Mother glanced in the direction of the rising bread dough. Strangely enough, the tablecloth was not to be seen although the bowl still remained in its usual place and position. Then I discovered that Peter, the house cat, becoming chilly during the night, had jumped upon the bowl. His weight had gradually carried the cloth downward into the dough while the sponge had risen high around him, making a warm and springy mattress.

"As ours was a thrifty Yankee family, Mother shooed Peter off the tablecloth, removed the covering, decided that no harm had been done, and baked the bread as usual."

PARKER HOUSE ROLLS

[Parker House, Boston, Mass.]

½ cup scalded milk
½ cup boiling water
1 teaspoon salt
1 teaspoon sugar
1 tablespoon butter
½ yeast cake dissolved in ¼ cup lukewarm water
3 cups bread flour, or enough to knead

Put milk, water, salt, butter and sugar into mixing bowl and mix well. Add yeast. Then add flour until it is stiff enough to knead. Cover and let it rise to double its bulk, shape into balls, put into buttered pan and cover. Let it rise in a warm place again to double its bulk. With the floured handle of a wooden spoon press the balls through the center almost cutting in half. Brush one-half with butter, fold other half over and press together like a pocketbook. Let rise again and bake in a hot oven (400° F.) for 15 minutes. Brush the tops with butter after baking. This recipe will make about 2 dozen rolls.

Lost to gustatory history is the story of how Parker House rolls came into being. Definitely established, however, is the fact that a crisp, golden folded roll was conceived by Harvey D. Parker, founder of the Boston hostelry which bears his name.

BANANA BREAD

[*A favorite at Echo Lake Camp, Appalachian Mountain Club, Me.*]

1¾ cups sifted flour	⅓ cup shortening
¾ teaspoon soda	⅔ cup sugar
1¼ teaspoons cream of tartar	2 eggs, well beaten
	1 cup mashed banana (2 to 3
½ teaspoon salt	bananas)

Sift the flour, soda, cream of tartar and salt together 3 times. Rub the shortening to a creamy consistency with the back of a spoon. Stir the sugar, a few tablespoons at a time, into the shortening and continue stirring after each addition until light and fluffy. Add eggs and beat well. Add flour mixture, alternately with banana, a small amount at a time. Beat after each addition until smooth. Pour into a well-greased loaf pan and bake in a moderate oven (350° F.), about 1 hour or until bread is done. Makes 1 loaf, about 8½ x 4½ x 3 inches.

BLUEBERRY CAKE

[Durgin-Park, Boston, Mass.]

¾ cup sugar
2 eggs, beaten
3 cups flour
3 teaspoons baking powder
¾ teaspoon salt
1¼ cups blueberries, washed
and drained
1 tablespoon melted butter
1½ cups milk

Mix sugar with beaten eggs; sift flour, baking powder and salt and add; stir in blueberries, melted butter and milk. Beat just enough to mix; bake in hot oven (400° F.) about 30 minutes. Makes 1 large panful which cuts into 21 squares.

Durgin-Park, famous restaurant in the market district of Boston, has a venerable history.

VERMONT GRAHAM BREAD

1½ cups sour milk (or buttermilk)
2 tablespoons sour cream (or melted butter)
⅔ cup molasses and maple syrup (half of each or alone)
2 teaspoons soda
½ teaspoon salt
1⅓ cups graham flour
1⅓ cups flour, sifted
raisins may be added

Mix in the order given. Bake in greased bread tins in a moderate oven (350° F.) 45 to 50 minutes.

This recipe has been used for more than sixty years in Brattleboro, Vt. From Mrs. T. F. O'Brien.

POPDOODLE CAKE

[*Sometimes called coffee cake*]

2¼ cups flour, sifted
  2 teaspoons baking powder
  1 cup sugar
  ½ cup shortening (butter and
    lard mixed)

½ teaspoon salt
1 cup milk
1 egg, beaten
2 teaspoons cinnamon
½ cup sugar

Mix and sift dry ingredients; cut in shortening, combine with milk and egg and add. Spread dough on a greased layer pan. Before baking sprinkle top with sugar and cinnamon, mixed. Bake in a hot oven (400° F.) about 30 minutes. Makes 1 (9-inch) coffee cake.

RYE POPOVERS

¾ cup rye flour
¼ cup flour
¼ teaspoon salt

2 eggs
1 tablespoon melted shortening
1 cup milk

Sift the rye and white flour and salt; break the eggs into the dry mixture, add melted shortening and milk. Beat until smooth. Fill greased gem pans ⅓ full and bake in a hot oven (450° F.) about 20 minutes; then reduce heat to moderate oven (350° F.) and continue baking 15 to 20 minutes, or until popovers are firm. Makes 8 large popovers.

Old time cooks are surprised to learn that excellent popovers can be made by placing the pans (without pre-heating) in a cold oven and baking with the regulator at (450° F.) for 30 minutes; then reduce heat to 350° F. and continue baking 10 to 15 minutes longer.

VERMONT MAPLE ROLLS

2 cups flour	4 tablespoons shortening
2½ teaspoons baking powder	¾ cup milk (about)
½ teaspoon salt	butter
½ cup maple sugar	

Sift flour once, measure, add baking powder and salt, and sift again. Cut in shortening. Add milk gradually, stirring until soft dough is formed. Turn on lightly floured board and knead 15 seconds, or enough to shape. Roll in oblong piece, ¼-inch thick. Spread with softened butter and sprinkle with maple sugar. ½ cup chopped butternuts, walnuts or pecans may also be spread over sugar. Roll as for jelly roll and cut in 1-inch thick slices. Place slices on greased pan or muffin tins. Spread tops of slices with butter. Bake in hot oven (400° F.) 15 minutes. Makes 10 to 12 rolls.

CORN ROLLS

[Parker House, Boston, Mass.]

⅓ cup sugar	1 cup milk
¼ cup lard	1 cup yellow cornmeal
1 egg, unbeaten	1 cup flour, sifted
¾ teaspoon salt	3 teaspoons baking powder

Cream sugar and lard; add egg and beat. Add salt and milk and stir; add cornmeal, flour and baking powder. Bake in greased muffin tins in a hot oven (400° F.) 20 minutes, or until done. Makes 12 rolls.

CORN BREAD

[*Durgin-Park, Boston, Mass.*]

¾ cup sugar, sifted   ¾ teaspoon salt
2 eggs, beaten   1 cup yellow cornmeal
2 cups flour   1 tablespoon melted butter
3 teaspoons baking powder   1½ cups milk

Mix sugar and beaten eggs; sift flour, baking powder and salt and add; then add cornmeal, melted butter and milk. Beat just enough to mix. Bake in a hot oven (400° F.) about 30 minutes. This makes one panful which cuts into 21 squares.

At Durgin-Park's, in the market, straw-hatted butchers and professors from Harvard dine off red-checked table-cloths. Durgin-Park's is as famous for steaks and seafoods as it is for hot breads.

BEST NEW ENGLAND JOHNNYCAKE

Don't try to follow this recipe!
"To make this johnnycake," according to the "Model Cook Book," published in 1885, "take one quart of butter-milk, one teacup of flour, ⅔ of a teacupful of molasses, a little salt, one teaspoonful of saleratus, one egg (beat, of course). Then stir in Indian meal, but be sure not to put in too much. Leave it thin, so thin that it will almost run. Bake in a tin in any oven, and tolerably quick. If it is not first-rate and light, it will be because you make it too thick with Indian meal. Some prefer it without the molasses."

GRANNY'S APPLE CORNBREAD

2 cups yellow cornmeal	2 tablespoons shortening, melted
¼ cup sugar	2 eggs, beaten
1½ teaspoons salt	1 teaspoon soda
2 cups sour milk	1 tablespoon cold water

⅞ cup raw chopped apple

Mix in the top of a double boiler the cornmeal, sugar, salt, milk and shortening. Set over hot water and cook about 10 minutes. Cool, add eggs, soda dissolved in water, and apples. Bake in greased baking pan in hot oven (400° F.) about 25 minutes or until done. Makes 8 large squares.

MAPLE CORN BREAD

1⅓ cups flour	½ teaspoon salt
⅔ cup bolted cornmeal	⅓ cup maple syrup
3 teaspoons baking powder	½ cup melted shortening

2 eggs, slightly beaten

Sift dry ingredients; add the syrup, shortening and eggs. Stir until well-mixed, but do not beat. Turn into a greased pan and bake 25 minutes in a hot oven (425° F.). Makes 8 squares.

Mrs. G. H. Kerr, Bulfinch Place, Boston, stopped for breakfast at a quiet little inn in California some years ago. The hostess said, "I see from your number plates you're from New England, and I'm happy that I have New England Corncake on the menu this morning." That corncake was delicious, but it tasted different. So Mrs. Kerr inquired. The hostess replied, "My grandmother up in Royalton, Vermont, taught me how to make it over forty years ago. We call it Maple Corn Bread."

CRACKLING BREAD

[*Mrs. Harry W. Parker, Warren St., Westboro, Mass.*]

1½ cups cornmeal   2 tablespoons sugar
¾ cup flour   ¼ teaspoon salt
  1 teaspoon baking powder   1 cup sour milk
        1 cup diced salt pork cracklings

Mix and sift dry ingredients; add milk and stir in cracklings. Turn into two large pans or into 16-muffin tins. Bake in hot oven (400° F.) for 30 minutes.

Cracklings are thin slices of salt pork remaining after the fat has been rendered. In some households, children ate them as childen today eat popcorn or candy. Thin slices of salt pork were laid on brown paper in a baking pan which was placed in a slow oven. When they were hot a little salt was sprinkled over them.

Scraps left from the leaf in making lard may be substituted in this recipe as they are also known as cracklings. In that case increase the salt to ½ teaspoon.

MUFFINS

2 cups flour, sifted   ½ teaspoon salt
3 teaspoons baking powder   1 egg, well beaten
3 tablespoons sugar   1 cup milk
        3 tablespoons butter or butter substitute, melted

Mix and sift dry ingredients. Combine egg and milk, add to flour and stir only until mixed. Add shortening and blend, but do not beat. Bake in greased muffin tin in a hot oven (425° F.) about 25 minutes. Makes 12 muffins.

MAINE BLUEBERRY MUFFINS

2 cups flour
2½ teaspoons baking powder
½ cup sugar
½ teaspoon salt

1 egg, well beaten
¾ cup milk
¼ cup melted fat
¾ cup blueberries

Sift flour once, measure, add baking powder, sugar and salt and sift again. Combine egg and milk, add to flour and stir only until mixed. Do not beat. Add shortening and blend. Fold in blueberries. Mixture will be stiffer than usual muffin mixture. Bake in greased muffin tins in a hot oven (400° F.) 25 to 30 minutes. Makes 12 muffins.

Blueberries were frequently dried, after gathering, and spread on paper in a warm airy room. When winter swept down they were used in lieu of currants or were soaked and then made into sauce.

BERKSHIRE MUFFINS

[From the New England Kitchen of Louise Crathern Russell]

⅔ cup milk, scalded
½ cup yellow cornmeal
½ cup cooked rice
½ cup flour, sifted

2 tablespoons sugar
½ teaspoon salt
3 teaspoons baking powder
1 egg, separated

1 tablespoon melted butter

Pour hot milk over cornmeal and let it stand for 5 minutes. Add rice. Mix and sift dry ingredients. Combine with cornmeal, rice and egg yolk, well beaten, then add melted butter. Fold in stiffly beaten egg white. Bake in a hot oven (425° F.) about 25 minutes. Makes about 8 small muffins.

CRANBERRY MUFFINS

¾ cup cranberry halves	½ teaspoon salt
½ cup powdered sugar	4 tablespoons sugar
2 cups flour	1 egg, well beaten
3 teaspoons baking powder	1 cup milk

4 tablespoons shortening, melted

Mix cranberry halves with the powdered sugar and let stand while preparing muffin mixture. Sift dry ingredients, add egg, milk and shortening; then add the sugared cranberries. Mix but do not beat. Bake in a moderate oven (350° F.) for 20 minutes. Makes 12 muffins.

MAINE OATMEAL GEMS

[Mrs. Nellie Barrett, East Sumner, Me.]

2 cups rolled oats	¼ cup molasses
1½ cups sour milk	pinch of salt
1 teaspoon soda	1 egg, beaten

1 cup flour, sifted

Mix rolled oats and milk and let stand several hours or overnight. Add soda, molasses, salt, egg and flour. Blend well but do not beat. Bake in greased muffin tins in a hot oven (400° F.) 20 to 25 minutes. Makes 12 muffins.

Oliver Wendell Holmes, asked to express briefly his idea of happiness, said, "Four feet on a fireplace fender."

GRAHAM GEMS

[Thorndike Hotel, Rockland, Me.]

½ teaspoon soda
1 cup sour milk
1 egg, beaten

2 tablespoons molasses
2 tablespoons butter
½ teaspoon salt

2 cups graham flour

Stir soda into sour milk; combine with egg, molasses and melted butter; add graham flour and salt. Blend only enough to mix. Do not beat. Fill greased muffin tins ⅔ full and bake in a hot oven (400° F.) 20 to 25 minutes. Makes 12 muffins.

MAINE GINGERBREAD

½ cup sugar
½ cup shortening (lard, butter, bacon drippings or any combination of the three)
1 cup molasses
2 teaspoons soda

1 cup boiling water
2½ cups flour
1 teaspoon ginger
1 teaspoon clove
1 teaspoon cinnamon
½ teaspoon salt

2 eggs, well beaten

Cream sugar and shortening; add molasses; dissolve soda in boiling water and add to the sugar mixture. Sift the remaining dry ingredients and add this to the mixture, and beat until smooth. Add the eggs last. Pour into a greased pan 12″ x 8″ x 2″ and bake in a moderate oven (350° F.) about 45 minutes. Makes 1 panful.

This recipe has come down through three generations of the same family. It is now being made by Mrs. Carroll Curtis, Bethel, Maine.

MUSTER DAY GINGERBREAD

2½ cups flour, sifted	3 tablespoons butter
1 teaspoon ginger	1 teaspoon soda
½ teaspoon salt	3 tablespoons boiling water

1 cup light molasses

Sift the flour, ginger and salt together; work the butter into the flour mixture. Dissolve the soda in the water, add to the molasses and stir in dry ingredients. Knead well together. Let stand in a cold place until dough is thoroughly chilled. Roll out on floured board to ¾-inch thickness, adding just enough additional flour so that dough will roll. Bake in a moderately hot oven (375° F.) about 20 minutes. Makes 2 sheets 7 by 11 inches.

GLAZE

3 teaspoons milk mixed with 3 teaspoons molasses

After baking, while the gingerbread is still hot, brush over top with the glaze. The gingerbread is a crisp sheet of cooky-like pastry, delicious with a glass of milk. The longer it lasts the better it is.

In the early days of New Hampshire, between 1800 and 1850, there were great celebrations known as "Muster and Training Days." These were the heydays of the food peddlers who sold squares of delicious gingerbread, glazed on top. This recipe is just as it was over a hundred years ago. There are as many variations of this recipe as there are variations of corn bread. A recipe which has been in the family of L. M. Stevens, Colebrook, N. H., calls for the addition of 1 teaspoon alum, dissolved in boiling water. This makes the gingerbread golden. Mr. Stevens' grandmother sold Muster Gingerbread to the "Muster" on the Concord Camp grounds for 10 cents a "slab."

HARD GINGERBREAD

[*Mrs. B. S. Patt, River Ave., Providence, R. I.*]

1½ cups butter	1 teaspoon soda
2½ cups sugar	3 teaspoons ginger
6 eggs	1 teaspoon salt
¼ cup milk	8 cups flour, sifted

Cream butter, add sugar, eggs, milk and sift in dry ingredients. Spread ¼-inch thick on greased inverted dripping pan. Roll very thin, preferably with a greased rolling pin. Bake in hot oven (400° F.) about 10 minutes. Cut in squares and keep in a covered crock. This gingerbread was made in large quantities every year and served with home-made wines when the minister or a special guest called. Best when one day old. Makes 48 squares.

SOUTH GLASTONBURY GINGERBREAD

[*Celia Thomas, South Glastonbury, Conn.*]

1 cup lard	4 cups flour
½ cup sugar	2 teaspoons baking powder
3 eggs, well beaten	1 teaspoon soda
1 cup molasses	½ teaspoon cinnamon
1 cup buttermilk or sour	1½ teaspoons nutmeg
milk	1 tablespoon ginger

Cream shortening, add sugar and cream. Add eggs and molasses. Alternate buttermilk with the sifted dry ingredients. Pour into well greased floured cake pan and bake 40 to 50 minutes in a moderate oven (350° F.). Makes 2 (9-inch) square cakes.

More gingerbread is eaten in New England than in any other section of the country. It was probably one of the first breads baked in New England. A gingerbread recipe was brought over on the "Mayflower."

STRAWBERRY SHORTCAKE

[*Mrs. George D. Aiken, Montpelier, Vt. The favorite recipe of Vermont's governor and his family*]

2 cups flour

3 teaspoons baking powder

1 teaspoon salt

2 teaspoons sugar

½ cup shortening

¾ cup milk (about)

Mix and sift dry ingredients; cut in shortening until well mixed; add milk, stirring quickly to make a soft dough. Turn onto a lightly floured board and pat with hands just enough to shape. Cut in 2 cakes ½-inch thick. Bake in a hot oven (450° F.) for 15 minutes.

Slice 2 quarts large juicy ripe strawberries into a bowl. Add 1 cup sugar. Spread sugared berries on each buttered layer, topping the second layer with whipped cream. Serves 6.

Strawberries, until comparatively recently, grew wild in sunny fields, small and distinctly sweet. The Indians introduced the white men of the Plymouth Colony to them. The first strawberry shortcake was probably made of corn-meal.

———

Kate Douglas Wiggin wrote in 1911:
"Who would not rather make a delicious strawberry shortcake than play 'The Maiden's Prayer' on the piano? Where is the painted table scarf that can compare with an honest loaf of milk-white bread? Is a bunch of wax or paper flowers any more artistic than a ball of perfect butter stamped with a garland of daisies?"

NEW HAMPSHIRE SODA BISCUITS

2 cups flour
½ teaspoon soda
1 teaspoon cream of tartar

½ teaspoon salt
¼ cup lard
1 cup milk (about)

Sift flour once, measure, add soda, cream of tartar and salt, and sift again. Cut in shortening quickly and lightly until well mixed. Add milk until a soft dough is formed. Turn out on lightly floured board and knead with as few strokes as possible, working dough rapidly. Pat ½-inch thick, cut with floured biscuit cutter. Bake on ungreased baking sheet in hot oven (450° F.) 12 to 15 minutes. Makes 12 biscuits, marvels of lightness and sweetness. Soda biscuits still retain their flavor when they are warmed over in the oven. Old-fashioned New Hampshire cooks invariably prefer this recipe to all other biscuit recipes.

HASTY PUDDING

[Today it is more often called Cornmeal Mush]

6 cups boiling water
1 teaspoon salt
1 cup yellow cornmeal

Bring water to a rapid boil in top of double boiler; add salt. Slowly sift in cornmeal stirring constantly until mixture is smooth and boils. Set over hot water and steam for 30 minutes or longer. Serve hot with molasses or milk, or sugar and butter with nutmeg. Serves 8.

If mush is to be fried, mix 4 tablespoons flour with corn-meal. This makes it easier to slice. Empty baking powder tins or drinking glasses make excellent molds. Rinse with cold water before pouring in the mush. When ready to use, slice and lightly flour the slices before frying on a hot greased griddle. New Orleans molasses was the preferred old-time accompaniment. Butter and maple syrup are more often served with fried mush today.

Hasty Pudding was a favorite supper dish on New England farms where it was sometimes called Stir-about Pudding. It was cooked in a big iron kettle. As the hungry children waited for the fresh warm milk that was to be poured over it, they would watch it pop and sputter. Sometimes it was poured into a big yellow bowl and served for dessert. Any pudding that was not eaten was turned into a bread pan, sliced and fried for breakfast.

Mrs. F. A. Hagen, Atlantic St., Plymouth, Mass., says, "One old lady I knew when I was a little girl used to serve Hasty Pudding as a vegetable, with gravy. I remember once that unexpected guests came, and she, who was an ample provider, feared there might not be enough vegetables. She whisked together a Hasty Pudding in an iron kettle and poured it into a mold and turned it out the last thing before dinner was served. Hasty Pudding was given its name because it could be made and served in so short a time. Since it could be eaten as a vegetable, a dessert, the main dish for lunch or supper or served for breakfast, it saved the day for many a housewife in an emergency."

"Gap and Swallow" was another venerable emergency dish, not unlike Hasty Pudding.

SPIDER CORN BREAD

1 cup corn meal
⅓ cup flour
2 tablespoons sugar
1 teaspoon salt

2 teaspoons baking powder
1 egg
1¾ cups milk and water (half
of each)

1 tablespoon butter

Mix and sift dry ingredients. Beat the egg and add 1 cup of the milk and water mixture. Stir in dry ingredients. Turn into an iron spider (about 8 inches in diameter) in which butter has been melted. Pour the rest of the milk and water over the top, but do not stir. Bake in a moderately hot oven (375° F.) 25 to 30 minutes. Cut into 8 pie-shaped pieces.

Mrs. Helen B. Farnham, Church St., Watertown, Mass., was given this recipe by her great-aunt, Novella, who is 94 years old and still lives on Cape Cod. Spider bread should have a line of creamy custard through the center. It is sliced as a pie. A large piece of butter is placed on top of each slice and it is eaten with a fork.

VERMONT BANNOCK

[*Mrs. Isabel Phillips, Crescent St., Athol, Mass.*]

1 cup cornmeal
½ teaspoon salt

boiling water
2 tablespoons soft butter

Combine cornmeal and salt. Pour on boiling water to make cornmeal the consistency of thick cream. Add butter. Spread thin in large well buttered pan and bake in a moderate oven (350° F.) about 60 minutes. Serve with butter and maple syrup or with milk. Cut into 8 large squares.

CORNMEAL APPLESAUCE

[To serve with roast pork]

2 cups boiling water
1 teaspoon salt
1 cup yellow cornmeal

4 tart apples, sliced
(but not peeled)
and cored

Stir the cornmeal into the salted water. Add the apples and cook until the cornmeal is thick. Serve with roast pork gravy. Serves 5.

For moderns, this recipe takes the place of potatoes in the meal. It comes from Cora M. Vining, 48 Bedford St., Bridgewater, Mass., who says it is at least as old as her great-grandmother who was born about 1780 in Duxbury, Mass.

CORNMEAL SOUFFLÉ

[A variation of an old recipe]

⅓ cup Rhode Island white or
    yellow cornmeal
1 tablespoon butter
2 cups milk, scalded
4 tablespoons grated cheese

1 teaspoon salt
¼ teaspoon paprika
few grains cayenne
3 egg yolks, well beaten
3 egg whites, stiffly beaten

Place cornmeal and butter in a kettle, pour on milk. Cook until the consistency of mush. Add cheese, seasonings and egg yolks, cook slowly 1 minute longer. Cool. Fold in egg whites. Bake in an ungreased baking dish in a moderate oven (350° F.) about 25 minutes. Serve with green salad and ham, bacon or sausages for luncheon or supper. Serves 4.

BROWN BREAD

[A recipe in rhyme]

One cup of sweet milk,
One cup of sour,
One cup of corn meal,
One cup of flour,
Teaspoon of soda,
Molasses one cup;
Steam for three hours,
Then eat it all up.

A half teaspoon of salt should also be added, even though it does not rhyme.

BOSTON BROWN BREAD

1 cup rye flour
1 cup yellow corn
1 cup graham flour
¾ tablespoon soda
1 teaspoon salt

¾ cup molasses
2 cups sour milk or 1¾ cups sweet milk or water
1 cup raisins or dates (if desired)

Mix and sift dry ingredients, add molasses and milk; stir until well mixed, turn into a well-buttered mold, and steam 3½ hours. The cover should be buttered before being placed on the mold, and then tied down with string; otherwise the bread in rising may force off the cover. Mold should never be filled more than ⅔ full. A melon-mold or one-pound baking-powder tins make the most attractive shaped loaves, but a 5-pound lard pail answers the purpose. For steaming, place mold on a trivet in kettle containing boiling water, allowing water to come half-way up around mold, cover closely, and steam, adding more boiling water as needed. 1 cup of raisins or dates may be added if desired.

Baked Brown Bread was a popular old-time dish. The crust on this baked bread was so thick and tough that it was cut off and never eaten. The following baking day that crust would be softened in water and stirred into the new mixture to give the bread a rich, dark color. One family jokingly remarked that their brown bread was "primeval" because each batch contained remnants of a former baking, the original bread dating back so far that no one could remember when it had been baked.

YANKEE TOAST

[A country breakfast dish]

Slice lengthwise, but do not peel, about twice the number of McIntoshes you think your family should eat for breakfast, and fry them (the apples, not the family) in butter with 3 tablespoons water and ¼ cup sugar for every 5 apples. Serve on French or German toast with broiled bacon.

R U A YANKEE COOK?

Answers on page 368

31. What is Baptist bread? Bean porridge? Rum cherries?
32. What is the difference between a blueberry and a huckleberry?
33. What are "bean-hole" beans?
34. What is a "dido" and what is its purpose?
35. Can you make a clam pie? Parsnip stew? Barberry jelly?
36. How do you open clams?
37. What are the "bones of contention" in New England concerning: Clam chowder? Baked beans? Apple pie?
38. What is "garden sass"?
39. What is Slip-gut?
40. Repeat the verse in Yankee Doodle that mentions Hasty Pudding.

STORIES OF OLD NEW ENGLAND DISHES

Ella Shannon Bowles

Early in the nineteenth century, Major Jonathan Grout of a certain New England town gave two parties in honor of his marriage to an estimable widow. The first of these social gatherings had not pleased certain of the bridegroom's fellow townsmen for he had invited only the families who lived between the upper and lower mills on the river. The disgruntled neighbors who were not on his list declared that the Major was getting "high-toned," and their remarks, as such words have a way of doing, reached the good man's ears.

"I'll give another party and this time no one'll hev a chance to miscall me," he vowed.

So he harnessed up his best four-horse team, collected his guests and drove them up to his house with a flourish. Then, one by one, he presented the town's poor to his bride and she received them graciously and asked them to partake of a repast which a local historian describes as *not only bountiful but most inviting.*

We have no record of the dishes included in that feast, but knowing Major Grout's passion for pumpkin pies, we are certain that at least a dozen of the golden delicacies decorated the table.

As an eligible widower and the catch of the county, the Major had been pursued for months by various widows. "Which one of us do you intend to take?" a coquettish damsel asked him.

The besieged man's eyes twinkled. "Wait 'til Thanksgivin' and I'll show ye," he answered.

True to his word, the Major did show them and on Thanksgiving day sent to each widow a pumpkin and a pint of New Orleans molasses to make herself a genuine old-fashioned "punkin pie."

How those forehanded ladies must have mixed and rolled the

pie-crust to form the fluted edges encircling the filling made of pumpkin stewed for hours in an iron kettle and pressed through a colander into good, rich milk sweetened with the molasses and seasoned with just the right pinches of ginger and cinnamon and dashes of salt! They used no eggs in those pies, for eggs were scarce just before Thanksgiving and the pumpkin made the filling of the right consistency.

"Pumpkin pie was an indispensable part of a good and true Thanksgiving," wrote Sarah Josepha Hale, the authority on the great feast day.

Mrs. Hale knew whereof she spoke, for, as the editor of the famous *Godey's Lady's Book,* she had been tireless in her efforts to establish a national Thanksgiving and her words put pumpkin pie in its rightful place.

Pumpkins or *pompions,* as the Pilgrims called them, were used in various ways on colonial tables. Josslyn called pumpkin stewed with a little butter, spice and vinegar the *ancient New England standing-dish,* and Edward Johnson said in 1651, *"Let no man make a jest of pumpkin, for with this fruit the Lord was pleased to feed his people till corn and cattle were increased."*

For many years, in rural districts, baked pumpkins shared the honors with "rye and injun," berries, roasted apples and hasty pudding to be eaten with milk as the proper supper dish for a growing child. In preparing this dish, a small and very ripe pumpkin with a hard shell was chosen and the stem end was sliced off to form a cover with a handle. Then the seeds and the stringy substance were scooped out until only the solid meat remained. New milk was poured in, the cover was clapped on and the pumpkin was popped into the tin baker or the brick oven to roast for six or seven hours when it was removed to be filled again with milk and eaten straight from the shell.

Pumpkins, however, were not the only "pie timber" used in making the standard New England dessert. Their circular slices hung from poles suspended from the rafters in old-time farmhouse kitchens, but apples also dried on racks above the fireplaces, berries shriveled on cloths spread on the floors of open chambers and great crocks of mincemeat stood in the butteries.

The week before Thanksgiving, housekeepers made dozens of mince pies and set them in the cheese-presses in the cold pantries to freeze. There, in the fashion of Miss Abigail's forty mince pies in *The Story of a Bad Boy,* they waited, *"each one more delightful than the others, like the Sultan's forty wives,"* until they were brought out two or three at a time to be warmed for the mid-day dinner.

Just as essential as pies to the success of the Thanksgiving feast were the puddings which accompanied them. They were of many varieties ranging from the aristocratic plum-pudding of English vintage to the lowly "Gap and Swallow" with its sauce of thick maple syrup.

Among the jewels of the pudding family were the floating islands, sweetened with rosewater, the flummeries made by turning rich custard over cake and topping it all with the beaten whites of eggs, and the syllabubs with their foundations of *good sweet cream* and *double refined powdered white sugar.*

In 1808, Lucy Emerson of Montpelier, Vermont, told *"the rising generation of Females in our Country"* who consulted her book, *The New England Cookery,* exactly how "To Make A Fine Syllabub From The Cow."

"Sweeten a quart of cyder with double refined sugar and grate nutmeg into it," quoth Lucy. *"Then milk your cow into your liquor. When you have thus added what quantity of milk you think proper, pour half a pint or more, in proportion to the quantity of syllabub you make, of the sweetest cream you can get all over it."*

However, no pudding for Thanksgiving, or any other day for that matter, was better liked than the *"Tasty Indian Pudding."* Such a dish, fit for the proverbial king, reached the peak of perfection through the right mingling of Indian meal, molasses and whole milk, the slow baking in the brick oven, and the occasional addition of cold milk to the bubbling concoction.

The brick oven was heated only for the Wednesday and Saturday bakings. A fire was built of dry pine wood and at the end of two hours the hot coals were removed and the ashes swept out with a husk broom and a turkey's wing. Then loaves of rye and Indian bread, commonly called "rye and injun," were lifted with the wooden shovel or *peel* and slid to the further edge of the oven floor. Chicken and meat pies and other pies went in next. The pot of beans and the dish of Indian pudding were placed where they could be easily refilled and the cakes were arranged in front. Finally the iron door was shut with a bang to remain closed for at least an hour when the cakes and pies were removed. Then the chicken pies and bread were drawn out but the beans and Indian pudding were left in all night to be made more delectable by the long slow cooking.

When the great oven was cold, "Hard Injun Puddings" were boiled for hours in linen bags. They were so well-liked in the eighteenth century that the historian of Hadley, Massachusetts, tells of one or two families of the town who consumed three hundred and sixty-five such puddings yearly.

Hasty Pudding, stirred up with corn meal in a big pot of boiling water, was another standby which might be eaten in the form of mush and milk or could be molded, cut in slices, and fried in pork fat in a heavy iron skillet.

Neither was it necessary to heat the brick oven to bake bread. "Rye or injun" might be put in a covered iron pan upon the hearth with coals heaped upon the lid and the loaves left to bake through the night, and the mixture for Rhode Island jonnycakes could be spread on boards placed at just the right angle before the blaze of the fire to turn into crispy tid-bits to be served with wild grape jelly or maple syrup.

The New England colonists learned the value of corn as a food from the Indians and from them assimilated such words as *samp, sagiminity* and *hominy* into their language and the various forms of the grain into their diet. The Indian name *nokehick* for a meal of parched corn *turned almost inside outward and white and floury* was pronounced "ho-cake" by the English.

M'sickquatash, the Indian word for corn boiled whole, became the *succotash* of the Pilgrims when they combined corn and beans. As time went on, however, succotash developed into a more elaborate dish made of large white beans, hulled corn, corned beef, salt pork, chicken, white turnip and potatoes and in this form was a famous food of Plymouth, Massachusetts, where it was served again and again at celebrations of Forefathers' Day on December 21.

If you are a New Hampshire Yankee, you have heard about and perhaps have eaten bean-porridge and salt-rising bread. The porridge was made by boiling beans in corned beef liquor and thickening the mixture with Indian meal. It was hardened in quart bowls and when taken out each one of the molds was hung up in the buttery by means of a loop of strong string laid over the edge of the bowl before the porridge was turned in. When eaten, slices were cut off and heated in a skillet. Salt-rising bread was prized because it required no yeast to make it rise but was started from a batter which fermented in about five hours.

Although wheat flour was used sparingly in the back country, nearly every family tried to keep a little on hand to make cakes and hot biscuits for neighborhood tea-parties and for the Thanksgiving cooking. By the late eighteenth century white flour had ceased to be a luxury among the well-to-do families of the Piscataqua region. Certain hostesses were famous for foods they served. Lady Pepperell of Kittery, the granddaughter of Chief-Justice Samuel Sewell of Massachusetts Bay Colony and wife of the American baronet, Sir William Pepperell, was lavish with her rusks made by a rule preserved in the family for many years. Ten pounds of *flower* and twenty eggs were used in making them. The culinary reputation of "Lady" Langdon, wife of John Langdon and the best known hostess of her day, rested upon her delicate pound cake.

At prim New England tea-drinkings when the best china, linen and silver were brought out in honor of neighbors who might have driven miles over the drifts of snow for a friendly visit, seed-cake supplemented the pies, doughnuts and cheese and cold meats set out for the guests. It was made in various ways. In the country— eggs made it light, but in the towns where there were bakeries, yeast was purchased to leaven it. To assist the readers of *Godey's* in producing the popular tea-cake, Mrs. Hale formulated the following directions in rhyme:

A SEED CAKE

Get a tin, and as soon as you've buttered it o'er,
To assist it in turning out nicely procure
Half a quartern of dough which your baker will bring
When he comes round with bread, if he has such a thing,
And he must be a curious tradesman indeed
If he cannot supply it at once. To proceed,
Set it down by the fire to rise for a time,
Then obtain half a pound of fresh butter—mind, prime—
And three pounds of powdered loaf sugar—the best—
With some caraway seeds—say an ounce—with the rest,
Mix them up in the usual way, and the cake
May be placed in a moderate oven to bake.

The old New England dishes carried with them a tradition of intimate kitchen knowledge that many of our modern dishes do not. Today, perhaps even Mrs. Hale herself might be inclined to something more like this:

A SEED CAKE

Call up the grocer and ask for a cake
"Something like Mother use to bake"
It won't be the same ... won't taste as good,
But that won't matter, it'll still be food.

VI. PUDDINGS, PIES AND CAKES

ORIGINAL INJUN' PUDDIN'

[One of the oldest of New England's desserts]

5 cups milk	¾ teaspoon cinnamon
⅔ cup dark molasses	⅜ teaspoon nutmeg
⅓ cup granulated sugar	1 teaspoon salt
½ cup yellow cornmeal	4 tablespoons butter

Heat 4 cups of the milk and add molasses, sugar, cornmeal, salt, spice and butter to it. Cook 20 minutes or until mixture thickens. Pour into baking dish, add remaining cold milk. Do not stir. Put into slow oven (300° F.) and bake for 3 hours without stirring. Serve warm with cream or Hard Sauce (page 203), or vanilla ice cream. Serves 8. This pudding is also called Whitpot (also Whitspot) Pudding.

Frosty morning, when the first leaves float lazily down, when the squirrels bark in glee and it's cool enough to build a fire in the kitchen range, then it's Baked Injun' Puddin' time.

Most Yankee cooks agree that authentic Injun' Puddin' is made according to the recipe above. There are, however, as many variations to this basic recipe as there are days of the year. Rhode Islanders insist on Rhode Island white cornmeal. The famous Durgin-Park recipe which follows calls for an egg and a pinch of baking powder; tapioca is sometimes added, also a few tablespoons of white

QUIET HARVEST

flour to increase the whey. Some cooks add seeded raisins, and spices vary slightly according to individual preference. One of the most delicious of all variations calls for the addition of 1 pint of sliced sweet apples or home-grown pears. These translucent sweet slices rise to the top and form delicious islands in a sea of red brown juice. Serve in a soup plate with thick, yellow sweet cream.

BAKED INDIAN PUDDING

[*Durgin-Park, 30 North Market St., Boston, Mass.*]

3 cups milk
¼ cup black molasses
2 tablespoons sugar
2 tablespoons butter

¼ teaspoon salt
⅛ teaspoon baking powder
1 egg
½ cup yellow cornmeal

Mix all the ingredients thoroughly with one-half of the milk and bake in a hot oven (450° F.) until mixture boils. Stir in remaining half of hot milk and bake in a slow oven (300° F.) for 5 to 7 hours. Bake in a stone crock well greased inside. Serve warm with whipped cream or vanilla ice cream. Serves 6.

60-MINUTE BAKED INDIAN PUDDING

1 quart milk, scalded
5 tablespoons yellow cornmeal
2 tablespoons butter
1 cup dark molasses

1 teaspoon salt
¾ teaspoon cinnamon
½ teaspoon ginger
2 eggs

1 cup cold milk

Put milk in double boiler, add meal slowly, stirring constantly. Cook 15 minutes, then add butter, molasses, seasonings, and eggs, beaten well. Turn into buttered dish and pour cold milk over mixture, but do not stir. Bake 60 minutes in a moderate oven (350° F.). Serve with cream, vanilla ice cream or Hard Sauce (page 203). Serves 8.

APPLE PANDOWDY

[From a cook book published in 1880]

"Fill a heavy pot heaping full of pleasant apples, sliced. Add 1 cup molasses, 1 cup sugar, 1 cup water, 1 teaspoon cloves, 1 teaspoon cinnamon. Cover with baking powder biscuit crust, sloping it over the sides. Bake overnight. In the morning cut the hard crust into the apple. Eat with yellow cream or plain."

Miss Theodate Bates, Somersworth, N. H., writes: "My grandmother had been praising the apple pandowdy which our family enjoyed for breakfast. A neighbor asked her to send a dishful. When the neighbor's daughter returned the dish she said, 'Mother thanks you.' Was that all her mother had to say? Daughter replied, 'Mother hopes you will never send her any more.'"

Modern recipes for pandowdy call for 5 apples, sliced; 3 tablespoons sugar, 3 tablespoons molasses, ¼ teaspoon nutmeg, cinnamon and salt. Bake in casserole until apples are soft. Prepare a rich soft biscuit dough. Turn out over apples and bake 15 minutes longer in a hot oven. Serve with Hard Sauce (page 203), Lemon Sauce (page 200), Nutmeg Sauce (page 180) or cream. Serves 6. Pandowdy is also called "Apple Jonathan" and "Apple Pot-Pie."

Maine apple pandowdy is something else again. "Try out 3 slices of home-raised salt fat pork in a dinner kettle which already has in it enough water to more than cover 8 or more tart apples sliced and ⅔ cup molasses. Make a dozen dumplings as for soup and drop in, cook 20 minutes, being careful that the mixture does not 'catch on.' Serve hot."

Apple Brown Betty is made according to the modern recipe for pandowdy. In place of the biscuit crust 1½ cups bread crumbs combined with ½ cup sugar are sprinkled in layers on top of the sweetened apples. Dot crumbs with bits of butter. Bake in a moderate oven (350° F.), 45 minutes.

APPLE DUMPLINGS

[A Massachusetts recipe]

2 cups flour, sifted	¾ cup milk
2½ teaspoons baking powder	8 small apples, pared and
½ teaspoon salt	cored
½ cup shortening	butter, cinnamon, sugar

Sift flour, baking powder and salt; cut in shortening. Add milk, stirring until a soft dough is formed. Knead on slightly floured board and roll ⅛-inch thick. Divide into 8 parts. Place apple on each part. Fill each hollow with 1 tablespoon sugar and 1 teaspoon butter. Fold dough up over apple, pressing edges together. Place apples on pan, sprinkle with cinnamon and sugar and dot with ¼ teaspoon butter. Bake in moderately hot oven (375° F.) 30 to 40 minutes. Serve with cream or Hard Sauce (page 203). Serves 8.

Left-over apple jelly may be used in addition to sugar to fill centers of apples. Grandmother's recipe reads: "Tie dumplings in loose cloths which have been dipped in water and floured on the inside. Boil steadily in plenty of water 1 hour." Dumplings may be steamed, too, but modern Yankee cooks usually prefer theirs baked.

APPLE CRUMB

4 cups apples, sliced	½ cup butter
¼ cup hot water	½ cup flour
	½ cup sugar

Butter baking dish and cover with sliced apples; pour water over apples. Work butter, sugar and flour together until mixture is like crumbs. Spread over apples. Bake in hot oven (450° F.) 10 minutes. Reduce heat to moderate (350° F.) and bake 30 minutes longer. Serve with cream. Serves 4.

YANKEE APPLE JOHN

[Mrs. Henry Doucette, 348 Main St., Lewiston, Me.]

6 tart apples, thinly sliced	2 cups flour, sifted
¾ cup sugar	3 teaspoons baking powder
¾ teaspoon cinnamon	pinch salt
½ teaspoon nutmeg	½ cup shortening
⅛ teaspoon salt	⅔ cup milk (about)

Grease shallow baking dish and fill with sliced apples. Mix sugar, spices and salt and sprinkle over apples. Sift flour with baking powder and salt. Cut in shortening until mixture is fine. Add milk, mixing until a soft dough is formed. Knead lightly on floured board, roll to fit over pan; brush with milk, bake in a hot oven (450° F.) about 25 minutes, or until apples are tender. Serve with Nutmeg Sauce. Serves 5.

NUTMEG SAUCE

1 cup sugar	dash salt
¼ teaspoon nutmeg	2 cups boiling water
2 tablespoons flour	1 tablespoon butter

1 tablespoon vinegar

Mix sugar, nutmeg, flour and salt in saucepan: Add boiling water, stirring constantly until blended. Add butter and boil 5 minutes. Remove from fire, add vinegar.

APPLE SEVENTH HEAVEN

6 apples	¼ teaspoon cinnamon
2 tablespoons sugar	½ cup brown sugar
⅛ teaspoon salt	½ cup butter

1 cup finely chopped or shaved nuts

Spread bottom and sides of oblong cake pan 8″ x 12″ generously with butter. Peel apples, cut into 8 equal parts and place in parallel rows closely in pan. Mix sugar, salt and cinnamon and sprinkle over apples. Cream brown sugar and butter; add nuts. Spread over and between apples, then pat to make a smooth surface. Bake for ½ hour in quick oven (450° F.) or until apples are tender. Serve with thick cream. Serves 6.

MY GRANDMOTHER'S APPLE TURNOVER

[*Norma Roberts, Bristol, N. H.*]

Bake a rich biscuit shortcake; split, butter and fill in between and on top with hot applesauce, seasoned with nutmeg and sweetened to taste with sugar and dotted lightly with butter. Serve cut in squares with Butter Sauce.

BUTTER SAUCE

½ cup butter   1½ tablespoons flour

2 cups boiling water

Blend butter and flour, stir in hot water gradually and cook until it thickens. No sugar is added. Makes 2 cups sauce.

"Charles Flogg, who lived nearby, often came to help grandmother, who was a widow. She always put the turnover in a large oval-shaped dish with a cover. If that was on the table he would eat little else in his haste. Came one April first he was there. Grandmother put the dish on the table. Charlie ate very little, passing his plate soon for turnover. Grandmother 'histed' the cover off the empty dish shouting, 'April Fool.' Madder than a wet hen, he did not come to the house again for two years."

APPLE TAPIOCA

¼ cup pearl tapioca   5 medium apples, peeled and
2 cups water   quartered
¼ teaspoon salt   ½ cup sugar

Soak tapioca in water overnight or for several hours. Then place over direct heat to cook for 20 minutes or until tapioca is transparent. Add salt. Pour tapioca over apples and sugar in baking dish. Bake in a moderate oven (350° F.) until apples are tender, about 45 minutes. Serves 6.

"FRESHMAN'S TEARS"

[A cream tapioca pudding popular in Western Massachusetts]

3 tablespoons pearl tapioca   3½ cups milk, scalded
1 cup water   1 tablespoon cornstarch
⅛ teaspoon salt   ½ cup sugar
3 eggs, separated   1 teaspoon vanilla

Soak the tapioca several hours, add the water and salt, and cook in the top of a double boiler about 2 hours, or until the tapioca is transparent. Beat the yolks of the eggs, add the milk, and combine with the tapioca. Mix the constarch and sugar and add. Return to the double boiler and cook until thick and creamy, about 15 minutes. Just before serving, fold in the whites of the eggs, beaten stiff, and vanilla. Serve cold. Serves 8.

Tapioca pudding was appropriately named "Freshman's Tears" by the undergraduates at Mount Holyoke College, South Hadley, Mass. This particularly delicious version is from Mrs. Silas Snow, Williamsburg, Mass. In the home of Mrs. Clifton Johnson, Hockanum, Hadley, Mass., "grandma" made this pudding until she was nearly ninety.

She made it in a milk pan, added raisins, and called it
"plum pudding." But the boys of the family had their own
name for it. They called it "Pill Pudding," much to
grandma's disgust.

APPLE SNOW

[*Mary N. Cabral, 3495 Riverside Ave., Somerset, Mass.*]

Peel and grate a large sour apple, sprinkling ¾ cup powdered
sugar over it. Break into this the whites of 2 eggs and beat all constantly until pudding is light and frothy. Take care to make in a
large bowl as it beats very stiff and light. Heap into a glass dish
and pour a custard around it and serve cold. Serves 4.

Easy to make with an electric beater; otherwise, long and
tedious. A very delicate dessert.

MRS. HAYNES' APPLE DESSERT

[*Mrs. John Haynes, 105 Charlotte St., Hartford, Conn.*]

2 apples, peeled and chopped fine	1 cup sugar
	2 tablespoons flour
½ cup nuts, chopped	1 teaspoon baking powder
1 egg, beaten	⅛ teaspoon salt

Combine all the ingredients and mix. Bake in a shallow greased
pan in a moderate oven (350° F.) about 25 minutes or until a
macaroon-like crust forms on top. Remove from pan while warm.
Place in sherbet glasses. Serve cold with whipped cream. Serves 4.

BLUEBERRY SLUMP

[Mrs. M. S. Newcomb, 160 Coyle St., Portland, Me.]

2 cups blueberries, washed   1 cup flour, sifted
½ cup sugar   2 teaspoons baking powder
1 cup water   ¼ teaspoon salt
                ½ cup milk (about)

Stew blueberries, sugar and water. Mix and sift flour, baking powder and salt; add milk, stirring quickly to make a dumpling dough that will drop from the end of a spoon. Drop into the boiling sauce. Cook 10 minutes with the cover off and 10 minutes with cover on. Serve with plain or whipped cream. Serves 4. On Cape Cod they call this pudding Blueberry Grunt. A steamed berry pudding is also known as a Grunt.

Apple Slump is made in the same way, substituting apples for blueberries. Stew 6 well-flavored apples with ¼ cup molasses, ¼ cup sugar and ½ cup water and proceed as above.

BLUEBERRY UPSIDE-DOWN CAKE

[A delicious Maine recipe]

2 tablespoons butter   1 cup sugar
1 cup brown sugar   5 tablespoons blueberry syrup
½ cup blueberry syrup   1 cup flour, sifted
1 medium sized tin of blue-   1 teaspoon baking powder
    berries, drained   1 teaspoon salt
3 egg yolks, beaten   3 egg whites, beaten stiff
                whipped cream

Cook together butter, sugar and ½ cup blueberry syrup from a tin of blueberries until sugar is dissolved. Cover the bottom of a 10-inch baking dish with all the blueberries. Pour the cooked syrup over berries. Make a batter by beating together egg yolks, sugar and the 5 tablespoons blueberry syrup. Sift flour, baking powder and salt and add. Fold in egg whites. Pour mixture over the blueberries and bake in a moderate oven (350° F.) 45 minutes. Serve upside down, topped with sweetened whipped cream or Berry Sauce (page 211). Serves 5.

CRANBERRY UPSIDE-DOWN CAKE

[*A modern Cape Cod recipe*]

3 tablespoons butter	½ teaspoon vanilla
1 cup brown sugar	1 egg, well beaten
1 can cranberry sauce	1¼ cups flour, sifted
1 small (number 2) tin apricots	2 teaspoons baking powder
½ cup sugar	½ teaspoon salt
¼ cup shortening	½ cup milk

Melt butter in a skillet or upside-down cake pan. Add sugar and cook slowly 2 or 3 minutes; add cranberry sauce and apricots. To make batter: cream sugar and shortening; add vanilla and egg, sift flour with baking powder and salt. Add alternately with milk. Pour batter over fruit in skillet. Bake in a moderate oven (350° F.) about 25 minutes. Turn out onto large plate so that fruit is on top. Serve with whipped cream. Serves 6.

MOTHER'S BLUEBERRY BREAD AND BUTTER PUDDING

8 thin slices white bread	1 cup sugar
¼ cup butter	pinch of salt
1 quart blueberries	¾ cup cream, whipped

Remove crusts of bread. Butter each slice. Stew berries, sugar and salt for 15 minutes. Butter a deep baking dish. Alternate slices of bread and stewed berries until all are used. Bake in a moderate oven (350° F.) for 15 to 20 minutes. Serve very cold with whipped cream. Serves 6.

MOLLY'S PLEASANT PUDDING

A layer of bits of butter   One of applesauce
One of grated bread   One of sugar

Repeat the layers until a medium sized buttered baking dish is filled. Make a custard of 3 eggs, 2 cups milk, ¼ teaspoon salt. Pour over. Bake in a moderate oven for half an hour. Serves 4 to 6.

This recipe was copied by Mrs. Lennart W. Bjorkman, 16 Hillcrest Circle, Swampscott, Mass., from an old wooden covered account book dated 1821 in which her great-aunt had neatly pasted recipes. The book came from Hopkinton, N. H. The same treasure chest of old-time hints and recipes reveals the following: "Oranges and lemons keep best wrapped alone in soft paper and laid in a drawer of linen" —so highly prized were the fruits which we use every day.

CARAMEL BREAD PUDDING

1 cup brown sugar   ⅛ teaspoon salt
5 slices of bread   2 eggs, beaten
3 cups of milk   1 teaspoon vanilla

Place sugar in bottom of a buttered casserole or baking dish. Butter bread, remove crusts, cut slices into quarters, and place on top of sugar. Mix the milk, salt, eggs and vanilla and pour over the bread. Bake in moderate oven (350° F.) about 40 minutes or until a knife inserted in the middle does not adhere. Serve with top milk, cream or ice cream. Serves 4.

This recipe comes from an old Portsmouth, N. H., family where it was served almost every Sunday for dessert. From Helen Kane, 256 Danforth St., Portland, Me.

MARTHA'S VINEYARD GREEN CORN PUDDING

[Mrs. E. W. Foote, W. Tisbury, Mass.]

24 ears of corn	2 tablespoons butter, melted
milk	1 teaspoon salt
3 eggs, well beaten	4 tablespoons sugar

Cut each row of corn lengthwise through each kernel. Then grate with grater and scrape each ear, taking care not to scrape too close to the cob. Sometimes the corn will be milky, at other times dry. The amount of milk to add depends on the corn. The mixture should be about the consistency of cornbread mixture after the milk, eggs, butter, salt and sugar are added. There will be about 4 cups of the mixture. Turn into a greased baking dish. Bake 2 to 3 hours in a very slow oven (250° F.) or until pudding is set and light brown. It should be dry enough when done to cut into squares. Butter each individual serving. Serves 6 to 8.

Vineyarders serve this corn pudding either as the main course or as dessert. A noble dish.

BROWN BREAD BREWIS

[Mrs. F. A. Hagen, Atlantic St., Plymouth, Mass.]

Take hard crusts from brown bread, put in a pan with a little salt and cold water. Cover pan and set over low fire to simmer. Add a small piece of butter and a little cream or rich milk. Cook until mixture is the consistency of thick mush. Serve with cold meats, or as a pudding with milk or syrup. New England Hard-Scrabble is another name for this dish.

A beverage called Crust Coffee was made from the hard crusts from brown bread. Hot water was poured over the crusts and the resulting liquid was served as a coffee substitute.

GOOSEBERRY FOOL

1 quart ripe gooseberries	dash of salt
2 cups water	4 egg yolks
1 tablespoon butter	4 egg whites
1 cup sugar	2 tablespoons powdered sugar

Top and stem the gooseberries, stew in water until tender. Press through a colander to remove skins. Add butter, sugar, salt and egg yolks beaten together until light. Pour into a glass bowl. Beat egg whites, stiff, add powdered sugar. Heap on berries. Serve cold without sauce. Serves 6 to 8.

"As a little girl on 'gram's' farm this was a Saturday night treat to finish off our baked bean supper," reports Mrs. Stanley Macey, 7 Lyndon St., Concord, N. H.

A dictionary definition of a fool is "a dish of crushed fruit with whipped cream and sugar."

MAPLE HICKORY NUT WHIP

¾ cup maple syrup	1 cup heavy cream
2 egg yolks, well beaten	2 egg whites
1 tablespoon gelatine	2 tablespoons powdered sugar
¼ cup cold water	½ cup hickory nuts, broken
½ teaspoon salt	

Cook maple syrup and beaten egg yolks in double boiler until slightly thickened, about 5 minutes. Soak gelatine in cold water for 5 minutes, dissolve over hot water, and add to custard. Remove from fire and cool. Whip cream until stiff. Beat egg whites until stiff but not dry, fold in powdered sugar; fold cream and eggs into the cooled custard as soon as it begins to thicken. Add nuts and salt. Serve in sherbet glasses. Serves 6.

DOWN EAST SIZZLERS

1 cup flour, sifted	2 tablespoons butter
1 tablespoon sugar	½ cup milk
1 teaspoon baking powder	1 egg, beaten
½ teaspoon salt	canned blueberries, drained

Sift flour, sugar, baking powder and salt. Cut in butter until mixture is consistency of coarse cornmeal. Combine egg and milk and stir into dry ingredients. Roll thin on a floured board and cut about the size of a saucer. Place 1 tablespoon blueberries on each pastry and seal edges with water. Fry in hot deep fat (370° F.) until a golden brown. Serve hot. Makes 20 sizzlers.

This is an old Maine recipe from Mrs. Daniel Gannon, South Main Street, Fall River, Mass.

PLUM DUFF

½ cup brown sugar	½ cup pastry flour, sifted
¼ cup melted butter	¼ teaspoon soda
1 egg, well beaten	¼ teaspoon baking powder
1 cup cooked, seeded	¼ teaspoon salt
unsweetened prunes	1 tablespoon milk

Add sugar to melted butter, cool slightly and stir in the egg. Cut prunes into small pieces. Mash and measure. Mix and sift dry ingredients. Add fruit pulp to first mixture, sift in dry ingredients and add the milk. Bake in well greased muffin tins filled ⅔ full in a moderate oven (350° F.) about 25 minutes. Serve warm with Foamy Sauce (page 196). Serves 4.

The original Plum Duff (i.e., plum dough), named by seamen, was a stiff flour pudding with raisins or currants, boiled in a bag. This one has a lighter flavor and will be welcomed by landlubbers, too.

UNCOOKED SNOW CREAM

[A child's delight; some children call it "Snow Mush"]

Fill a tall glass with light new clean snow. Pour in rich milk. Add a tablespoon of sugar, a few drops of red (vegetable) coloring, 2 or 3 drops of vanilla to taste. Beat mixture with long-handled silver spoon and serve immediately.

QUEEN OF PUDDINGS

[Also called Princess Pudding]

2 cups fine dry bread crumbs	grated rind 1 lemon
4 cups milk	jam, jelly, or berries
2 tablespoons butter	4 egg whites, beaten stiff
1 cup sugar	¾ cup sugar
4 egg yolks, well beaten	juice of ½ lemon

Soak crumbs in milk 5 minutes. Cream butter, stir in sugar and add egg yolks and lemon rind. Stir into soaked crumbs. Turn into greased casserole, place in a pan of hot water and bake in a moderate oven (350° F.) until firm, about 1 hour. Spread a layer of jam or jelly or fresh raspberries on top of the pudding. Add sugar and lemon juice to egg whites, spread on pudding and replace in oven until meringue is lightly browned. Serve without sauce. Serves 6.

"I'll never forget that my 'granny' always had this wonderful pudding for my Sunday night meal when I stayed with her week ends," writes Mrs. Eva C. Mitchell, 849 Riverside St., Portland, Me., whose recipe this is.

BIRD'S NEST PUDDING

8 tart apples, peeled and
   sliced
¾ cup sugar

½ teaspoon cinnamon
baking powder biscuit dough
   (recipe page 164)

Fill deep buttered dish with tart apples to within 2 inches of top. Add sugar mixed with cinnamon. Roll biscuit crust 1-inch thick and cover. Bake in a moderate oven (350° F.) for 40 minutes. Serve with Sour Sauce. Serves 6.

SOUR SAUCE

½ cup sugar
 1 tablespoon flour

¾ cup water
 2 tablespoons butter

2 or 3 tablespoons vinegar

Cook sugar, flour, water and butter until smooth and thick. Remove from fire; add vinegar. If vinegar is strong, 2 tablespoons will be enough.

"This is not Crow's Nest, Apple Cobbler or even Apple Shortcake! It is Bird's Nest Pudding, just as my mother used to make it," writes Frances A. Bush, Brandon, Vermont.

Yankees differ widely as to what a Bird's Nest Pudding should taste like. The only ingredient on which all agree is apples. In Connecticut they pour a baked custard mixture over apples and bake 1 hour. In Vermont, where maple sugar is widely used, they serve a sour sauce over the pudding. In Massachusetts, where there are comparatively few maple trees, they serve it with shaved maple sugar.

HONEYCOMB PUDDING

[A Tamworth, N. H., recipe]

3 tablespoons butter

2 tablespoons milk

3 eggs, separated

1 cup molasses

1 tablespoon lemon juice

1 cup flour

⅛ teaspoon salt

½ teaspoon cinnamon

Melt shortening, add milk, beaten yolks of eggs, molasses and lemon juice. Sift together flour, salt and cinnamon and add. Fold in stiffly beaten whites. Pour into a greased casserole and bake in a very slow oven (250° F.) for 1 hour. Serve with whipped cream or Hot Lemon Sauce (page 200).

POVERTY PUDDING

[Hartwell Farm, Lincoln, Mass.]

1 quart cornflakes

1 quart milk

2 eggs

¼ cup molasses

¼ cup sugar

1 teaspoon ginger

1 teaspoon salt

1 teaspoon cinnamon

Put cornflakes in greased pudding dish, mix remaining ingredients and pour them over the cornflakes. Set pudding dish in a pan of hot water and bake in a moderate oven (350° F.) 30 minutes. Serves 4.

NEW HAMPSHIRE "PLATE CAKE"

Fill a pie tin with any fresh fruit, such as berries, sliced apples or peaches. Sprinkle with sugar. Cover with a biscuit crust rolled

½-inch thick. Bake in a hot oven (450° F.) until crust is brown and fruit soft, about 15 to 20 minutes. Loosen the crust around the edge, invert the dish and serve upside down with the cooked fruit on top. Cover with sweetened whipped cream. Especially good made with blueberries, raspberries or wild strawberries.

BAKED RICE PUDDING

[Mrs. Raymond E. Baldwin, Judson Place, Stratford, Conn. A favorite recipe of the Governor of Connecticut and his family]

⅓ cup uncooked rice
6 cups milk
1 cup sugar

½ teaspoon salt
1 cup seedless raisins
1 teaspoon vanilla

Wash rice, add milk, sugar and salt and place in a greased baking dish. Bake, uncovered, in a very slow oven (250° F.) for 3 hours, stirring mixture well with a fork 3 times during the first hour of baking. Add raisins and vanilla and continue baking, stirring whenever a brown film forms on top. Serve with cream. Serves 8.

VERMONT RICE PUDDING

¼ cup rice
¼ teaspoon salt
2 cups milk

½ cup sugar
½ cup heavy cream
maple syrup

Place rice, salt and milk in the top of a double boiler and cook over water for 3 hours. Stir in the sugar, cool. Whip the cream and fold in the cold rice. Serve with a small pitcher of hot maple syrup. Serves 4.

STEAMED BLUEBERRY PUDDING

[*Eva E. Pratt, Water Village, N. H.*]

2 cups flour, sifted	2 tablespoons butter
4 teaspoons baking powder	2 tablespoons molasses
½ teaspoon salt	⅞ cup milk
2 tablespoons sugar	1 cup blueberries, floured

Mix and sift dry ingredients; cut in butter, combine molasses and milk and add gradually; add blueberries and turn into a greased mold. Steam 1½ hours. Serve with Colonial Pudding Sauce (page 211) or Hard Sauce (page 203). Serves 5. On Cape Cod this pudding is called Blueberry Grunt.

For steamed Blackberry Pudding substitute blackberries for blueberries.

> *Pudding bags were made of muslin or knit out of cotton yarn. Those that were knit looked like a man's stocking top. (One New England cook says that until she was a big girl she thought that is what they were.)*
>
> *Before the bags were used, they were dipped into boiling water, floured, and filled while hot. Apples and raisins were favored in the puddings. Half the room in the bag was allowed for the pudding to swell. Whether or not you allowed room, the pudding did swell, just the same!*
>
> *Puddings were either steamed on top of the vegetables in the great black iron kettles or dropped into rapidly boiling water. Pudding dishes were called Twifflers.*
>
> *Some cooks made a new bag each time they made a pudding; others used the same bag. It was indeed a chore to clean a pudding bag!*
>
> *At one period, when pudding was part of the dinner, it was served first, which explains the old saying, "I came early in pudding time."*
>
> *Fat little boys were called "pudding bags."*

BLACKBERRY FLUMMERY

[Mrs. John Haynes, 105 Charlotte St., Hartford, Conn.]

1 pint blackberries	3½ tablespoons cornstarch
2 cups water	¼ cup cold water

½ cup sugar

Simmer the blackberries and the 2 cups water; do not stir. The berries should be tender in 10 minutes. Dissolve cornstarch in ¼ cup water and stir carefully into berries. Simmer for 5 minutes, add sugar and when cold, pour into a glass dish. Serve very cold with sugar and cream. Serves 4.

LEMON SPONGE PUDDING

1 cup sugar	pinch of salt
1 tablespoon flour	rind and juice of 1 lemon
2 tablespoons butter	1 cup milk
2 egg yolks	2 egg whites, stiffly beaten

Sift the sugar, flour and salt and blend with the beaten egg yolks. Add the milk, lemon juice and rind, beating thoroughly. Melt butter and add. Fold in the stiffly beaten egg whites and bake with pudding dish set in a pan of hot water for ¾ hour in a moderate oven (350° F.). The pudding has a layer of lemon jelly, a topping of cake-like consistency, and nice brown crust. Serve cold. Serves 6.

STEAMED CRANBERRY PUDDING

[A Cape Cod recipe]

1 cup flour, sifted	⅔ cup suet, chopped
1 teaspoon baking powder	1 cup cranberries, washed
½ teaspoon salt	and picked over
⅓ cup brown sugar	1 egg
½ cup bread crumbs	⅓ cup water

Mix ingredients, turn into a greased mold. Steam 2 hours. Serve with Hard Sauce (page 203) or Foamy Sauce (page 196). Serves 6.

CRACKER PUDDING

7 large common crackers, rolled   1 cup raisins
4 eggs, slightly beaten   ¼ cup butter
7 cups milk

Mix these ingredients, pour into a steamer or the top of a double boiler and steam for about 2 hours. Serve with Foamy Sauce. Serves 8 to 10.

FOAMY SAUCE

½ cup sugar   2 teaspoons water
½ cup butter   1 egg, beaten
½ teaspoon vanilla

Stir the sugar, butter and water together in a saucepan over low heat until well blended. Keep warm. Just before serving, stir in the beaten egg and vanilla.

This recipe comes from Mrs. Allan A. Houston, Auburn, Me., who copied it from her grandmother's cook book where it is written in fine script. As a child this was always Mrs. Houston's Thanksgiving and Christmas pudding. It was not until she was grown that she tasted plum pudding. The recipe came either from her great-grandmother, Elizabeth Newman, who brought it to Winthrop, Me., from Newburyport, Mass., in 1816, or from her grandfather's family, the Webbs, who settled in Winthrop, Me., from Braintree, Mass., before the Revolution. Either way it has a noble history. The pudding is the consistency of curds and all the sweetness is derived from the raisins and the sweet foamy sauce served with it.

OATMEAL PUDDING

[*Mrs. Carrie Castle Francis, 1 W. Main St., Norwalk, Conn.*]

The following recipe was taken from "In The Kitchen," written by Elizabeth S. Miller, Geneva, N. Y., in 1875 and dedicated to the Cooking Class of the Young Ladies' Saturday Morning Club of Boston, Mass.

The book was a wedding present to Mrs. Francis' mother, 63 years ago, and although yellowed with age, is still in service. This recipe is a favorite in her family to this day.

4 cups milk	¼ pound seedless raisins
2 cups oatmeal	¼ pound currants
3 eggs	1 teaspoon salt
½ pound suet, chopped fine	½ cup sugar
1 teaspoon nutmeg	

Scald the milk at night and pour it over the oatmeal. Stir, cover, and let remain overnight. Next day beat the eggs, stir in the other ingredients, and pour into the overnight mixture, mixing well. If you are old-fashioned lay a pudding cloth in a bowl and pour the pudding into it, tying it tight but leaving room to swell, and plunge it into boiling water, cover tight, and boil for 2 hours. If you are not old-fashioned, steam it in the top of a double-boiler. In any event, serve it with Maple Sugar Sauce. Serves 8.

MAPLE SUGAR SAUCE

½ pound maple sugar	4 tablespoons hot water
¼ pound butter	

Crack the sugar in small bits, add hot water and let simmer a few minutes until clear. Take from fire and stir in the butter.

SNOW BALLS

[A Rhode Island recipe]

2 cups flour, sifted   ½ cup butter
½ teaspoon salt   1 cup sugar
2 teaspoons baking powder   ¾ cup milk
              4 egg whites, beaten stiffly

Sift the flour, salt and baking powder. Cream the butter, stir in the sugar gradually. Stir in the dry ingredients alternately with the milk. Fold in the beaten egg whites. Fill buttered custard cups ⅔ full; fasten waxed paper over the top and tie securely. Steam 50 minutes. Unmold and serve with sliced peaches, crushed strawberries or Raspberry Sauce. Serves 6 to 8.

RASPBERRY SAUCE

1 cup canned or fresh raspberries
¼ cup sugar

Crush berries, strain to remove seeds. Add sugar and cook to a heavy syrup.

RHUBARB ROLY POLY

[Easier to take than the usual sulphur and molasses spring tonic]

2 cups flour, sifted   ¾ cup milk
2 teaspoons baking powder   2 cups rhubarb,
1 teaspoon salt   cut in pieces
2 tablespoons sugar   1 cup sugar
4 tablespoons shortening   butter

Sift flour, baking powder, salt and sugar. Cut in shortening. Add milk to make a soft dough. Knead on slightly floured board and roll ⅛-inch thick. Spread with rhubarb, dot generously with butter, sprinkle with sugar and roll like a jelly roll. Bake in a moderate oven (350° F.) 30 to 40 minutes. Serve with cream or Hard Sauce (page 203). Serves 6.

HUCKLEBERRY PUDDING

2 cups flour, sifted
4 teaspoons baking powder
2 teaspoons sugar

½ teaspoon salt
⅔ cup milk
1 cup huckleberries

¾ cup sugar

Sift dry ingredients, add milk; pat dough into a square, about ½-inch thick. In the center of the dough place huckleberries, washed and sugared. Roll or fold dough, keeping the berries in the center until berries are entirely surrounded by dough. Tie or sew in a white cloth or bag, allowing room for swelling. Plunge bag in boiling water and steam 1 hour. Serve hot on a large platter with Pudding Sauce or Berry Sauce (page 211). Serves 5.

PUDDING SAUCE

¾ cup sugar
⅛ teaspoon salt
1 tablespoon cornstarch

1 cup boiling water
1 tablespoon butter
¼ teaspoon vanilla

Mix sugar, salt and cornstarch. Cook in boiling water until clear. Add butter and vanilla. Serve hot.

The ancestors of Mrs. H. E. Thrasher, So. Attleboro, Mass., who contributed this recipe, settled in Topsfield, Mass., in the early 1700's and then came to Attleboro in 1730. Mrs. Thrasher can trace this recipe to her father's mother who made it often.

Apple Pudding is made in the same way, substituting apples for huckleberries.

APPLE PUFFETS

[Mrs. Neils C. Anderson, Cumberland Center, Me.]

2 cups flour, sifted
1½ teaspoons baking powder
½ teaspoon salt

2 eggs, beaten
1 cup milk
2 cups chopped apples

Sift dry ingredients, add eggs and milk and beat until smooth. Fill baking cups alternately with a layer of batter and then of chopped apples until cups are ⅔ filled. Steam 1 hour. Serve hot with sweetened and flavored cream. Other fruits may be substituted for the apple. Serves 4.

STEAMED FIG PUDDING

[Mrs. Abner Lowell, Gorham, Me.]

1 pound chopped figs
1 cup suet, chopped
1 cup molasses
¾ cup milk

½ cup sugar
2 eggs
1 teaspoon soda
3 cups pastry flour, sifted

¼ teaspoon salt

Mix ingredients, turn into greased mold or covered baking dish and steam 5 hours. Serve with Hot Lemon Sauce or whipped cream sweetened and flavored with rum or brandy. Serves 6 to 8.

HOT LEMON SAUCE

½ cup sugar
1 tablespoon cornstarch
⅛ teaspoon salt

1 cup boiling water
1 teaspoon grated lemon rind
3 tablespoons lemon juice

3 tablespoons butter

Mix sugar, cornstarch and salt; stir in hot water, gradually; bring to a boil and cook 15 minutes, stirring until thick and clear. Remove from fire, stir in lemon rind, juice and butter. Makes 1¼ cups sauce.

HARRIET'S SUET PUDDING

1 cup soft bread crumbs
½ cup chopped suet
½ cup seeded raisins
1 cup sugar
2 cups flour, sifted
½ cup molasses

½ cup shredded citron
2 apples, chopped fine
3 eggs, beaten
1 teaspoon soda
1 teaspoon allspice
1 teaspoon cinnamon

1 teaspoon salt

Combine ingredients, mixing well. Fill well-greased mold half full. Steam 3 hours. Serve with Hard Sauce (page 203), or Foamy Sauce (page 196). Serves 8.

DESIRE'S BAKED PLUM PUDDING

[*"My great-grandmother's Thanksgiving pudding"—Edith W. Webber, 16 Thorndyke St., Beverly, Mass.*]

1 quart milk, heated
3 tablespoons butter
3 cups bread crumbs
½ teaspoon salt
3 eggs, beaten
1 cup brown sugar

¾ cup molasses
1 pound raisins
½ pound currants
½ teaspoon mace
½ teaspoon cinnamon
⅔ teaspoon clove

Pour hot milk in which butter is melted over bread crumbs, add remaining ingredients and bake 3 to 4 hours in a moderately slow oven (325° F.). Stir once or twice before the crust forms. Serve with Hard Sauce (page 203), or Foamy Sauce (page 196). Serves 8.

DEACON PORTER'S HAT

[Recipe from the Office of the Steward, Mount Holyoke College, South Hadley, Mass.]

1 cup ground suet	2 teaspoons baking powder
1 cup molasses	½ teaspoon salt
1 cup raisins	1 teaspoon cloves
1 cup currants	1 teaspoon cinnamon
3 cups flour, sifted	1½ cups milk
¾ cup chopped nuts (optional)	

Combine suet, molasses, raisins, and currants. Mix and sift dry ingredients. Add to suet mixture alternately with milk, beating until smooth after each addition. Turn into a greased 2-quart mold, cover tightly, and steam 3 hours. Serve hot with hard sauce. Send to the table whole. Serves 10 to 12.

This dessert is well known to students of Mount Holyoke College. Deacon Porter, an early trustee of the college, wore a stovepipe hat, style 1837. This pudding, when it came to the table whole, was given this epithet by some college wag. A light-colored steamed pudding, made in a similar mold, was called Deacon Porter's Summer Hat. Mount Holyoke College, when it was Mount Holyoke Seminary, used to be called "The Minister's Rib Factory" because it turned out so many wives for ministers and missionaries.

Thursday, Sept. 21st. A Boston lady received this day in 1827 a letter from an eminent Bostonian visiting in the South. It was hot down there, he reported, and apologized for writing to her in his shirt sleeves.

From "An Almanac for Bostonians"

YANKEE CHRISTMAS PUDDING

1 loaf day-old bread, with crusts discarded
1/4 pound citron, cut in small pieces
3/4 pound suet, chopped
1 pound currants
1 pound raisins

grated rind 1 lemon
1/4 teaspoon cloves
1 1/2 cups sugar
1 teaspoon salt
3 apples, chopped fine
1 wine glass brandy
6 eggs, beaten

Crumb the bread, mix all ingredients in the order given. Turn into greased 1 1/2-quart mold, cover and steam 6 hours (or steam 4 hours if placed in 2 molds). Serve with Hard Sauce or Foamy Sauce (page 196). Serves 12.

HARD SAUCE

4 tablespoons butter
1 cup confectioners' sugar

1/8 teaspoon salt
1 tablespoon heavy cream

1 teaspoon vanilla, rum, whisky or brandy

Cream butter thoroughly, add sugar gradually and cream together until fluffy. Add cream and vanilla, beating well. Makes about 3/4 cup.

CHOCOLATE MINT CREAM

[From the New England Kitchen of Louis Crathern Russell]

1 cup milk
1 1/2 squares cooking chocolate
4 cream mints
1 tablespoon gelatine

2 tablespoons cold water
1/2 cup sugar
1/4 teaspoon salt
1 cup heavy cream

Scald the milk; in it, dissolve the chocolate and the mints. When dissolved, beat with egg beater to blend the mixture. Add gelatine, previously softened in cold water; then sugar and salt. Cool. Add the cream. Chill until the mixture begins to harden. Whip until the mixture holds its shape. Serve with whipped cream. Serves 4.

MAINE CHOCOLATE PUDDING

1 square chocolate, cut in pieces	⅓ cup sugar
2 cups milk, scalded	⅛ teaspoon salt
2 tablespoons cornstarch or 4	¼ cup cold milk
tablespoons flour	½ teaspoon vanilla

Combine chocolate and scalded milk in top of double boiler until chocolate has melted. Beat with rotary egg beater until well blended. Mix cornstarch (or flour), sugar and salt; stir in the cold milk to make a smooth paste. Stir into the scalded chocolate-milk and continue to stir over boiling water until mixture has thickened. Cover, cook 15 or 20 minutes, remove from stove; add vanilla. Serve cold with thick cream poured gently over the top of the pudding so that delicate scum will not be broken. Serves 4.

LITTLETON PUDDING

[Mrs. R. H. Sawyer, Littleton, Mass.]

2 cups milk	¼ teaspoon salt
2 tablespoons cornstarch	1 egg white, stiffly beaten
¼ cup cold water	⅓ cup shredded coconut
½ cup sugar	1 square chocolate
	1 cup cream, whipped

Heat milk in double boiler; add cornstarch dissolved in cold water, sugar and salt; cook until thick. Remove from stove, add beaten egg white. Divide mixture into 2 parts. To one add coconut, to the other the melted chocolate. Fill sherbet glasses half full of the coconut mixture, top with chocolate mixture. Before serving add sweetened whipped cream. Serves 4.

VERMONT BAKED CUSTARD

[In France they call it Crême Brûlée]

2 cups heavy cream	4 eggs
3 tablespoons maple sugar,	⅛ teaspoon salt
shaved	¼ cup maple sugar, shaved

Put the cream into a saucepan and bring to the boiling point. Beat the eggs slightly with the 3 tablespoons of sugar and salt. Pour the hot cream slowly over this mixture, stirring constantly. Then put in a double boiler over hot water and cook for 5 minutes beating all the time with an egg beater. Pour into a pudding dish and cool. When ready to serve cover the top, gently, with ¼ cup finely shaved maple sugar and place under the broiler until the sugar melts and becomes smooth and glossy and forms a thin hard crust over the soft custard. Serve without sauce. Serves 4 to 6.

PUMPKIN CUSTARD

[From the New England Kitchen of Louise Crathern Russell]

2 cups milk	½ cup light brown sugar
1 teaspoon butter	¾ teaspoon salt
3 eggs, beaten	¾ teaspoon cinnamon
1 cup pumpkin, strained	

Scald milk, add butter, eggs, sugar, salt, cinnamon and pumpkin. Pour into baking dish or individual molds and set in a pan of hot water. Bake in a moderate oven (350° F.) about 40 minutes or until blade of a knife inserted in center does not adhere. Serve warm or chilled.

SALEM CUSTARD SOUFFLE

2 tablespoons butter
2 tablespoons flour
1 cup milk
4 eggs, separated

3 tablespoons sugar
½ teaspoon vanilla
¼ teaspoon almond extract
⅛ teaspoon salt

Cream the butter and the flour; heat the milk and pour it gradually over the butter and flour. Cook 8 minutes in a double boiler, stirring often. Beat egg yolks well; add sugar, flavorings and salt and stir in. Fold in egg whites stiffly beaten. Turn into greased baking dish and place in a pan of hot water. Bake in a moderate oven (350° F.) 50 to 60 minutes or until firm. Serve at once from baking dish with sweetened whipped cream, flavored with sherry, strawberry sauce or soft maple sugar. Serves 6.

QUAKING CUSTARD

[*A 100-year old recipe from Westfield, Mass. Also called Spanish Cream.*]

1 tablespoon gelatine
2 tablespoons cold water
⅓ cup sugar
½ teaspoon salt

2 egg yolks, slightly beaten
2 cups milk, scalded
2 egg whites, stiffly beaten
1 teaspoon vanilla

Soak gelatine in cold water for 5 minutes. Mix sugar and salt and egg yolks and pour the scalded milk over this mixture. Return to top of double boiler, stir over hot water until mixture coats spoon. Pour over gelatine and stir until gelatine is dissolved. Chill until slightly thickened, then fold in egg whites and vanilla. Turn into mold. Cool until firm. Unmold. Serve with cream. Serves 6.

Add a half a cup of macaroon crumbs to the cooked custard and pour over macaroons for a variation. Replace vanilla with ¼ teaspoon almond extract.

MAPLE CUSTARD

[*Mrs. R. H. Sawyer, Littleton, Mass.*]

3 eggs, beaten   2 cups milk
½ cup maple syrup   dash of salt

Combine eggs, syrup, milk and salt. Pour into individual molds. Set molds in a pan of hot water. Bake in a moderate oven (350° F.) about 40 minutes, or until blade of a knife inserted in center does not adhere. Serve warm or chilled. Serves 4.

Although not popular today, a favorite dessert several generations ago was Minute Pudding. Scald 3 cups milk and pour over mixture of 1 cup cold milk blended with ¾ cup flour and 1 teaspoon salt. Return to double boiler for 20 minutes. Serve with maple syrup or honey. Serves 6 to 8.

SEA MOSS BLANC MANGE

½ cup sea moss   ⅛ teaspoon salt
3 cups milk   1 teaspoon vanilla or lemon

Soak moss 15 minutes in cold water; pick out discolored pieces. Add moss to milk and cook in double boiler 25 minutes. Strain. Add salt and flavoring. Turn into individual molds. Chill, unmold and serve with crushed, sweetened berries or sliced bananas and cream. Serves 5.

Our forefathers used to gather sea moss, dry it and keep it for years.

TIPSY PARSON

Arrange slices of sponge cake on individual plates. Moisten each piece with 2 tablespoons sherry. Pour chilled custard sauce over each serving.

MAPLE CHARLOTTE

1 tablespoon gelatine   2 cups maple syrup
½ cup cold water   2 cups heavy cream, whipped

Dissolve gelatine in cold water. Heat maple syrup and add gelatine. Let stand until the mixture begins to thicken. Fold in whipped cream. Pour into individual serving glasses. Sprinkle with chopped butternuts, if desired, and serve ice cold. Serves 6.

SYLLABUB

[Mary N. Cabral, 3495 Riverside Ave., Somerset, Mass.]

1 pint heavy cream, beaten stiff   whites 2 eggs, beaten stiff
½ cup confectioners' sugar   1 glass white wine (sweet
                                      Madeira or Sauterne)

Fold in half the sugar with the cream, the remainder with the eggs. Mix well, add the wine slowly. Serve over Trifle, lady fingers, macaroons, sponge cake or sliced bananas.

TRIFLE

Put slices of sponge cake together, sandwich fashion, with strawberry jam. Cover with a soft custard, delicately flavored with almond extract. Serve with Syllabub. Trifle is also made with macaroons softened with custard and served with Syllabub.

CIDER JELLY

[From the New England Kitchen of Louise Crathern Russell]

2 tablespoons gelatine   2 cups boiling sweet cider
½ cup cold water   ¾ cup sugar
              ⅓ cup lemon juice

Dissolve gelatine in cold water for 5 minutes. Add remaining ingredients in order given. Pour in a mold and chill. Unmold and serve with whipped cream. Sprinkle with nutmeg. Serves 4.

※※

MAPLE MOUSSE

2 eggs, separated   ½ cup maple syrup
⅛ teaspoon salt   ½ pint cream, whipped

Beat yolks of eggs until lemon-colored; add salt, add maple syrup and cook in top of double boiler until mixture thickens. Cool. Beat egg whites, until stiff. Combine maple syrup mixture, egg whites and cream. Freeze. Serves 6.

Smith College girls in the early 1900's were fond of this dessert.

※※

COFFEE MOUSSE

[Grace Ross, Northampton, Mass.]

1 cup strong coffee   ⅛ teaspoon salt
1 cup milk   ½ tablespoon flour
1 cup sugar   4 eggs, separated
1 pint cream, whipped

Use 4 tablespoons of coffee to 1 cup water in making coffee so that it will be very strong. Add milk to coffee and heat. Combine sugar and salt and flour and stir into coffee mixture. Cook, stirring constantly, until it reaches the boiling point. Pour over the well-beaten yolks of the eggs and cook in the top of double boiler until mixture thickens. Cool. Add egg whites, beaten stiff, and cream. Freeze. Serves 8 to 10.

RHUBARB ICE CREAM

[Parker House, Boston, Mass.]

2 cups water   2⅓ cups sugar
2½ pounds rhubarb, cut in pieces   4 cups heavy cream, whipped

Add water to rhubarb and boil 5 to 10 minutes. Add sugar; cool and add cream. Pack in freezer in finely chopped ice and rock salt and freeze. Makes about 2 quarts ice cream.

CONCORD GRAPE ICE CREAM

[Parker House, Boston, Mass.]

1 pound Concord grapes   ½ pound Tokay grapes
½ pound Malaga grapes   2⅓ cups sugar
½ pound seedless grapes   4 cups heavy cream, whipped

Pick grapes from stems; wash. Heat the grapes but do not boil; press the mixture through a sieve. Combine grape juice, sugar; cool and add cream. Pack in freezer in finely chopped ice and rock salt and freeze. Makes about 2 quarts.

ORANGE PINEAPPLE ICE CREAM

[Grace Ross, Northampton, Mass.]

1 cup crushed pineapple   1½ cups sugar
1 cup orange juice   1 cup milk
            ½ pint cream, whipped

Mix pineapple, orange juice and sugar and let stand overnight. Add milk and cream. Freeze. Serves 6.

LEMON SHERBET

[Mrs. Silas Snow, Williamsburg, Mass.]

2 cups sugar	juice 2 lemons
½ teaspoon lemon extract	4 cups milk
2 egg whites, beaten stiff	

Mix sugar, extract and juice. Add milk and egg whites. Pack at once in freezer in finely chopped ice and rock salt and freeze. Serves 8.

BERRY SAUCE

[Miss Lillian V. Dearborn, 55 Beach Ave., Melrose, Mass.]

1 cup sugar	1 cup mashed berries
¼ cup soft butter	(strawberries, raspberries,
1 egg white	blueberries)

Beat sugar and butter to a cream; add egg white beaten to a froth. Stir in mashed berries. Makes 2 cups sauce.

MAPLE SAUCE FOR VANILLA ICE CREAM

[Mrs. Silas Snow, Williamsburg, Mass.]

Boil maple syrup to 227° F. or until it spins a fine short thread when dropped from spoon. Cool slightly and pour over ice cream.

COLONIAL PUDDING SAUCE

[To eat on Deep Dish Apple Pie or Steamed Blueberry or Apple Pudding or Bean Pot Apples]

3 cups rich heavy cream   ⅔ cups soft maple sugar

Stir cream and maple sugar and thoroughly blend. Flavor with grated nutmeg.

IN THE NAME OF THE GREAT JEHOVAH
AND THE CONTINENTAL CONGRESS
—Ethan Allen.

Frederic F. Van de Water

The first New Englanders brought to this land a dismal culinary heritage. They found on arrival that they must apply the rules, if any, of English cooking to the odd provender on which the Indians managed to live. Some of the Pilgrim Fathers starved to death but none of them as far as I am aware perished of dyspepsia, wherein lies the substance of miracle.

Yankee subjugation of an excessively inhospitable wilderness was an accomplishment no more valorous and resourceful than the creation by early New Englanders of more than savory foods out of less than palatable materials.

Britishers who have been reared in the midst of plenty for fifty generations persist, even now, in the ritualistic murder of foodstuffs. New Englanders who inhabit a grudging and infertile land have confronted from the first staples which in their native state were insipid or worse and have transformed these into some of the fairest adornments of the American table.

No one knows the name of the psalm-singing Lucullus who first blended materials so discordant as dry beans, salt pork, and molasses into mighty culinary harmony. The rash adventurer who laid hold upon pumpkin and glorified it in pie also remains anonymous. So do the original authors of brown bread, codfish balls, cranberry sauce, hasty pudding.

Nothing in the Yankee epic is more edifying than the canto which deals with his kitchen prowess. Despite his reputed scorn of matters of the flesh, the New Englander always has fed himself well in the face of tremendous handicaps. If the rest of the nation sees in the lean, short-spoken native of the North East no trace of the sybarite, that is America's and not the Yankee's fault. Wherever he has gone, the New Englander's "rule"—not "recipe"—book has accompanied him.

Vermont, latest of the New England states, shared from the beginning in a common culinary heritage. We accord due honor to traditional Yankee dishes. We even still observe the generally outmoded custom which decrees that boiled salmon and fresh green peas are the only proper elements for Fourth of July's dinner. In the production of typical New England fare we sometimes outstrip our sister commonwealths. Vermont turkeys surpass all rivals in succulence and flavor. We have altered other viands the better to suit the Green Mountaineer's acute sense of taste. Our epicurean appreciation of maple syrup runs straight from the sugar house into the kitchen.

Syrup, like wine, has its vintage years. The variation may not be perceptible to the untutored but the Vermonter knows and keeps the best in store.

We regard most highly that pale golden fluid—and the paler the better—which the earliest sap run yields. It has delicate bouquet perceptible to the trained taste. When the Philistine customer turns back the first run syrup he has received and demands more body and color to his purchase, Vermont scorn is unutterable, though I have heard men strive to voice it.

As for the nefarious practice of blending maple with cane or corn syrup, the very thought makes Vermonters shudder. It is iniquity comparable to brightening Romanée Conti with a lacing of vanilla extract.

Esteem for maple syrup influences much of Vermont's cooking. We use it instead of molasses in our baked beans and these, in consequence, have flavor not to be found elsewhere. Maple sugar gives squash and pumpkin pies additional savor that raises them to ambrosia's level. Maple cream, produced by checking sugaring just before the mass solidifies, is another typical Vermont delicacy.

During the sap run, "sugar-on-snow suppers" burgeon in this region. Boiling sap is poured to congeal upon bowls of mounded snow. These are served with doughnuts which form stomachic foundation for such intense sweetness and with pickles to preserve appetites that otherwise might be cloyed. Technically, this constitutes a meal; more accurately, it is an adventure in the intricacies of taste.

Further adventures wait him who comes humbly into a Vermont kitchen. There is the crock of "filled cookies," fat crumbly cakes with interiors of chopped and lemon-flavored raisins. Cider jelly, brown, tart, flavorous, is rated by the old line Vermonter above cranberry sauce as an accompaniment to turkey. Vermont corn, ground to meal between the stones of a water mill, has distinctive fragrance and palatability.

No one has written a poem to sliced salt pork, fried brown and then drenched in cream gravy; or to creamed codfish with a yellow star of molten butter in the middle of the bowl and a baked potato gaping open on your plate and awaiting inundation. There are worse and more tediously exploited lyrical subjects.

When the hog has been butchered in the fall and the lard has been tried and the kettle's contents have been strained into pails, the wise Vermonter rescues the scraps of solid matter that remain, salts them and spreads them on paper to dry. Crisp, golden, savory, these ultimate vestiges of pig are ordained to be nibbled between draughts of hot buttered rum. The god who has Vermont appetites in his care is a lavish and ingenious deity.

"Sarm" Wallace was a well-to-do farmer with only two children to raise. His barns were well filled with stock and his gardens were made to yield a-plenty. Mrs. "Sarm" was a famous cook and did full justice to Sarm's supplies. A poor neighbor, Lyme Millen, who had numerous boys and girls, often worked for him. On one occasion Mrs. "Sarm" invited Lyme to eat dinner with them. Lyme was a bit diffident about accepting. His would-be hostess spoke up, "Better come eat; ye can git yer goodies when yer git home." Telling it afterward Lyme remarked, "Consarned old fool knew I didn't have anything but salt pork an' 'taters."

SOUR MILK CHEESE

[Called also Dutch, Curd, Cottage Cheese and Connecticut Pot Cheese]

1 quart thick sour milk   ½ teaspoon salt
1 tablespoon soft butter   pepper
     1 tablespoon cream

Place the milk in a pan on the back of the stove or over hot water until curd has separated from the whey. Spread a cheese cloth over a strainer, pour in the milk, lift the edges of the cloth and draw them together; drain or squeeze quite dry. There will be about ⅔ cup of curd. Add the butter, salt, pepper and cream. A little minced onion or chopped parsley or chives may also be added.

In Connecticut they call thick sour milk "loppered" milk. In Massachusetts they refer to it as "clabbered" milk.

There is an old tale, probably unfounded, but none the less charming, about the Island groups and how they got their names. The fable has it that they were owned by a man with three daughters. He was getting old and parceled them off to his daughters thus: to his favorite he gave his most productive island—Martha's vineyard; and to his next he gave the islands near to home—Elizabeth's islands; to his last daughter, Nan, he offered what was left and so— Nan-tuck-it!

PIES

YANKEE PIE CRUST

[for 1 two-crust (9-inch) pie]

2½ cups flour, sifted
¾ teaspoon salt

¾ cup shortening
¼ cup cold water (about)

Mix and sift flour and salt; cut in shortening until the size of a pea. Add water gradually, stirring with a fork. Use only enough water to hold dough together, putting to one side pieces of dough as soon as formed. Shape into a ball and chill thoroughly, first wrapping dough in waxed paper. Roll on lightly floured board, using as little flour as possible. Roll the dough in one direction only and do not stretch the dough. Pie crust may be made in advance and kept in a cool place.

Do not grease the pan. Remember the old saying, "A good pie crust greases its own tin."

TO MAKE A PYE WITH PIPPINS

[The Compleat Cook's Guide—1683]

"Pare your pippins, and cut out the cores, then make your coffin of crust. Take a good handful of quinces sliced and lay at the bottom, then lay your pippins on top, and fill the holes where the core was taken out with syrup of quinces, and put into every pippin a piece of orangado, then pour on top the syrup of quinces, then put in sugar, and so close it up, let it be very well baked, for it will ask much soaking, especially the quinces."

MAPLE APPLE PIE

1½ quarts apples, peeled and
    sliced thin
1 cup soft maple sugar
¼ teaspoon salt

¼ teaspoon cinnamon
1 tablespoon flour
2 tablespoons butter
cream

Have pie pan lined with pastry. Put in sliced tart apples. Spread over them maple sugar, salt, cinnamon, and flour; dot with butter. Cover with perforated top crust, brush with cream and bake in a hot oven (450° F.) for 10 minutes; then reduce heat to moderate (350° F.) and bake 40 to 50 minutes longer. Makes 1 two-crust (9-inch) pie.

PRIZE NEW ENGLAND APPLE PIE

[*The apple pie state champions of the six New England states met at Worcester, Mass., January 5, 1939, to compete for New England honors. First prize went to Connecticut; second to New Hampshire and third to Maine. The prize winner, Mrs. Henry Delay, Harwinton, Conn., contributes her recipe as follows*]:

⅔ cup lard
2 cups all-purpose flour, not sifted
1½ teaspoons salt
¼ cup cold water

6 to 8 tart apples
1 cup sugar
cinnamon and nutmeg
2 tablespoons butter
2 tablespoons heavy cream

Mix lard, flour and salt, leaving a few lumps the size of a pea in order to make crust flaky. Pour water over mixture gradually, working it in with a fork. With hands shape mixture into a ball. Divide into two parts for upper and lower crust. Pare, core and slice apples, fill pan to slightly rounding. Pour sugar on top of apples. Add a shaking of both cinnamon and nutmeg. Cut butter into small pieces and dot the top. Shake a little additional salt over all. (If apples are juicy a sift or two of flour and a little additional sugar on lower crust should be added before apples are placed in pie.) Moisten edges of crust and put top crust in place. Press and crimp edges. Gloss crust with heavy cream. Bake in a hot oven (450° F.) 15 to 20 minutes. Reduce heat to (350° F.) and bake 30 to 40 minutes longer.

MAINE CRAB APPLE PIE

[*Mrs. Merle Towle, Intervale, Me.*]

3 cups unpeeled crab apples, cored and quartered
1½ cups sugar
¼ teaspoon salt
¼ cup cold water

Have a pie pan lined with pastry. Put in apples. Sprinkle sugar and salt and water over them. Cover with top crust and bake in a hot oven (450° F.) for 10 minutes; then reduce heat to moderate (350° F.) and bake 40 to 50 minutes longer. Makes 1 two-crust (8-inch) pie. The flavor is delicious and the color a lovely pink.

PORK APPLE PIE

[Mrs. Wm. Dodge, Alderdale Farm, Canterbury, N. H.]

> 8 to 10 tart apples, peeled, cored and sliced
> 20 pieces of fat salt pork, cut the size of peas
> ¾ cup sugar (maple sugar preferred)
> ½ teaspoon cinnamon
> ¼ teaspoon nutmeg
> ¼ teaspoon salt

Fill a deep dish with apples. Mix salt pork, sugar, spices and salt and sprinkle the mixture over the apples. Cover with pie crust. Cut slits for steam to escape. Bake in a hot oven (450° F.) for 10 minutes; then reduce heat to moderate (350° F.) and bake 30 to 35 minutes longer. If crust becomes brown, cover with brown paper so that it will remain a golden brown. While pie is baking, blend a package of cream cheese with 1 tablespoon thick cream and allow to become firm in refrigerator. Serve pie warm with slice of cheese.

Old-time New Englanders used salt pork from soup to dessert. This recipe is said to have been made first by an old fisherman who used dried apples, salt pork and molasses. His wife improved upon it, using fresh apples and maple sugar. It became a popular dish, often served in Vermont homes for the Sunday evening meal. Calvin Coolidge, in the White House, extolled its goodness. Pork Pie has a more succulent flavor than ordinary apple pie.

VERMONT FRIED APPLE PIES

[Mrs. A. A. Durham, 200 Fern St., W. Hartford, Conn.]

½ teaspoon salt
2 cups flour

3 tablespoons butter
½ cup milk (about)

Add salt to flour, cut in shortening; add milk to make a dough a little softer than pie crust. Roll thin and cut in rounds about the size of a saucer. In the center of each place a spoonful of thick spiced applesauce. Fold over, wet edges with milk and seal with fork. Fry in hot deep fat (370° F.) until golden brown. Drain. May be dusted with powdered sugar and served hot with maple syrup or cream; may also be stored in a jar and warmed over when needed. Makes 4 turnovers.

These pies were often made with dried apples. Early in the fall apples were peeled, sliced in eighths, strung on twine and hung on the clothesline in the sun or laid on the oven after the heat was turned off. Or, sometimes a sheet was spread on a piazza roof and the apples were placed on the sheet for 4 days, but always taken in at night, in case of rain. Some of the old recipes call for the addition of 1 egg and 1 teaspoon baking powder to the milk. Doughnut dough is also used by many old-time cooks.

MINCE PIE

Use 2 cups mincemeat. Bake between 2 crusts.

In Colonial days New England housewives often baked as many as 100 pies at a time, stacked them in big jars, and stored them in a shed where they'd freeze. When a pie was wanted it was placed in the pie cupboard in the fireplace chimney and thawed out.

MINCEMEAT

[Mrs. B. S. Patt, 161 River Ave., Providence, R. I.]

3 pounds lean beef, chopped fine
2 pounds suet, chopped fine
3 quarts apples finely chopped
3 pounds seeded raisins, chopped
2 pounds currants
1 pound citron, cut in small
 pieces
½ cup candied orange peel,
 chopped
½ cup candied lemon peel,
 chopped
½ cup lemon juice

¼ cup orange juice
2 tablespoons salt
4 cups sugar
1 cup coffee
2 cups cider (not too new)
1 teaspoon cloves
1 teaspoon allspice
2 teaspoons cinnamon
3 cups brandy (1 bottle about
 ¼ size)
1 cup sherry
1 cup currant jelly

Mix all ingredients except brandy and sherry, and cook 2 hours; when cool, not cold, add liquor; let stand in crock a week before using. This makes about 12 quarts and will keep indefinitely in a cool place. This recipe came from Maine and is very old.

> *Most old-timers make mince meat more or less "by guess and by gory," or, as one cook put it, "I just hove a little of this and a little of that in my mincemeat. Came out first rate, too."*

CRANBERRY MINCE PIE

[A modern Cape Cod recipe]

Stir contents 1 can cranberry sauce until it is broken into pieces. Combine with 1 cup mince meat. Fill an 8-inch unbaked pastry shell and criss-cross the top with strips of pastry making a lattice-work upper crust. Bake in a hot oven (450° F.) 10 minutes; then reduce heat to moderate (350° F.) and bake 25 minutes longer. Makes 1 two-crust (8-inch) pie.

COOLIDGE MINCE MEAT

[Household Department of the Boston "Post"]

½ peck apples
½ pound currants
2 pounds seeded raisins
½ pound citron, diced small

2 pounds sugar
2½ quarts cider
1 pound boiled beef, diced
1 pound suet, cut small

½ teaspoon salt

Pare, core and chop the apples fine. Chop together the currants, raisins and citron; add the apples, sugar and cider and boil about 4 minutes. Add meat and suet and simmer about 1 hour, stirring frequently to prevent burning. Add salt, last. Season to taste with cinnamon, cloves and nutmeg. A little jelly or fruit juice will improve the flavor. Use 2 cups for a 9-inch pie. Makes about 5 quarts.

This is the recipe of Miss Aurora Pierce, who was housekeeper for Col. John C. Coolidge, father of the President.

CRANBERRY RAISIN PIE

[A Cape Cod recipe, sometimes called Mock Cherry Pie]

1 cup cranberries, coarsely
   chopped
1 cup raisins, coarsely chopped
1 cup sugar

1 tablespoon flour
¼ cup boiling water
⅛ teaspoon salt
¼ teaspoon vanilla

Line pie plate with pastry. Mix sugar, flour, and salt; add water and vanilla, then raisins. Beat smoothly and add cranberries and turn into pastry-lined plate. Top with a lattice of pastry strips. Bake in a hot oven (450° F.) 10 minutes; reduce heat to moderate (350° F.) and bake 30 to 40 minutes longer. Makes 1 two-crust (8-inch) pie.

MOCK MINCE PIE

[An 80-year-old recipe]

1 cup rolled cracker crumbs	½ cup butter
1 cup vinegar	1 teaspoon cinnamon
1 cup water	1 teaspoon cloves
1 cup raisins	¼ teaspoon salt
1 cup molasses	⅔ cup sugar

Cook slowly a few minutes until it is the consistency of mince meat. Bake between 2 crusts, following directions for baking mince pie.

"One of the brothers in my grandmother's family had some Mock Mince Pie at the home of a friend, and he liked it so much that he brought the recipe home. My grandmother made it, also my mother, and now I use it," writes Clara E. Langdon, 66 Elizabeth Street, Pittsfield, Mass.

GREEN TOMATO MINCE MEAT

8 quarts green tomatoes	2 pounds seeded raisins
3 pounds brown sugar	1 tablespoon clove
1 cup vinegar	1 tablespoon cinnamon
1 teaspoon salt	1 tablespoon nutmeg
1 pint boiled cider	1 tablespoon allspice

Cook all together about 2¼ hours. Put in jars and seal. Makes 5 quart jars.

UNCOOKED BLUEBERRY PIE

1 pastry shell previously baked   2 cups berries, washed and
1 cup whipped cream   drained
½ cup powdered sugar

When ready to serve, fill shell with berries, sprinkle with the powdered sugar, cover with the whipped cream.

BLUEBERRY PIE

4 cups blueberries, washed and   1½ cups sugar
    drained   1½ tablespoons flour
⅛ teaspoon salt   1 tablespoon butter
milk

Mix all ingredients thoroughly. Line plate with pastry, fill with blueberries and dot with butter; adjust top crust, brush with milk and bake in a hot oven (450° F.) 10 minutes; then reduce heat to moderate (350° F.) and bake 25 minutes longer. Makes 1 two-crust (9-inch) pie.

DEEP BLUEBERRY PIE

[From the New England Kitchen of Louise Crathern Russell]

4 cups blueberries   ¼ teaspoon salt
1½ cups sugar

Combine berries, salt and sugar in a deep baking dish with no under crust. Put an inverted cup in the middle. This serves to keep the crust up so that it will not be soaked with the juices. Put on top crust. Bake in a hot oven (450° F.) 10 minutes; then reduce the heat to moderate (350° F.) and bake 35 minutes longer. Serve hot with cottage cheese. Makes 1 deep dish (9-inch) pie.

CHERRY PIE

[*A Vermont recipe*]

3 cups cherries
⅔ to 1¼ cups sugar (according
   to the acidity of the fruit)
¼ teaspoon salt

1 tablespoon quick cooking
   tapioca
1 tablespoon butter

Place the cherries in an unbaked pie shell. Sprinkle over them a mixture of sugar, tapioca and salt and stir quickly until they are well coated. Dot with butter. Cover with a top crust or lattice crust. Bake in a hot oven (450° F.) for 10 minutes; then reduce heat to medium (350° F.) and bake 25 minutes longer. Makes 1 two-crust pie.

Rhubarb, Gooseberry, Blueberry, Strawberry may be made following this same recipe. For Rhubarb Pie use peeled diced rhubarb.

MOCK CHERRY PIE

1 cup cranberries, washed and
   looked over
¾ cup raisins
1 cup sugar

2 teaspoons flour
⅛ teaspoon salt
1 tablespoon butter

Cut cranberries in halves; mix together cranberries, raisins and dry ingredients and turn into an unbaked pastry shell; dot with butter and adjust top crust or criss-cross lattice crust. Bake in a hot oven (450° F.) 10 minutes; then reduce heat to moderate (350° F.) and bake 25 minutes longer. Makes 1 two-crust (7-inch) pie.

Greta Henderson, Winter Street, Portland, Me., says in a dog-eared book belonging to her grandmother she found this note appended to the recipe for Mock Cherry Pie. "Here is a good pie to go with fried potatoes for breakfast."

CAPE COD CRANBERRY PIE

3½ cups cranberries, washed and   1½ tablespoons flour
    looked over   ¼ teaspoon salt
1½ cups sugar   3 tablespoons water
2 tablespoons melted butter

Chop cranberries and mix with remaining ingredients. Fill an unbaked pie crust with the mixture and arrange strips of pie crust criss-cross over the top. Bake in a hot oven (450° F.) 10 minutes; then reduce heat to moderate (350° F.) and bake 40 minutes longer. Makes one (9-inch) pie.

A cranberry pie wouldn't taste right to a Cape Codder unless it was covered with a criss-cross lattice crust.

PRUNE AND APRICOT PIE

1½ cups cooked prunes   1 teaspoon lemon juice
½ cup cooked apricots   2 tablespoons prune juice
½ cup sugar   2 tablespoons apricot juice
1 tablespoon flour   1 tablespoon butter

Cut prunes and apricots in small pieces, add sugar. Place in an unbaked pie shell, sprinkled with flour. Combine lemon juice, prune juice and apricot juice and pour over fruit. Dot with butter. Place top crust on pie and bake in a hot oven (450° F.) 10 minutes, then reduce heat to moderate (350° F.) and bake 20 to 25 minutes longer. Makes 1 two-crust (7-inch) pie. If fruit is sweetened omit the sugar.

PEACH PIE

[The Howland Family, South Dartmouth, Mass.]

Line a deep pie dish with unbaked pastry. Peel ripe, juicy peaches, do not remove the pits. Fill pie dish with the peaches. Sprinkle

½ cup sugar over peaches. Lay the upper crust on very gently. Do not press it to the lower crust on the edge. When the pie is baked lift the upper crust carefully and pour in a filling.

FILLING

2 egg whites, stiffly beaten   1 tablespoon sugar
¾ cup rich milk, scalded   ½ teaspoon corn starch
2 tablespoons milk

Stir the egg whites into the milk, add the sugar and the corn starch dissolved in the 2 tablespoons milk. Cook in the top of a double boiler 5 minutes. Cool. This filling should be cold when poured over hot pie. Replace the crust, allow pie to cool, eat while slightly warm.

Apple pies are often baked in a similar manner. The apples are sliced and placed in the pie without sugar or spices. The top crust is removed, sugar, cinnamon and nutmeg are added and the top crust replaced. The uncooked sugar gives a fresher flavor to the apples and there is no juice to cook out. Honey is sometimes used in place of sugar.

CONCORD GRAPE PIE

1 cup sugar   1 egg, beaten
2 tablespoons flour   2 cups Concord grapes, cut
¼ teaspoon salt   and seeded but not skinned
2 tablespoons butter

Combine sugar, flour and salt; add egg and mix with grapes. Place in an unbaked pie shell and dot with butter. Add upper crust. Bake in a hot oven (450° F.) for 10 minutes. Reduce heat to moderate (350° F.) and bake 20 minutes longer. Makes 1 two-crust (7-inch) pie.

STRAWBERRY CHIFFON PIE

[Toll House, Whitman, Mass.]

1 tablespoon gelatine	½ teaspoon salt
¼ cup water	1 cup strawberry pulp and
4 eggs, separated	juice
½ cup sugar	¼ cup sugar
1 tablespoon lemon juice	whipped cream
garnish of strawberries	

Soak gelatine in water for 5 minutes. Beat egg yolks, slightly; add ¼ cup sugar, lemon juice and salt. Cook over boiling water until of custard consistency. Add softened gelatine, stirring thoroughly. Then add strawberry pulp. (A little red coloring gives a pleasing color to the pie.) Cool, and when mixture begins to congeal fold in the stiffly beaten whites of the eggs to which has been added the ¼ cup sugar. Fill baked pie shell and chill. Before serving spread a thin layer of whipped cream over pie and garnish with strawberries. Makes 1 one-crust (9-inch) pie.

RHUBARB PIE

[A Rhode Island recipe]

1 tablespoon butter	2 eggs, separated
1¼ cups sugar	1 tablespoon flour
2 cups rhubarb cut in ½-inch	4 tablespoons sugar
pieces but not peeled	

Melt the butter, add 1 cup of the sugar and rhubarb, cook until the rhubarb is slightly softened and the sugar melted. Add the egg yolks, beaten slightly. Mix the remaining ¼ cup sugar with the flour and add. Cook until rhubarb is of a jelly-like consistency. Pour into baked pie shell and top with meringue made by gradually beating sugar into beaten egg whites. Brown in a slow oven (300° F.) about 15 minutes. Makes 1 one-crust (8-inch) pie.

For Strawberry Rhubarb Pie substitute 1 cup strawberries for 1 cup of the rhubarb.

GREEN CURRANT PIE

1 scant quart mixed green and half-ripe currants	1½ cups sugar 2 tablespoons flour

Wash and stem currants. Mix sugar and flour and sprinkle over currants. Line a pie plate with pastry; fill with fruit and adjust top crust, sealing edges carefully as this pie is very juicy. Bake in a hot oven (450° F.) 10 minutes; then reduce heat to moderate (350° F.) and bake 25 to 30 minutes longer. Makes 1 two-crust (9-inch) pie.

This recipe was given to Mrs. Clifton Johnson, Hockanum, Hadley, Mass., by her mother-in-law. Mrs. Johnson comments: "Pie timber is often scarce on a farm in the spring and early summer and I imagine this recipe was born of necessity but it surely is good! My oldest son was in the Marines during the World War. A favorite topic of the boys at the time was what they would like to eat when the war was over. His longing was for green currant pie. Convalescents in the family, when asked what they would relish, often answered, 'Green Currant Pie,' thereby startling the doctor or nurse. I would say this pie has 'it' if anything culinary has that elusive thing."

Spring Fashion Note: In 1880 the "Traveller" announced that Miladies' new hats looked "like crushed hansom cabs."

PRIZE-WINNING DATE PIE

[Mrs. Hazel C. Johnson, Stoneham, Mass.]

1 pound pitted dates	2 eggs, slightly beaten
3 cups milk	¼ teaspoon salt
	1 tablespoon sugar

Cook dates in 2 cups of the milk in the top of a double boiler until tender. Press through a sieve. Add remaining cup of milk, eggs, salt and sugar. Pour into an unbaked pie shell. Bake in a hot oven (450° F.) 10 minutes; then reduce heat to moderate (350° F.) and bake 25 minutes longer, or until knife comes out clean when inserted in custard. Cool. Makes 1 one-crust large (10-inch) pie.

Some cooks cover this pie with meringue; others with whipped cream. Many prefer it plain.

APPLE CUSTARD PIE

1½ cups applesauce	3 eggs, beaten
½ cup sugar	¼ teaspoon salt
½ teaspoon cinnamon	1½ cups milk

Mix applesauce, sugar, cinnamon, eggs, salt and milk. Line a pie plate with pastry. Pour apple custard mixture into crust and bake in a hot oven (450° F.) 10 minutes. Then reduce heat to moderate (350° F.) and bake 25 to 30 minutes longer or until knife inserted comes out clean. Makes 1 one-crust (9-inch) pie.

Adapted from recipes contributed by Mrs. G. E. Plummer, Route 5, Portland, Maine, and Mrs. A. A. Banton, 67 Palm St., Bangor, Maine, who report: "This is the kind of pies to which the girls treated their 'best fellers' fifty years ago, when Pa was courtin' Ma."

CUSTARD PIE

[A Rhode Island recipe]

2 whole eggs and 2 egg yolks,
    slightly beaten
½ cup sugar
¼ teaspoon salt

⅛ teaspoon nutmeg
½ teaspoon vanilla
2 cups milk, scalded

Combine eggs with sugar and salt. Flavor with nutmeg and vanilla, add hot milk. Line pie plate with pastry; brush with egg white and allow to dry in refrigerator. Pour in custard filling; bake in a hot oven (450° F.) for 10 minutes, then reduce heat to moderate (350° F.) and continue baking 30 minutes longer or until knife inserted comes out clean. Cool. Makes 1 one-crust (9-inch) pie.

MAPLE CUSTARD PIE

1 cup maple sugar, packed
2 tablespoons butter
1½ cups milk, scalded
1 tablespoon cornstarch

½ cup milk
3 eggs, slightly beaten
½ teaspoon salt
sprinkling of nutmeg

Have pie pan lined with pastry with fluted edge. Fill with custard prepared thus: heat maple sugar and butter until they bubble, add scalded milk and stir until sugar is dissolved. Add cornstarch which has been dissolved in cold milk, eggs, and salt. Sprinkle nutmeg over top. Bake 10 minutes in a hot oven (450° F.), then reduce heat and finish baking in moderate oven (350° F.) for about 25 minutes, or until knife inserted comes out clean. (Grandmother used to test this pie with a broom straw.)

THE "MASON GIRLS" ROSE CUSTARD PIE

[A New Hampshire recipe]

4 egg yolks	¼ teaspoon salt
2 egg whites	3 cups milk, scalded
1 cup sugar	½ teaspoon rose flavoring
1½ teaspoons flour	2 egg whites, beaten stiff
¼ teaspoon ginger	2 tablespoons sugar

Line a 9-inch pie plate with unbaked pastry. Combine yolks and 2 egg whites and beat; mix sugar, flour, ginger and salt and add the eggs; stir in milk gradually. Add flavoring. Pour into pastry and bake in a hot oven (450° F.) 10 minutes; then reduce heat to moderate (350° F.) and bake 25 to 30 minutes longer or until knife inserted comes out clean. Cool, frost with meringue made by adding sugar to beaten egg whites. Brown in oven (300° F.). Makes 1 one-crust (9-inch) pie.

This pie was made by the "Mason Girls" who were forever playing with a ouija board. One night (so the story goes) it moved forcibly when they were playing and spelled out that a dear relative was dead—which proved true. Years later, when the house was remodeled, the ouija board was found hidden in a partition. They had never used it since that night.

COOLIDGE LEMON CUSTARD PIE

2 eggs, separated	⅛ teaspoon salt
juice and grated rind 1 lemon	4 teaspoons flour
1 cup sugar	1 teaspoon melted butter
1 cup milk	

Beat the egg yolks until thick and lemon colored. Add the lemon juice and rind, sugar, salt, flour and milk. Last, fold in the egg whites, beaten stiff. Pour into an unbaked pastry shell (with the edges fluted) and bake in a hot oven (450° F.) 10 minutes; reduce heat to moderate (350° F.) and bake 20 minutes longer.

This recipe was contributed by Miss B. B. Forsyth, 226 Beech Ave., Melrose, Mass. It came from Vermont and was a favorite custard pie of the late President Coolidge.

LEMON MERINGUE PIE

[*Parker House, Boston, Mass.*]

¾ cup sugar
⅛ teaspoon salt
3 tablespoons cornstarch
1 cup boiling water

⅓ cup lemon juice
2 egg yolks, slightly beaten
1 teaspoon butter
meringue

Mix the sugar, cornstarch and salt; stir in the boiling water gradually, pour the mixture into a saucepan and stir until it thickens. Beat the egg yolks slightly; add the lemon juice, stir the mixture into the saucepan; cook one minute. Remove from the stove; stir in the melted butter. Cool slightly, pour into baked shell; cover with meringue. Makes filling for one (7-inch) pie.

MERINGUE

2 egg whites   ⅛ teaspoon salt
3 tablespoons confectioners' sugar
or
2 tablespoons fine granulated sugar

Beat the egg whites until peaks will form when beater is lifted from the bowl. Add the salt and 1 tablespoon of the sugar; beat; continue until all the sugar is used. Pile the meringue lightly on the lemon filling. Bake in a slow oven (300° F.) for 15 to 20 minutes or until delicately browned.

TWO-CRUST LEMON PIE

[Mrs. Lucy Kimball Ide, Charlton City, Mass.]

1 tablespoon cornstarch	juice and grated rind of 1
1 cup sugar	lemon
1 cup water	1 egg slightly beaten

Combine cornstarch and sugar, add lemon juice and rind, water and egg. Cook for a few minutes and cool. Place mixture in unbaked pie shell; place crust on top and bake in a hot oven (450° F.) 10 minutes; then reduce heat to moderate (350° F.) and bake 20 to 25 minutes longer. Makes 1 two-crust (7-inch) pie.

PUMPKIN PIE

[Mrs. Alice G. Burke, West Falmouth, Mass.]

1 cup steamed, strained pumpkin	3 eggs, well beaten
⅔ cup brown sugar	2 cups cream
½ teaspoon ginger	(rich milk will do)
1 teaspoon cinnamon	½ teaspoon salt

Mix all together. Pour into an unbaked pastry shell and bake in a hot oven (450° F.) 10 minutes; then reduce heat to moderate (350° F.) and bake 20 to 25 minutes longer, or until knife comes out clean when inserted in custard. Makes 1 one-crust (9-inch) pie.

One secret of good pumpkin pie is to include at least ½ teaspoon ginger among the spices. Some cooks substitute nutmeg (½ teaspoon) for the cinnamon. A delightful variation is to add 1½ teaspoons ground coriander seeds to the recipe; or ½ cup finely cut butternut meats.

SQUASH PIE

Substitute squash for pumpkin. Vermonters will tell you the proper sweetening for squash or pumpkin pie is 1 cup of maple syrup instead of brown sugar.

Cooks of Concord, Mass., fail to agree as to whether spice or rose water is the more suitable flavoring for squash pie. Advocates of spice find rose water insipid. Rose water champions find spice lacking in subtlety. This argument is one of long-standing in the town and never fails to bring on heated discussions at club suppers and church luncheons.

CHOCOLATE CREAM PIE

[*A Rhode Island recipe*]

1 square chocolate	¼ cup sugar
1½ cups milk, scalded	⅛ teaspoon salt
4 tablespoons flour	1 tablespoon butter
⅓ cup milk	¼ teaspoon vanilla extract
1 egg yolk	whipped cream, or meringue

Add chocolate to milk in top of double boiler and melt. Mix flour and ⅓ cup milk to a smooth paste and stir into hot mixture. Cook until thickened, stirring constantly. Cover and let cook about 10 minutes. Mix egg yolk with sugar and salt, combine this with the hot mixture and cook 2 minutes longer; add butter and flavoring. Allow mixture to cool. Turn into a baked pie shell. Top with whipped cream or meringue. Makes 1 one-crust (9-inch) pie.

Alternate layers of sliced bananas and cooled filling (with a topping of bananas) makes Chocolate Banana Cream Pie. Omit chocolate and increase flour to 5 tablespoons for Banana Cream Pie. For Coconut Pie omit chocolate, add ⅔ cup shredded coconut to the filling. Sprinkle ⅓ cup plain or toasted coconut over the top.

VINEGAR PIE

[Heloise Parker Broeg, Boston "American"]

2 egg yolks
2 cups water
½ cup vinegar

1 tablespoon melted butter
1½ cups sugar
4 tablespoons flour

½ teaspoon lemon extract

Line a pie plate with pastry. Combine egg yolks, water, vinegar and melted butter. Add flour to sugar and combine with vinegar mixture. Add flavoring and pour into pastry-lined pie plate and bake in a hot oven (450° F.) 10 minutes; then reduce heat to moderate (350° F.) and bake 20 to 30 minutes longer. Cool. Makes 1 one-crust (8-inch) pie.

Vinegar pies were very popular in New England a generation ago.

BOILED CIDER PIE

[A recipe as old as New England Boiled Dinner]

1 cup sugar
¼ cup water
2 tablespoons butter

7 tablespoons boiled cider
2 eggs, separated
few gratings nutmeg

Combine sugar, water, butter and thick boiled cider, and simmer about 10 minutes. Cool. Add egg yolks, well beaten. Fold in egg whites, beaten stiff.

Line a plate with unbaked pie crust. Pour in filling. Dust with nutmeg. Add a top crust and bake in a hot oven (450° F.) for 10 minutes; then reduce the heat to moderate (350° F.) and bake for 25 to 30 minutes. Makes 1 (8-inch) pie.

Plain cider will not do. Use old-fashioned boiled cider made in the fall from sweet cider boiled until it is thick and dark and rich. Cider pie will be "runny." It does not "set" like other pies.

OLD-FASHIONED CREAM PIE

[*This recipe originally appeared in "Godey's Lady's Book"*]

Line a deep pie plate with unbaked pastry. Over it spread a layer of butter the thickness of a nickel. Over this sprinkle a layer of sugar, the same thickness. Next another layer of butter the same thickness. Next, a layer of flour also the thickness of a nickel. Pour 1 pint of cream flavored with ½ teaspoon vanilla and ⅛ teaspoon nutmeg over all. Bake in a hot oven (450° F.) 10 minutes; then reduce the heat to moderate (350° F.) and bake for 40 minutes or until knife inserted comes out clean. The butter bubbles up through the layer spread above it, making the pie a delicious confection.

MAPLE CREAM PIE

1 pint milk, scalded	2 eggs, beaten
1 cup maple sugar, packed	½ teaspoon salt
3 tablespoons cornstarch	1 tablespoon butter
¼ cup milk	1 teaspoon vanilla
whipped cream	

Heat milk and maple sugar in double boiler until sugar is dissolved. Add cornstarch dissolved in cold milk. Let cook ½ hour, stirring occasionally. Add to beaten eggs, return to double boiler and cook 1 minute. Remove from fire; add salt, butter, and vanilla. Cool. Pour into baked pastry shell. Cover with whipped cream before serving.

Some Vermonters add a speck of black pepper to this filling before pouring it into the pastry shell. Others bake it in 2 crusts and omit the whipped cream.

COTTAGE CHEESE PIE

[From the New England Kitchen of Louise Crathern Russell]

2 cups cottage cheese

3 eggs

rind 1½ lemons

juice 1½ lemons

juice 2 oranges

1 cup sugar

¼ teaspoon salt

Put cottage cheese through a sieve, strainer or colander. Add eggs, fruit juices and rind, sugar and salt. Mix and pour into pastry lined pie plate and bake in a hot oven (450° F.) 10 minutes; then reduce heat to moderate (350° F.) and bake 25 to 30 minutes longer, or until inserted knife comes out clean. Makes 1 one-crust (8-inch) pie. Serve cold.

WHITE NAVY BEAN PIE

[Mrs. Mae Bangs Twite, Oak Bluffs, Mass.]

2 cups navy bean pulp

1 cup evaporated milk
  (undiluted)

2 tablespoons cornstarch

¼ cup water

½ teaspoon nutmeg

½ teaspoon cinnamon

¾ cups sugar

3 egg yolks

3 egg whites

Cook the beans until very soft. Put them through a sieve to have 2 cups of pulp. Mix cornstarch with water; add spices to sugar. Mix with the bean and milk mixture. Add beaten egg yolks. Put in an unbaked pie shell and bake in a hot oven (450° F.) for 10 minutes; then reduce heat to moderate (350° F.) and bake 25 minutes longer or until "set." Remove from the oven and top with egg whites beaten stiff with 3 tablespoons sugar; then return to oven until delicately brown. Makes 1 one-crust (9-inch) pie.

BUTTERSCOTCH PIE

[A Massachusetts recipe]

2 tablespoons butter
¾ cup brown sugar, firmly
    packed
1½ cups milk

4 tablespoons flour
¼ teaspoon salt
2 egg yolks or 1 egg, beaten
    slightly

whipped cream, or meringue

Put butter, sugar and 1 cup milk in the top of double boiler; heat until milk is scalded. Mix flour and salt and stir in ½ cup cold milk. Stir into mixture in double boiler. Stir constantly until mixture thickens; cover and cook 10 minutes. Stir a little of the hot mixture into the eggs, pour into the double boiler; cook 2 minutes. Cool, fill baked pie crust (8-inch) with the mixture. Top with whipped cream or meringue.

MAPLE BUTTERNUT CHIFFON PIE

¾ cup maple syrup
2 egg yolks, beaten
½ teaspoon salt
2 teaspoons gelatine

¼ cup cold water
2 egg whites, beaten
3 tablespoons sugar
½ cup whipped cream

½ cup butternut meats, broken

Heat maple syrup in double boiler, add to egg yolks, return to double boiler and cook until mixture thickens. Add salt. Soak gelatine in cold water 5 minutes, set over hot water until it dissolves, then add to first mixture. Cool. Beat egg whites until frothy, add sugar gradually and beat until stiff but not dry. Fold in whipped cream. When first mixture begins to set, fold in egg and cream mixture. Pour into baked pie shell. Sprinkle butternut meats over top.

SOUR MILK PIE

[Mrs. Priscilla L. Jones, Wrentham, Mass.]

1 egg, slightly beaten
1 cup sour milk (or cream)
1 cup sugar
1 tablespoon vinegar

1 teaspoon cinnamon
½ teaspoon cloves
½ teaspoon allspice
1 cup seedless raisins

⅛ teaspoon salt

Combine all the ingredients, stirring until thoroughly mixed. Let stand 45 minutes so that the raisins will absorb some of the liquid. Turn into an unbaked pie shell. Cover with another crust, or not, as desired. Bake in a hot oven (450° F.) 10 minutes, then reduce heat to moderate and bake 25 to 30 minutes longer. Cool. Makes 1 (7-inch) pie.

ICE CREAM PIE

[Toll House, Whitman, Mass.]

3 egg whites, beaten
½ cup sugar

1 teaspoon vanilla
1 pint ice cream

Cover an inverted pie plate with pastry, bringing pastry well onto the sides and trimming off at edges of plate. Prick pastry several times on bottom and sides of plate and bake at 450° F. for 20 minutes or until brown. Cool crust. Beat egg whites until stiff, add sugar, slowly beating all the time. Lastly add vanilla. Fill pastry shell with ice cream (chocolate or coffee is delicious) cover with meringue and brown under broiler until meringue is "set" and a golden brown color. Pastry shells may be made by covering inverted muffin tins if desired. These make individual pies. One pint of ice cream will fill 6 muffin tin shells.

MAINE MOLASSES PIE

[*Mrs. Gladys P. Anderson, Cumberland Center, Me.*]

3 cups molasses	1 tablespoon melted butter
1 cup sugar	juice 1 lemon
3 eggs, beaten	½ teaspoon nutmeg
¼ teaspoon salt	

Beat all ingredients together and turn into unbaked pastry shell. Bake in a hot oven (450° F.) 10 minutes; then reduce heat to moderate (350° F.) and bake 30 minutes longer, or until knife inserted comes out clean. Makes 1 one-crust (9-inch) pie.

TRANSPLANTING

By E. Harriet Donlevy

We left New England many years ago,
And came to live and build on mid-West land;
I planted lilacs in a hedge below
The shed; they blossomed purple against sand.

I brought my braided mats and pewter ware,
A Pilgrim warming pan, and feather bed,
My highboy, Sandwich glass, and Winthrop chair;
My recipe for succotash and bread.

I had baked beans for supper Saturday,
And put white shells about the garden walk;
We never lost our clipped New England way
Of answering direct to neighbors' talk.

Here in the sandy country, I remember woods,
Of lady-slippers, sweeter than this sage;
New England isn't place, or neighborhood—
It's part of coursing blood, and heritage.

THE FARM KITCHEN

Margaret Carmichael

When the lumbering gray snow clouds have snuffed out the last flickers of light from the worn-out winter sun, when a bristling North-Easter begins to flap the old shingles on the barn roof and swoop about up among the rafters, when the cattle stamp and chew and swish their tails as if to keep warm, there is no place on earth that looks quite so good to a man as his own old-fashioned farm kitchen. The dog, too, knows what that final shutting of the barn door means, and rising from his bed in the hay, follows his master's lantern between the snow drifts to the shed door, where the cat whines on the cold granite step. There is food, warmth, and a corner for each one of them within the four sturdy walls of the farmer's kitchen. Let the city-folk have their big living-rooms and parlors with their noisy radiators tucked away in corners. What radiator ever baked a crock of beans on a Saturday night, or had an oven door that a man could let down to warm his feet on? In the farm kitchen, where the big black range is, there, also, is the very essence of *home*.

Country parlors change with the times, putting on city airs. The furniture is always stiff and uncomfortable in its stolid plush or wicker dignity; the mantelpieces over the bricked-up fireplaces are loaded with nonsensical gadgets and family photographs—unnoticed after the first week of novelty—which serve as excellent dust-catchers. Periodically, the old gadgets and pictures, seen to be hopelessly out of date, are replaced by new ones. Carrie Belle, aged eight, in her heart-shaped gilt frame is banished to the old horsehair trunk, making room for Carrie Belle's daughter in a wide burnt-wood frame, who, in time, is whisked away in favor of Carrie Belle's grand-daughter, very modern in Shirley Temple curls and a chromium setting. . . . The parlor *must* be up to date.

Not so with the farm kitchen; comfort is first there. For convenience's sake, the oil lamp may give way to electricity, the

wheezy pump to running water, but the old wood-range remains
the great black Mogul of domestic affairs. Year in and year out
it stands pat and firmly on its four squat legs, feeding and warming people, the very heart of the farm kitchen and this thing we
call home. All during the winter months, when the snow covers
the north windows, or when the farmyard is soupy with cold mud,
the shining stove radiates a comforting warmth mingled with the
delicious brown odors of coffee and of pies and cakes hidden away
in the depths of its cavernous oven.

Opposite the stove, the kitchen table catches up the waves of
warmth in its red and white checked cloth, flinging them out again
with renewed cheer. The geraniums on the window ledge hold
the glow of the afternoon sun long after it has dropped from sight.
The air of settled complacency here is as frank as the sunlight itself,
and just as mellow. Mother's worn rocker still rests in the same
spot next to the window where Grandmother kept it when she
was mistress of the house, performing miracles in molasses cookies
and partridge pies with the aid of the same old stove. How many
tired, fretted babies have been rocked to sleep in that chair, how
many socks darned there, and how many sweaters knit! The cat
curls there now in a drowsy ball, purring her content. But to the
farmer who has been working in the cold all day, the armchair
drawn up to the stove looks better than the rocker. Here he may
steep himself in the comforting warmth, his pipe in his mouth,
his stocking-feet toasting on the open oven door. The dog, too, has
his favorite spot between the stove and the mammoth wood-box
behind it. His tail, thumping the floor lazily, catches the quick
eye of a kitten hiding in the wood-box. She creeps to the edge and
hurls herself at the tail ferociously, only to bounce away at the first
low growl.

Cats and dogs are not allowed in modern city kitchens where
Efficiency has replaced Comfort as the household god. These kitchens are like compact, smoothly-run business offices in their cool
precision; there is nothing of home in them. The friendly giant
stove has been replaced by a pert, enameled gas or electric range;

the red and white checked table cloth on the old kitchen table, by a shining white porcelain top. The walls, cupboards and furniture painted a bright green, yellow, or blue, shriek their newness. The spotless tiled linoleum on the floor dares anyone to set a muddy foot on it. Children and cumbersome fathers are shooed out of the kitchen along with the dogs and cats. It has become a hallowed temple to the gods of Hygiene and Domestic Science, with a uniformed cook as high priestess.

The farm kitchen, despite modern improvements, can never become quite as devoid of comfort and cheer as its sophisticated cousin; its part in farm life is too integral. But lately, a new factor, a new "Jack-the-Giant-Killer" has appeared in country homes, threatening to rob the kitchen of its position as head room in the farm-house and the friendly giant stove of its dominance over household affairs. This menace is the radio. There being no place for it in the already crowded kitchen, it has found its place in the dining-room beside that other modern necessity, the telephone. The old stove still warms muscles and bones chilled by winter's buffeting, still provides that snug, tucked-away-from-the-world feeling, but the radio brings the world to the farm, ignoring alike mud, ice, piled drifts and impassable roads. The farmer and his family, too long shut away from the world, spend more and more of their time in the dining-room. No more drowsy evenings around the kitchen stove! Cold toes and chapped hands are forgotten after supper as the whole clan crouches about the radio, tapping out the rhythm of the "Continental" or listening raptly to Lady Hester's words of wisdom concerning the care of a lily-white skin. . . .

And out in the deserted kitchen, the old black Mogul still rumbles courageously to itself as it boils tomorrow's breakfast cereal; "R-r-radio can't feed 'em. R-r-radio can't feed 'em. . . ."

CAKES AND COOKIES

ONE-EGG CAKE

2 cups cake flour, sifted	4 tablespoons butter or other
3 teaspoons baking powder	shortening
¼ teaspoon salt	1 egg
1 cup sugar	¾ cup milk
1 teaspoon vanilla	

Sift together three times flour, baking powder and salt. Cream butter, add sugar gradually and cream together. Add unbeaten egg and beat thoroughly. Add flour alternately with the milk, beating after each addition until smooth. Add vanilla. Bake in 2 well greased (8-inch) layer tins in a moderate oven (350° F.) about 25 minutes. Frost with any desired frosting. Makes 2 (8-inch) square layer cakes or 18 cup cakes.

A New Hampshire farmer sold a piece of property to some city folk who had decided to buy a few chickens. The lady came to the farmer and asked him how long a hen should sit on eggs for hatching. Wishing to be thoroughly helpful, the farmer told her that a hen sits three weeks for chickens and four weeks for ducks. So the lady went off and got the clucking hen started nicely. Now it so happened that the city folk had hired a local girl to act as maid of all work, and after this same hen had been sitting on her eggs patiently for two weeks, the amateur farmers were called back to the city on urgent business. "Now remember," Mrs. City Folk said to her maid of all work, "if the hen sits more than another week you're to take her off; I don't want any ducks."

BOSTON CREAM PIE

Spread Cream Filling between the layers of One-Egg Cake. Sift powdered sugar over top. Cut in pie-shaped wedges.

CREAM FILLING

½ cup sugar	2 eggs (or 4 egg yolks),
½ cup flour	slightly beaten
¼ teaspoon salt	½ teaspoon vanilla
2 cups milk, scalded	1 tablespoon butter

Combine sugar, flour and salt and mix with egg yolks; stir in hot milk slowly, to form a smooth paste. Cook over boiling water 10 minutes, stirring constantly the first 5 minutes. Cool and add vanilla. Add butter last.

PARKER HOUSE CHOCOLATE CREAM PIE

Frost Boston Cream Pie with chocolate icing and cut in pie-shaped wedges.

Quite adept at respectfully wriggling out of tight places are the famous colored waiters in the dining rooms of Boston's Parker House, as one delighted guest who was recently party of the second part in such a situation can testify.

Having ordered chocolate cream pie in the Parker House Grill one evening, the guest expressed his surprise at an unfamiliar looking dish which was set before him. "Are you sure this is what I ordered?" he asked. "Yes, sir," said the waiter. "This is chocolate cream pie."

"Why, chocolate cream pie is an open pie crust filled with chocolate pudding and covered with whipped cream."

"That is true in some places, sir. But at the Parker House, this is chocolate cream pie," replied the waiter with finesse

and finality. The fact is that throughout New England, chocolate cream pie is made as a layer cake, with icing on top, custard cream between layers. Washington Pie differs from Boston Cream Pie in that raspberry jam is spread between the layers.

※

OLD MAINE LOBSTER CAKE

[Old-fashioned marble cake]

3 cups flour, sifted	1 cup butter
¾ teaspoon cream of tartar	2 cups sugar
½ teaspoon soda	1 cup milk
¼ teaspoon salt	4 eggs, beaten

Sift flour, cream of tartar, soda and salt together 3 times. Cream butter thoroughly. Add sugar gradually and cream together well. Add eggs one at a time and beat well. Add flour alternately with milk, beating until smooth. Divide mixture into 2 bowls. To one part add ½ cup molasses, ½ teaspoon cloves, ¼ teaspoon nutmeg. To the other part, add ½ cup chopped raisins; ½ cup chopped citron. Put by tablespoons into greased loaf pan (15 x 9 x 2 inches) alternating light and dark mixture. Bake in moderate oven (350° F.) about 1 hour. Frost or not, as desired.

Mrs. D. Lusignan, 9 Monroe St., Concord, N. H., whose recipe this is, got it from her aunt who was raised outside of Portland. She, in turn, says her mother made it when she was a girl and that was some time ago as Mrs. Lusignan's aunt was 65 her last birthday. No one knows why this cake is called Lobster Cake.

ONE-EGG MOCHA CAKE

[Mrs. L. G. Young, 58 Preston St., Windsor, Conn.]

2 tablespoons butter	1 cup flour, sifted
1 cup sugar	¼ teaspoon salt
1 egg, separated	1½ teaspoons baking powder
¾ cup milk	½ teaspoon vanilla

2 squares chocolate, melted

Cream butter, add sugar and cream together. Add egg yolk and beat; add milk alternately with remaining dry ingredients, sifted together. Beat in chocolate and vanilla then fold in egg white beaten stiff. Turn into 2 greased layer pans and bake in moderate oven (350° F.) about 20 minutes. Makes 2 thin (8-inch layers). Put Chocolate Filling between layers and Mocha Frosting on top.

CHOCOLATE FILLING

¾ cup water	½ teaspoon butter
1 tablespoon cornstarch	1 square chocolate
½ cup sugar	½ teaspoon vanilla

⅛ teaspoon salt

Place all the ingredients except vanilla into a saucepan over boiling water. Cook over low heat, stirring constantly until thick and smooth. Cook 10 minutes longer. Cool, add vanilla.

MOCHA FROSTING

¼ cup butter	⅛ teaspoon salt
1½ cups confectioners' sugar	2 tablespoons hot, strong coffee
1 teaspoon vanilla	(about)

2 teaspoons cocoa

Cream butter until soft; gradually stir in the cocoa and half the sugar, then add vanilla and salt. Add remaining sugar alternately with coffee, beating until smooth after each addition and adding enough coffee for proper consistency to spread.

ANGEL SPONGE CAKE

[Mrs. Annie E. Bumpus, 466 Main St., Brockton, Mass.]

4 eggs, separated	1½ cups cake flour, sifted
1¼ cups sugar	3 times
¾ cup water	¼ teaspoon salt
1 teaspoon baking powder	1 teaspoon vanilla

Beat the egg yolks in a large bowl until lemon-colored. Add sugar, beat again, add water and beat thoroughly. Sift flour, baking powder and salt and add to the egg mixture and beat with a spoon until smooth. Add vanilla and fold in stiffly beaten egg whites. Turn into ungreased cake pan and bake in a moderate oven (350° F.) about 1 hour. Invert pan 1 hour, or until cold.

JOHANNA CAKE

[Marion Smith, Tamworth, N. H.]

1⅔ cups flour, sifted	1¼ cups sugar
1 teaspoon cream of tartar	3 eggs, separated
¼ teaspoon salt	½ cup milk
½ teaspoon soda	½ cup thinly sliced citron
½ cup butter	½ teaspoon vanilla

Sift together flour, cream of tartar, salt and soda. Cream butter, add sugar and cream thoroughly. Add egg yolks and beat; add flour alternately with milk, a small amount at a time. Stir in citron, add vanilla and fold in stiffly beaten egg whites. Bake in 2 greased (8-inch) layer pans in a moderate oven (350° F.) about 25 minutes. Spread with any desired frosting.

COCONUT CREAM LAYER CAKE

3 cups cake flour, sifted

3 teaspoons baking powder

¼ teaspoon salt

1 cup shortening

3½ cups confectioners' sugar

4 eggs separated

1 cup milk

1 teaspoon vanilla

1 cup shredded coconut

Sift flour, baking powder and salt together 3 times. Cream butter, add sugar gradually and cream together thoroughly. Add egg yolks and beat well. Add flour alternately with milk, a little at a time, beating until smooth. Add vanilla and coconut. Fold in stiffly beaten egg whites. Bake in 3 greased (9-inch square) layer pans in a moderate oven (350° F.) about 30 minutes. Frost with 7-minute icing or boiled icing and sprinkle 1½ cups coconut between layers and over the cake while frosting is soft. With the addition of the coconut, both the 7-minute icing and the boiled icing given below make enough frosting for this 3-layer cake if used sparingly between the layers.

7-MINUTE ICING

2 egg whites, unbeaten

1½ cups sugar

5 tablespoons water

1½ teaspoons light corn syrup

¼ teaspoon salt

1 teaspoon vanilla

Combine egg whites, sugar, water, corn syrup and salt in the top of a double boiler. Place over rapidly boiling water, beat constantly with rotary egg beater, and cook 7 minutes or until frosting will stand in peaks. Remove from boiling water, add flavoring and beat until the right consistency to spread. Makes enough frosting to cover top and sides of a 2-layer (9-inch) cake or 2 dozen cup cakes.

BOILED ICING

1½ cups sugar
½ teaspoon light corn syrup
⅔ cup water

¼ teaspoon salt
2 egg whites, beaten stiff
1 teaspoon vanilla

Combine sugar, corn syrup, water and salt. Bring to a boil, stirring only until sugar is dissolved. Boil rapidly until syrup spins a long thread when dropped from top of spoon (240° F.). Pour syrup slowly over egg whites, beating constantly. Add vanilla. Continue beating until frosting is the right consistency to spread. Makes enough frosting to cover top and sides of a 2-layer (9-inch) cake or 2 dozen cup cakes.

1-2-3-4 CAKE

[Sarah Lee Whorf, Provincetown, Mass.]

1 cup butter
2 cups sugar
3 cups flour, sifted
4 eggs

1 cup water or milk
3 teaspoons baking powder
¼ teaspoon salt
1 teaspoon vanilla

Cream the butter, add the sugar and cream thoroughly. Add the eggs one at a time, and beat well. Sift the remaining dry ingredients twice, and add alternately with the water or milk. Beat well, add the vanilla. Turn into greased pan or pans and bake in a moderate oven (350° F.) 25 minutes (in layers) to 1 hour (in 1 square pan). Makes 1 large loaf cake or 2 (9-inch) layers.

Norma Roberts, Bristol, N. H., says of this cake: "Still fresh in my memory is the day a neighbor came to spend the day with my mother and proudly brought with her this recipe which was new to her then. Women thought nothing of visiting each other for an entire day years ago, and swapped everything but their babies."
This cake is also known as Park St. Cake.

CONNECTICUT RAISED LOAF CAKE

*[Also called Election Cake, March Meeting Cake
and Dough Cake]*

2 cups milk, scalded	¾ cup shortening
½ cup brown sugar, tightly	2 eggs
packed	1½ cups raisins
½ teaspoon salt	¼ pound citron sliced thin
1 compressed yeast cake	(optional)
5 cups flour, sifted	½ teaspoon nutmeg
1½ cups sugar	½ teaspoon mace

Place milk, brown sugar and salt in a mixing bowl. When luke-warm add crumbled yeast cake and 4½ cups of the flour; beat thoroughly and let rise overnight. In the morning cream the sugar and shortening and add. Stir in the eggs, raisins, citron, nutmeg, mace and remaining ½ cup flour. Mix thoroughly using hands if necessary. Place in greased bread tins lined with waxed paper and again greased. Rise until double in bulk. Bake in a moderately hot oven (375° F.) until brown, about 50 minutes. Makes 2 loaves.

In the old days of long drawn out March Town meetings, nearby taverns were heavily patronized during the noon hour. Sometimes meetings would drag along until the following day. In the evening town paupers would be auctioned off in the tavern to anyone who "would keep them a few degrees above starvation."

March Meetin' or 'Lection Cakes were sold in the village stores all day at four pence a baker's dozen. These cakes were about the size of an ordinary pancake, but thicker. The dough was cut down in the middle of the night so that it would not rise too fast. Housewives vied with one another to see which could bake the best cake. No two cakes were alike as the recipes called for "flour to mix stiff but not too stiff."

Election cake is said to have originated in Hartford, Conn., a century ago and was served to all who voted the straight ticket.

Raised Cakes were also made frequently around Thanksgiving. They were proudly carried to church suppers or bestowed on married daughters home for the holiday feast.

PORK CAKE

1 pound fat salt pork	2 teaspoons cloves
2 cups boiling water	2 teaspoons allspice
8 cups flour, sifted	2 teaspoons nutmeg
2 teaspoons soda	2 cups raisins, chopped
¼ teaspoon salt	4 eggs
2 teaspoons cinnamon	2 cups sugar
	2 cups molasses

Put pork through food chopper, using finest knife; pour boiling water over pork and let stand 15 minutes. Mix and sift flour, soda, salt and spices and mix with raisins. Combine eggs, sugar and molasses and add the pork mixture; gradually stir in flour-fruit mixture and mix thoroughly. Turn into 4 greased deep loaf pans, lined with waxed paper and again greased. Bake in slow oven (300° F.) for 1¼ hours. Makes 4 loaves. Recipe can be easily halved or quartered.

This is the favorite recipe of Mrs. Howard S. Martin, 49 Ascadilla Rd., Worcester, Mass. Mrs. Martin's mother got it from her mother-in-law one hundred years ago. This cake conserves the more expensive shortenings and uses salt pork of which the supply was plentiful. It is a delicious cake and keeps fresh for months if carefully wrapped and placed in a stone crock. In fact it improves in flavor if kept for some time.

AUNT MAY'S SPICE CAKE

[Eleanor St. George Sybilholme, Quechee, Vt.]

½ cup butter and lard mixed	1 teaspoon cloves
1 cup sugar	1 teaspoon cinnamon
1 egg, beaten	1 teaspoon nutmeg
2 cups cake flour, sifted	1 cup sour milk
1 teaspoon soda	1 teaspoon vanilla extract
¼ teaspoon salt	1 teaspoon lemon extract

½ cup seedless raisins

Cream shortening and sugar; beat in egg. Mix and sift flour, soda, salt and spices. Add to sugar mixture alternately with the sour milk. Add lemon and vanilla and raisins. Bake in moderate oven (350° F.) for 50 minutes or until done. Makes 1 loaf.

> *Grandaunt May lived in Aroostook County, Maine. Granduncle Frank had five wives. She was the fifth. He must have been a good "chooser" for all five are said to have been notable cooks. This recipe is proof of No. 5's skill and economy.*

MY GRANDMOTHER'S SOUR CREAM SPICE CAKE

[Mrs. Arthur Graves, South Ashfield, Mass.]

1 egg	¼ teaspoon salt
⅞ cup sour cream (about)	½ teaspoon cinnamon
1 cup sugar	½ teaspoon nutmeg
2 cups flour, sifted	¼ teaspoon cloves
1 teaspoon soda	½ cup raisins

Break the egg into a cup and fill cup with sour cream. Pour into a bowl and beat thoroughly with Dover egg beater. Add sugar and beat. Sift remaining dry ingredients twice and add to egg, cream and sugar mixture. Pour into a greased baking sheet and bake in a moderate oven (350° F.) 45 minutes. Makes 1 (8-inch) square cake. Or pour into muffin tins and make into cup cakes. Makes 12 cup cakes. Stewed prunes, cut into pieces, may be added, and ¼ cup prune juice substituted for ¼ cup of the sour cream. Nuts may also be substituted for the raisins. Serve with a big pitcher of creamy milk.

BLACK CAKE

[A delicious spice cake]

4 cups flour, sifted	1 cup seedless raisins, chopped
1 teaspoon soda	1 cup butter
½ teaspoon salt	1½ cups sugar
1 teaspoon cream of tartar	½ cup molasses
1 teaspoon cloves	1 cup milk
1 teaspoon nutmeg	3 eggs

Mix and sift flour, soda, salt, cream of tartar, cloves and nutmeg; mix ½ cup with raisins. Cream butter until soft, add sugar, creaming until fluffy, and beat in thoroughly one egg at a time. Add flour mixture alternately with combined molasses and milk, beating until smooth after each addition, then beat in raisins. Turn into greased square pan and bake in moderate oven (350° F.) about 45 minutes. Makes 2 loaf cakes.

UNCOOKED ICING

When cake has cooled, frost with an icing made by beating whites of 2 eggs until stiff; gradually beat in 2 cups sugar, 1 teaspoon cream, 1 tablespoon grated orange rind. Beat vigorously until smooth. If frosting becomes too thick, add a little orange juice.

This recipe has been in the family of Miss L. Maude Cate, 152 South Main St., Wolfeboro, N. H., ever since she can remember. It was given to her mother by her great-aunt Lucy Crawford, daughter of Ethan Allen Crawford of Crawford's Notch, N. H.

HOT WATER CAKE

[A spice cake without eggs]

½ cup shortening
½ cup sugar
1 cup molasses
2½ cups flour, sifted
1½ teaspoons soda

½ teaspoon salt
½ teaspoon cinnamon
½ teaspoon allspice
½ teaspoon cloves
1 cup boiling water

Cream shortening, add sugar and cream again. Add molasses and remaining dry ingredients sifted together. Last of all add boiling water. Bake in a moderate oven (350° F.) about 35 minutes. Makes 1 (10-inch) square cake.

Recipe is from Mrs. Ellen M. Bliss, Attleboro, Mass., and has been in her family for years. On her mother's side Mrs. Bliss is a direct descendant of Roger Williams.

BETTY ALLEN'S WEDDING CAKE

4 cups pastry flour, sifted
1½ teaspoons baking powder
½ teaspoon salt
1 teaspoon cinnamon
1 teaspoon nutmeg
½ teaspoon cloves
½ pound butter
3½ cups sugar

6 eggs, beaten
juice 1 orange
2 pounds seeded raisins
(cut)
1 pound currants
½ pound citron, finely cut
¾ cup orange juice or other
fruit juice

½ pound walnut meats, chopped

Mix and sift flour, baking powder, salt and spices. Cream butter, add sugar gradually, creaming until fluffy. Add eggs, beating thoroughly, then put in fruits, fruit juices and nuts. Add dry ingredients gradually, beating well after each addition. Turn into greased bread tins (lined with heavy paper) and again greased; bake in very slow oven (275° F.) about 2 hours. Makes 3 loaves.

"Betty Allen, née Elizabeth Parsons, lived in Northampton, Mass.," according to Mrs. Clifton Johnson, Hadley, Mass., who contributed this recipe. "She sent six stalwart sons to the Revolution. The local Chapter of the D. A. R. is named for her. A descendant, Miss Clara Allen, is still living in Northampton. My youngest son, Captain Irving Johnson, who sails his own ship 'Yankee,' and cruises around the world, is fond of this cake as it keeps in any climate. I send him some wherever he is on his birthday, which is July 4, and for Christmas. He saved some to eat 'rounding the Horn,' when he sailed on the 'Peking.' It was also served when he married a Pitcairn Islander to a girl from Manga Reva on the deck of the 'Yankee.' "

VERMONT SCRIPTURE CAKE

[Mrs. Charles E. Woods, Lunenburg, Mass.]

1 cup butter	Judges 5:25
2 cups sugar	Jeremiah 6:20
3½ cups flour	I Kings 4:22
2 cups raisins	I Samuel 30:12
2 cups figs	I Samuel 30:12
1 cup almonds	Genesis 43:11
1 cup water	Genesis 24:20
6 eggs	Isaiah 10:14
a little salt	Leviticus 2:13
1 tablespoon honey	Exodus 16:31
spice to taste	I Kings 10:2

Follow Solomon's advice for making good boys (Prov. 23:14).

In some places the cookbook is one's Bible ... or again the Bible is one's cookbook.

WELLESLEY FUDGE CAKE

2 cups cake flour, sifted
2 teaspoons baking powder
½ teaspoon soda
¼ teaspoon salt
½ cup butter
1¼ cups firmly packed brown
  sugar

1 egg, well beaten
2½ squares chocolate,
  melted
¾ cup milk
1 teaspoon vanilla
½ cup walnuts, chopped

Sift flour, baking powder, soda and salt 3 times. Cream butter, add sugar and cream thoroughly. Add egg and chocolate and beat well. Add flour, alternately with milk, beating well. Add vanilla. Turn into 2 layer pans (8 x 8 inches) and bake in a moderate oven (350° F.) about 25 minutes. Cool and frost with Fudge Frosting between layers and on top and sides of cake. Sprinkle chopped nutmeats on top.

FUDGE FROSTING

1½ cups sugar
¾ cup water
1 tablespoon light corn syrup

⅛ teaspoon salt
3 squares chocolate
3 tablespoons butter

1 teaspoon vanilla

Combine sugar, water, corn syrup and salt. Boil without stirring, until mixture forms a very soft ball in cold water (235° F.) Remove from stove, add chocolate (it is not necessary to cut it fine) and cool to lukewarm. Add butter and vanilla. Beat until frosting is the right consistency to spread. Makes enough frosting to cover tops and sides of an 8-inch layer cake.

Rocelia asked her husband, Jim, to watch the cake she had put in the oven and take it out when it was done. When she came home two hours later, she found the cake burned to a crisp. Commenting on it later, to one of her neighbors she remarked, "It's terrible what these men do. After all, all Jem had to do was set and remember!"

CHOCOLATE "WEARY WILLIE" CAKE

[A Vermont inn called "The Weathervane" originated this recipe contributed by Minnie L. Lawton, 33 Silver Lake Ave., Lakewood, R. I.]

1 cup flour, sifted	1 egg
1½ teaspoons baking powder	⅞ cup milk (about)
¼ teaspoon salt	2 squares chocolate
1 cup sugar	2 tablespoons butter
	1 teaspoon vanilla

Sift the flour, baking powder, salt and sugar into a mixing bowl. Break egg into a measuring cup and fill cup with milk; add the flour and beat well. Add chocolate, melted with the butter, and beat again. Add vanilla. Pour into greased 8-inch pan lined with waxed paper and bake in a moderate oven (350° F.) for about 35 minutes. Makes 1 (8-inch) square cake. Frost with Marshmallow Icing.

MARSHMALLOW ICING

2 tablespoons milk	1 square chocolate
1 cup confectioners' sugar	1 teaspoon butter
2 tablespoons marshmallow fluff	½ teaspoon vanilla

Add milk to sugar and stir until smooth. Add marshmallow fluff and beat. Then add the chocolate and butter which have been melted together and mix thoroughly. Spread on cake.

WATERMELON CAKE

[Mrs. Annie L. Grant, 4 Pelham St., Worcester, Mass.]

3 cups flour, sifted
3 teaspoons baking powder
¼ teaspoon salt
½ cup shortening
1½ cups sugar

3 egg whites, beaten stiff
1 cup milk
1 teaspoon vanilla
½ teaspoon red coloring
½ cup raisins

Sift together flour, baking powder and salt. Cream shortening, add sugar gradually and cream together thoroughly. Add flour, alternately with the milk, beating until smooth. Add vanilla and fold in egg whites. Divide batter into 2 parts. To one part add the red coloring and well-floured raisins. Grease a melon mold. Put a layer of the white batter in the bottom, then the red in the center and a layer of the white batter on top. Bake in a moderate oven (350° F.) about 30 minutes. Ice with boiled icing or butter icing, tinted green.

APPLE SAUCE CAKE

[Mrs. Ardene Hunt, Farmington, Conn.]

1 cup sugar
½ cup shortening
1 cup apple sauce (warm)
1 teaspoon soda
1⅔ cups flour, sifted

1 teaspoon cinnamon
½ teaspoon cloves
¼ teaspoon nutmeg
¼ teaspoon salt
1 cup raisins, floured

Cream sugar and shortening; add apple sauce in which soda has been dissolved; add flour and spices and salt sifted together and lastly floured raisins. Turn into a greased loaf tin and bake in a moderately slow oven (325° F.) about 45 minutes. Makes 1 loaf. Keeps moist a week if stored in closely covered cake box.

DATE CAKE

2 cups flour, sifted
1 teaspoon soda
¼ teaspoon salt
½ teaspoon cloves
⅛ teaspoon nutmeg

½ cup butter
1 cup sugar
1 cup sour milk
½ pound dates or prunes, cut
up fine

Sift together flour, soda, salt and spices. Cream butter, add sugar and cream again thoroughly. Add flour to creamed mixture, alternately with the sour milk, beating well. Add dates or prunes. Turn into a well-greased loaf pan and bake in a moderate oven (350° F.) about 1 hour. Makes 1 loaf (8 x 4 inches).

Mrs. Frank A. Pickering, 5 Quincy St., Methuen, Mass., has used this recipe since 1895. It was given to her mother-in-law many years before that with the compliments of F. M. Barney & Co., Wholesale and Retail Grocers, Lowell, Mass., a firm which has long been out of business.

CIDER CAKE

6 cups flour, sifted
1 teaspoon soda
½ teaspoon salt
1 grated nutmeg

1 cup butter
3 cups sugar
4 eggs beaten
1 cup cider

Mix and sift flour, soda, salt and nutmeg; cream butter well, add sugar gradually, creaming until fluffy, then eggs and beat thoroughly. Add flour mixture alternately with cider, beating until smooth after each addition. Turn into greased loaf pan (4 x 9½ x 9½) and bake in a moderate oven (350° F.) about 1 hour. Keep moist in a glass jar with apples.

Mary B. Hutching, 101 School St., Brookline, Mass., who has made this cake many times, says, "It will keep for a year. It is not unlike pound cake. Nuts, cherries, figs or citron may be added." This recipe is 100 years old.

JELLY ROLL

[An old Rhode Island recipe]

¾ cup cake flour, sifted   4 eggs, separated
 1 teaspoon baking powder   ¾ cup sugar, sifted
 ¼ teaspoon salt   1 tablespoon lemon juice
                    1 cup jelly

Mix and sift flour, baking powder and salt. Beat egg yolks until thick and lemon-colored; gradually beat in sugar and lemon juice. Fold in 2 of the stiffly beaten egg whites; gradually fold in flour, a few tablespoons at a time, then fold in the remaining egg whites. Turn into pan (15 x 10 inches) which has been greased and lined with waxed paper and again greased. Bake in moderately hot oven (375° F.) about 15 minutes. Quickly turn from pan on paper sprinkled with powdered sugar. Cut off crisp edges and remove wax paper; spread with jelly (beaten enough to spread easily) and roll lengthwise. Wrap in cloth and cool on rack. Makes 1 roll.

MAPLE BUTTERNUT TEA CAKES

[A Vermont recipe]

2½ cups flour, sifted   2 eggs
  2 teaspoons baking powder   ½ cup hot water
  ½ teaspoon baking soda   1 cup maple syrup
  ½ teaspoon salt   ½ teaspoon vanilla
  ½ cup butter   1 cup butternut meats, finely
  ½ cup sugar   cut

Sift together flour, baking powder, soda and salt. Cream butter, add sugar and cream thoroughly. Add eggs and beat well. Combine maple syrup and water and add alternately with the flour, beating well after each addition. Add vanilla and butternut meats. Bake in greased cup-cake pan in a moderate oven (350° F.) about 20 minutes. Makes 16 to 20 cakes. Frost or not, as desired.

MAPLE FROSTING

2 cups maple syrup   2 egg whites, stiffly beaten

Boil syrup without stirring until it spins a long thread (240° F.). Pour syrup slowly over egg whites and beat until stiff enough to spread. Makes enough frosting for 24 cup cakes or tops and sides of a 2-layer (8-inch) cake.

In olden days maple sugar was about the consistency and color of brown sugar today and was the only sugar used by the early settlers.

PIE, JAM AND CAKE TART

[Bernice Bailey, Hanover, Mass.]

Line muffin pans with pie crust. Add one heaping tablespoon of jam or jelly. Fill remaining space with the following cake mixture:

½ cup shortening   2 cups flour
1 cup sugar   2 teaspoons baking powder
2 eggs   ¼ teaspoon salt
¾ cup milk   1 teaspoon vanilla

Cream shortening and sugar. Add egg yolks; beat. Sift flour, baking powder and salt. Add alternately with milk to creamed mixture. Add vanilla and stiffly beaten egg whites. Bake in a moderate oven (350° F). about 25 minutes. Makes 12 cakes.

LACE MOLASSES WAFERS

[Marjorie Mills, "Herald-Traveler," Boston, Mass.]

½ cup molasses
½ cup sugar
½ cup butter

1 cup flour
½ teaspoon baking powder
¼ teaspoon soda

Slowly heat molasses, sugar and butter to boiling point. Boil 1 minute and remove from fire. Add flour, baking powder and soda, which have been sifted together. Stir well. Set pan in vessel of hot water to keep batter from hardening. On buttered baking sheets or inverted dripping pans drop quarter teaspoons of batter 3 inches apart. Bake in moderate oven (350° F.), until brown, about 10 minutes. Cool slightly, then lift carefully with thin knife. If desired, roll around the handle of a spoon to shape while still warm. Makes about 4 to 5 dozen cookies.

BRANDY SNAPS

½ cup molasses
½ cup butter
⅔ cup powdered sugar

1 cup flour
1 teaspoon lemon juice
½ teaspoon grated lemon rind

Heat the molasses, butter and sugar together. Add the flour, juice, rind and mix well. Drop the mixture from the tip of a small spoon in patties about three inches apart to allow for spreading. Bake in a hot oven (400° F.), 10 to 15 minutes. If desired, they can be rolled while still hot about a greased spoon or knife handle. Serve plain or filled with whipped cream. Makes about 3 dozen snaps.

GINGER SNAPS

[Mrs. Lillian Stock, 55 Lancaster St., Providence, R. I.]

1 cup lard
1 cup molasses
1 teaspoon soda

2 teaspoons ginger
½ teaspoon salt
2½ cups flour, sifted (about)

Boil lard and molasses 2 minutes and cool. Add soda, ginger, salt and flour to make a stiff dough. Chill in refrigerator several hours or overnight. Roll very thin. Bake in a moderately hot oven (375° F.) for about 8 minutes. Makes about 50 cookies.

SOFT GINGER COOKIES

[Mrs. L. G. Young, 58 Preston St., Windsor, Conn.]

1 cup sugar	2 teaspoons soda
½ cup butter	1 teaspoon cinnamon
½ cup lard	1 teaspoon ginger
1 egg	¼ teaspoon each, cloves,
1 cup molasses	allspice, nutmeg
1 cup sour milk	1 teaspoon salt

5 cups flour, sifted (about)

Cream sugar and shortening; add egg and beat well. Add molasses, then milk, then remaining ingredients, adding flour until dough is just stiff enough to roll. Chill thoroughly. Roll ⅛-inch thick and cut in desired shape. Bake on greased baking sheet in a moderately hot oven (375° F.) about 12 minutes. Makes about 12 dozen cookies. Store in covered cooky jar.

MAPLE GINGER SNAPS

[A Vermont recipe]

2 cups soft maple sugar	4 cups flour (about)
1 cup butter	1 tablespoon ginger
2 eggs, beaten	1 teaspoon soda
¼ teaspoon salt	1 cup sour cream

Cream the maple sugar and butter and add the eggs. Sift the salt, flour and the ginger together. Add the soda to the cream. Add the flour and ginger to the first mixture alternately with the cream. Roll thin and bake in a moderately hot oven (375° F.) about 8 minutes. Makes about 5 dozen cookies.

CALAIS COOKIES

["This recipe makes soft, medium or crisp cookies, according to thickness to which dough is rolled"—Gretchen McMullen, "Yankee Network," Boston]

1 cup lard	½ cup cold water
1 cup sugar	4 cups flour
1 egg	1 teaspoon ginger
½ cup molasses	1 teaspoon salt
	1 teaspoon soda

Cream the lard and sugar. Drop in egg and beat well. Stir in molasses. Add cold water. Add flour sifted 3 times with ginger, salt and soda. Mix to a soft dough, kneading as little as possible. Roll out ½-inch thickness for soft cookies, ¼-inch thickness for medium crisp, and ⅛-inch for very crisp. With a 2½-inch cutter, the rule makes 6 dozen medium crisp cookies. Bake in moderately hot oven (375° F.) about 10 minutes. If stored as soon as cool, crisp cookies remain crisp and soft cookies soft.

PEANUT BUTTER COOKIES

[Mrs. Myron Duefrene, 7 Francis Ave., Conimicut, R. I.]

½ cup butter	1 egg, well beaten
½ cup peanut butter	1¼ cups flour, sifted
½ cup sugar	¼ teaspoon salt
½ cup brown sugar	½ teaspoon baking powder
	¼ teaspoon soda

Cream butter and peanut butter; add sugar gradually, add egg and combine with peanut butter mixture. Sift together flour, salt, baking powder and soda and add. Mix well. Chill dough. Roll out cookies and bake 10 to 15 minutes in a moderate oven (350° F.). Makes 24 cookies.

CHOCOLATE COOKIES

[*A Massachusetts recipe*]

½ cup butter
1 cup sugar
1 egg, beaten
3 squares chocolate, melted

⅛ teaspoon soda
¼ cup milk
2 cups flour, sifted
2 teaspoons baking powder

½ teaspoon salt

Cream the butter, add sugar, egg and chocolate, soda (dissolved in the milk), flour, baking powder and salt. Chill dough, then roll to ⅛-inch thickness. Cut in desired shape and bake on a greased baking sheet in a moderately hot oven (375° F.) about 8 minutes. Makes about 3 dozen cookies.

CHOCOLATE RAISIN DROP COOKIES

[*A Rhode Island recipe*]

1 cup cake flour, sifted
1 teaspoon baking powder
¼ teaspoon salt
4 tablespoons butter or other
    shortening
⅔ cup sugar

1 egg, well beaten
2 squares, unsweetened
    chocolate, melted
½ cup finely cut raisins
½ cup chopped walnut meats
¼ cup heavy sour cream

1 teaspoon vanilla

Sift flour once, measure, add baking powder and salt, and sift again. Cream butter thoroughly, add sugar gradually, and cream well. Add egg and beat thoroughly; add chocolate and blend; then raisins and nuts, and mix well. Add flour, alternately with cream, beating well after each addition. Add vanilla. Drop from teaspoon on ungreased baking sheet and bake in moderate oven (350° F.) 15 minutes, or until done. Makes 30 cookies.

CARAWAY COOKIES

[*Norma Roberts, Bristol, N. H.*]

1 cup butter
2 cups sugar
2 eggs, beaten slightly
1 cup sour cream
¾ teaspoon caraway seed

1 teaspoon soda
½ teaspoon salt
flour to roll as soft as possible
(about 4 cups)

Cream butter and sugar, add eggs, cream (in which soda is dissolved) and salt. Sift flour and add gradually. The less flour used, the more tender the cooky. Add caraway seed and chill. Roll to ⅛-inch thickness. Bake in a moderately hot oven (375° F.) about 8 minutes. Makes about 8 dozen cookies.

Caraway cookies are to New England butteries what orchids are to an evening dress. Full of the flavor of June fields, starred with daisies and washed with golden sunshine, they cling to a man's memory all the days of his life.

NEW MEADOWS INN COOKIES

[*Mrs. Annie Trusant, Portsmouth, N. H.*]

½ cup butter
1 cup sugar
1 egg
⅓ cup milk
2½ cups flour

1 teaspoon cream of tartar
½ teaspoon soda
½ teaspoon salt
½ teaspoon nutmeg
¼ teaspoon mace

Cream shortening, add sugar, egg and milk. Mix and sift dry ingredients and add. Let stand overnight. Roll very thin and bake in a moderately hot oven (375° F.). Makes 10 dozen 3-inch cookies.

MOTHER'S SUGAR COOKIES

[*Mrs. Jennie Duke, 53 Ferry St., Everett, Mass.*]

1 cup shortening
1 teaspoon salt
1 teaspoon vanilla
¼ teaspoon soda

2 cups sugar
1 egg, well beaten
5 cups flour, sifted
4 teaspoons baking powder

1 cup milk

Combine shortening, salt, vanilla and soda. Add sugar gradually and cream well. Add beaten egg and mix thoroughly. Sift flour with baking powder. Add to creamed mixture, alternately with milk mixing well. Drop from teaspoon on baking sheet. Let stand a few minutes then flatten cookies. Bake in moderately hot oven (375° F.) 12 to 15 minutes. Makes about 8 dozen cookies.

OATMEAL COOKIES

[*Mrs. John Connors, 136 West St., Gardner, Mass.*]

2 cups flour, sifted
½ teaspoon salt
½ teaspoon soda
1 teaspoon baking powder
½ teaspoon cinnamon
¼ teaspoon cloves
¼ teaspoon nutmeg
1 cup quick-cooking oatmeal

⅔ cup walnuts, chopped fine
¾ cup butter or other
    shortening
1 cup brown sugar, firmly
    packed
2 eggs
3 tablespoons molasses
2 tablespoons hot water

Add salt, soda, baking powder and spices to flour and sift again. Mix in the oatmeal and the chopped walnuts. Cream the shortening. Add sugar gradually, creaming well together. Beat in eggs one at a time. Add molasses and hot water. Gradually mix in the dry ingredients. Drop by teaspoon onto greased baking sheet, about an inch apart. Bake in a moderately hot oven (375° F.) 8 to 10 minutes. Makes about 36 cookies.

FILLED COOKIES

[Mrs. Harold S. Bowker, 201 June Street, Worcester, Mass.]

½ cup butter (or lard)　　　2 teaspoons cream of tartar
1 cup sugar　　　　　　　　1 teaspoon soda
1 egg, beaten　　　　　　　3 cups flour, sifted (about)
1 teaspoon vanilla　　　　　½ teaspoon salt

½ cup milk

Cream butter, add sugar, egg and vanilla. Mix and sift dry ingredients and add to the first mixture alternately with the milk. The dough should be stiff enough to roll out thin. Cut with a cooky cutter. Place filling on one cooky and then place another cooky on top of filling. Press down edges. Bake in a moderate oven (350° F.) about 12 minutes. Makes about 20 cookies.

FILLING

½ cup sugar　　　　　　　　1 cup raisins
2 tablespoons cornstarch　　　½ cup water

Combine sugar and cornstarch, add water and raisins. Cook in top of double boiler until thick.

BRAMBLES

[Norma Roberts, Bristol, N. H.]

pastry　　　　　　　　　　　1 cup sugar
1 cup seeded raisins,　　　　1 egg, beaten
　　chopped fine　　　　　　juice and grated rind 1 lemon

Roll pastry ⅛-inch thick; cut in 4-inch oblongs. Combine raisins, sugar, egg and lemon juice and rind. Cook slowly over low heat until thick; place a heaping teaspoonful on each oblong. Wet edges with cold water and fold over. Press edges together with floured fork, prick top and bake in a hot oven (450° F.) about 15 minutes. Makes about 20 brambles.

BROWNIES

½ cup flour, sifted	1 cup sugar
½ teaspoon baking powder	2 eggs, beaten
¼ teaspoon salt	2 tablespoons milk
2 squares chocolate	1 teaspoon vanilla
⅓ cup butter, melted	1 cup walnuts, broken

Sift flour, baking powder and salt. Melt chocolate and add butter. Add sugar to eggs, then add chocolate mixture and beat well. Stir in flour, milk, vanilla and nuts, spread on greased pan 8 x 8 inches. Bake in a slow oven (300° F.) 50 minutes. Cool. Cut in strips and remove from pan. Makes 16 brownies.

MAPLE NUT COOKIES

[*A Vermont recipe*]

3 cups flour, sifted	1 teaspoon soda
1 teaspoon baking powder	½ cup hot water
½ teaspoon salt	1 cup walnut meats,
1½ cups soft maple sugar	chopped
3 eggs, beaten	1½ cups dates, cut in pieces

Mix and sift flour, baking powder, salt. Beat maple sugar into egg, stir in dry ingredients; add soda dissolved in hot water, nuts and dates. Drop from a teaspoon on baking sheet and bake in a moderately hot oven (375° F.) about 12 minutes. Makes about 5 dozen cookies.

SNICKERDOODLES

[Mrs. Clara Rose Hadfield, 19 Putnam Rd., Somerville, Mass.]

2 cups sugar, sifted	1 teaspoon salt
2 eggs, well beaten	1 cup chopped raisins
4 tablespoons butter	1 cup milk
4 cups flour	1 tablespoon vanilla
4 teaspoons baking powder	sugar and cinnamon

Add sugar to eggs, then stir in butter which has been softened but not melted. Mix and sift dry ingredients; add raisins and add to first mixture alternately with the milk. Beat well, add vanilla. Drop by teaspoonfuls on greased cooky sheet. Sprinkle cookies generously with sugar and cinnamon mixed together. Bake 20 minutes in a moderate oven (350° F.). Do not place snickerdoodles close together on cooky sheet as they spread. Makes 36 cookies.

BUTTERSCOTCH COOKIES

[From the New England Kitchen of Louise Crathern Russell]

4 cups flour, sifted (about)	1 cup shortening (butter and lard)
1 teaspoon soda	2 cups brown sugar
1 teaspoon cream of tartar	2 eggs
½ teaspoon salt	1 teaspoon vanilla
1 cup nutmeats (optional)	

Mix and sift dry ingredients; cream shortening until soft; beat in sugar, eggs, vanilla and nuts. Stir in dry ingredients and knead into two rolls. Chill several hours or overnight in refrigerator. Slice paper-thin and bake in a moderately hot oven (375° F.) for 8 minutes. Makes about 8 dozen cookies.

THERE ARE ALWAYS COOKIES IN GRANDMA'S KITCHEN

LEMON WAFERS

½ cup flour, sifted
¼ cup butter
¼ cup sifted powdered sugar

½ teaspoon grated lemon rind
1 teaspoon lemon juice
2 tablespoons milk

Sift flour once, measure, and sift again. Cream butter thoroughly, add lemon rind and juice and blend. Add flour, alternately with milk, mixing well. Drop ¼ teaspoon on an ungreased baking sheet, placing about 2 inches apart. Bake in moderate oven (375° F.) about 5 minutes. Makes about 3 dozen wafers.

ROCKS

[Mrs. E. Petrin, 20 Lafayette St., Biddeford, Me.]

3 eggs
1½ cups brown sugar
⅓ cup lard, melted
⅓ cup butter, melted

½ cup raisins
½ teaspoon salt
2 cups flour, sifted
1 teaspoon baking powder

1 teaspoon cinnamon

Beat the eggs, add the sugar and beat. Add melted shortening, raisins, and dry ingredients sifted together. Mix thoroughly. Drop from teaspoon on greased baking sheet and bake in moderately hot oven (375° F.) about 12 minutes. Makes about 3 dozen cookies.

When the price of food was high and bills accumulated and a widow with debts wanted to marry again, New England (as well as New York and Pennsylvania) had a custom known as the shift marriage. Such a marriage, performed according to law, with a woman dressed only in her shift, was made to avoid hampering the new husband with old debts. A favorite spot for many of these marriages was three miles from Kingston, R. I., where three town lines meet.

COOKING IN MAINE—AND ELSEWHERE

Laura E. Richards

I do not know that Maine has any special State Dietary. Until 1820 she was a part of Massachusetts. Today, the whole country overflows her every summer. She is playground and breathing place. To be sure, the players have to be fed, and they seldom bring their food with them. What one and all expect in Maine is sea food, chiefly shell-fish. They expect chowder; fish and clam. We can give them this; the best, we rather think, to be had anywhere.

When I ask the excellent friend who prepares our own fish chowder for her recipe, she has none to give me; but the result is mirific. This is the way with many, if not most, good cooks. They know how to make a thing, they have perhaps little sympathy with those who do not know. Here in Maine we make our chowder, either fish or clam, with good rich milk (it does no harm to add a little cream); two or three onions shredded fine; potatoes and salt pork, diced; butter, pepper, and salt. The addition of tomatoes and other ingredients may (and does) suit New York; perhaps other States; it is not for Maine.

As for the lobster, he is the friend of all the world; and, for our Maine lobster stew, I will only say that it cannot be excelled. Probably each good cook has some little trick or quirk of her own, so I will not attempt to give a recipe.

Oysters and clams are beyond question, I suppose, the best of bivalves, but I wish to put in a word for the mussel, well known on European coasts, but largely neglected, even contemned, in this country. The mussel, boiled or stewed in its beautiful dark blue shell, is of a pleasing buff or yellow color, agreeable both to look at and to taste.

Mussels are invariably connected in my mind with Newport Island. I see a troop of rosy children, making their way through the fields after their swim in the bay, tugging a pail or pails of mussels, dripping and gleaming in the sunlight. There are no such mussels as those in Narragansett Bay. We used, I think, simply to boil them till the shells opened easily, then squeeze lemon juice on them, and so eat them, with great pleasure. In Bermuda they give you a mussel pie, much esteemed, but I think I like the plain way better.

For a more elaborate recipe for cooking mussels, I quote, by kind permission of a cousin, Mr. R. H. Gardiner, from the cookbook of my husband's great-great-grandmother, Mrs. Silvester Gardiner. It is a vellum-bound volume, with the title "Mrs. Gardiner's receipts from 1763." The original has lain for over a hundred years in the ancestral sideboard in the dining-room at Oaklands, in Gardiner, Maine. Recently it has been privately printed, in exact duplicate, by three of her great-great-great-grandchildren.

Mrs. Gardiner was born and lived in Boston; her married life passed in a large house on the corner of Winter and Washington Streets. Her portrait by Copley shows her one who, I should imagine, enjoyed the good things of life. She certainly was a notable housewife. This is the way she cooks mussels.

MUSSELS TO STEW

Wash them very clean from Sand, in two or three waters; then put them into a Stewpan, which cover close and let them stew until all the Shells are opened; then take them out and pick them out of their Shells. When they are all picked, and the little Crabs which may have been in any of them, are thrown away, put them into a Saucepan, and to every quart of Mussels put half a pint of the Liquor that came from them in stewing, which you must strain through an hair Sieve; add a blade of Mace and a piece of butter, as big as a Wallnut, rolled in Flour. Let them stew, and when done sufficiently, toast some Slices of Bread cut triangular, brown, and lay them round the Dish, pour in the Mussels, and send them hot to Table.

In those days of few and small inns and taverns, keeping open house was often a necessity, and the proportions of some of the recipes are somewhat staggering today. Moreover, Dr. Gardiner's estates in Maine caused much travelling back and forth from Boston to the Kennebec, a journey which must be made either on horseback or by water, and which took a week or even longer. Special preparations must be made for these journeys, as witness the following:

PORTABLE SOUP, FOR TRAVELERS, ETC.

Take three Legs of Veal, one Leg of Beef, and the lean part of half an Ham; cut them into small pieces; put a quarter of a pound of Butter at the Bottom of a large Cauldron; then lay in the Meat and Bones with four ounces of good Anchovies and two ounces of Mace. Cut off the green leaves of five or six heads of Celleri, wash the Heads of the Celleri clean, and then cut them up small, put them in, with three large Carrots, cut thin, then cover the Cauldron close and set it over a moderate Fire. When you find the Gravy begins to draw, take it up, and so continue taking up all the Gravy as it draws, and untill you can draw no more. Then put Water in sufficient to cover the meat, and set it upon the Fire again, & there let it stew for four hours when you must strain it, into a clean Pan, through an hair Sieve. Set the Pan on the Fire, and let it boil three parts away; then strain your Gravy also, which you draw from your meat into the Pan or Pot, & set it again on the Fire, and let the Soup boil gently untill it looks thick like Glue, observing to skim it the whole time it is on the Fire very carefully, so as to skim off all the Fat. You must take great care, when it is near enough done, that it don't burn. Put in Chyan Pepper to your taste, pour it upon flat Dishes, a quarter of an Inch thick and there let it stand untill the next Day; when you must cut it out with round Tins, a little larger than a Crown piece. Lay the Cakes thus cut on Dishes and set them in the Sun to dry. It will answer best to make the Soup in frosty weather. When the Cakes are dry, put them into Tin

Boxes, or a Tin Box, with writing Paper between every Cake, and keep them in a dry Place.

Pour a pint of boiling Water on one Cake, add a little Salt, and you have immediately a Bason of good Broth. A little boiling Water poured upon one of the Cakes will make Gravy sufficient for a Turkey or Fowls.

The longer the Cakes are kept the better.

N.B. As the Cakes are drying, be carefull to turn them.

When Mrs. Gardiner and Dr. Gardiner were quietly at home, she may have entertained him with Marrow Pasties.

MARROW PASTIES

Cut half a pound of marrow in little Lumps, and throw Salt upon them; skin shred six apples small and mix them therewith; to which, add a quarter of a pound of Sugar. Season with beaten Mace, Cinnamon, and Nutmeg; mix half a pound of currants ready washed and plumpt, well with all the other Ingredients, with Sack, Rose Water, or Orange Flower Water, to make them into turn-over Pasties with Puff Paste.

She is the only person who has ever told me how to prepare a Mutton Ham, a thing of which I have read, in books about Australia, through the years since I first found it in "Geoffrey Hamlyn."

MUTTON HAMS

Cut an hind quarter of Mutton like an Ham; mix an Ounce of Saltpetre, a pound of brown Sugar and a pound of common Salt and therewith rub your Ham well, and then lay it in an hollow Tray with the Skin-side down, and baste it every Day, for a Fortnight, with this Pickle; after which roll it in Bran and smoak it for a fortnight; then boil it, and hang it in a dry Place. It eats well broiled.

I hope I may try this recipe some day, but I am not sure.

All of the recipes are what one might call arduous ones. There is no dallying with anything. Even a pudding is a matter of severe labor. Witness:

A TANSEY PUDDING

A Pint of Cream, sixteen Eggs, throwing away the white of one half of them, beat the Yolks, and the Whites separately, and when beat thoroughly mix them and strain them thro' a coarse hair Sieve, then beat them again with one pound of Sugar, a little Salt and a grated Nutmeg; then add a pound of grated Naples Biscuit or fine French Bread, stir it well untill all the Lumps are broken and the whole is smooth and perfectly mixed; then pour in your Cream and put in a Pint of the Juice of Spinage, half a Gill of the Juice of fresh Tansey, and stir them well together. Then put a quarter of a pound of fresh Butter into a Bell Skillet, and let it just melt; then pour it in your Tansey and keep stirring it over a clear Fire untill it thickens and curdles; then pour it into an hair Sieve, and let all Whey drain off; after which put it into a Dish and smooth it over with a Knife or Spoon, and bake it in a slow Oven. Stick some Almonds upon the Top of it which have first been blanched and sliced, and some Citron.

Besides her Sea Food, I suppose Maine's most important culinary contribution is her wealth of camping and sporting cookery—and her pies! If I quoted from my fisherman son's admirable recipes for camp cooking, it would perhaps be misleading—I myself camp no more! I may however give his Camp Johnnycake recipe, since it is in constant use in my own household.

COBBOSSEE JOHNNYCAKE

1 cup corn meal	2 teaspoons baking powder
¼ cup sugar	2 eggs
½ tablespoon salt	1 cup milk
1 cup flour	1 tablespoon melted butter

For Pies, I will say against all comers that the following recipe, of the good friend who sees to my table for me, is the perfect Squash Pie:

SQUASH PIE

1½ cups of squash, put through a colander	2 egg yolks, beaten
¼ cup flour	1 tablespoon molasses
1½ cups of milk, "more or less"	sugar to taste
	ginger and nutmeg to taste

Last, add the beaten whites of the 2 eggs, and beat in well. Bake in lower crust only.

All these recipes, however, are those of newcomers to Maine— pale-faces! I am fortunate in possessing two really indigenous recipes, though the first belongs of right not to Maine, but to the South.

SEMINOLE SOUP

Take a squirrel, cut it up and put it on to boil. When the soup is nearly done add to it one pint of picked hickory-nuts and a spoonful of parched and powdered sassafras leaves—or the tender top of a pine tree, which gives a very aromatic flavor to the soup.

Valuable as the above is, my most interesting recipe, by far, is that kindly sent me by my good friend the Princess Watawaso, whose father was long Chief of our Penobscot Indians, at their reservation at Oldtown, Maine, and who is herself an admirable and devoted worker with and for her people. She writes me that her people much delight in muskrat stew, and look forward to this delicacy every spring and fall. She adds,

"Most people, because of the name 'rat,' shiver, but the muskrat lives only on roots, grasses and such things."

MUSKRAT STEW

When dressing the muskrat, one must be very careful not to burst the musk bag. All fat must be cut off, particularly under the front and back legs. Cut up (as for chicken stew), soak overnight. Wash well the next morning, parboil, wash again. Try out in an iron kettle 4 pieces of fat salt pork, sear the muskrat, put in 2 cups of water and cook slowly for ½ hour. Peel about 4 good-sized potatoes and cut in half, place on top and season with salt and pepper. When potatoes are almost done, remove lid until all liquid is evaporated. Serve hot.

I am so fortunate as to live where hunting friends kindly bring gifts of game in season: partridge, duck, woodcock, venison, rabbits. Beyond the avoidance of over-cooking, these require no special recipes. But do not let a *bad* cook touch any of them! The same is true of Maine's peerless fish, both salt and fresh water: smelts, shad, trout, bass, white perch.

I have tried raccoon, and found it rather too fat; and, once or twice, bear meat, which is like coarse beef. Candor compels me to admit that I have not yet tried muskrat, but I mean to do so.

BOILED HAM

My last word is given me by my beloved Uncle Sam Ward. I cannot give the whole of his wonderful recipe for boiling a ham; I can only say that a quart of champagne and a wisp of new-mown hay were indispensable. Circumstances, largely economic, have hitherto prevented me from trying this recipe, yet I doubt not that it is the best I have to offer.

The Ward Family has always liked its good *food*. Behind the jovial figure of Uncle Sam, I seem to see that of Great-Uncle John, of happy and hospitable memory, and to hear him say to my mother, "My dear Julia, all compounds of eggs and milk are rendered more palatable by the addition of a little white wine." Which nobody can deny!

It was easy enough to begin this screed; I find it more difficult to end it. Memories come crowding into my mind, many of them with a tag of association attached to them. How dear Cousin So-and-So liked Kedgeree! How many mussels did the Reverend Blank eat at a sitting? And so on, and on! But there must be an end of cookery, and I resolutely close the kitchen door.

Breakfast Habits

The late "Tommy" Hunt of the Boston Public Library staff, used to tell a story that shows how urban habits are carried, like the seeds of exotic plants, into regions where they begin to encroach upon deeper rooted native growths.

A summer resident was mowing his lawn one morning when a farmer drove along with a load of garden truck. As he drew opposite the yard, he stopped his horse and called, "Howdy! Want any cantaloupes this mornin'?"

"No, thank you; I guess not today."

"Got some nice ones."

"Yes, they look good, but I don't think we need any just now."

"Folks are usin' them a lot."

"So I understand."

"Yes. Don't seem natural, but I hear there's some that uses them in place of pie, for breakfast!"

R U A YANKEE COOK?

Answers on page 369

41. What is the design of the weathervane on Faneuil Hall Tower?
42. How do you pronounce Billerica, Concord, Groton, Quincy, Rehoboth?
43. What is Massachusetts' most famous fish?
44. What city is the locale of "The Old Clock on the Stairs"?

VII. SAUCES, PRESERVES, PICKLES, JELLIES AND JAMS

VERMONT BOILED-CIDER APPLE SAUCE

[An original old recipe]

"Boil yr. cider on the stove till it's down to a thick mush. This will require lots of replenishing. It takes a terrible lot of cider. Either use this in mincemeat, so, or mix it with straight apple sauce to eat."

BOILED CIDER APPLE SAUCE

[A later recipe]

2 quarts sweet apples, cored and pared
1 quart sweet cider reduced by boiling one-half

Put apples in a kettle, add cider, simmer 3 or 4 hours. If cider is sour add maple sugar or brown sugar to taste.

Some families used to make this sauce by the barrel, keeping it in the cellar and allowing it to freeze and dipping it out as needed.

APPLE BUTTER

2 gallons cider
8 quarts apples, pared and
    quartered

6 cups sugar
2 tablespoons cinnamon
1 teaspoon cloves
1 teaspoon allspice

Let cider boil until it cooks down to half its original volume. Add apples, a quart or two at a time; cook over low fire 4 or 5 hours. Add sugar and spices, stirring frequently lest apple butter "catch on." Makes about 6 quarts.

SWEET PICKLED APPLES

[Mrs. L. Rust, Beverly, Mass.]

Select tart, well-flavored apples. Cut in halves and remove core but do not peel. Put 3 cloves in each half. Make a syrup of equal parts sugar and water, using 1 pound sugar to 2 pounds apples. Simmer apples in syrup until tender. Store in a stone crock.

BAKED APPLES

Choose firm apples; core and cut ½-inch band of skin about their equators before baking. Place in baking dish. Add boiling water to ¼ the depth of the apples. Bake covered or uncovered in a hot, medium or slow oven until apples are tender. If uncovered, baste occasionally with the water in the pan. Remove apples, boil syrup until thick and pour over apples. Apples may have many different fillings to give variety—brown sugar and butter, raisins, nuts or cranberry jelly. Serve with cream.

CHRISTMAS APPLES

12 apples   2 cups water
3 cups sugar   1 cup quince jelly
                  ½ cup brandy

Pare and core perfect apples. Simmer (in a syrup made from the sugar and water) until firm but tender. Place apples in a shallow serving-dish, taking care to keep them whole and unbroken. Fill the centers with quince jelly. Boil down the syrup in which the apples were cooked until thick. Pour over the apples. Just before serving, pour the brandy over the apples, light, and bring to table. Serves 8 to 10.

Do you remember the clove-apple on grandmother's parlor whatnot long ago? Call it a "pomander" today, but it still remains an apple solidly embedded with cloves and guaranteed to last half a century.

APPLE BALL SAUCE

Pare apples and shape into 3 cups of balls, using vegetable cutter. Make a syrup by boiling 2 cups sugar, 1½ cups water, 10 cloves and 4 shavings of lemon rind for 7 minutes. Remove rinds and cloves, add ⅓ of the balls and cook until soft. Repeat twice. Cook syrup until reduced ½ and pour over balls. Serves 6.

BLUSHING APPLES

[To serve with roast pork or fowl—or as a salad or dessert]

½ cup red cinnamon candies   6 firm cooking apples, pared
½ cup sugar   and cored
 1 cup water

Dissolve sugar and candies in water. Put apples in a casserole with cover. Pour syrup over, cover and bake slowly, in an oven

300° F. for 1 to 1½ hours, basting frequently. Lacking the candies, substitute 2 sticks cinnamon, a few drops red vegetable coloring and 1 cup sugar.

BEAN POT APPLE SAUCE

[Mrs. George S. Bishop, 295 Whiting Ave., Dedham, Mass.]

Peel, quarter and core apples. Place in a bean pot, sprinkle layers with sugar and cinnamon (½ cup sugar and ½ teaspoon cinnamon to 8 apples is a good proportion). Cover with sweet cider and bake in a slow oven (250° F.) 2 to 3 hours or until fruit is tender but has not lost its shape.

BAKED PRUNES

[Mrs. Edward O'Donnell, 15 Wall St., Middletown, Conn.]

Wash 20 to 30 large prunes and put in a bean pot, barely covering them with hot water. Add sugar to taste, 3 cloves and the rind of ½ lemon. Bake slowly with cover on jar until prunes have almost candied, about 1 hour. Serve cold with whipped cream, thick cream or rich milk. Serves 4.

BAKED PEARS

Fill an earthen bean pot with Sheldon or Seckel pears, left whole and unpeeled. Add to each quart of fruit—

½ cup brown sugar   ½ cup hot water
½ cup maple sugar   ¼ teaspoon ginger

Bake slowly (300° F.) for 1½ hours, replacing water as needed in order to keep the pears from burning and to make a syrup in the bottom of the bean pot.

TEN-MINUTE CRANBERRY SAUCE

½ cup sugar   2 cups water   4 cups cranberries

Boil sugar and water 5 minutes. Add cranberries and boil without stirring until the skins pop open (5 minutes is usually sufficient). Remove from fire and allow the sauce to remain in the vessel until cool. Makes 4 cups.

GRANDMOTHER'S CATSUP

[Avis Williams, Brunswick Rd., Gardiner, Me.]

1 peck ripe tomatoes (about)   2 tablespoons mustard
2 cups sharp vinegar   1 tablespoon powdered cloves
6 tablespoons salt   1 teaspoon black pepper
4 tablespoons allspice   ¼ teaspoon red pepper

Cook and rub tomatoes through a sieve into a kettle until there is 1 gallon of liquid, free from seeds. Mix the vinegar and spices, and stir them into the tomato juice. Simmer until mixture thickens (about 3 hours) stirring constantly. Remove kettle from fire and allow to stand until cold. Stir and pour into small-necked bottles. Makes about 8 pints.

> *Sweetened catsup in Maine is regarded, to quote Kenneth Roberts who is an authority on "down east" cooking, "as an abomination against God and man, against nature and good taste." But when it comes to a clear red color the Massachusetts recipe which follows wins. A recipe for catsup dated 1860 calls for 1 pint of brandy 10 minutes before removing catsup from the fire.*

TOMATO CATSUP

[A Massachusetts recipe]

1 gallon tomato stock	⅛ teaspoon cayenne pepper
½ pint vinegar	⅓ cup salt
3½ teaspoons cinnamon	2 cups sugar

Cook 1 peck washed ripe tomatoes until soft without removing peel. (There should be about one gallon of stock.) Let stand for a few days in a crock. Force through wire sieve. Add the other ingredients. Simmer with tomato stock until proper thickness, adding sugar when nearly ready to bottle (in order to prevent burning). Bottle and keep in a cool place.

This recipe was used about 75 years ago by Joshua Davenport who manufactured and sold vinegar, catsup, and many kinds of pickles. His brother, Otis J. Davenport, lived in Colrain, Mass., and grew and harvested the materials for the business. This recipe was given to Mrs. A. O. Davenport, Main St., Shelburne Falls, Mass., by her mother, Fidelia, who secured it from Joshua.

GRAPE CATSUP

[Mrs. P. John Finnan, 80 Elmwood Ave., Waterbury, Conn.]

5 pounds grapes, cleaned and stemmed	1 tablespoon cloves
	1 tablespoon cinnamon
2 pounds sugar	1 tablespoon allspice
1 pint vinegar	1 teaspoon pepper
1 teaspoon salt	

Boil grapes in enough water to keep from burning. When soft, strain through a sieve. Add remaining ingredients. Boil until catsup thickens. Makes about 6 pints.

CURRANT CATSUP

[Mrs. Russell G. Cameron, 5 Seeall St., Gloucester, Mass.]

5 pounds currants	1 teaspoon cinnamon
3 pounds sugar	1 teaspoon salt
½ pint vinegar	1 teaspoon allspice
1 teaspoon cloves	½ teaspoon black pepper

dash red pepper

Boil all ingredients about 1½ hours or until thick. Bottle.

BREAD AND BUTTER PICKLES

[Eleanor Taylor, 382 Ward St., Newton Centre, Mass.]

4 quarts cucumbers	5 cups sugar
8 small white onions, thinly sliced	1 teaspoon turmeric powder
	½ teaspoon cloves
2 green peppers, shredded	2 tablespoons mustard seed
½ cup salt	1 teaspoon celery seed

5 cups mild vinegar

Select small crisp cucumbers. Wash and slice (do not peel) in paper-thin slices. Add onions, peppers and salt; cover with a weighted lid and let stand overnight. Then make a pickling syrup of the sugar and spices. Add the vinegar and pour over sliced pickles. Place over low heat and stir occasionally. Heat the mixture to scalding point but do not boil. Pour into hot sterilized jars and seal. Makes about 6 quart jars.

One quart of cracked ice added to the vegetables and salt before adding the pickling syrup makes a crisper pickle.

BRINE FOR CUCUMBER PICKLES

Wash small pickling cucumbers as soon as picked. Place in a crock and cover with a brine of 1 cup salt to each 4 quarts water.

Let stand 2 days completely covered with brine. Then make into sweet or sour pickles.

SOUR CUCUMBER PICKLES

Place cucumbers that have stood in brine (see above) in mixture 1 part vinegar to 3 parts water, covering pickles completely. Simmer 3 minutes, pack in jars, add 6 whole cloves and fill jars with boiling vinegar and seal at once. Or pack fresh from vines into jars and add hot vinegar and spice mixture. Seal at once. Longer method gives crisper pickles.

SWEET CUCUMBER PICKLES

Prepare cucumbers that have stood in brine (see above) in mixture 1 quart vinegar, 1 cup sugar, 1 stick cinnamon, 12 whole cloves. Heat to boiling, boil three minutes, turn into jars and seal. This mixture is the amount for 10 medium sized cucumbers and will approximately fill 1 quart jar.

OIL CUCUMBER PICKLES

[Mary A. Martin, 24 John St., Springfield, Mass.]

24 small (6-inch) cucumbers	1 cup olive oil
2 quarts boiling water	¼ pound white mustard seed
1½ cups salt	¼ pound black mustard seed
	6 cups vinegar

Wash, dry and slice cucumbers in very thin slices without paring. Cover with a brine made of water and salt and let stand overnight. Drain thoroughly, place in a crock. Mix olive oil, mustard seed and vinegar and pour over cucumbers. Stir frequently. Makes 4 pint jars.

MAINE SWEET MIXED PICKLES

[Mrs. Roland B. MacConnell, Adams Ave., Saugus, Mass.]

2 quarts green tomatoes
2 quarts cauliflower
2 quarts firm cucumbers
2 quarts onions

1½ quarts vinegar
2½ pounds brown sugar
2 tablespoons mixed pickling
    spice

Wash, trim and cut in pieces but do not slice the vegetables. Soak overnight in 4 quarts water and 1 cup salt. Drain. Heat to the boiling point in 2 parts water and 1 part vinegar to cover. Drain again. Make a syrup of the 1½ quarts vinegar, brown sugar and pickling spice. Boil 5 minutes, add well-drained vegetables and cook until well heated through or until desired tenderness is reached. (Cucumbers will look white when done.) Seal in jars. Makes about 8 quarts.

CHOW CHOW

[Mrs. Vinie Watts, Machiasport, Me.]

4 peppers
12 ripe cucumbers
4 pounds cabbage
1 bunch celery
1 quart onions

½ cup salt
1 cup flour
2 tablespoons mustard
1 teaspoon turmeric
3 quarts vinegar

Chop vegetables fine, sprinkle with salt and let stand overnight. Drain well. Make a paste of the flour, mustard, turmeric and about 1 cup of the vinegar. Add to remaining vinegar. Cook in double boiler until mixture thickens. Pour over chopped vegetables. Cook 10 minutes. Pour into jars and seal. Makes about 5 quart jars.

MUSTARD PICKLES

[Mrs. L. G. Young, 58 Preston St., Windsor, Conn.]

2 quarts green tomatoes	1 cup salt
1 large cauliflower	1 quart small white pickling
6 red peppers	onions
1 dozen small sweet gherkins	

Dressing:

3 tablespoons flour	1 cup water
3 tablespoons mustard	2 cups sugar
½ tablespoon turmeric	1 quart vinegar

Cut tomatoes, cauliflower and peppers in small pieces. Add onions whole, add salt, cover with water and let stand overnight. In the morning bring to a boil and cook 3 minutes. Drain. Make mustard dressing by mixing the flour, mustard and turmeric to a paste with the water. Add the vinegar and sugar and bring to boiling point. Add vegetables and gherkins and simmer 5 minutes. Pack in sterilized jars and seal. Makes about 7 pints.

PICKLED ONIONS

[Celia M. Mooney, Georgetown, Mass.]

1 quart small silver-skinned	1 tablespoon salt
pickling onions	2 cups vinegar

Peel onions and cover with water to which salt is added. Let stand overnight. Scald in this brine to keep onions white. Pack in jars, covered with hot vinegar. Makes about 4 half-pint jars.

GRANDMOTHER'S FRUIT PICKLE

[From the New England Kitchen of Louise Crathern Russell]

10 peaches	2 sweet green peppers
6 pears	2 hot peppers
4 large onions	5 cups sugar
30 ripe tomatoes	2 tablespoons salt
1 bunch celery	1 ounce pickling spice
3 sweet red peppers	1 pint vinegar

Cut up all fruits and vegetables except hot pepper; mix all together including whole hot peppers; add sugar, salt and vinegar and spice tied in a bag. Cook until thick, about 2 hours. Remove hot peppers and spice bag before sealing in jars.

PICCALILLI

1 peck green tomatoes, sliced	1 cup salt
3 pounds onions, sliced	2 cups sugar
3 large green peppers, cut into strips	1½ quarts vinegar
3 red peppers, cut into strips	1 cup whole mixed pickling spice
2 cups water	

Put vegetables into a kettle in layers with salt sprinkled between the layers. Let stand overnight. Drain. Rinse with cold water and drain again. Cook vegetables with sugar, vinegar, pickling spice and water until mixture has thickened slightly. Turn into sterilized jars and seal. Makes about 7 quart jars.

This recipe is from Gretchen McMullen, "Yankee Network," Boston, Mass. It belonged to her grandmother, Maria

Helen Ware Fenelon who first made it before the Civil War. There has never been a year since then when this relish has not been made, which gives it at least 77 years to its credit.

RUMMAGE PICKLES

[*Mrs. R. H. Sawyer, Littleton, Mass.*]

2 quarts green tomatoes
1 quart ripe tomatoes
3 sweet green or red peppers
6 onions
1 small cabbage
1 bunch celery

1 cauliflower
2 pounds sugar
1 quart vinegar
½ cup salt
1 teaspoon pepper
1 teaspoon mustard

Put all vegetables through food chopper, add salt, let stand over-night and drain. Heat sugar, vinegar and spices to boiling; add vegetables. Simmer 5 minutes and seal. Makes about 5 quart jars.

GREEN SLICED TOMATO PICKLE

[*To accompany baked beans*]

1 peck green tomatoes
1 cup salt
1 dozen large onions
1 cup sugar
6 red sweet peppers

2 tablespoons celery seed
1 tablespoon ground allspice
1 tablespoon cinnamon
1 teaspoon clove
1 tablespoon mustard
vinegar

Slice tomatoes, sprinkle with the salt and leave overnight. In the morning drain off the liquor, slice the onions; combine tomatoes, onions, and other ingredients. Place in kettle, cover with cider vinegar and simmer until tender, about 20 minutes. Pour into clean hot jars and seal at once. Makes 8 quart jars.

CHILI SAUCE

[Mrs. Chester A. Knowlton, 20 Maple St., Saugus, Mass.]

18 ripe tomatoes, chopped
6 onions, chopped
3 green peppers, chopped
1 cup sugar

2 teaspoons salt
1 teaspoon cinnamon, allspice
  and nutmeg
½ teaspoon cloves

2½ cups sharp vinegar

Cook chopped vegetables until tender then add sugar, salt, spices and vinegar. Simmer until thick. Then place in sterilized jars, and seal. Makes about 3 pints.

RHODE ISLAND RELISH

[Mrs. John E. O'Reilly, 466 Prairie Ave., Providence, R. I.]

20 large ripe tomatoes, cut in small pieces
6 tart apples, pared and cut in small pieces
6 large pears, pared and cut in small pieces
6 large onions, chopped fine
6 large peaches, cut in small pieces
3 large green peppers, chopped fine
4 cups white corn, cut from the cob
2 tablespoons salt
1 quart vinegar
2½ tablespoons mixed spice, put in a bag

Put tomatoes on to cook; simmer 15 minutes. Add remaining ingredients and simmer together about 2 hours; seal in jars. Makes about 6 quart jars.

The first local peaches were put on the market in Boston in 1828 for such as were able to pay 3 cents a dozen.

PEPPER RELISH

[A Vermont recipe]

24 sweet peppers   3 cups sugar
2 hot peppers   2 tablespoons salt
18 large onions   1 quart vinegar
            2 tablespoons celery seed

Seed peppers and chop with onions. Cover with boiling water and let stand 10 minutes. Drain, put in a kettle, add sugar, salt, vinegar and celery seed. Simmer 30 minutes. Bottle in small bottles. Makes approximately 6 half-pint bottles.

POTSFIELD PICKLES

["Old New England Recipe"—Mrs. William O. Abbott,
125 Chestnut St., Wakefield, Mass.]

3 pints chopped green tomatoes   ½ cup horse-radish
3 pints chopped red tomatoes   ½ cup salt
3 pints chopped cabbage   2 quarts vinegar
3 pints chopped onions   3 cups sugar
6 red peppers   ½ teaspoon cinnamon
2 bunches celery   ½ teaspoon cloves
            ½ cup white mustard seed

Combine vegetables and cover with salt. Let stand overnight. Drain and add vinegar, sugar and spices. Cook 20 minutes and seal in jars. Makes about 6 quarts.

GRANDMOTHER'S SAYINGS

He doesn't know beans when the bag's untied.
Small potatoes and few in a hill.

AUNT MELISSA'S YELLOW TOMATO CONSERVE

[Norma Roberts, Bristol, N. H.]

2 quarts small yellow
   tomatoes
1 lemon, cut in thin slices

½ pound candied ginger,
   chopped (optional)
8 cups sugar
1 cup water

Do not peel or slice the tomatoes. Combine all ingredients and cook until thick. Seal while hot in sterilized glasses. Makes about 8 pints.

The yellow tomatoes used for this preserve are no bigger than crab apples and look like drops of sunshine. Delicious in winter with hot biscuits.

RIPE TOMATO PICKLE

[May E. Foley, Massachusetts State College, Amherst, Mass.]

1 quart tomatoes, skinned and
   quartered
2 cups granulated sugar
¾ cup cider vinegar

½ teaspoon salt
spice bag
2-inch stick cinnamon
½ piece whole mace
12 whole cloves

Place ingredients in kettle and boil slowly until tomatoes are transparent and juice the consistency of 30% cream. Pour into jars and seal. If pickle is to be used immediately, place in crocks and place in refrigerator until time for serving.

Tomatoes should be firm and not too ripe. Allow ¼ pound

waste for every pound of tomatoes as purchased. Makes about 2 pint jars.

From the "Pocumtuc Housewife" published in Old Deer-field more than a century ago, comes this recipe for ripe tomato pickle. Perhaps its original title was Love Apple Pickle. The use of tomatoes at this early date was daring indeed as this vegetable was looked upon with suspicion until comparatively recent years.

REED FAMILY TOMATO RELISH

3½ pounds sugar
1 pint vinegar
7 pounds tomatoes
1 tablespoon whole cloves,
    ground in food chopper

1 tablespoon allspice
1 stick cinnamon, ground in
    food chopper
3 large or 4 small red peppers,
    cut in strips

Boil sugar, vinegar and tomatoes. As soon as skins break, take out tomatoes and let drain 3 days; then put them back into syrup and boil several hours. Add spices in a spice bag; also add red peppers. Boil until thick and dark red colored. Seal in jars. Makes 6 pint jars. Pieces of ginger added to this make it taste similar to chutney.

WINTER CHILI SAUCE

[Mrs. E. N. Bailey, Salisbury, Mass.]

2 onions
2 peppers (no seeds)
1 large can tomatoes
1 cup vinegar
1 tablespoon salt

½ teaspoon cinnamon
½ teaspoon allspice
¼ teaspoon clove
½ cup brown sugar
1 teaspoon pepper

Chop or grind onions and peppers. Combine all and simmer 2 hours. Makes approximately 3 cups chili sauce.

CHUTNEY SAUCE

2 red or green peppers	1 quart vinegar
6 green tomatoes	2 tablespoons salt
4 small onions	2 tablespoons celery seed
2 cups brown sugar	2 tablespoons mustard
1 cup raisins	12 large sour apples

Remove seeds from peppers. Cut vegetables in fine pieces, add raisins and cook slowly 1 hour with vinegar and spices. Add apples, cored and quartered. Cook slowly until soft and thick. Bottle and seal. Makes about 4 pint jars.

Great-grandmother's recipe from Miss Winifred M. Kelley, Willimantic, Conn.

UNCOOKED SACCHARINE PICKLES

[Mrs. Charles L. Keene, West Poland, Me.]

Wash and dry cucumbers (large ones may be split lengthwise and small ones left whole). Pack into dry, clean jars and fill to overflowing with the following *uncooked* syrup:

2 quarts vinegar	½ teaspoon allspice
¼ cup salt	3 tablespoons mustard
1½ teaspoons cinnamon	2 teaspoons powdered alum
½ teaspoon cloves	1 teaspoon saccharin
½ cup prepared horse-radish	

Syrup to make 4 quarts; pickles may be used in 2 weeks.

PICKLED NASTURTIUM SEEDS

Gather nasturtium seeds when they are small and green, before the inner kernel has become hard. Remove the stems and let stand in salted water overnight. Freshen in cold water, pack in small bottles, cover with boiling vinegar. Use as substitute for capers. Some cooks sweeten and spice the vinegar.

STRING BEAN PICKLE

[Mrs. Henry Morris, Proctorsville, Vt.]

1 peck butter beans or string beans, cut fine
1 dozen onions, chopped
2 bunches celery, chopped
2 quarts vinegar

3 pounds brown sugar
1 cup mustard
1 cup flour
2 tablespoons turmeric
2 tablespoons celery seed

Boil vegetables together in lightly salted water, to cover, about 30 minutes, then drain. Bring to a boil in a separate kettle vinegar and brown sugar; mix the mustard, flour and turmeric with a little cold water and add gradually to hot mixture as in making gravy. Add celery seed and simmer all together 20 minutes, stirring constantly. Then add vegetables and simmer 10 minutes. Fill jars to overflowing and seal at once. Makes about 14 quart jars.

CORN RELISH

[Mrs. Lena F. B. Reed, Saco, Me.]

18 large ears corn
4 large onions, chopped
2 green peppers, seeded and chopped
1 red pepper, seeded and chopped

1¼ pounds light brown sugar
¼ cup salt
3 tablespoons celery seed
3¼ tablespoons dry mustard
2 quarts vinegar

Cut corn from cob but do not scrape the ear, mix with onions and peppers and add remaining ingredients. Cook slowly 15 to 20 minutes. Turn into sterilized jars and seal. Makes about 5 pint jars.

RED CABBAGE RELISH

[Mrs. R. S. Tucker, 16 Longwood Ave., Fitchburg, Mass.]

1 large red cabbage	2 tablespoons whole cloves
½ cup salt	¼ teaspoon pepper
1 quart sharp vinegar	1 teaspoon allspice

Quarter the cabbage, cutting out the hard core; shred finely and place in a wooden or earthen bowl with ½ cup salt. Place in a cool place for 24 hours, stirring occasionally. Rinse in cold water and drain through a colander. Add vinegar; also cloves, pepper, and allspice, tied in a piece of muslin. Bring to a boil, add cabbage. Simmer 10 to 12 minutes, then allow to cool, with cover on kettle. Will be ready to use in 2 or 3 days. Keep in a covered crock in a cold cellar. Will keep several weeks. Makes about 2 quarts.

CELERY SAUCE

15 small ripe tomatoes	2 large celery heads
1 small green pepper	1½ tablespoons salt
2 onions	¾ cup sugar
	2 cups vinegar

Chop all the vegetables. Mix with the salt, sugar and vinegar. Boil until thick. Bottle. Makes about 2 half-pint jars.

HORSE-RADISH JELLY

[Mrs. Joseph Catanzaro, 39 Wildmere Ave., Waterbury, Conn.]

½ cup horse-radish	½ cup vinegar
3¼ cups sugar	½ cup liquid pectin

Mix horse-radish, sugar and vinegar until the sugar is dissolved. Bring to a boil, then at once add the pectin, stirring constantly.

Let come to a full rolling boil and boil for ½ minute. Remove from the fire, skim and pour quickly into small jelly molds. When firm, unmold as a garnish for beef pot roast. Makes 5 small molds.

DEDHAM RHUBARB RELISH

[Mrs. George S. Bishop, 295 Whiting Ave., Dedham, Mass.]

1 quart rhubarb, diced	1 teaspoon salt
1 pint vinegar	1 teaspoon pepper
1 quart onions, chopped fine	1 teaspoon cinnamon
2 pounds brown sugar	1 teaspoon cloves
1 teaspoon celery salt	

Cook rhubarb and vinegar 20 minutes; add the remaining ingredients and cook slowly about 1 hour. Seal. Makes about 4 pint jars.

This recipe won a prize in a national contest conducted by a leading women's magazine. It is a very old recipe.

❧

February Eats:
"The Household Magazine" (*published in Brattleboro, Vt.*) *in February, 1884, suggested the following:*

Breakfast: Roast beef, warmed in gravy; baked and stewed potatoes; hot rolls and butter; oatmeal porridge and milk; tea, coffee and milk.

Dinner at 1 p. m.: Pea soup, beef steak, broiled rare; stewed tomatoes; baked potaotes; baked sweet potatoes; mixed pickles; apple tapioca pudding; nuts, raisins, apples, grapes, and oranges; tea.

Tea at 6 p. m.: Bread and butter; stewed prunes; soda and graham biscuit and cheese; tea.

SWEET PICKLED GOOSEBERRIES

[*Mrs. L. Rust, Beverly, Mass.*]

6 pounds gooseberries   1 pint vinegar
6 pounds sugar

Remove the little blossom end of the gooseberries. Add vinegar and ½ of the sugar. Cook 20 minutes. Add remaining sugar and cook 20 minutes longer. Seal in glass jars. Makes about 6 pint jars.

AMBER MARMALADE

[*A Martha's Vineyard recipe*]

1 grapefruit   3 lemons
3 oranges   water
sugar

Cut fruit into pieces and remove seeds. Measure, add 3 times as much water as fruit. Let stand overnight. Drain, reserving water. Cut fruit in very thin shreds, return to water, boil 10 minutes and let stand overnight. The second morning add 1 cup sugar for each cup of fruit and juice and boil until it sheets from the spoon. Makes about 10 glasses.

NEW ENGLAND APPLE MARMALADE

[*Norma Roberts, Bristol, N. H.*]

2½ pounds sugar   2½ pounds tart apples, peeled
1¼ cups water   1 orange
1 lemon

Heat the sugar and water until the sugar is dissolved. Slice and core the apples; add the juice of the orange and lemon and the peel sliced very thin. Simmer until mixture is thickened, about 1¼ hours. Turn into glasses and when cold cover with paraffin. Makes about 6 large glasses.

ROSE HONEY

[Norma Roberts, Bristol, N. H.]

5 pounds white sugar
6 cups water
lump of alum, size of a cherry

petals of 8 double, fragrant roses
12 red clover blossoms
20 white clover blossoms

Boil the sugar and water until thick and clear (232° F.). Add the alum and boil 4 minutes longer. Remove from fire. Add the petals and blossoms. Let stand 10 minutes; strain and pour into sterilized jars while hot. Makes about 6 jars. Delicious with soda biscuits and gems.

ROSE PETAL JAM

[Norma Roberts, Bristol, N. H.]

2 cups rose petals
2 cups warm water
2¾ cups sugar

2 tablespoons strained honey
1 teaspoon lemon juice
pink coloring

Cut the rose petals into strips with kitchen shears, discarding the tough white base. Pack tightly in measuring cup but do not bruise. Add warm water and cook about 10 minutes, or until tender. Lift the petals carefully, allowing them to drain. Measure 1 cup rose petal liquid; add sugar and honey and cook until sugar spins a fine short thread (220° F.). Add the drained petals and cook very slowly about 40 minutes. Add lemon juice and simmer until thick. Add a suggestion of pink coloring and seal at once. Makes 3 or 4 small glasses.

COOLIDGE TOMATO MARMALADE

[*A Plymouth, N. H. recipe*]

4 quarts tomatoes (measure them whole)	2 lemons
	½ ounce cinnamon stick
3 oranges	¼ ounce whole cloves

Blanch the tomatoes with boiling water and pare them. Slice into a shallow kettle. Slice the oranges and lemons very thin and quarter the slices. Pour off half the juice from the tomatoes. Weigh the sliced tomatoes and add an equal weight of granulated sugar. Stir until the sugar is dissolved. Now add the oranges, lemons, cinnamon stick and whole cloves.

No more than 4 quarts of tomatoes (dry measure) should be boiled at one time. In order to preserve the beautiful color, a large shallow kettle should be used over high temperature so that the marmalade will reach boiling point quickly. Stir often and reduce the heat somewhat after the marmalade has begun to boil. Test by cooling a teaspoon in a saucer. When the mixture shows the crinkling signs of jellying it is ready for the jars. Makes about 6 pint jars.

APPLE JELLY

Wipe apples, remove stem and blossom ends, cut in quarters and put in large kettle; add cold water until apples are nearly covered. Cover and cook slowly about 25 minutes, or until apples are soft; turn into a jelly bag of canton flannel or several thicknesses of cheesecloth and allow juice to drain. (Do not squeeze, as squeezing makes a cloudy juice.) Measure juice; boil 5 minutes; add ¾ cup sugar for every cup of juice; continue boiling until jelly sheets from the spoon (220° F.). Skim and turn into glasses, cover until jelly has set; then cover jelly with a layer of hot melted paraffin. Porter apples make a sweet jelly; Gravensteins a spicy jelly. 2 pounds apples makes about 4 glasses of jelly. For best results cook only 4 or 5 cupfuls of juice at a time. Some cooks heat the sugar before adding; others do not.

COMBINATION APPLE JELLIES

Equal parts of apple and cherry, apple and rhubarb, apple and strawberry, apple and cranberry make delicious jellies. Three parts apple to one part barberries or quince also makes a satisfactory jelly.

MINT JELLY

Follow recipe for apple jelly. Before removing jelly from the fire bruise the leaves of a bunch of fresh mint and add. Add a small amount of green coloring. Remove leaves when desired strength of mint flavor is obtained.

QUINCE JELLY

Wash and quarter quinces. Remove the seeds. Follow the recipe for Apple Jelly.

QUINCE HONEY

[Marjorie Mills, "Herald-Traveler," Boston, Mass.]

6 quinces   sugar

Pare the quinces and drop them in cold water. Cover the skins with boiling water and boil rapidly for half an hour. Drain. Grate the quinces and add to liquor drained from skins. Cook mixture for 20 minutes. Skim and add an equal amount of sugar. Simmer for 10 minutes and then pour into clean hot jars and seal. Makes about 3 pint jars. Serve on hot biscuits or muffins.

CURRANT JELLY

Wash currants, but do not stem. Place in a kettle. Add ¼ as much water as fruit. Cook until currants are soft and colorless. Drain through a jelly bag. For each cup of juice allow ¾ cup sugar. Follow recipe for Apple Jelly.

MOCK GUAVA JELLY

[Mrs. Mary A. Lewis, 329 Wayland Ave., Providence, R. I.]

1 pound dried apples   5 cups sugar (about)
water   ¾ cups lemon juice

Wash apples and soak overnight in cold water to cover well. Cook apples in the same water until soft; strain through a jelly bag. Measure. There should be about 5 cups of juice. Add an equal quantity of sugar that has been heated, and lemon juice. Boil until jelly sheets from edge of spoon. Pour into glasses and cover with paraffin when cool. Makes about 12 glasses.

PARADISE JELLY

[Norma Roberts, Bristol, N. H.]

20 cooking apples   12 quinces
3 quarts cranberries   sugar

Cut the apples and quinces in quarters, but do not peel. Add the cranberries. Cover with water, boil until soft. Strain through a jelly bag. Measure juice and add 1 cup of sugar for each cup of juice. Boil until jelly sheets from spoon. Pour into glasses and when cold cover with paraffin. Makes 12 to 16 glasses.

GRAPE JELLY

[Mrs. Herbert Buttrick Hosmer, Elm St., Concord, Mass.]

Select Concord grapes that are not fully ripe. Wash and drain, place in a preserving kettle, mash well and heat until the juice flows freely. Strain through a jelly bag and add to the juice ¾ cup sugar for each cup juice. Boil until sugar sheets from edge of spoon, about 10 to 20 minutes. Pour into sterilized glasses. When cool, cover with hot melted paraffin. 2 pounds of grapes make 3 to 4 glasses of jelly.

Residents of Concord, Mass., point with pride to the "Grapevine Cottage," home of Ephraim Wales Bull. Mr. Bull, a Boston goldbeater, moved to Concord in 1836 where he purchased a home on Lexington Road adjoining Hawthorne's "Wayside." Here he devoted the major portion of his time to horticulture and the search of a hardy grape that would withstand the early frost and the severe winters of New England. Finding on his own property a wild vine that bore a grape of good flavor, he planted the seeds and cultivated the seedlings for six years. Soon his grape, "The Concord Grape" was in the hands of every nurseryman in the country. Mr. Bull's important contribution brought him fame but little money. On the bronze tablet over his grave in Sleepy Hollow Cemetery in Concord are the words— "He sowed—others reaped."

BEACH PLUM JELLY

[Sarah Lee Whorf, Provincetown, Mass.]

Wash beach plums that are red (not ripe), pick over and place in a kettle. Cover with water, heat to scalding. Pour off and discard this water and start all over again! Pour on fresh hot water so that it can be seen among the fruit but does not cover it. Cook until fruit is soft. Strain liquid through jelly bag. Measure. Add 1 cup sugar for each cup of juice. Proceed as for apple jelly.

Attached to a very old recipe for beach plum jelly is this note: "Never make this jelly on a damp day."

BEACH PLUM JAM

[Mae Bangs Twite, Oak Bluffs, Martha's Vineyard, Mass.]

Follow recipe for Beach Plum Jelly. When fruit is soft, press through sieve. Measure fruit, add 1 cup sugar for each cup of fruit and boil until jam is thick and clear, stirring to prevent burning. When sufficiently cooked, jam will sheet from spoon like jelly. Pour into sterilized glasses and seal.

The beach plum is found rooted in the dunes along the beaches of Cape Cod and Martha's Vineyard where excavations bring nothing to light but coarse beach sand. Where its nourishment comes from is a matter to marvel over.

As beach plum pickers know, there is something of the grape, the plum and the cherry about the beach plum. It is as though nature had combined the best features of all three. The thick tough skin of the ripe beach plum is much like that of the wild purple grape. There is a resemblance in the pulp and also in the shape of the fruit, to that of the cultivated plum, although it is much smaller. And its firmness and bitter flavor are not unlike those of the wild cherry.

There is an old Indian legend that the Great Spirit created the beach plum especially for man because the birds flocked to eat all other fruits in their season, thereby depriving him of his just share. Be that as it may, in the autumn when the beach plum bushes hang full of ripe fruit, no birds sit among the branches to feast, although they devour the bitter wild cherry.

Beach plum pie was once a popular dish. The plums were not pitted. The diner might take a first tiny bite and finding it free from pits, sweet and toothsome, be misled to take a larger deeper bite. Often his entire skull would be jarred to its foundations when his teeth came together upon five or six bullet-hard obstacles concealed within the pink sweetness of the filling. Later, when pie makers went to the trouble of removing the pits, beach plum pie became much less common, and no wonder.

The beach plum is today considered primarily a jelly fruit.

A newspaper writer on the "Martha's Vineyard Gazette" philosophizes on the beach plum in this wise:

"There is something peculiarly remindful of human life in the beach plum, its bush and fruit. The blending of bitter and sweet in the flavor of the fruit, the obvious fight against odds that is waged by the bush in order to maintain life and bear fruit. And the tinge of bitterness that is noticeable in the ripest of the plums is as though the bush was conscious of having always labored under the most serious of handicaps, beaten by the winds, undernourished, and that in disappointment at having been deprived of the beauty, size and symmetry of a real plum tree, the bitterness of failure has tinctured the sweetness of the fruit, even as bitterness in human nature is revealed beneath a kind and genial exterior."

GRAPE CONSERVE

[Mrs. Walter E. Purdy, 12 Ware St., Dorchester, Mass.]

4 pounds grapes
1 pound seeded raisins

2 oranges
3 pounds sugar

Cook the grapes until soft and sieve. Add raisins, the pulp of the oranges and the skin, cut fine and the sugar. Cook until thickened, stirring to prevent burning. Nutmeats may be added if desired. Makes about 6 half-pint jars.

CRANBERRY CONSERVE

4 cups cranberries
2 cups raisins
4 tablespoons chopped orange
    rind

1 tablespoon chopped lemon
    rind
2 tablespoons lemon juice
½ cup orange juice
6 cups sugar

Mix ingredients; let stand 30 minutes; boil quickly 10 minutes; lower fire and simmer until mixture thickens. Pour into sterilized jars and seal. Makes 6 jars.

CRANBERRY GINGER RELISH

[A modern Cape Cod recipe]

2 tablespoons candied ginger
1 can cranberry sauce (2½ cups)

2 tablespoons orange rind

Chop candied ginger and cut orange rind in very thin strips. (Use only the orange-colored portion of the peel.)

Break the cranberry sauce with a fork and combine with the ginger and orange peel. Makes about 2 cups relish.

CRANBERRY ORANGE RELISH

[*Uncooked*]

4 cups cranberries, washed and looked over

2 oranges
1¾ cups sugar

Put cranberries through food chopper; peel oranges, remove seeds and put rind and oranges through chopper. Mix with cranberries and sugar. Let stand for a few hours before serving. Makes 4 cups relish.

BLUEBERRY JAM

4½ cups blueberries
juice and grated rind 1 lemon

7 cups sugar
1 cup liquid pectin

Crush the berries; add lemon juice, rind and sugar. Bring to a hard boil and boil 2 minutes. Remove from fire and stir in pectin. Skim and stir for 5 minutes. Pour into glasses; when cold seal with paraffin. Makes about 6 glasses.

QUINCE AND APPLE PRESERVES

[Marjorie Mills, "Herald-Traveler," Boston, Mass.]

1 pound of fruit,—quince and sweet apple	1⅔ cups sugar water

Peel, core, slice and then cook quinces until tender in about 4 times their measure of water. Pare, and core apples and cut into medium thick slices and cook in a small amount of water until tender. Drain off the juice from both apples and quinces, add sugar to the juice and boil mixture for 5 minutes. Add fruit and boil mixture until it is thick and clear. Pack immediately into hot jars and seal at once. Makes 4 to 5 glasses.

PUMPKIN PRESERVE

4 quarts raspberries	9 cups sugar

Wash berries, sprinkle with sugar. Let stand 12 hours. Cook about 10 minutes. Pack in clear glasses and let stand in the sunshine two days. Makes 4 half-pint jars.

Strawberries may be substituted for raspberries.

RHUBARB JAM

6 pounds rhubarb, cut in small pieces	6 lemons sliced thin 6 pounds sugar

Put fruit in a large bowl, cover with sugar and let stand 24 hours. Boil gently for about 45 minutes or until desired thickness is obtained. Do not stir more than necessary so that fruit will be unbroken. Turn into scalded glasses and cover with paraffin. Makes about 8 glasses.

STRAWBERRY-PINEAPPLE CONSERVE

2 cups fresh pineapple, cut in pieces

6 cups sugar

2 quarts strawberries, hulled

Combine pineapple and sugar; simmer slowly 10 minutes; add strawberries, and continue to cook until thick and clear. Makes about 6 glasses.

HEAVENLY JAM

[A Rhode Island recipe]

3 pounds ripe peaches
3 pounds sugar

juice and grated rind 1 orange
pulp and juice of 2 oranges

3-ounce bottle maraschino cherries

Peel and mash peaches with potato ricer, discarding pits. Add sugar and let stand overnight. Add orange rind, juice, pulp and cherries cut in small pieces, also cherry juice. Cook until thickened. Makes about 6 pint jars.

SALEM CURRANT CONSERVE

5 quarts currants, stemmed
1 quart red raspberries
juice 6 oranges

pulp and peel of 1 orange, cut in small pieces
2 pounds seeded raisins

5 pounds sugar

Wash fruit, combine ingredients and cook until syrup sheets from spoon. Remove from fire, cool about 5 minutes, stirring frequently to prevent floating fruit. Pour into glasses when cool and set, cover with paraffin. Makes about 15 glasses.

SUNSHINE STRAWBERRIES

Fine-flavored, large strawberries are most delicious when pre-served in the sunshine. Hull, measure and allow an equal quantity of sugar. Dissolve sugar in just enough water to melt it, then cook it almost to the thread stage (220° F.). Add berries and sim-mer gently about 10 minutes or until fruit is tender. Do not stir; try to keep the fruit whole. Pour strawberries onto large platters or shallow pans, cover with mosquito netting or glass and stand in the hot sunshine for 2 or 3 days when mixture should thicken and jelly. Bring in each night. Put into sterilized jars and seal with paraffin.

Sweet pitted cherries, raspberries and blackberries may be pre-served in the same way. Fruit may also be dried in a very slow oven (110° F.) instead of by sunshine.

PUMPKIN PRESERVE

[From the New England Kitchen of Louise Crathern Russell]

1 medium-sized pumpkin   1 pound sugar
½ cup lemon juice

Cut pumpkin in half, remove seeds, peel off the rind. Slice in ⅜-inch pieces. Pack the slices in a crock, alternating layers of pumpkin with layers of sugar. Pour the lemon juice over it. Let stand for 2 days. Drain. Make a syrup of 3 pounds of sugar and 1 pint of water. Boil the pumpkin in this until the pieces are very soft. Pour off the syrup, and boil the syrup until thick. Then pour the syrup over the pumpkin and seal in jars. If desired, boil with the syrup a little ginger root and fine lemon peel. Makes about 4 quart jars.

The pale amber pieces of preserve make an interesting addition to the Thanksgiving feast.

SWEET PICKLED PEARS

1 pint vinegar
2 pounds brown sugar

2-inch stick cinnamon
4 quarts pears

Boil vinegar, sugar and cinnamon for 20 minutes. Stick 2 cloves in each pear. Place pears in the syrup and cook until soft. Can and seal. Makes about 4 pint jars.

GINGER PEARS

[From the New England Kitchen of Louise Crathern Russell]

10 pounds hard pears
3 lemons

5 pounds sugar
3 ounces Canton ginger

Peel pears, core and slice thin. Cut lemon rind into strips and add rind and juice. Add sugar and ginger. Simmer about 3 hours or until juice sheets from spoon. Remove from fire, cool 5 minutes, stirring frequently to prevent floating fruit. Fill pint jars and seal at once. Makes about 8 pint jars.

PICKLED PEACHES

2 quarts peaches
2 cups vinegar
5 cups brown sugar, firmly packed

stick cinnamon (4 inches)
1 teaspoon whole cloves
½ teaspoon allspice

Scald peaches and remove skins. Boil vinegar, sugar and spices (tied in a spice bag) for 10 minutes. Add peaches to the syrup (a few at a time) and cook until tender. Pack in clean hot jars, boil syrup 5 minutes longer, pour over fruit and seal. Makes about 4 pint jars.

CANDIED TOMATOES

[Mrs. L. S. Hapgood, 47 Sparks St., Cambridge, Mass.]

2 cups sugar   2-inch stick cinnamon
4 cups water   4 pounds tomatoes

Mix sugar and water, add cinnamon and bring to a boil. Peel tomatoes, add the syrup and cook slowly about 45 minutes, or until thickened. Remove cinnamon. Makes 3 small glasses.

PRESERVED CITRON

6 pounds fresh citron, weighed   3 pounds sugar
    after preparing   3 pints water
              4 lemons, sliced thin

Peel citron and cut in sections, removing all the seeds. Slice the citron about ¼-inch thick and cut into 1-inch square pieces. Boil the sugar and water to a heavy syrup; add the citron and lemon and cook slowly until tender. Keep in crocks or seal in jars.

Norma Roberts, Bristol, N. H., who sends this recipe adds: "Great-grandfather Prescott and his family lived with his son Frank and family and every Thanksgiving afternoon was dedicated to preparing citron for preserves. That huge old kitchen held a happy assembly around the big red painted table."

Candied angelica and sweet flag were among other early confections. Mountain cranberry, a small dainty species of bog cranberry, was used when the others were scarce.

WATERMELON RIND PICKLE

[Helen N. Upson, West Cheshire, Conn.]

8 pounds watermelon rind	several broken cinnamon sticks
1 quart vinegar	2 teaspoons whole cloves
3 pounds sugar	1 teaspoon allspice

Remove outer skin from rind and cut in medium thin slices. Weigh, and cook rind until tender. In a second kettle boil together vinegar and sugar and a spice bag containing the cinnamon, cloves and allspice. After the mixture has boiled, add the watermelon rind. Simmer slowly until rind is clear. Pack in clean hot jars, fill to overflowing with syrup and seal. Makes about 4 quart jars. 1 or 2 sliced lemons may be added with the watermelon rind.

Many Yankee cooks start their pickling season July 5th by making watermelon rind pickle from their 4th of July watermelon.

R U A YANKEE COOK?

Answers on pages 369-370

45. What Bay State College was founded by a tin-peddler?
46. Explain the expression— "He has too many shingles to the weather."
47. Why is Connecticut called "The Nutmeg State"?
48. For what vegetable is Maine famous?
49. Give the origin of the following:
    Beacon Hill
    Milk Street
    Brimstone Corner
    Damnation Alley
    The Common
50. Complete the following stanza:
    "Where the Lowells talk to the Cabots—"

VIII. BEVERAGES: HARD AND SOFT

RHUBARB TONIC

[A drink children like]

2 pounds rhubarb 　　　　 3 cups water

⅓ cup sugar

Wash rhubarb and cut in small pieces. Add water and cook slowly, about 20 minutes. Strain. Add sugar, heat again to dissolve sugar. Drink when cooled.

RASPBERRY PUNCH

[Mrs. Louise Staples, Winthrop, Mass.]

1 quart strong cold tea 　　　 1 quart raspberry shrub

1 quart water 　　　　　　　 juice 12 lemons

3 cups sugar

Combine all ingredients ½ hour before serving; add 4 pickled limes cut in slices, if desired. Strain and serve.

HAYMAKERS' SWITCHEL

[Mrs. Henry Kahl, Pittsfield, Mass.]

1 gallon water   1 cup molasses
2 cups sugar   1 cup vinegar
              1 teaspoon ginger

Stir the ingredients together thoroughly, "put in a stone jug," says the old recipe, and "hang in the well to cool."

Switchel—that good old Yankee drink—is nothing more than water seasoned to taste. It is thirst-quenching and inexpensive and the ingredients are always at hand; furthermore, it holds its own, lacking ice, better than most drinks of its kind.

SODA BEER

2 ounces tartaric acid   whites of 2 eggs
2 tablespoons flour   2 quarts water
2 pounds white sugar   juice of 1 lemon

Mix cream of tartar and flour with the sugar. Combine all ingredients. Boil about 3 minutes. When wanted for use put ½ teaspoon soda in a glass. Dissolve in ½ glass water. Pour into it about 2 tablespoons of the lemon mixture and it will foam to the top of the glass.

Mrs. Charles W. Gain, Steep Falls, Me., remarks that this is sometimes called "The Deacon's Summer Drink" and flavored with wintergreen instead of lemon.

RASPBERRY SHRUB I

4 quarts raspberries   1 quart vinegar
                    sugar

Add vinegar to berries and let stand 4 days. Strain. To each pint of juice add 1 pint of sugar. Boil 20 minutes. Bottle and keep in a cool place. A tablespoonful added to a glass of water makes a refreshing drink.

From "The Lady's New Book of Cookery" (published 1852) by Sarah Josepha Hale under chapter titled "Liquors and Summer Beverages." Contributed by Mrs. Thomas F. Fahey, R. D. 2, Scotia, N. Y.

RASPBERRY SHRUB II

1 cup raspberries   2 cups water
½ cup sugar   2 tablespoons vinegar

Crush the raspberries, add the sugar, water and vinegar. Serve very cold with a few whole raspberries for garnish.

"My grandmother was a Quaker and very, very temperate," writes Mrs. Clinton Mewer, 32 Old Orchard Ave., Old Orchard Beach, Maine. "However, she got thirsty now and then even as you or I, and so she made raspberry shrub. She used to cool it in the well."

GRAPE JUICE

Wash Concord grapes and pick them from the stems. Barely cover with water. Boil until skins are broken and seeds are separated. Strain through a colander and then through a jelly bag. Measure the juice. Allow 1 cup of sugar to each 4 cups of juice.

Boil the juice and the sugar for 15 minutes. Pour into sterilized bottles, cool, and seal bottles.

UNCOOKED GRAPE JUICE

Wash Concord grapes and remove them from their stems. Place 2 cupfuls in a quart fruit jar. Add 1 cup sugar and cover with boiling water. Seal and allow to stand several weeks before using. When ready to use, strain the contents of the jar.

YANKEE MEAD

[*Mrs. Volney E. H. Cone, 28 Providence St., Springfield, Mass.*]

4 pounds brown sugar	4 ounces cream of tartar
½ pint molasses	1 ounce checkerberry
3 quarts boiling water	1 ounce sassafras

Mix the sugar, molasses and boiling water; when lukewarm add the cream of tartar. When cold add the checkerberry and sassafras. Use about 2 tablespoons of this mixture to a glass of water and add ⅓ teaspoon soda, stir and drink immediately.

In grandmother's day mead was as common as ginger ale is today.

RAISIN WINE

[*Mrs. George Whelpley, 430 West St., Reading, Mass.*]

2 pounds raisins, seeded and chopped	1 pound sugar
	juice of 1 lemon
2 gallons boiling water	rind of ½ lemon, grated

Put into stone jar or crock and stir every day for a week. Strain and bottle. Do not use for 10 days.

From "Old Dr. Carlin's Recipes."

ELDERBERRY WINE

[Mrs. Alice Richardson, Dover, N. H.]

4 quarts elderberries
3 gallons boiling water
3 pounds sugar
½ ounce ground ginger
6 cloves

1 pound raisins
¼ pint brandy (if desired) to
    each gallon of liquid
1 yeast cake to each 4 gallons
    of liquid

Pour boiling water on berries which have been removed from the stalks. Let stand 24 hours. Strain through coarse bag or cloth, breaking berries to extract all possible juice. Measure and add other ingredients except yeast and brandy in proportion to amount. Boil for 1 hour skimming often. Let cool to "milk-warm" then measure again and add yeast in proportion to amount, and brandy if to be used. Let ferment with yeast 2 weeks and keep several months before using.

A rich bodied wine.

ELDER BLOSSOM WINE

[Mrs. Oliver Moore, Spencer, Mass.]

1 quart elder blossoms
3 gallons water
9 pounds sugar

3 pounds raisins
½ cup lemon juice
1 yeast cake

Pick blossoms from stems. Pack measure full, pressing firmly. Boil water and sugar 5 minutes, add blossoms and mix well. Cool to lukewarm. Add raisins, lemon juice and yeast. Put in crock for 6 days. Stir 3 times each day. Strain and let stand till December in covered crock. Bottle or put in fruit jars.

A light bodied wine suggestive of champagne.

BEET WINE

8 pounds beets   5 pounds sugar
12 quarts water   2 pounds raisins

2 yeast cakes

Wash, clean and cut beets into small pieces, boil in 6 quarts water until soft. Drain and put the liquid in a crock. Put the other 6 quarts of water on beets and boil until they are white. Drain again and to all the lukewarm liquid add the sugar, raisins and yeast. Let stand 3 weeks, then bottle.

Recipe given to Mrs. C. H. Tewksbury, Halifax, Mass., by a lady over 80 years old, whose mother first used it.

DANDELION WINE

[*Mrs. Russell G. Cameron, 5 Seeall St., Gloucester, Mass.*]

2 quarts dandelion blossoms   3 lemons, sliced, peel and all
   (no stems)   1 yeast cake
3 oranges, sliced   5 pounds sugar

4 quarts water

Pour 4 quarts boiling water over the blossoms, and let stand 3 days. Stir each day. At the end of the third day strain. Add 3 oranges sliced, 3 lemons sliced, peel and all, 1 yeast cake and 5 pounds sugar. Stand 3 days and stir each day. At the end of third day strain. Let stand in crock 4 weeks, in not too cold a place. Strain, bottle and cap.

Dandelion wine was made by the barrel in Colonial days. Many a child was kept at the picking of these brilliant little flowers in the early summer days, clearing broad green swaths across a yellow field.

CONCORD GRAPE WINE

[*Minnie M. Laing, 9 Winter St., Penacook, N. H.*]

Stem grapes, crush, measure, add an equal quantity of sugar and water. Let stand 3 or 4 days, stirring occasionally. Strain, put in crocks, let stand 6 months. Syphon off, bottle and cap. This wine improves with age.

½ bushel grapes makes about 6 gallons wine.

RHUBARB WINE

4 pounds rhubarb cut fine	4 pounds sugar
1 teaspoon almond extract	½ yeast cake
1 gallon boiling water	¾ tablespoon gelatine

Combine rhubarb, extract and water. Let stand 3 days and strain. Add the sugar and yeast, and the gelatine dissolved in a little water. Let stand for 2 days. Put into jug and cork. After three months strain and bottle.

SPRUCE BEER

[*Norma Roberts, Bristol, N. H.*]

1 gallon boiling water	¾ teaspoon oil of wintergreen
¾ teaspoon oil of spruce	4 gallons cold water
¾ teaspoon oil of sassafras	3 pints molasses
2 cakes compressed yeast	

Pour boiling water over oil of spruce, sassafras and wintergreen. Add cold water, molasses and yeast cakes. Let stand 2 hours, bottle, let stand 48 hours before using. Place on ice before serving. Makes 25 quart bottles.

POTATO WINE

[Mrs. Donald Shirtcliffe, Turner's Falls, Mass.]

10 medium-sized potatoes, grated   6 pounds sugar
     or ground   4 pounds seeded raisins
 2 gallons warm water   1 yeast cake

Combine and stir twice daily for 2 weeks. Strain and bottle.

GRANDMA'S GINGER BEER

2 cups sugar   1 compressed yeast cake
2 lemons, juice and rind   1 tablespoon cream of tartar
6 quarts boiling water   1 tablespoon Jamaica ginger

Put sugar and scraped (or grated) rind and juice of lemons into a large bowl. Pour the boiling water over them and let it stand until milk-warm. Dissolve the yeast in a little warm water with the cream of tartar and ginger. Add to first mixture and stir thoroughly. Bottle and tie down corks. Lay bottles on their sides in a cool place for three days. Fasten corks in securely or the working beer will force them out. Beer should be put into stone bottles if you have them. 2 tablespoons of ginger powder may be used instead of the extract but makes a slightly cloudy drink.

Hay-makers find this a refreshing drink when they come in from the fields.

This "written in" recipe belonging to the Kimball family of Hampton, Conn., is by Mrs. Lucy Kimball Ide, Charlton City, Mass.

METHEGLEN

[Norma Roberts, Bristol, New Hampshire]

3½ pounds honey to each 1 gallon of water. Boil 45 minutes. Pour this while boiling hot over some walnut leaves (bruised) 2 ounces to the gallon. Let stand overnight. Take out the leaves. Add a piece of toast on which a cake of yeast is spread; let it stand 3 days. Then close the hole of the keg with a sand bag, and let it stand undisturbed for 3 months. Then draw off in bottles, or a clean keg, and cork.

> *This was a choice drink that was kept in the closet in grampa's room for a little treat when influential friends called; or perhaps an extra vote or two were won through its potency.*

KOUMISS

2 quarts milk
¼ yeast cake in 1 tablespoon warm water
4 tablespoons sugar

Heat milk to lukewarm. Combine milk, yeast and sugar and bottle, filling each pint bottle to within 3 inches of top. Fasten tightly. Keep in cool place. After 2 days, lay bottles on sides. Best on fifth day. Made chiefly for convalescents.

BLACKBERRY VINEGAR

2 quarts blackberries   sugar   2 quarts cider vinegar

Combine and let stand 4 days. Mash and strain through cloth. For every 3 quarts of juice add 5 pounds sugar. Boil 8 minutes. Skim. When cool, bottle and seal. To serve, add one tablespoonful to a glass of water.

> *From "Grandma's Cook Book." Bottles were placed on*

their sides on cellar floor and covered with sawdust. Recipe is by Helen N. Upson, R. F. D. 1, West Cheshire. Mrs. Upson's ancestors were among the founders of Chatham, Mass., New Haven and Hartford, Conn.

HOT BUTTERED RUM

Heat medium-sized tumbler and dissolve therein 1 teaspoon powdered sugar in a little boiling water. Add one wineglass New England rum and 1 tablespoon butter. Fill glass with boiling water. Stir well and sprinkle grated nutmeg on top.

Generations ago when the early settlers of New England, due to the rigors of the climate and the hardships of life, required fortifying and stimulating beverages, rum was the most popular and beneficial drink. In the eighteenth century the rum industry was well established in New England and a flourishing business was carried on between the West Indies and the states of Massachusetts, Connecticut, and Rhode Island. The rum trade played an important part in the economic and social life of early New England. Molasses imported from the West Indies was converted into rum in the many New England distilleries not only for local consumption but large exports of rum were sent to the African coast in exchange for slaves who were transported to the West Indies for labor.

MINT JULEP

Using a silver mug (very important in order to obtain condition of proper frosting) place ½ teaspoon granulated sugar in the mug. Add enough water to make a paste. Grind fresh mint leaves into paste. Fill mug up to the top with finely scraped ice. Add Bourbon whiskey, pouring it through the ice. Stir with spoon until mug is frosted. Add sprigs of fresh mint.

CHAMPAGNE PUNCH

2 bottles champagne or dry sparkling white wine (Saumur or
   Vouvray)
1 large bottle (28 ounce) sparkling water
1 jigger (2 ounces) cognac or other good brandy *
1 jigger (2 ounces) curaçao or other orange cordial *
1 jigger (2 ounces) maraschino or other cherry cordial *
2 lemons, sliced
2 oranges, sliced
½ basket fresh strawberries

Have all ingredients thoroughly iced. Mix a short time prior to
serving. Place block of ice in bowl or, better still, have ice outside,
surrounding bowl. The proportion of champagne to water may vary
from equal parts of each to champagne alone, according to taste.
Makes about 24 4-ounce glasses.

* One, two or all of these may be used; the total used should be 6 ounces.

OLD-FASHIONED EGGNOG

Beat separately the whites and yolks of 12 eggs. Mix yolks in
punch bowl with 2 quarts cognac, 1 pint New England rum, 1½
pounds sugar. Add slowly 2 gallons milk. Stir constantly to prevent curdling. Place beaten whites of eggs on top. Sprinkle with
grated nutmeg. Place in tub of ice 2 hours before serving. This
recipe makes approximately 3 gallons.

*Every Christmas Eve Boston's Beacon Hill turns back
the pages of history and offers an enchanting scene.
From the brilliantly illuminated State House to Charles
Street, from aristocratic Beacon Street right over the Hill
into the slum districts, old houses beam holiday tidings to
all and hospitality reigns.
Caroling groups stream up and down the Hill past Bull-*

finch mansion fronts which are gaily illuminated with vari-colored lights. Good fellowship flourishes as luxuriantly as Yuletide greetings. At Louisburg Square, the focal point of the celebration, guests toast each other with eggnog.

Householders come to their doors as the carolers halt out-side. With them, as a gesture of democracy, the servants are permitted to stand. A few homes invite small groups of carolers to enter and warm themselves before the open fire. The custom of Beacon Hill carols was originated by Fred-erick W. Briggs, of Newtonville, Mass., in 1895 after spending a merry and musical evening in an English town. In recent years some 150,000 Christmas Eve celebrators have joined the wandering minstrels in celebrating Joyous Yule-tide on the Hill.

NEW ENGLAND BAKED APPLE TODDY

Dissolve 1 teaspoon of sugar in 2 ounces boiling water. Pour into medium-sized tumbler and add 1 wineglass applejack and half of a baked apple. Fill glass ⅔ full of boiling water. After stirring well, sprinkle with grated nutmeg. Serve with spoon.

TOM AND JERRY

Beat separately the whites and yolks of 12 eggs until the whites are stiff and the yolks lemon-colored. Mix in a punch bowl. Add 2 ounces Jamaica rum, 1 teaspoon ground cinnamon, ½ teaspoon ground cloves, ¼ teaspoon ground allspice. Stir well. Add sugar until the mixture reaches the consistency of light batter. In order to prevent the sugar from settling, use a dash of soda or cream of tartar.

To serve, place 1 tablespoon of the mixture in a small glass and add 3 ounces brandy. Fill the glass with boiling water and add grated nutmeg.

A mixture of ½ brandy, ¼ Jamaica rum, and ¼ Santa Cruz rum, may be substituted for the straight brandy.

SHERRY COBBLER

A great summer drink, refreshing as an east wind, is a Sherry Cobbler.

To make:
Half fill a tall glass with cracked ice
Add 1 tablespoon of powdered sugar
Add 1 sherry glass of sherry
Stir with a spoon until glass is frosted
Decorate with fruit, sliced orange, sliced
lemon, sliced pineapple, cherries, etc.
Serve with straws.

Cobblers are of American origin and are great favorites in all warm climates.

OCTOBER ALE

"Adam and Eve were rightly damned for eating the appelle in the Garden of Eden," wrote the old Yankee. "They should have made cyder." "Or apple jack," a modern Yankee adds, "that's a potent drink!"

That some of it was potent, a New Hampshire farmer once proved. The story goes that he was carrying a jug of it along a railroad and was caught on a trestle, with trains approaching in either direction. In his fright, he dropped the jug, which exploded, blew up the bridge, wrecked both trains and killed all the fish in the river for three miles in both directions. All the searchers could find of the farmer were his stomach and his gullet. Those organs, because of an almost continuous diet of applejack, were so heavily lined with copper, that when they were sent to the mint, $14.20 in pennies was returned.

CLARET PUNCH

2 bottles claret
2 large bottles sparkling water
1 jigger (2 ounces) cognac or other good brandy
1 jigger (2 ounces) curaçao or other orange cordial
1 jigger (2 ounces) sherry
¼ pound sugar
    rind of one lemon
4 slices cucumber (not peeled)

Mix claret, sugar, lemon and cucumber, and ice for several hours. Place block of ice in punch bowl, pour in the iced mixture and the remaining ingredients. Stir gently. Makes about 25 4-ounce glasses.

RUM PUNCH

1 bottle rum (New England Rum or Jamaica Rum may be used. The New England makes a less heavy punch)
½ pint Virgin Island rum (for added flavor)
½ pint cognac or other good brandy
½ pint claret
½ pint cold strong tea
1 bottle sparkling wine (champagne or Sparkling Saumur, etc.)
    or 1 large bottle sparkling water
3 oranges, sliced
1 pineapple, sliced
¼ pound sugar (½ pound if a sweeter punch is desired)

Mix all ingredients except sparkling wine or water at least 12 hours before serving. Place block of ice in punch bowl. Add previously mixed ingredients and sparkling wine or water. Stir well. Makes about 22 4-ounce glasses.

CIDER CHAMPAGNE

Make cider about November 25th from perfect apples without rot. Do not use apples which have been frozen. Delicious or Baldwins are best. Put cider in a new whiskey barrel. To a 50-gallon barrel add 10 pounds white sugar and 10 pounds light brown sugar. Be sure to have 2 extra gallons of cider to fill in barrel as pumice works out. Keep a piece of burlap over bung hole while cider is working. Cider should be kept in a cool place at all times. It will be ready to bottle in about 8 weeks. Do not draw it from the bottom of the barrel but syphon it out.

No one in all New Hampshire makes more sparkling cider champagne than C. H. Weeks, Peterboro, N. H., whose directions are given above.

THE MULLS

3 bottles wine (usually claret, port, sherry or madeira)
6 teaspoons mixed powdered cloves, cinnamon and nutmeg
6 cups water
12 fruit sugar cubes, assorted flavors

Boil spices in water until steam becomes pungent. Stir in sugar cubes and wine and bring to a boil. Serve steaming hot. Makes about 25 4-ounce glasses of hot punch.

BRANDY PUNCH

2 bottles cognac or other good brandy
½ bottle orange curaçao
2 jiggers grenadine

2 bottles sparkling water
1¼ pounds sugar
juice of 15 lemons
juice of 4 oranges

Place a large block of ice in punch bowl. Add above ingredients. Stir well. Makes about 35 4-ounce glasses.

WHISKEY PUNCH

2 bottles whiskey
(rye or bourbon)
1 bottle sparkling water

½ pound sugar
juice of 3 lemons
2 lemons, sliced
1 orange, sliced

Place large block of ice in punch bowl. Add above ingredients. Mix well.

CHAMPAGNE COBBLER

⅓ glass fine ice

½ teaspoon powdered sugar
1 piece orange peel

To the ice add the sugar and orange peel. Fill with dry champagne or great western. Decorate with fruit. Serve with straw.

HOT BRANDY SLING

[Mrs. Mary O'Brien, Pleasant Street, Otter River, Mass.]

1 lump sugar dissolved in hot water
1 wine glass brandy

Fill glass with hot water, grate nutmeg on top. Serve at once.

CHERRY BOUNCE

[Mrs. F. A. Hagen, Atlantic St., Plymouth, Mass.]

Fill a gallon jar with wild cherries and pour in enough whiskey to cover. (Rum is preferred by some Yankees.) Let stand for 3 weeks. Then pour off the clear liquor and set aside. Mash the cherries, breaking the stones, and drain in a jelly bag. Add this to the first pouring off. For every 2 quarts of liquor from the cherries, take 1 pound of white sugar dissolved in a gill of water, bring to boil and mix with the liquor, stirring well. Then bottle and let stand several weeks before using. As the lady who gave this recipe to Mrs. Hagen used to say:—"Hifalutin people call this cherry cordial, but I say it's cherry bounce."

OLD IRONSIDES RUM AND SODA

Into a large bar glass put the juice of 1 lemon, 2 dashes orange bitters, 1 wine glass New England rum, and 3 small lumps ice. Fill up with plain soda water. Mix and remove ice.

André Simon, President of the Wine and Food Society of England, once described a bottle of old rum from the renowned stock of Medford, Mass., as "a steel fist in a velvet glove."

FISH HOUSE PUNCH

The following is believed to be the authentic recipe for this famous old punch as served at the famous Fish House Club in Philadelphia. This punch was often served in New England.

Dissolve ¾ pound of loaf sugar in a little water in punch bowl. When it is entirely dissolved, add a bottle of lemon juice. Next add 2 bottles Jamaica rum, 1 bottle cognac, 2 bottles of water and a wine glass of peach cordial. Put a big cake of ice in the punch bowl. Let Punch stand about 2 hours, stirring once in a while. In winter, when ice melts more slowly, more water may be used; in summer less. The melting of the ice dilutes the mixture sufficiently. Makes about 60 4-ounce glasses.

PLANTERS' PUNCH

The basis for nearly all West Indian rum drinks is:
1 of sour, 2 of sweet, 3 of strong, 4 of weak.
Any of the best West Indian rums may be used in mixing this punch.

½ bottle (12 ounces) fresh lime or lemon juice
1 bottle sugar syrup (or 1¼ pounds sugar)
1½ bottles rum
2 bottles water (or its equivalent in ice-and-water or ice alone, about 3 pounds).

Mix all ingredients well. Decorate with fresh fruit as desired. Makes about 30 4-ounce glasses.

OLD SALEM SMASH

Into a large bar glass put 2 tablespoons sugar, 2 tablespoons water, 4 sprigs fresh mint, rubbed to bring out the flavor, ½ glass shaved ice, and 1 wine glass New England rum. Mix well.

HOT APPLEJACK

⅓ applejack   juice ¼ lemon
⅔ boiling water   2 teaspoons sugar
                          1. slice lemon
Stir together.

A Maine logger was treating one of his cronies to apple-jack. Because he was very choice of it, they were to have only one drink apiece.

After the jug was back in the cupboard the logger smacked his lips, settled back in his chair and waited for his friend to speak. . . . After a long silence the logger went to the cupboard and with a sheepish grin, said, "Well, fella, a bird can't fly with only one wing."

MULLED CIDER

½ teaspoon allspice   1 quart cider
2-inch stick cinnamon   ⅓ cup brown sugar
6 whole cloves   nutmeg

Tie allspice, cinnamon and cloves in a cheesecloth bag. Drop bag into kettle of hot cider with sugar added and let it simmer until cider is spicy enough. Serve in mugs with dash of nutmeg. Serves 4.

FAMILY TONIC—1848

"Take myrrh, 12 ounces; cayenne pepper, 10 ounces; pickling ash berry, 2 ounces; sculcap and peach-meat, 4 ounces; alcohol, one gallon. Put into convenient vessel and shake several times a day for 10 days. Will be found useful in feeble or languid states of the system, colic, hysteria, rheumatism, mortification, and in all violent attacks of Disease. Dose: a tablespoonful, more or less according to circumstances." And be it said that great-granddad knew his "circumstances."

MAPLE SUGARING

"SAP'S RISIN'"

Sydney Wooldridge

The manufacture of maple syrup is not a process, but a ritual—a ritual of mysticism that has all the appurtenances of paganism and the Black Arts. The very metamorphosis of a thin, colorless, insipid, sweetish liquid of no particular character into a rich and delicate flavor, a distinctive table personality, partakes of alchemy. It could not be more marvelous were it done with the aid of unicorn horn, mummy dust, and bezoar stone. The mysterious offering of the trees, thousands, each its patient drip and drip; the attendance of the weather, its rhythm of freeze and thaw by night and day; the votive fire, its bottomless nap of coals endlessly devouring eight-foot logs, its roaring draft dominating and seemingly activating every movement within the sap house for days and weeks on end, constantly attended, never allowed to die; the oxen; the patchwork of snow in the naked orchard; the spiles and buckets, expressive symbols—all these are the trappings of a cult. A whole building, one of the most important and best loved on the farm, is set aside, a chapel, for the exclusive use of the god of sapping and his priests.

Priests is the word, for any one who once participates in the rites of sugaring-off becomes a quiet fanatic who yearly, at the season of Easter and the Passover and the pagan festivals of the rebirth of the world, returns to the sap house with a lilting heart, or, far away in years or miles, feels twinges of nostalgia.

Weeks before the first thaw, when the frost is still six feet in the ground and marbles are unthought of, when Christmas and New Year's are barely gone and the seed catalogues have only begun to arrive, old weather wiseacres, knowing better even while they say it, try to wish the season into the present by remarks of, "Well, it'll soon be time for sugarin'-off," and, "Sap's about due to rise," remarks accompanied by wistful gazings over the hills on the horizon, introduced into conversations without preamble or apparent motivation and accepted by the hearer with the same momentary religious exaltation. Buckets are repaired and washed and set by the evaporator so long they have to be washed again before they are hung. Spiles are counted and furbished; wood, twenty, thirty cords of it, is piled in the open end of the sap house to form a fourth wall while the snow still lies heavy on the side hills. Spontaneously the fervor rises and, lacking the encouragement of the weather, dies, to rise and die again.

And then one morning, when, perhaps, no one about the farm has mentioned or thought of sapping for a week or more, Matt, the son of the family, wakes. Still wallowing in the warmth of sleep, he realizes suddenly (how he does not know; the knowledge springs into his head full born) that this is the day. He's off through the house spreading the tidings with a shout, and out to the big maple in the yard in his pajamas—making the first tap before sunup, when the sap will hardly start to rise before noon.

The ritual begins. The oxen, Buck and Broad, trace through the orchard with the sledge load of buckets and spiles. Father and the hired man and Uncle John and Allie from back of the mountain, the Coffin boys and Pops Talley and Jean, the Canuck, bore and hang, estimate the run, hazard weather predictions—there is no lack of willing hands during the sapping season.

Matt sucks the first drops from the first spile and, although it is hardly worth the effort from an economic point of view, once more Buck and Broad trace through the orchard, this time drawing the fifty gallon gathering tank while the crew collects the few hours' offering. There is no profit in kindling the great fire to boil down these few gallons of sap that will make a scant quart of syrup—but farmers would sap if there were no profits at all; many do. The first run is sacred; the first born upon the altar, the wine upon the ground. Profits or no profits, the fire is lighted; the draft roars; steam rolls under the ridge ventilator, steam that sweetens hair and stiffens clothes with a sizing of sugar. Duke, the setter, sleeps under the fire box. Stories of runs almost forgotten fly while the sap bubbles and froths. A dozen pairs of eyes, not trusting the watcher's, needlessly inspect the thermometer in the last tray of the labyrinthed evaporator a dozen times every five minutes.

And when the first run is drawn off—

Tomorrow night the syrup will be clear, golden, light, delicate, fancy. Tonight it has served to wash the conduit pipes and the evaporating trays. It is brown, sluggish, almost dull in taste. It would hardly test B.

There is an adage that the first run is the best run. It is true, if you can be in the sap house when it is drawn off. The tin cup passing silently and reverently from hand to hand, from the straining bucket to the woodpile, is an orgy as truly as any ancient revel of Dionysus. Not a man in the sap house then will admit that this is not the choicest brew of the season.

When the farmer assures you that the syrup he sells you is the first run, do not believe him. The first run is gone as soon as it is cool enough to drink. You would not have liked it, anyway; but it was the best of the season.

It was.

HOW TO MAKE A ROSE POTPOURRI

[Household Department, Boston Sunday "Post"]

First of all the roses should be just blown, of the sweetest smelling varieties and gathered as dry as possible. After each gathering spread the petals out upon a sheet of paper and leave until they are free from all moisture. Then place a layer of petals in your jar, sprinkling with very coarse salt, and so on, alternating layers of petals and sprinklings of salt until jar is almost filled. Leave for a few days until a froth is formed, then mix thoroughly, adding more petals and salt and repeat mixing operation daily for a week.

The next step is the addition of various aromatic gums and spices, such as benzoin, cassia buds, cinnamon, cloves, cardamon and vanilla beans, all of which may be obtained at any drug store. Five cents each of benzoin, cassia buds (or ½ teaspoon ground cinnamon) and 5 cents worth cardamon beans will be sufficient for an ordinary jar. Cloves should be used sparingly, probably half dozen whole ones bruised in a mortar, or not more than a half a teaspoon of the ground spice. One vanilla bean will suffice.

After these have been added, mix again and leave for a few days more when you may add the essential oils. Those of the jasmin, violet, tuberose and attar of rose are best, with just a hint of ambergris and musk, and all of these must be procured from a perfumer, although a druggist could get them for you if he chose to. Ten cents worth of each of these is enough, with the exception of attar of roses, these drops being so exceptionally pleasing for a rose jar that twice the amount may be used.

Mix the oils in thoroughly and keep covered except when you wish to perfume your room.

If these directions are followed carefully, you will have a rose jar which will be a joy forever.

IX. CANDIES AND SWEETMEATS

OLD-FASHIONED BUTTERSCOTCH

2 cups brown sugar   ½ cup milk
¼ cup molasses   2 tablespoons water
                 2 tablespoons vinegar

Combine ingredients; cook until mixture cracks when tried in cold water (290° F.). Pour candy into buttered tins and mark into squares as it hardens. Makes 18 squares.

CANDIED CRANBERRIES

[*A Cape Cod recipe*]

½ cup firm cranberries   ½ cup sugar
                 ½ cup water

Wash and dry berries and prick each with a needle. Boil sugar and water until syrup spins a thread (234° F.). Add berries and continue cooking until syrup forms a hard ball in cold water (250° F.). Lift berries from syrup, remove to wax paper and let stand until well dried. Roll in granulated sugar. Use like candied cherries.

FUDGE

2 cups sugar	2 tablespoons light corn syrup
¾ cup milk	2 squares chocolate
⅛ teaspoon salt	1 teaspoon vanilla
¾ cup walnuts, broken in pieces	

Combine sugar, milk, salt and corn syrup. Place over low heat, bring to a boil and boil gently until mixture forms a soft ball in cold water (238° F.). Remove from heat and add chocolate. (It is not necessary to cut chocolate in pieces.) Cool fudge for 10 minutes. Add butter and beat until fudge is thick and begins to lose its glossy appearance. Add vanilla and nuts and pour into buttered pan (8" x 8"). Cut in squares while still soft.

APPLETS

[A modern Yankee recipe]

8 medium firm cooking apples	2 tablespoons unflavored
or	gelatine
2 cups unsweetened apple pulp	1 cup chopped walnut meats
½ cup cold water	1 tablespoon lemon juice
2 cups white sugar	powdered sugar

Peel and core apples; cut in small pieces. Cook in sauce pan with ¼ cup of the cold water until tender; force through sieve; add white sugar, cook until thick, about 30 minutes, stirring occasionally to prevent burning. Soak gelatine in remaining ¼ cup cold water; add to apple mixture, stirring until dissolved. Cool slightly by placing pan in cold water for 15 to 20 minutes; add walnut meats and lemon juice; mix well. Pour into flat pan to ½-inch thickness. Place in automatic refrigerator or let stand on ice overnight. Cut in squares and roll in powdered sugar. 1 tablespoon cornstarch added to each ½ cup sifted powdered sugar will prevent stickiness.

MOLASSES TAFFY

[The kind children love to pull]

1 cup sugar
¾ cup brown sugar
2 cups molasses

1 cup water
¼ cup butter
⅛ teaspoon soda

¼ teaspoon salt

Cook white and brown sugars, molasses and water together until brittle (272° F.) stirring frequently to prevent burning. Remove from heat, add butter, soda and salt, stirring just enough to mix. Pour into large greased pans and allow to stand until cool enough to handle. Butter fingers, and pull taffy until firm and light yellow. Stretch into a rope, twist and cut into 1-inch lengths. Makes 50 pieces.

MOLASSES BRITTLE

2 cups sugar   2 cups molasses   ⅛ teaspoon soda

Boil sugar and molasses in a heavy iron skillet (295° F.) until it cracks when tested in cold water. Remove from fire and stir in soda. Don't revel long in the beautiful blending of color, but pour immediately into well-buttered tins. Cool, crack up and munch. If you are fortunate enough to have butternuts, place a layer of nutmeats on the pans after they are buttered.

Directions for making this candy are given by Irene Boulton, Hollis, N. H., who says, "My father often made this candy which even his most sophisticated children always relished."

BUTTERNUT PANOCHA

[*A Vermont recipe*]

3 cups light brown sugar	2 tablespoons butter
¼ teaspoon salt	1 teaspoon vanilla
½ cup milk	⅔ cups coarsely chopped butternuts

Combine sugar, salt and milk and cook over low heat until a soft ball can be formed (238° F.). Remove from stove; add butter, set aside to cool without stirring. When cool, stir in vanilla. Beat until candy becomes creamy. Stir in nut meats. Turn into buttered dish, when candy is thick. Cut into squares when cold. Makes 24 large pieces. Walnuts or pecans may be substituted for butternuts.

MAPLE CARAMELS

¼ cup white sugar	¼ cup corn syrup
¾ cup maple sugar	⅛ teaspoon salt
½ cup heavy cream	1 tablespoon butter
¼ cup brown sugar	⅓ cup whole nut meats

Cook the first five ingredients until a soft ball is formed when a little of the mixture is dropped in cold water (250° F.). Remove, add the salt, butter and nut meats and pour into buttered pan. When cold, cut into squares.

Today, thirty per cent of this country's maple crop comes from Vermont. There is a tendency for maple sugar to become stronger in flavor the farther north the region in which the trees grow. Why, no one can say. But Vermont is happily located so that its syrup carries a distinctive flavor that is neither flat nor too strong.

The first run syrup is generally considered the finest of the crop. Vermonters believe in treating the "home folks" before giving the "furriners" a taste. Of course, some goes to Cousin Hattie who moved to Wisconsin and "can't get the right kind of syrup from any place but home."

TAFFY APPLES

[*Often called Lollipop Apples*]

1 cup brown sugar	1 tablespoon butter
½ cup granulated sugar	¼ teaspoon salt
½ cup light corn syrup	1 stick cinnamon
½ cup water	few drops red vegetable coloring

6 red eating apples

Cook sugars, corn syrup, water, butter, salt and stick cinnamon until syrup crackles in cold water (300° F.). Remove from fire, take out stick cinnamon, add red coloring. Stick a wooden skewer in the stem end of apples, dip one at a time into the hot syrup, coating thoroughly. Place on oiled paper to cool. Makes 6 apples. Apples may also be colored green and flavored with mint or wintergreen.

MAPLE SYRUP CAKES

Boil maple syrup down to 231° F., or until it forms a very soft ball in cold water. Beat with a sugar beater, made for that purpose (or an egg beater if cakes are made in small quantities). Pour into molds 1½ x 3 inches. Do not wet molds.

This recipe is vouched for by Mrs. Silas Snow, on whose farm in Williamsburg, Mass., maple products have been made for 45 years.

We have no record of the making of the first maple sugar, for it was the Red Man's discovery, centuries before Columbus. When the first settlers came to New England, they learned the art of sugaring-off. In fact the sugar of the maple trees was the only sugar they knew, cane sugar being a luxury beyond their simple means.

A SUGAR-ON-SNOW PARTY

[A Vermont recipe]

A maple-sugar-on-snow party is a unique way of serving refreshments to a group. Such a party is most satisfactorily managed when fresh, clean snow is available.

Preparing the Snow

Gather a quantity of snow, providing a panful for each couple. Pans ten to twelve inches in diameter are best. Pack the snow solidly in the pans. In cold weather these pans may be prepared with the snow beforehand and left out of doors. Soup plates packed full of snow may be used in place of pans, if preferred. In this case, prepare one dish of snow for each person.

Preparing the Syrup

Allow one quart of syrup for six people. Pour the syrup into a large kettle; when it begins to boil it will bubble up and boil over rapidly. Boil the syrup until when dropped on the snow it remains on the surface and becomes waxy. Until it is of the right consistency it will dissolve into the snow. If a thermometer is used boil until 236° F. It is well to boil down the syrup partially before the party as it takes quite a time before it reaches the proper consistency.

Serving

Provide each person or couple with a pan of snow, a small pitcher of hot syrup and a fork. Pour the syrup on the snow, a little at a time. Some will prefer to make hollows in the snow and fill them; others will string the syrup out in fine lines. Some people call the syrup "sheepskins"; others refer to it as "leather aprons" or "maple wax." As soon as the snow cools the syrup, each person takes his fork and gathers up the syrup to be eaten and then the process is repeated.

MENU FOR SUGAR-ON-SNOW PARTY

Sugar on Snow
Plain Doughnuts—Sour Pickles—Coffee

For a real Vermont maple sugar party, doughnuts and pickles are necessary to complete the menu. The tartness of the pickles makes it possible to enjoy and consume more "leather aprons." Coffee clears the taste and doughnuts naturally follow along with coffee. Some Vermonters insist on cheese and at "elegant" parties butternuts are rolled with the sugar on the fork.

Sugaring Off

When the enthusiasm for the waxed sugar begins to wane, usually someone begins creaming what he has left in his dish. If this syrup is still warm it may be stirred until a nice creamy consistency and then picked up in the fingers and eaten as candy. Any syrup which has been boiled down and not served may be restored to its original consistency by adding water and bringing to a boil. It may then be used in cooking or served with pancakes.

A good maple sugar season is characterized by several good "runs." A "run" simply refers to the flow of sap which is fostered by alternately cold and warm periods. Those who like to get outdoors in the early spring to witness the fascinating phenomenon usully take a trip to a genuine sugar camp. It may be necessary to drive over a rutted muddy road, but the experience amply repays the effort. If they are "boiling" at the camp, a profusion of escaping steam will greet the eye and the essence of maple is readily apparent. Inside the shelter someone is tending the evaporator, an iron monster with a rather confusing series of pans and siphons and valves.

When the syrup in the finishing pan boils, it is drawn off and passed through a very fine felt strainer. The strained syrup is then ready for market.

BUTTERNUT SEA FOAM

[*A Vermont recipe*]

2 cups sugar
¼ teaspoon salt
⅔ cup light corn syrup

½ cup water
2 eggs, stiffly beaten
1 teaspoon vanilla

½ cup butternuts or pecans

Combine sugar, salt, corn syrup and water; cook over low heat until mixture boils, stirring constantly. Continue cooking without stirring, until mixture spins a long thread (240° F.). Pour very slowly over egg whites, beating constantly, until candy holds its shape. Add vanilla and nuts, cut in pieces. Turn into greased pan. Cut in squares. Makes 18 pieces.

POPCORN BALLS

[*Mrs. Carl Rustemeyer, Williamsburg, Mass.*]

1 cup molasses
1 cup sugar
1 tablespoon vinegar

2 tablespoons butter
½ teaspoon soda
12 cups salted popcorn

Combine molasses, sugar, vinegar and butter; cook, stirring occasionally until a small amount of mixture forms a very hard ball in cold water; add soda. Remove from heat and pour over corn; cool slightly. Butter fingers lightly and mold corn into balls; cool on greased surface. Makes about 18 balls.

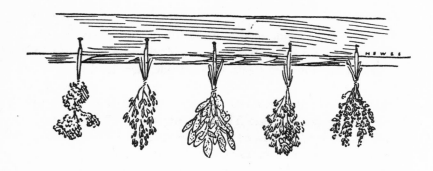

X. HERBS

Marjorie Mills, Boston, "Herald-Traveler"

No Yankee cook book would be complete without a chapter, however brief, on the herbs and simples that were cherished by early New England settlers, some of the seeds brought in little packets by the Pilgrims. Bees worked among the thyme and hyssop and hung in the tall sprays of lavender under the hot July sun that first summer in Plymouth. Women, a little homesick perhaps for the gardens they had left behind, saved the medicinal herbs to dry carefully, sage and winter savory and dill for seasoning, the coriander seeds for seed cakes and the leaves of innumerable herbs for tisanes both medicinal and refreshing to weary humankind.

The Indians taught the Pilgrims the medicinal and culinary uses of the plants, roots and berries in the New World and the early settlers guarded their herbals by Tusser, Culpeper, Coles and John Parkinson. They also clung to a sturdy belief in the benign effect of certain herbs, southernwood or Lad's Love, rosemary, lavender, hyssop and angelica. The herbs that invoked the evil spirit were vervain, betony, yarrow, mugwort and St.-John's-wort.

Oil from the plants of sweet marjoram and lavender were used to polish the oaken tables and chairs which must have left a spicy scent about the rooms even if the sprays of herbs, laid away with linens and with woolens to guard against moths, had not kept the rooms fragrant.

From the seventeenth to the nineteenth century New England women depended for the most part on their home-grown herbs and condiments for seasoning foods, for medicines, for the fragrant pot-pourris and lotions which they must have loved then as now. Parsley, thyme and celery root seasoned their stews; rose water gave flavor to pound cake. The first edition of "The American Frugal Housewife," published in Boston in 1829, mentions nasturtium and peppers from Mexico, as new and desirable condiments.

Not until steamships replaced clipper ships were spices like mace, cloves and allspice available to more than a few, so patches of pot herbs flourished near the doorway of every New England home or gave off their fragrance under the summer sun in clumps along the garden wall.

And there you'll still find herbs growing with the lilacs, the cinnamon roses and Queen Anne's lace near the crumbling cellar holes of many an old New England homestead. For herbs have a mysterious vitality and tenacity; they ask little encouragement to flourish and they persist as though they knew we needed their quiet healing and refreshment in a hurried and harried generation.

Perhaps we are beginning to realize our need of the simples, the pot and nose herbs of another day, for herb gardens flourish again the length and breadth of New England. You may read any one of a dozen fascinating books on herbs, their history, their culture, their use and significance. The legend, fantasy and superstition clinging around herbs is endless. We read again and again "Herbs and the Earth" by Henry Beston whose herb garden, growing against an ancient stone wall beneath a gnarled apple tree in Nobleboro, Maine, is one of the pleasantest spots we have ever visited. The book is sheer poetry.

Start an herb garden and you'll find yourself treading a fragrant path to adventure and discovery. You'll make rose geranium jellies, herb soups and salads and fascinating beverages; you'll strew herbs in omelets and stews and fricassees; you'll miss basil if it's lacking in tomato dishes and your cottage cheese will be aromatic with chives; you'll candy mint leaves and sweet flag and perhaps blue borage blossoms. You'll inevitably make your own potpourri and insist all your friends sniff it while you look on proudly as though you had invented the idea.

In case you haven't a tiny plot of ground for an herb garden or the quiet, gentle little plants seem too dull to you, blended herb powders may be bought or the dried thyme, basil, chervil, marjoram, mint, sage and savory. The secret of success in using fresh or dried herbs is subtlety. One should never be conscious of the lusty flavor of herbs, only of a mysterious enhancement of savor and aroma in food or a beverage.

In spring, country women find their pot herbs and savory greens along every New England roadside and in every marsh and field. No one needs tell them that narrow-leafed dock, bright new shoot of dandelion, gray-green, furry sprouts of milkweed, mullen and the first cowslip, chicory, kale and sorrel can go into a round-bellied pot with a piece of salt pork, ham hock or lean bacon and come out good beyond the telling.

Gathering field greens you sniff the fragrance of moist brown earth in springtime, sense the rhythm of life stirring around you and feel as renewed as the earth itself. Eating properly cooked tender shoots of New England greens, you'll enjoy one of the savoriest foods Nature spreads out on her green tablecloth.

If you're a cliff dweller in a city apartment and neither the patch of home-grown herbs nor the sprightly waifs of the field are available for your gathering basket, do grow a small window box of spicy plants to lend zest and romance to urban menus. Mint, cress, marjoram, basil, chives and rose geranium will flourish on a sunny window sill and supply both the savor to food and the poignant link with old New England ways which herbs, wherever grown and cherished, can't fail to yield.

The recipes listed are a few of our favorites, one or two from Helen Morgenthau Fox's "Garden With Herbs," one from Helen Noyes Webster of Lexington who is a sort of patron saint for herb enthusiasts in New England, and the candied mint leaf recipe from Caroline Torry of the Wenham Herb Center.

CANDIED MINT LEAVES

[Caroline Torry, Wenham Herb Center]

Thin gum arabic with water and brush each fresh green mint leaf with the mixture, using a good sized firm, clean paint brush. Then dip the leaves in sugar and let them crisp and harden on wax paper. Pack in air-tight tin boxes in layers with wax paper between each layer—and you can regale your friends with your own candied mint leaves next winter at tea, or adorn a huge layer cake with pink peppermint icing and a wreath of candied peppermint leaves.

BLUE BORAGE STARS

Treat the petals the same as sugared mint leaves. The gum arabic may be painted on with a camel's-hair brush.

TARRAGON VINEGAR

Pick fresh green leaves of tarragon herb, wash, dry slightly, fill a jar with them, cover with a good grade of vinegar. Cover the jar closely and let it stand 2 to 4 weeks, strain and bottle.

CORIANDER SEED ROLL

Roll rich pie pastry very thin. Spread it with butter, brown sugar, spices and coriander seeds. Roll up and cut into slices. Bake in hot oven (400° F.) until pastry is brown.

CORIANDER SEED CAKES

2 cups flour
1 cup sugar

2 egg yolks
1 tablespoon coriander seeds

1 tablespoon sour cream

Combine and roll, press mixture into shapes like little pretzels or any shape desired. Bake in moderate oven.

HOREHOUND CANDY

[From "Herbs" by Helen Noyes Webster]

1 ounce dried horehound herb,   1 teaspoon cream of tartar
    leaf, stem, flowers   2 cups horehound tea
2½ quarts boiling water   1 teaspoon butter
   3 cups granulated sugar   1 teaspoon lemon juice

Steep herb in boiling water for 2 minutes. Strain and squeeze through cheesecloth. Allow tea to settle, then decant. Add sugar and cream of tartar. Boil to 240° F., add butter and continue boiling without stirring until the temperature reaches 312°. Remove from fire and add lemon juice. Pour into buttered pan. When cool, block in squares; roll in confectioners' sugar; pack in airtight jars.

CANDIED SWEET FLAG

Dig root in the fall when it is fully ripe. Clean, scrape and cut crosswise into sections. Boil gently in water to cover for several hours. Pour off the water and crystallize the root sections in a boiling sugar syrup. Lovage root may be candied in the same way.

SAFFRON BREAD

4 cups flour   3 eggs
1 cup butter   ¼ teaspoon cloves
1 pint milk, scalded and   ¼ teaspoon mace
    cooled   ½ teaspoon cinnamon
1 yeast cake, soaked in ¼ cup   1 cup sugar
    tepid water   1 tablespoon rosewater
½ teaspoon salt   1 teaspoon saffron, soaked in
1½ tablespoons caraway seed   warm milk

Pour hot milk over the sugar, butter and salt. When nearly cool add yeast and saffron juice. Add slightly beaten eggs and flour sifted with spice, rosewater and caraway seed. Beat well and let rise for six hours. Cut down and put dough into buttered pan, let rise until double in size. Bake 1 hour in moderate oven (350° F.).

CHIVE OMELET

1 tablespoon flour
½ cup milk
6 eggs, well beaten

¾ teaspoon salt
pepper
⅓ cup chives, finely cut

Stir flour into milk until mixture is smooth; add eggs, salt and pepper. Turn into a buttered hot frying pan and place over moderate heat. As omelet cooks, lift edge towards center and tip pan so the uncooked mixture flows under the cooked portion. When portion is lightly browned, sprinkle chives over top. Fold over and slip on to hot plate. Serves 5.

CHICKEN WITH FINES HERBES

[Lexington Field and Garden Club]

½ cup water
5 tablespoons butter
5 tablespoons flour
¾ cup milk

¾ cup chicken broth
½ teaspoon salt—few grains
pepper

Make cream sauce as usual with proportions given above and add

> ½ teaspoon finely chopped burnet
> 1 teaspoon finely chopped chives
> ¾ teaspoon finely chopped rosemary
> ⅛ teaspoon finely chopped tarragon
> 1 teaspoon finely chopped chervil
> 2 cups cut up boiled fowl
> 1 cup finely cut celery

Let it stand in double boiler for at least half hour before serving so that the different flavors may blend. A longer time will improve it. If you haven't all these herbs in your garden, experiment with those you do have. It's really lots of fun, try it and see for yourself.

CARROTS WITH LEMON JUICE AND MINT

[Helen Webster]

Melt a generous piece of butter and add juice of 1 lemon, 1½ tablespoons chopped spearmint. Combine well with 1½ quarts cooked and diced hot carrots.

ROSEMARY BISCUITS

[Helen Webster]

Any standard recipe for baking powder biscuit with chopped rosemary added in the proportion of 1 tablespoon to 2 cups of flour.

GREEN SALAD

[Weathered Oak Herb Farm]

Wash and crisp in the usual way lettuce, water cress, chicory, young dandelions, lovage and sorrel. To this add celery, chives, onion rings, sweet pepper, radishes, cucumber, and a little fresh marjoram and ¼ cup chopped bread-and-butter pickles. Leaves must be fresh and dry, cold and crisp when salad is tossed together in salad bowl. Dress with herb dressing before serving. Garnish with violets.

MINT SAUCE FOR GRAPE FRUIT OR FRUIT CUP

½ cup mint tips packed hard   ½ cup water

1 cup sugar

Boil about 5 minutes, strain and add green coloring as desired. When cool add to fruit and let stand at least 2 or 3 hours. If you prefer a sweeter sauce add more sugar when making syrup. Vary with different kinds of mint.

THE KING'S MEAD

For a small amount, take one quart of water, one cup of honey, one lemon cut in slices, one half a tablespoon of nutmeg. Boil until no scum comes to the top, removing the scum as it rises. Add a pinch of salt, the juice of half a lemon. Strain and cool. This is a good drink as it is, but should stand until it is fermented.

—*"The Queen's Closet Opened."*

GREEN PEA SOUP WITH MINT

1 quart of fresh peas	1 teaspoon salt
1 onion	1 teaspoon sugar
1 large or 2 small sprigs of	4 tablespoons butter
mint	2 egg yolks
1 teaspoon spinach juice	½ cup cream

Shell the peas, and break up the pods; wash the pods and boil for two or three hours in the water in which other vegetables have been cooked if possible. Strain and add the peas, the onion, mint, salt and sugar, and three pints of water in which the pods were cooked. Cook until the peas are tender, then rub through a sieve, add butter, spinach juice (for color) and bring to boiling point. Season more if needed, and just before serving add the egg yolk diluted with the cream. Cook, stirring constantly for five minutes, but do not allow the liquid to boil. Strain and serve with croutons.

—*Helen Fox, "Gardening with Herbs."*

ROSE GERANIUM JELLY

Prepare the pulp of apples as for a plain jelly. Boil the juice thus obtained for twenty minutes. To each pint of juice add one pound of sugar and place in a preserving kettle over the fire. Stir until all the sugar has melted, then add two or three rose geranium leaves, bring to the boiling point, and boil rapidly for two minutes, removing any scum which may rise to the surface. Turn into jelly glasses, removing the leaves, but place a fresh leaf in each glass.

—Helen Fox, "Gardening with Herbs"

HERB DRESSING

[Florence Bratenahl]

Rub bowl with garlic. Cut one onion in thin slices. Add 1 cup of comb honey, ½ cup tarragon vinegar, juice of 1 lemon, season with dry mustard, red pepper, paprika, dash of Worcestershire. Beat well—stand overnight and then strain. (Mrs. Webster adds 2 glasses of rhubarb and mint jelly to the vinegar.)

Herbs cut up in dressing:

> ½ teaspoon finely chopped burnet
> 1 teaspoon finely chopped chives
> ½ teaspoon finely chopped lemon thyme
> 1 teaspoon Neapolitan parsley

BALM WINE

1 peck of balm leaves	2 pounds granulated sugar
(Melissa officinalis)	4 egg whites
	1 yeast cake

Take a peck of balm leaves, put them in a tub or large pot, heat four gallons of water scalding hot, ready to boil, then pour it through the leaves, let it stand so all night, then strain them through a hair sieve, put to every gallon of water two pounds of fine sugar, and stir it very well; take the whites of four or five eggs, beat them very well, put them into a pan and whisk it very well before it be overhot, when the skin begins to rise take it off and keep it skimming all the while it is boiling, let it boil three quarters of an hour then put into the tub, when it is cold put in a little new yeast upon it, that it may head the better, so work it for two days, then put it into a barrel and stop it up close and when it is fine, bottle it.

—Moxon, "English Housewifery," 1775.

FRENCH HERB SOUP

3 tablespoons butter
1 small head lettuce (shredded)
1 small bunch water cress
　(cut fine)
1 cup sorrel (cut fine)

2 sprigs chervil (finely
　chopped)
6 cups chicken stock
½ cup cream
1 egg yolk

1 teaspoon salt and a little pepper

Cook the herbs in the butter, for 5 minutes, being careful not to brown the herbs; add chicken stock, salt and pepper, and cook for ½ hour; add cream mixed with egg yolk, and stir until heated, but not boiled. Season to taste, serve without straining, with croutons.

—*Mrs. LeBoiteaux in the Garden Club of American Bulletin.*

RECIPE FOR HERB POWDER

Take fresh marjoram, basil, bay leaf, and parsley and dry in the sun until crisp. Pick carefully off the stalks and rub into fine powder. Add a small quantity of dried and powdered lemon peel, allowing to each ounce of herbs in powder one small saltspoon of salt and half this quantity of ground pepper. Sift through a piece of coarse muslin and store for use in small bottles.

This makes an excellent herb powder for flavoring purposes.

—*Grieve, "Culinary Herbs."*

ODDITIES

[from "The Pocumtuc Housewife," published in Deerfield in 1805]

SUBSTITUTES FOR TEA AND COFFEE

The leaves of currant bushes picked very small and dried on tin can hardly be distinguished from green tea. Peas roasted and ground are an excellent substitute for coffee and you would hardly know which was best.

ELDERBLOW TEA

Is peculiarly efficacious for babes or for grown people in digestive disorders.

SKUNK CABBAGE

Promotes expectoration, quiets the nerves, is very useful in asthma.

THOROUGHWORT

Yellow Dock and Golden Thread are good in bitters.

CAUDLE TO GIVE AWAY TO POOR FAMILIES

Set three quarts of water on the fire. Mix smooth, enough oatmeal to thicken it with a pint of water. Pour this into the boiling water with twenty powdered Jamaica peppers. Boil to a good middling thickness, then add sugar, half a pint of well fermented table beer and a glass of gin. Boil all.

SYRUP FOR THE SPRING OF THE YEAR

Boil together, dock root, thoroughwort, yarrow, mullein, sarsaparilla, coltsfoot, spearmint, May weed, dandelion root, and any other herbs you like. Boil down the water and add molasses to make a syrup. Put in brandy to keep. Make a good deal of this, and give all the family a tablespoon before breakfast as a preventive of Spring fevers.

CATNIP

Promotes perspiration.

SAFFRON

Makes a valuable tea for children afflicted with measles, chicken pox, and all eruptive diseases.

MOTHERWORT

Is very quieting to the nerves. Students and wakeful people find it useful.

HAVE YOU A YANKEE CELLAR?

(AND WHAT DO YOU KEEP IN IT?)

Answers on pages 370, 371

51. Why were cellar doors made so wide in old houses?
52. What is a swinging shelf?
53. What is a candle chest, and why was it kept down cellar?
54. Identify a preserve closet; cheese closet; screen closet.
55. With what kind of mortar did the early masons fasten the cellar stonework together?
56. Why were wells placed in cellars?
57. From what wood were salt pork barrels made? How was the density of the brine determined? How was the pork kept from floating on top of the brine? What was the method of placing the pork in the barrel?
58. What fuel was used in the cellar smoke-oven to cure the hams and bacon? to heat the brick baking ovens? to make charcoal?
59. What is a milk cellar? vegetable cellar? fruit cellar?
60. In what was cider applesauce placed? How were turnips stored? Where was corned beef placed for curing? In what were hams pickled? How was butter kept sweet? How was lard stored?
61. What was a cellarway?
62. And a question which worried many a thrifty Yankee house-wife on a cold winter night:
    "Will it freeze down cellar?"

INSTRUCTIONS FOR BAYBERRY CANDLES

[Household Department, Boston Sunday "Post"]

Remove berries from twigs; pick them over again to remove any leaves or small pieces of twigs. Put a few berries in colander and shake back and forth to remove all dust. Put berries in kettle filled with water. Use a large kettle so wax will float to the top. Set in middle of stove (not over direct heat else sediment will cook into wax) and leave overnight. In the morning, set in a cold place, preferably out of doors, and wax will form in a solid cake. This will take all day.

Remove wax and brush or pick off any sediment, and put in a small kettle filled with water. Set it on the stove again (not over direct heat), and when entirely melted, pour through strainer, then through cheesecloth. Set out of doors again to harden. If it is not clean enough, melt it again in water and strain. Be sure to have wax perfectly clean. In straining warm wax, work in a warm place, else wax will begin to harden. Work over the back of the range but be careful not to get too close to the fire.

Now your wax is ready for the molds, or to dip by hand. If you use a mold, have wicks longer than mold, so you can pull out candles. Put wick in mold, and dip the tip of wick into warm wax and let it harden (this will take but a moment). Then pour your wax into the mold. If you use a teapot, wax will be easier to handle. Hold the mold in upright position or tie it to faucet. Let this stand in a cold place half a day. Then take a sharp pointed knife and loosen candles at the base, and pull out. Here is where a long wick is handy. If candles do not come out readily, it is because your wax was not clean enough, and you will have to pour boiling water over the molds to loosen them. Then hold them until they are firm enough to lay down.

10 lbs. bayberries makes 1 lb. wax
1 lb. wax makes 2 good size candles.

GLOSSARY OF COOKING TERMS
AND NEW ENGLAND COLLOQUIALISMS

Baste. To keep food moist by pouring juices from the pan or additional fat or liquids over food while baking or roasting.

Beat. A motion made by lifting the mixture over and over by means of a spoon, fork or whisk.

Bind. To thicken slightly, usually with flour mixed with melted fat or liquid.

Blend. To mix ingredients thoroughly.

Braise. To brown in a small amount of hot fat; and then to add desired seasonings and liquid and cook slowly in closely covered dish on top of the stove or in the oven.

Broil. To cook food on a greased rack exposed to a direct flame.

"Catch on." A New England expression meaning to allow food to stick to the pan slightly so that meat or mixture browns but does not burn. (See Yankee Pot Roast, page 70.)

Chop. To cut with a knife. It does not mean to put through a chopper.

Cobbler. A deep-dish fruit pie made with rich biscuit dough, with top and side crusts or with top crust only.

Common Cracker. A large old-fashioned lightly salted cracker also called Boston cracker.

Cracklings. The crisp, golden brown pieces that remain after salt pork has been sliced and heated and the fat extracted. (See Crackling Bread, page 157.)

Cream. To make soft and smooth by rubbing against the side of a bowl with the back of a spoon; usually applied to shortening and sugar.

Cream together. To blend ingredients until they are light and fluffy.

Cut. (1) To slice down through mixture. (2) To combine fat with dry ingredients, using two knives, a fork or blender. (3) *Cut and fold.* A gentle motion which incorporates egg whites with a minimum loss of air imprisoned in the whites.

Dice. To cut into small cubes.

Dot. To scatter small bits, as butter, over surface of food.

Dredge. To sprinkle or coat with flour.

Drop Cakes. A Yankee dish not unlike a fritter.

Entrée. A small made dish served as a separate course at a formal dinner or as the chief dish of a main course at an informal meal.

Fricassee. To stew or braise.

Fried Cake. A thick griddle cake sauté in hot fat, usually made of cornmeal. (See Indian Fried Cakes, page 134.)

Fried Pie. Fruit turnover made with doughnut dough or pastry and fried in deep fat. (See Vermont Dried Apple Fried Pie, page 220.)

Fritter. Pieces of fruit or vegetables or fish enclosed in a batter and fried in deep fat.

Fool. A dish of crushed fruit with whipped cream and sugar.

Fry. To cook in hot fat.

Grind. To put through food chopper or meat grinder.

Griddlecakes. Flat batter cakes baked on a griddle on top of a stove. Larger and thicker than pancakes.

Grunt. Cape Cod name for a steamed berry pudding. (See recipe page 184.)

Lard. To insert long, narrow strips of salt pork or bacon, through meat in gashes which have been made over the surface of lean meat or fish before roasting or baking it. This is done to prevent dryness.

Marinate. To soak in French dressing or similar mixture.

Mince. To cut in tiny pieces.

Mix. To combine ingredients, usually by stirring.

Oyster liquor. If oysters do not have sufficient liquor to meet requirements of recipe, place in a large sieve and pour water over them, carefully catching the liquid as it runs through.

Pancake. Same as griddlecake except smaller and thinner.

Pan-fry. To cook in small amount of fat.

Pandowdy. A fruit dessert topped with a biscuit crust.

Parboil. To boil only until partly cooked, about one-half total length of cooking time.

Parch. To dry and brown with dry heat; usually applied to corn.

Pudding bag. A bag in which puddings are steamed. (See page 194.)

Purée. A thick smooth liquid made by rubbing cooked foods through a sieve.

Sauté. To fry and lightly brown in a small amount of fat.

Scald. To bring to a temperature just below the boiling point. To scald milk, heat, covered, in a double boiler until foamy on top.

Score. To cut narrow grooves or gashes.

Sear. To brown surface quickly with intense heat to hold in juices.

Sift. To mix dry ingredients by putting through a sieve once or several times. Use two pieces of paper or two bowls, sifting from one to the other.

Simmer. To heat below the boiling point (184° F.)—"to keep water smiling but not laughing."

"Sizzlers." A New England dessert similar to a fried pie.

Slump. What State-of-Mainers call cooked fruit topped with dumplings or biscuit dough.

Sponge. A yeast batter.

Steam. To cook in steam. This is frequently done in a double boiler or steamer.

Stew. To cook in liquid in a covered dish over low heat for a long time.

Stifle. A Cape Cod name for a meat or fish stew.

Stir. To mix with a circular motion.

Stock. The liquid in which meat, fish, poultry or vegetables have been cooked.

*Try out.** To render or melt the fat of salt pork (or any animal fat) by cutting in small pieces and frying over very slow heat or heating in double boiler. Fat should not brown. Pieces that remain when fat is separated from membrane are called cracklings.

Truss. To tie a fowl or other meat so that it will hold together.

Until set. Until a liquid has become firm. Usually applied to a gelatine mixture.

Whip. To beat rapidly to incorporate air and produce expansion.

White Sauce. A sauce made by blending shortening and flour and adding milk and seasonings.

---

* Many of the recipes in this book call for salt pork. If this is not readily available, butter may be substituted without materially affecting the recipe. ¼ pound salt pork when tried out is the equivalent of approximately 4 tablespoons melted butter or other melted fat.

ANSWERS TO QUIZ

1. *maple syrup* pronounced sur-up
   sumach pronounced shoo-mak
   raspberry pronounced rasp-berry (with the *p* sounded)
   saleratus pronounced sal-e-*ra*-tus
2. Bean porridge: pronounced to rhyme with Norwich thus:
   "There was a young man from Nor-itch
   Who burnt his mouth on Bean Por-ritch."
3. *Switchel* is a drink consumed in great quantities on the haying
   fields of New England. It could be drunk on the hottest days
   without bad effect on the imbiber. For recipe see page 319.
   Johnnycake (Johnniecakes) derive their name from "journey
   cakes," probably because they could be cooked anywhere
   along the trail. See pages 132-134.
   Butternuts.
4. Lemons. Our forefathers (or foremothers) used to steep the
   tiny, red dried berries in hot water, and drink the acrid
   decoction.
5. New snow contains ammonia enough to make batter rise
   quickly.
6. Dried codfish (soaked to remove some of the salt) chopped
   with boiled potatoes. Recipe page 33.
7. The crisp skin of roast turkey, chicken, goose or other fowl;
   also the crisp bits left when lard is fried out of pork.
8. Pigs' feet, cheeks, etc., in a brine pickle. See recipe page 78.
9. Small balls of raised bread-dough fried in deep fat. Eat with
   butter. Recipe page 138.
10. "Emptyin's" (which contained the yeasty property) were the
    settlings in beer barrels. The whitest of breads of long ago
    were called "milk emptyin's."

11. Cook sweet cider down to half its volume. Add quartered sweet apples and cook until tender. This used to be stored in New England cellars by the tub, barrel and crock. It was sometimes allowed to freeze. See page 282.

12. Substitute maple sap for the water in brewing coffee.

13. Easily. See recipe page 324.

14. A delicious vegetable served with butter, salt and pepper. Recipe page 106.

15. Crust coffee is another name. It is also the name of a pudding. See page 187.

16. *Lifting—airing:* particular methods of stirring with wooden paddles. *Graining:* method of stirring syrup until it forms little grains. *Stirring-off:* stirring syrup until it hardens into sugar when poured out into a pan. *Granulating:* grains of sugar (as opposed to loaf or cake sugar).

17. Instrument made from iron or tin used to fill sausage cases.

18. *Trencher:* wooden plate or platter with slightly raised edges. *Piggin:* a small wooden pail or tub with an upright stave for a handle. *Skeel:* a shallow wooden vessel used to "set" milk until the cream gathers. *Losset:* wooden container for holding milk. *Keeler:* similar to losset. *Noggin:* small bowl or mug with a short heavy handle whittled at the side.

19. *Splinter broom:* in New England often made of yellow birch, close-shaved, and turned back on itself.

20. She burns a couple of bushels of hard wood for about two hours; then rakes out the coals and deposits them in the chamber under the oven, and starts baking.

21. The berries for "lemonade"; the bark for dye; the wood for sap-spiles.

22. *Catnip:* remedy for gas on the stomach—Babies! *Pennyroyal:* remedy for sick-stomach, colic, and bowel-trouble. *Thoroughwort:* remedy for fresh cold or sore throat. *Yarrow:* remedy for run-down condition; disordered digestion. *Hoarhound:* debility, colds, laxative. *Flag-root* (*Calamus*): root is chewed as a stomach tonic.

23. *Cheese-basket:* a tin or wicker pan with large holes to allow the whey to drain out. *Tallow-dip:* the method of dipping wicks into hot tallow, allowing to dry, then re-dipping until a candle of the proper length and thickness was formed. *Cracker-stamp:* a sharp, pointed instrument used to prick cracker dough before baking. *Scotch-kettle:* shallow iron kettle with rounded bottom, used for frying. *Swizzle-stick:* wooden stick to stir up hot toddy.

24. Of small consequence.

25. Salt settles when the container is kicked; hence, the purchaser would get too much for his money.

26. Maple sugar.

27. *Baked crullers:* baked, raised doughnut dough.
    Cherry cider: juice pressed out from cherries and bottled.
    Fried pies: balls of doughnut dough filled with a spoonful of dried-apple sauce, and fried in deep fat. See recipe page 220.
    Sage cheese: common cheese with sage mixed through it (greenish yellow in color).
    Election cake: see recipe page 252.

28. *Menhaden:* a fish used for making oil, fertilizer and bait.
    Porgy: a sparoid edible fish.
    Squinteague: an esculent fish.
    Quahog: the common American hard shelled clam.
    Turbot: the common American flounder.

29. *Bean swagger:* stewed dried beans cooked with small pieces of salt pork.
    Scraps: small squares of pork from which the lard has been "tried" (pressed out).
    Bloaters: large herring, cured by being salted, smoked and half-dried.

30. Shad.

31. *Baptist bread:* small irregular pieces of raised bread-dough fried in deep fat; served with maple syrup. See recipe page 138.
    Bean porridge: see recipe page 104.
    Rum cherries: small wild black cherries. Our forefathers were

wont to cover these cherries with rum for a day or two. Then drank the rum thus flavored.

32. Among many differences in appearance of bush and berry and leaf and taste, is the difference in seeds; the blueberry containing many tiny ones, the huckleberry 10 nutlets only. But New Englanders know them "on sight."

33. Beans baked for 24 hours in a hole, lined with coals and covered with earth. See recipe pages 102-103.

34. An irregular slash in the top piecrust to let out steam.

35. See recipes. Pages 63, 64; 117; 305.

36. Place them on hot coals, steam, or use a *sharp* knife.

37. *Clam chowder:* whether or not tomatoes (or other foreign substance) can be added.

    Baked beans: whether to use brown sugar or molasses for sweetening.

    Apple pie: whether cinnamon or nutmeg should be the outstanding flavoring in the pie.

38. Rhubarb.

39. An old-time pudding made of boiled milk and flour and usually served with Molasses Sauce.

40. But Father and I went down to camp,
    Along with Captain Goodwin,
    And there we saw the men and boys,
    As thick as Hasty Pudding.

41. A grasshopper.

42. (a) Billerica pronounced like Bill-rikker.
    (b) Concord pronounced like Con-cord.
    (c) Groton pronounced like Graw-ton.
    (d) Quincy pronounced like Kwin-zi.
    (e) Rehoboth pronounced like Re-ho-both.

43. Codfish.

44. Pittsfield, Massachusetts.

45. Worcester, Massachusetts, Polytechnic Institute.

46. He is trying to do too many things at the same time and doing none of them well.

47. A Connecticut peddler sold wooden nutmegs to unsuspecting housewives.

48. Potato.

49. (a) *Beacon Hill:* a beacon, erected on a high pole, acted as a guide to ships entering Boston Harbor at night.

(b) *Milk Street:* the farmers are said to have taken their milk to a spring on this street to "water" it before selling the milk to the people of the city.

(c) *Brimstone Corner:* corner of Park and Tremont Streets; named for the fiery sermons which were preached in Park Street Church.

(d) *Damnation Alley:* wide enough for one ox-cart only. When two teamsters met in this alley, the air was often blue with oaths—hence the name.

(e) *The Common:* for use of all the people. Used "in common" for pasturing cattle.

50. "And this is good old Boston,
    The home of the bean and the cod,
    Where the Lowells talk to the Cabots,
    And the Cabots talk only to God."

51. *Cellar doors* were made very wide so that kegs of cider could be rolled lengthwise through the door and over planks into the cellar.

52. *A swinging shelf* consists of two pieces of board, one end of which is nailed to the overhead cellar beams; the other to the board proper which is the shelf.

53. *A candle chest* or *box* is a shallow wooden container with a hinged cover in which tallow dips were stored. As candles melt and bend in ordinary summer temperature, the cellar coolness kept them hard and firm.

54. *Preserve closet:* wooden closet with tight-fitting door to hold preserved fruit. Light spoils the color of the fruit.

Cheese closet: wooden closet with screened back and front used for the curing of cheeses.

Screen closet: wooden closet with screened front—often used to hold pans of milk.

55. Common blue clay.
56. Cellar wells used when the kitchen was in the cellar; also a place to secure water if the place was attacked by the Indians.
57. Usually oak whiskey barrels.
   Density of the brine sufficient to float an egg half out of the brine.
   A clean flat rock, thoroughly scrubbed with soap and water, was placed across the top layer of the pork.
   Alternate layers of salt and pork; then water was poured in until it reached well above the last layer of pork.
58. Corncobs (dried) used to smoke hams and bacon.
   Dried bunches of black alder twigs, in this day hardwood staves from a wooden barrel. (To heat brick oven.)
   Black alder wood.
59. *A milk cellar* was a one-story brick building placed about one half story below the surface of the ground with a stone floor and one small window to the north. Kept milk cool in summer.
   A vegetable cellar comprised a separate section of a cellar, usually closed off by a partition, for vegetable storage.
   A fruit cellar was often a cavelike affair dug out of the side of a hill for fruit storage.
60. *Cider applesauce* placed in barrels in the cellar, and allowed to freeze as a delicacy.
   Turnips stored in a long deep wooden box—"turnip-box."
   Corned beef was cured in hogsheads.
   Hams were pickled in wooden tubs of "pickle" brine.
   Butter was packed in wooden firkins or earthenware crocks; then a salt brine was poured over it.
   Lard was poured into small wooden kegs.
61. A cellarway is the closet-like opening at the head of the cellar stairs—usually lined with shelves for food storage.
62. Depends upon how well the housewalls are banked with earth and hemlock boughs.

INDEX